Praise for *Cleopatra and Frankenstein*:

'Positively inhalable. I was intensely consumed by the world of *Cleopatra and Frankenstein* for a few happy days'   *Evening Standard*

'New York at the start of the 21st century is captured with near-devotional lushness in this nostalgic debut. Mellors proves herself a poetic chronicler of inky gloom'   *Observer*

'Friends who couldn't get enough of Sally Rooney's *Conversations with Friends* will fall head over heels for Coco Mellors' debut novel'
                                        ES Magazine

'Recalls Hanya Yanagihara's heart-tugging epic *A Little Life*, with its exploration of male friendship, masculinity, and trauma, although with rather more levity'   *Sunday Times Style*

'A love story that is by turns devastating and funny. You won't be able to put this book down'   *The Sun*

'Coco Mellors' sprightly, sophisticated novel opens like a quirky indie film. A stellar debut – smart, shrewd and deliciously melancholy'
                                        Daily Express

'New York makes for a scintillating backdrop to pain, disenchantment and growth'   *Financial Times*

'Luminous. A great, swooning love story, a shattering depiction of how addiction and mental illness warp our lives and a perceptive, witty portrait of globalized New York. Mellors has written a devastatingly human book, at turns sharp and tender, that marks her as the rare writer whose sentences are as beautiful as they are wise. An unforgettable read'
SAM LANSKY, author of *The Gilded Razor* and *Broken People*

'A character-driven epic, thoroughly engrossing and entirely magnificent. Sometimes you can just tell that a debut novel has been percolating and perfecting inside an author's mind until it is ready to leap into – and ultimately change – the world'

ADAM ELI, author of *The New Queer Conscience*

'Remarkably assured and sensitive. A canny and engrossing rewiring of the big-city romance'   *Kirkus Reviews*

'Insistent, stylish and utterly captivating, the prose just sings'

HEIDI JAMES, author of *The Sound Mirror*

'If you are a fan of Sally Rooney's work, you will adore the way that Coco Mellors writes. Her craft is full of the same wit and life that we continue to enjoy in Rooney's work'   *The Courier*

'There is a lot to enjoy about this novel: the charmingly drawn New York backdrop; the impossibly witty banter between the lovers; the beauty and the fashion. But Mellors does darkness just as well as she does light, and it's the coexistence of these that makes the story so relatable and compelling'   *The Debut Digest*

'Mellors is a dynamic writer who infuses her work with wordplay, jokes, spiky dialogue, tense scenes and lyrical descriptions. *Cleopatra and Frankenstein* is an impressive, muscular read'   *Business Post*

Cleopatra and Frankenstein

Coco Mellors

4th ESTATE • London

4th Estate
An imprint of HarperCollins*Publishers*
1 London Bridge Street
London SE1 9GF

www.4thEstate.co.uk

HarperCollins*Publishers*
Macken House, 39/40 Mayor Street Upper
Dublin 1, D01 C9W8, Ireland

First published in Great Britain in 2022 by 4th Estate
First published in the United States by Bloomsbury in 2022
This 4th Estate paperback edition published in 2023

4

Copyright © Coco Mellors 2022

A catalogue record for this book is
available from the British Library

ISBN 978-0-00-842179-3

Set in Bembo MT Pro
Printed and bound in the UK using 100%
renewable electricity at CPI Group (UK) Ltd

For my mother, who believed

Halve me like a walnut
Pry the part of me that is hollow
From the part that yields fruit.

—OMOTARA JAMES

Let's be hungry a little while longer.
Let's not hurt each other if we can.

—MAYA C. POPA

CHAPTER ONE

December

S he was already inside the elevator when he entered. He nodded at
her and turned to pull the iron gate shut with a clang. They were in
a converted factory building in Tribeca, the kind still serviced, unusually, by freight elevators. It was just the two of them, side by side, facing
forward as the mechanism groaned into motion. Beyond the metal crisscross of the gate, they watched the cement walls of the building slide by.

"What are you getting?" He addressed this to the air in front of him,
without turning toward her.

"I'm sorry?"

"I've been sent for ice," he said. "What do you need?"

"Oh, nothing. I'm off home."

"At ten thirty on New Year's Eve? That is either the saddest or the
wisest thing I've ever heard."

"Let's indulge me and say wisest," she said.

He laughed generously, though she didn't feel she'd been particularly
witty. "British?" he asked.

"London."

"Your voice sounds like how biting into a Granny Smith apple feels."

Now she laughed, with less abandon. "How does that feel?"

"In a word? Crisp."

"As opposed to biting into a Pink Lady or a Golden Delicious?"

"You know your apples." He gave her a respectful nod. "But it's insanity to suggest you sound anything like a Golden Delicious. That's a midwestern accent."

They reached the ground floor with a soft thud. He cranked the door open for her to pass.

"You are an odd man," she said over her shoulder.

"Undeniably." He ran ahead to open the building door. "Accompany this odd man to the deli? I just need to hear you say a few more words."

"Mm, like what?"

"Like aluminum."

"You mean aluminium?"

"Ah, there it is!" He cupped his ears in pleasure. "That extra syllable. A-luh-mi-nee-uhm. It undoes me."

She tried to look skeptical, but she was amused, he could tell.

"You're easily undone," she said.

He surprised her by stopping to consider this with genuine earnestness.

"No," he said eventually. "I'm not."

They were on the street. Across from them a store selling neon signs bathed the sidewalk in splashes of yellow, pink, and blue. MILLER LITE. LIVE NUDES. WE WILL DYE FOR YOU.

"Where is it?" she asked. "I could use some more cigarettes."

"About two blocks that way." He pointed east. "How old are you?"

"Twenty-four. Old enough to smoke, if you were thinking of telling me not to."

"You are the perfect age to smoke," he said. "Time stored up to solve and satisfy. Is that how the Larkin poem goes?"

"Oh, don't quote poetry. You might accidentally undo *me*."

"'I sing the body electric'!" he cried. "'The armies of those I love engirth me and I engirth them'!"

"Sha-la-la! I shan't listen to you!"

She pressed her palms to her ears and sprinted ahead of him up the street. A car blasting a jubilant pop song shot by. He caught up with her at the light, and tentatively, she released her hands from her head. She was wearing pink leather kid gloves. Her cheeks were pink, too.

"Don't worry, that's all I remember," he said. "You're safe."

"I'm impressed you remember any at all."

"I'm older than you. My generation had to memorize these things in school."

"How old?"

"Older. What's your name?"

"Cleo," said Cleo.

He nodded.

"Appropriate."

"How so?"

"Cleopatra, the original undoer of men."

"But I'm just Cleo. What's your name?"

"Frank," said Frank.

"Short for?"

"Short for nothing. What on earth would Frank be short for?"

"I don't know." Cleo smiled. "Frankfurter, frankincense, Frankenstein . . ."

"Frankenstein sounds about right. Creator of monsters."

"You make monsters?"

"Sort of," said Frank. "I make ads."

"I was sure you were a writer," she said.

"Why?"

"Crisp," said Cleo, raising an eyebrow.

"I started an agency," said Frank. "We're where the people who don't make it as writers go."

They walked until they found the twenty-four-hour bodega glowing on the corner, flanked by buckets of heavy-headed roses and frothy carnations. Frank pulled the door open for her with a jingle. In the bright fluorescence of the shop's interior they looked at each other openly for the first time.

Frank was, she estimated, in his late thirties or early forties. Kind eyes, was her first thought. They crinkled automatically as they met hers. Long, feathery lashes that brushed against his spectacle lenses, lending his angular face a surprising softness. Curly dark hair, spry as lamb's wool, thinning a little on the top. Now, sensing her eyes on this, he ran a hand through his hair self-consciously. The skin on the back of his hand and face was freckled, still tanned despite the winter. It matched his tan cashmere scarf, tucked into a well-tailored topcoat. He had the slight, energetic build of a retired dancer, a body that suggested economy and intelligence. Cleo smiled approvingly.

He smiled back. Like most people, he noticed her hair first. It hung over her shoulder in two golden curtains, sweeping open to reveal that much-anticipated first act: her face. And it was a performance, her face. He felt instinctively that he could watch it for hours. She'd drawn thick black wings over her eyelids, 1960s style, finishing each flick with a tiny gold star. Her cheeks were dusted with something shimmering and gold too; it spar-kled like champagne in the light. A heavy sheepskin coat encased her, paired with the pink kid gloves he'd noticed earlier and a white woolen beret. On her feet were embroidered cream cowboy boots. Everything about her was deliberate. Frank, who had spent much of his life surrounded by beautiful people, had never met anyone who looked like her.

Embarrassed by the directness of his stare, Cleo turned to examine a shelf filled, inopportunely, with cans of cat food. She was wearing too much makeup, she worried, and looked clownish in the light.

"My brother," said Frank to the man behind the counter. "Happy New Year."

The man looked up from his newspaper, where he was reading about more government-sanctioned tortures in his country. He wondered what made this white man think they were brothers, then smiled.

"And to you," he said.

"Where's the ice?"

"No ice." He shrugged.

"What kind of deli doesn't sell ice?"

"This one," said the man.

Frank lifted his hands in surrender.

"Okay, no ice." He turned to Cleo. "You want your smokes?"

Cleo had been scanning the cigarette prices on the shelf. She pulled out her wallet, which, Frank noted, was not really a wallet at all but a velvet pouch stuffed with papers and wrappers. Her long fingers halt-ingly picked through its contents.

"You know what?" she said. "I have a few rolling papers in here. I'll just get a bag of tobacco. A small one. How much is that?"

Frank watched the man's whole posture relax forward as she addressed him. It was like watching the front of an ice glacier dissolve into the sea; he melted.

"Beautiful girl," he murmured. "How much you want to pay?"

A red blush was rising up her neck to her chin.

"Let me get this," said Frank, slapping down his credit card. "And—" He picked up a bar of milk chocolate. "This too. In case you get hungry."

Cleo gave him a grateful look, but she did not hesitate.

"Pack of Capris please," she said. "The magenta ones."

Back outside, Cleo scanned up and down the street.

"You'll never get a cab tonight," Frank said. "Where do you live?"

"East Village," she said. "Near Tompkins Square Park. But I'll just walk, it's not too far."

"I'll walk with you," he said.

"No, you mustn't," she protested. "It's too far."

"I thought it wasn't far?"

"You'll miss the countdown."

"Fuck the countdown," said Frank.

"And the ice?"

"You're right. The ice is important."

Cleo's face fell. Frank laughed. He began marching north, so she had no choice but to follow him. He looked over to find her trotting along beside him and slowed down.

"Are you warm enough?"

"Oh yes," she said. "Are you? Would you like my chapeau?"

"Your what?"

"My hat. He's a beret, so I usually speak to him in French."

"You speak French?"

"Only a little. I can say, like, 'Chocolat chaud avec chantilly' and 'C'est cool mais c'est fou.'"

"What does that mean?"

"'Hot chocolate with whipped cream' and 'It's cool but it's crazy.' Both surprisingly useful phrases. So, do you want him?"

"I don't think I was built to pull off a beret."

"Nonsense," said Cleo. "The world is your chapeau."

"You know what?" Frank plucked the hat from Cleo's head and pulled it gamely over his own. "You're right."

"Magnifique," she said. "Allez!"

They walked east toward Chinatown. A group of women all wearing silver top hats and novelty 2007 sunglasses wobbled past them. One blew a party horn by Frank's head, and the group exploded into whoops of delight. He pulled the beret back off his head.

"Would it be unfestive of me to say I hate New Year's?" he asked.

Cleo shrugged. "I usually only celebrate Lunar New Year."

Frank waited, but she didn't elaborate.

"So, what was the best part of last year for you?" he asked.

"Just one thing?"

"It can be anything."

"Gosh, let me think. Well, I switched to an antidepressant that actually allows me to achieve orgasm again. That felt like a win."

"Wow. Okay. I was not expecting that. That's great news."

"Both clitoral and penetrative." Cleo gave him two thumbs. "What about you? What was your favorite thing that happened last year?"

"God, nothing that can compare to that."

"It doesn't have to be that personal! Sorry, mine was weird. I'm embarrassed."

"Yours was great! That's a big deal. I just treat my misery the old-fashioned way, with large doses of alcohol and repression."

"How's that working for you?"

Frank mimicked her two thumbs up and kept walking.

"Anyway, I think it's really impressive that you're taking care of yourself," he said.

Another group of revelers had broken between them, drowning out this last statement. He clambered around them to return to her side, repeating himself.

"That's a kind thing to say. I just have a lot of . . ." She waved vaguely toward a pile of trash spilling onto the sidewalk next to them. "Stuff in my family. I have to be careful." She cleared her throat. "Anyway. Tell me about your year."

"Best moment from last year? Probably just work things. I won an award for an ad I directed. That felt really good."

"How wonderful! Which award?"

"It's called a Cannes Lion. They're kind of a big deal in my industry. It's stupid, really."

"No, it's not. I'd love to win an award for something."

"You will," he said confidently.

They passed two men, ostensibly strangers, pissing against a wall in comfortable silence. Frank offered Cleo his hand as she hopped over the twin streams of urine. She shook her head.

"Men!"

Her hand lingered in his, and then she pulled it away to rummage in her bag.

"So," he said. "Do you have someone in particular you're, um, having these orgasms with?"

Frank was straining for the tone of "curious friend," but worried he'd ended up more "concerned sexual health clinic counselor."

"Both clitoral *and* vaginal?" Cleo teased.

Frank cleared his throat.

"Yes . . . those."

Cleo gave him a sly, sidelong glance.

"Just myself right now."

His face cracked involuntarily into a grin. She laughed.

"Oh, you like that thought, do you? What about you? Isn't everyone your age supposed to be married?"

"No, they changed that law," said Frank. "It's optional now."

"Thank god," said Cleo and lit a cigarette.

They wound their way north to Broome Street, past storefronts selling houseplants and psychic readings, chandeliers and industrial-size kitchen mixers. They talked about New Year's resolutions and what's in an old-fashioned and who they'd known at the party (Cleo: one person; Frank:

everyone). They talked about the host of the party, a celebrated Peruvian chef named Santiago, who Frank had known for twenty years. Cleo's roommate was a hostess at Santiago's restaurant, which was how she'd been invited, though that roommate had absconded with an Icelandic performance artist soon after she arrived. They talked about Pina Bausch and Kara Walker and Paul Arden and Stevie Nicks and James Baldwin.

"There's this collection of essays I love by the curator Hans Ulrich Obrist," said Cleo. "It's called *Sharp Tongues, Loose Lips, Open Eyes* . . . I can't remember the rest."

"A man of few words."

"Oh, have you read him?"

"No, it's just, that title is—never mind. I keep meaning to read more," he conceded.

Cleo shrugged. "Just buy a book and read it."

"Right. I hadn't thought of that."

"Anyway, in one of the essays he talks about being able to tell how giving a person is as a lover by how curious they are. You're meant to actually *count* in your head how many questions they ask you in a minute. If they ask four or more, then they like to please."

"And if they ask none?"

"Then you can pretty much assume they don't eat pussy. Or, you know, dick, if that's your bag."

"Pussy," said Frank quickly. "Is my bag."

She gave him another of her amused looks.

"I sort of figured."

"And you?"

"My bag? Dick." She laughed, then tilted her head to consider this further. "Maybe with a side bag of pussy. But just a small one. Like one of those little clutches you wear to the opera."

Frank nodded. "An evening purse of pussy."

"Exactly. As opposed to, like, a duffel bag of dick."

"A portmanteau of penis."

"A carry-all of cock."

"A backpack of boners."

Cleo's face lit up with laughter, and then she burrowed it into her hands as though snuffing out a match.

"God, I sound carnivorous. Let's change the subject, please."

"So . . ." Frank took a deep breath. "What do you do? Where are you from? When did you move to New York? Do you have brothers and sisters? When's your birthday? What's your horoscope? Birthstone? Shoe size?"

Cleo exhaled another peal of laughter. Frank grinned.

"Go on then," he said. "Where are you from?"

"You really want to know all that about me?"

"I want to know everything about you," he said, and was surprised to find he meant it.

Cleo told him that she'd moved around a lot growing up, but her family eventually settled in South London. Her parents split up when she was a teenager, and her father, an affable but distant engineer, quickly remarried and adopted his new wife's son. Her mother died in Cleo's last year of university at Central Saint Martins. She still had not found a way to talk about it. She had no close family back home, which left her feeling untethered but also, she added quickly, completely free.

With nothing tying her to London and a small inheritance from her mother that could cover a flight and two years of cheap rent, she'd applied for a scholarship to study painting at a graduate program in New York. She arrived when she was twenty-one. For her, that MFA meant two years in a smooth orbit from her bed, to a canvas, to bars, to other people's beds, and back to a canvas. She'd graduated the previous spring and had been freelancing as a textile designer for a fashion brand ever since. The pay wasn't great, and they didn't provide benefits, but it gave her enough money and free time to rent a sizable room in the East Village, which she also used as her painting studio. Her biggest fear now was that her student visa was up at the beginning of the summer, and she had no plan for what to do next.

"Do you paint every day?" asked Frank.

"Everyone always asks that. I try to. But it's hard."

"Why?"

"Sometimes the process is like . . . Okay, you know when you're tidying up a cupboard—"

"Is that a closet?"

"Yes, you American, a closet. First, you have to pull everything out of it, and there's this moment when you're looking around and it's a total mess. And you feel like, *Shit*, why did I even start this? It's worse than before I began. And then slowly, piece by piece, you put it all away. But before you can create order, you have to make a mess."

"I'm following."

"That's what painting is like for me. Inevitably, there's a moment when I've pulled everything out of me, and it's just . . . it's chaos on canvas. I feel like I should never have started. But then I keep going, and somehow things find their order. I know when I've finished because I feel . . . I feel this *click* that means everything's in its place. It's all where it should be. Total peace."

"How long does that last?"

"Maybe seven-point-five seconds. And then I start thinking about the next piece."

"Sounds exhausting," said Frank.

"But those seven-point-five seconds are . . ."

She looked up at the sky dramatically. Frank waited.

"As you would say, they undo me," she said.

They passed a man wearing a tuxedo and a green feather boa, retching over a fire hydrant.

"I think feather boas should make a comeback," said Cleo.

"I think you are an exceptional person," said Frank.

"You don't know me well enough to say that," said Cleo, clearly delighted.

"I'm a good judge of these things."

"Then I'll just have to take your word for it."

They were in Little Italy, where the streets were lined with seemingly identical Italian restaurants with red-checkered tablecloths and plastic bowls of pasta stuck in the windows. Above their heads, strings of red, white, and green bulbs dropped lozenges of light onto the street below. In a third-floor apartment window, a group of people stood smoking out a window, their bodies silhouetted against the yellow light of the room behind them. "Happy New Year!" they shouted to no one in particular. Cleo and Frank passed a quiet pizza spot on the corner, where a lone man was stacking up plastic chairs for the night.

"You want to get a slice?" asked Frank.

Cleo fingered the tassels on her bag. "I don't have any cash."

"I'll buy you something," he said.

"Drop the *something*," she said lightly. "And you have the truth of the matter."

"You think I'm trying to buy *you*?"

"Aren't all men trying to buy women, deep down?"

"You really believe that?"

"I don't *not* believe it."

"That's incredibly unfair."

"Okay, tell me why I'm wrong."

He turned to face her and exhaled slowly. He really had just wanted to get a slice.

"I think men are taught to buy things for women, yes. Not because we want to own you or control you, but because it's a way to show we're interested or we care that doesn't require much, I don't know, vulnerability. We're not taught to communicate the way you are. We're given these very limited, primitive tools to express ourselves, and, yes, buying a fucking meal is one of them. But women also *expect* that from us—"

Cleo was hopping up and down in excitement to interrupt him, but he raised his hand, determined to finish. "It goes both ways. You say I'm trying to buy you, but you'd be offended if I didn't offer to pay."

"I would not!" she exploded. "And the only reason I'm going to *let* you pay is because I happen to be triple extra-broke right now."

"So now I *am* paying? See, that's where I call bullshit. You want it both ways. You want to be so principled and above it all, but as soon as that becomes inconvenient for you, you're fine with a man picking up the bill."

"Are you *kidding* me? Maybe I'm broke because of, I don't know, the gender pay gap, or years of systemic sexism limiting my job opportunities, or the fact I had to quit my last job as a nanny because the dad wouldn't stop hitting on me, or—"

Now it was Frank's turn to hop.

"That's not why you're broke! You're broke because you're twenty-four and an artist who works part-time! You can't blame all your problems on being a woman!"

Cleo put her face close to Frank's and spoke so quietly her words were just above a breath. He had the insane hope she was about to kiss him.

"Yes, I can," she said.

Frank turned and walked into the pizza shop. "You're cool," he said over his shoulder. "But you're crazy."

"Sounds better in French!" she shouted back.

Cleo lit another cigarette and stamped her feet against the sidewalk like a restless racehorse. She thought about leaving just to spite him, but she knew she would regret it instantly. There was nothing to do but stand and smoke. Frank ordered two slices of pizza, anxiously checking over his shoulder to make sure she was still outside. He'd already decided that if she left, he'd run after her and apologize. But the back of her blond head was still in view, surrounded now by a cloud of smoke.

Back outside, he handed her a slice. An amber stream of oil ran across the flimsy paper plate.

"Here," he said. "To make up for the years of systemic sexism."

"Wanker," said Cleo and took a bite.

"You're in America now," Frank said. "Here, I'm just an asshole."

They walked with their slices up Elizabeth Street. Ahead of them a couple stood outside a bar in a pool of lamplight, performing a timeless two-person drama. The woman was clutching her heels to her chest and crying in long, high wails while her boyfriend shook her shoulders, repeating, "Tiffany listen, listen Tiffany, Tiffany listen . . ."

"I hate to say this," whispered Frank as they passed. "But I don't think Tiffany's listening."

Cleo turned back to look at them. "You think they're all right?"

"They'll be fine. New Year's Eve is prime fighting night for couples. It's like fireworks and fights. The two staples of a good New Year's."

"Did we just have our first fight?" Cleo asked.

Frank handed her a napkin. "I don't know," he said. "You did keep your shoes on."

Cleo chuckled. "Would take a lot more than that to get me out of my cowboy boots." She screwed up her napkin and flicked it expertly into a trash can on the corner. "Fighting can be a good thing, anyway. Look at Frida Kahlo and Diego Rivera. They got divorced, got back together, split up again . . ."

"But did you ever think that they created their art in spite of the fighting, not because of it?"

"Who cares?" said Cleo between mouthfuls of dough. "Point is, they made it."

Frank nodded vaguely. He took her paper plate from her and folded it into a neat square with his own. He hoped they'd pass a place to recycle soon.

"I'm dying to go to their house in Mexico City," said Cleo.

"It's packed with lines of tourists," said Frank. "And Do Not Touch signs on every surface."

"Bummer." Cleo looked disheartened.

"But it's still worth seeing," added Frank quickly. "There's this framed collection of butterflies hanging above Kahlo's bed that Patti Smith wrote a poem about when she visited it. And all her clothes, of course. She had amazing style, kind of like you."

Cleo smiled happily at the compliment. "Those, I would love to see."

"Let's go next week," said Frank. "The whole city's full of art. It's the perfect place for you."

"Next week? Just like that?"

"Sure. Why not? I closed the office, and I've got thousands of air miles I need to use."

"Okay." She laughed. "I'm in." She shook out her hair. "Mexico fucking City!"

Frank, who had been planning to work all next week in the empty office, had never been much of a spontaneous traveler—but he liked the idea that he could be. He had the means, just not the incentive. And here was Cleo with the opposite. They both turned to each other at the same time. He hesitated, then pulled her in for a hug. Her hair smelled like soap and almonds and cigarettes. His chest smelled of damp wool and an expensive cologne she recognized, tobacco sweetened with vanilla.

"And I'm not trying to buy you," he added, releasing her. "I'd just like to see it with you."

"I know," she said. "I'd like to see it with you too."

They crossed the Bowery and wandered through the East Village, where the merriment on the street took on a subtle edge of aggression. People shouted outside bars and fell in and out of doorways. More couples fought on more street corners. At the entrance of the park, a group of crust punks, dressed in shabby military gear and studded leather jackets, gently waved sparklers above their matted heads. A pit bull wearing a neckerchief with the anarchy symbol drawn on it glanced up from the pillow of his paws to watch the sparks fall in mute wonder.

They arrived at a crumbling walk-up on St. Mark's. The smoked glass of the front door was scrawled with incomprehensible graffiti. Frank wondered, not for the first time, what mark these anonymous scribblers thought they were making. Cleo turned to him, shy again.

"Do you want to sit in my lobby with me?"

"Why your lobby?"

Cleo hid her face in her hands.

"It's nicer than my flat?" she said from between her fingers.

She slid her keys into the door and beckoned him in. Frank didn't feel it was polite to point out that her lobby was just a stairwell. Cleo sat on the scuffed linoleum steps and lit a cigarette.

"You smoke in here?"

She shrugged.

"Everyone does."

He watched her exhale twin streams of smoke from her nostrils. "I can't believe I didn't notice you at Santiago's," he said.

"I came late. I . . . It's stupid, but I couldn't decide what to wear. It's a kind of social anxiety, I think. If I'm nervous about going to something, I change like a hundred times. It gets later and later, which of course only makes me more anxious. Usually, I end up hyperventilating over a pile of clothes on my floor. It sounds silly, but it's actually quite terrible."

Frank nodded sympathetically. "So what did you end up wearing?"

"Tonight? Oh, just this thing I made."

"Can I see?"

Cleo raised an eyebrow. She pressed the cigarette between her lips and stood to unbutton the wooden toggles of her sheepskin. What she was wearing was not so much a dress as a net made of shimmering gold threads. It was woven just loosely enough to give a suggestion of the body within. He could see, very faintly beneath the shining lattice, the outline of her nipples and belly button. She was like a smooth, lithe fish caught in a glistening net.

"Let me come upstairs," he said.

"No," she said, sitting back down. "My roommates might be home. And"—she exhaled smoke seriously—"we'll have sex."

"What's wrong with that?"

"I'm leaving in a few months."

"I think we can finish before then."

Cleo suppressed a smile. "I just don't want to attach," she said.

She looked down between her knees. Frank crouched in front of her. "I'm afraid it might be too late for that."

"You think?"

"I attached the moment I heard you say aluminum."

Cleo looked up at him from beneath her winged eyelids.

"Al-um-in-ium," she said softly.

Frank clutched his heart. "See? I'm screwed."

"No, *I'm* screwed," she said. "I'm the one who has to leave."

"Where will you go?"

"I don't know. I heard Bali's cool."

She did not feel as casual about this as she sounded.

"Not back home to England?"

"England's not my home."

Cleo ground her cigarette out on the metal stair tread. He sensed there was more to the story there, but he didn't pry. She checked her watch to avoid further questioning.

"It's past midnight!"

"This isn't right," said Frank.

"Seriously," she said. "We've been talking for like—"

"No, I mean, *this*. New Year's Eve isn't meant to be this good."

"It's meant to be bad?"

"It's meant to be fine. You know? Just *fine*. It has never, not once in my life, exceeded my expectations."

"You know, in Denmark they jump off a chair to signify jumping into the new year."

"Are you Scandinavian?"

"Why? Because I'm blond?" Cleo rolled her eyes. "No, Frank. I just know some things."

"That you do." Frank stood up and dusted off his pant legs theatrically. "Okay, let's do it."

"Jump? But we don't have a chair."

"A stair is as good as a chair."

Cleo looked up at the stairwell behind them.

"But let's go all the way from the top," she said. "Start the year with a bang."

They climbed to the first landing. They had to clear roughly ten steps to land on the ground floor below. It was the kind of game children played, daring themselves to climb higher and higher. He took her hand. She squeezed it back. They both jumped.

CHAPTER TWO

June

C leo didn't want to wear white, but she had hoped for a wedding cake. She could have ordered it herself from one of the Italian bakeries on the Lower East Side, the kind of place where every surface was covered in either powdered sugar or dust, but she'd left the planning of the meal to Santiago, who was known for his ecstatic and orgiastic dinner parties. Santiago thought they should forgo a traditional cake, and since nothing else about her marriage to Frank was proving to be traditional, she did not insist otherwise.

In fact, Cleo didn't insist on anything about the wedding. She did buy a dress for the occasion, but the one she picked was blue. It was late June, too hot for anything elaborate, and the idea of wearing white had always seemed ridiculous to her. She hadn't been a virgin since she was fourteen. She'd let Frank slip his hands inside her underwear in her stairwell the first night they met. It had felt like he was tracing the alphabet on her clit. *L, M, N, O . . . POW!* No, there was no reason at all to wear white.

She found the dress she did wear buried at the back of an overpriced vintage store on Perry Street, a liquid silk slip so much cheaper than everything else, she worried afterward that it might actually be a nightgown. When she slid it over her head, she felt as if she had taken a knife to the surface of the sky, skimmed a little off the bottom, and worn the peel.

Frank still managed to outdo her, however, by showing up to City Hall in a three-piece ivory tuxedo. Cleo had been waiting on the steps, eating a hot dog from the street cart nearby—she'd never had one before, she reasoned, and today was a day of firsts—when she saw his white top hat bobbing above the gray street. She put down the half-eaten hot dog and threw her head back in delight.

"Well?" Frank heel-turned so she could take him in. Behind him, a family of tourists took his photograph.

"You are an incorrigible show-off."

"See, when you say it," said Frank, "that still sounds like a compliment."

He ran his hand down the silken slope of her back and cupped her behind.

"Do we look like we're going to two different weddings?" she asked.

"You look fantastic," said Frank. "Like a little lake."

"You look . . ." Cleo paused to fully take him in. "Like yourself."

It was true. Equal parts mad hatter and aging glam rock star, Frank looked surprisingly natural in the tux.

"Do I smell of mothballs?" Frank stretched his throat for her to smell, and she tucked her nose into the suntanned skin above his collar.

"Nope. Soap and . . ." She snapped her head back. "Gin?"

"Had a little one before I left. Had to! It's my wedding day! Come on, let's go in."

"*Our* wedding day, darling," said Cleo.

"Ours, yours, mine, theirs . . ." Frank launched into a singsong. He grabbed her hand, and they ran up the steps two at a time.

What is a wedding, Cleo wondered, if not a private dream made public, a fantasy suspended between two worlds like a cat's cradle? But Cleo had never dreamed about getting married. What she fantasized about was her first solo show as an artist, a day dedicated solely to her. What scared her was that recently it was easier to imagine the opening than the actual paintings. She worried that she was one of those artists who care more about being an artist than they do about making art. It was a fear so base, so desperately ordinary, that she never mentioned it to anyone, not even Frank.

Since they had not thought to invite a witness, Frank ran back outside and asked the hot dog vendor to join them. He surprised them both by quietly weeping through the entire ceremony, which lasted less than five minutes. Expelled back into the sunshine, Cleo embraced him while Frank insisted on crunching a $100 bill into his palm before saying goodbye. The couple wandered north to Canal Street, then stopped and smiled shyly at each other, unsure how to proceed. Frank lifted his hand, still clutching hers, to check his watch.

"Got a few hours till dinner. Want to get a drink?"

Cleo shook her head. They had invited thirty guests to the wedding dinner, but inevitably more would show up. The whole thing had been presented as a caprice, a giddy impersonation of adulthood. This wasn't unreasonable for Cleo, who had just turned twenty-five, but Frank was in his mid-forties. Too old, she thought, to consider himself too young to be married. She glanced around. Across the street, a storefront advertised $10 aura readings.

"What about that?"

Frank looked skeptical. "You think they'll make me a drink in there?"

They relinquished the sunshine of the street and stepped through a beaded curtain into the quiet, dark shop. It smelled of incense and takeout food. The high, needling sound of harp music replaced the discord of Canal Street outside. Behind a counter displaying an assortment of crystals and beaded jewelry, a middle-aged Chinese woman smiled at them.

"You married today?" she asked, pointing to Frank's tux. "It's good you come here."

She beckoned for Cleo to sit in a high-backed chair in front of an old-fashioned camera on a tripod and showed her where to place her palms either side, on two metal discs.

"So pretty," she said, looking at her. "Now, don't move."

She disappeared underneath a piece of black cloth attached to the back of the camera, pressed a button, which released a soft *poof*, then reappeared. Cleo had not expected to feel anything profound when the picture was taken, but she had hoped for a little more than the kind of brusque efficiency one might find at the DMV. Frank took her place, and she watched as he adjusted his bow tie. She saw a flash of his younger self, the anxious middle-schooler getting his yearbook picture taken. He looked up at the camera lens from beneath his long eyelashes and smiled, timidly, as if hoping to please. The contraption released another *poof*, and Cleo felt her heart contract. She did love him, she did.

Afterward they stood at the glass counter, looking down at their pictures. Cleo's aura was purple and yellow, while Frank's was red and green.

"Does that mean we're compatible?" asked Cleo anxiously.

"How long you been together?" asked the woman.

"Six months," said Frank.

The woman nodded.

"Eighty percent of relationship," she said, "is tolerating difference."

"What's the other twenty percent?" asked Frank.

The woman shrugged. "Fucking."

She performed the remainder of the reading with perfunctory brusqueness. Frank's aura suggested that he was creative, charismatic, and worried about money. Cleo's said she was intuitive, sensitive, stubborn, and needed to drink more herbal tea. That was it. Frank paid the woman and bowed affectedly before Cleo could pull him back out through the beaded curtains. She squinted up at him through the sunshine.

"What do you think?" she asked. "Are we compatible?"

"Well, we have at least twenty percent of the relationship down."

Then he hooked his arms around her and they kissed for a long time, without self-consciousness or ostentation, while all around them bright pyramids of fruit aged in the Chinatown heat, rows of diamante watches winked in the sun, and women flicked their fans open and closed like thoughts not quite realized.

———

"Felicitations and congratulations!"

Santiago beamed at them as he opened the door, his large body partially covered by a striped, sauce-stained apron. He was brandishing a bottle of champagne in one hand and a wooden spoon in the other. Wild-haired and robustly built, he reminded Cleo of some friendly mythological god. She submitted to being kissed wetly on each cheek, then spoon-fed a mouthful of golden beets. Behind him every surface of the large kitchen was covered in food. There were the beets with goat cheese, sliced filet mignon in a crushed black pepper sauce, lime-soaked ceviche, roasted asparagus, littleneck clams bathed in white wine, pearl couscous, shaved fennel and parmesan, and three other kinds of salad, one consisting entirely of edible flowers.

"Greatest chef in the world," Frank said, circling his arm around Santiago's wide girth. "Remember when you worked at that place that advertised processed meats like it was a good thing? And look at you now!"

Cleo caught Santiago's eye and smiled. Everyone Frank knew was the greatest *something* in the world. His half sister Zoe was the greatest actor, his best friend Anders was the greatest art director and amateur soccer player, and Cleo, well, Cleo was the most talented painter, the deepest thinker, the most beautiful woman on earth. Why? Because Frank wouldn't have married anyone else.

Frank plucked one of the edible flowers from the wooden bowl and placed it on his tongue, then gestured for Cleo to do the same. She bit into a cluster of yellow petals and closed her eyes. It tasted peppery and a little sweet, like licorice laced with paprika. Frank made an approving sound and took another.

"I knew I couldn't disappoint you," Santiago said, watching them. "You two understand pleasure." He motioned for them to sit at the dining table.

Santiago had recently opened his own restaurant and was riding a wave of critical and commercial success. His loft was a mix of faux found objects and exorbitant designer furniture; cinder-block side tables and vintage milk crates mingled with cowhide rugs and modernist lounge chairs. The effect was garishly impressive, like a dog walking on its hind legs.

"How was the ceremony?" he asked. "You know I got married at City Hall too." He winked at Cleo. "It's how this menace to society came to America."

"It was phenomenal," said Frank, using a dish towel to shimmy open the bottle of champagne. "Our witness was the guy from the street cart outside. Kamal. Nice guy. He cried!"

"You are lying to me." Santiago clapped his hands with delight.

"I'd bought a hot dog from him beforehand," said Cleo. "So he wasn't a complete stranger."

"You couldn't have asked someone from one of the other weddings to be your witness?"

"What would have been the fun in that?" asked Frank.

"Everything for the story," said Cleo, nodding toward Frank.

"And that's why we love him," said Santiago, slapping Frank's shoulder. "My mother-in-law was our witness. Looking like, excuse me for saying this but it's true, she was sitting on a kebab stick the whole time. Disapproving mothers, you know."

He smiled at Frank.

"Frank doesn't have to worry about that with me," said Cleo, and made a noise that was not quite a laugh.

Frank pecked the top of her head. Santiago took the bottle from him and poured three champagne flutes.

"We should send Kamal a bottle of this stuff," said Frank, swallowing most of his in one gulp.

"I didn't know you'd been married before," said Cleo to Santiago.

"For my visa," said Santiago. "She was a dancer I knew. But we were in love too, you know, for a moment."

"What happened?" Cleo asked.

Frank refilled his glass.

"Oh man, she died," said Santiago. "Overdose. Yeah, it was a real bummer. Beautiful woman, beautiful soul."

Cleo would have liked to ask another question, but Santiago got up to check on the food and Frank wanted to hear some music, and the conversation escaped like smoke.

By the time the wedding guests started to arrive, they had finished two bottles of champagne and sampled every dish. Cleo's former roommate, Audrey, came first. Slim-hipped, full-lipped, and covered in tattoos of quotes from books she'd only partially read, she was what Frank called one of Cleo's strays. Cleo went to kiss her, but Audrey stuck out her long pink tongue instead.

"That's how Tibetan monks greet each other," she said.

"I thought you were Korean?" said Frank.

Audrey rolled her eyes. Cleo covered Frank's mouth with her hand.

"Do Tibetan monks drink champagne?" she asked and handed Audrey a glass.

Audrey protruded her tongue again and pressed a pill onto it.

"Only when mixed with Klonopin." She swallowed it with a gulp, then went to find Santiago, whose restaurant she was a hostess at.

Next, Cleo's closest friend Quentin arrived. The two had met during Cleo's first weeks in New York and become inseparable, each as lonely and adrift as the other. Quentin had grown up between Warsaw and New York; his grandmother was a Polish heiress who believed gay people didn't exist in her country, which meant that Quentin would never have to work a day in his life but must also stay in the closet for the remainder of it. As far as his family was concerned, Cleo had been his girlfriend for the past two years.

"I still haven't forgiven you for not asking me to be your maid of honor," he said, kissing Cleo. "But I did get you a wedding present. It's *very* expensive."

"Honey, I don't think you're meant to tell them that."

This was Quentin's sometime boyfriend, Johnny. Johnny had the complexion of a naked mole rat and the same furtive expression, as though constantly looking for a hole through which to disappear. He was an odd choice of partner for Quentin, whose nature was like one extended grand entrance.

"I always thought you'd be the first to marry her," Frank said.

"So did I," said Quentin sadly.

The rest of the guests arrived, and Cleo took her place at the head of the table. She handed around plates and introduced acquaintances and accepted congratulations as the room became loud and gay. Most were friends of Frank's; advertisers and architects and designers, people who had found the intersection between creativity and economy, who made beautiful things but did not suffer for it. She smiled and filled glasses and tried to focus on the conversations happening around her.

"People don't know it, but Polish is a very poetic language," a bald academic, who did not speak Polish, was telling Quentin, who did. "You know when they translated *The Flintstones*, they put it all in rhyme?"

"Sorry I never called you back," exclaimed one guest to another across the room. "I threw my phone out the window after a bad haircut!"

Cleo stood up and tried making her way past the guests to the bathroom.

". . . And now all he wants to talk about is doing ayahuasca," a woman wearing a turban was saying to Zoe. "He goes down to Peru for the cere-monies and acts like it's some rare skill he's learned. I'm like, honey, it's a drug, not a degree."

"My acting teacher did say it completely neutralized his ego," said Zoe. "At least for a few weeks."

Zoe was the only family member they had invited. At nineteen she was also the youngest person there. Frank and Zoe looked almost nothing alike, despite being half siblings, in part because of the age difference, in part because Zoe's father was Black and Frank's, like their mother, was white. Bespectacled, freckled, and curly-haired, Frank was charmingly handsome, but he was rarely the best-looking person in the room. Zoe, on the other hand, was breathtaking. Her face had the symmetry of a Brâncuşi sculpture. Her hair was a tumble of curls streaked with copper and gold. She did not appear to have pores. Every time Cleo looked at her, she couldn't help searching for a flaw.

The turbaned woman turned to include Cleo in the conversation. Cleo could recall her job, food critic, but not her name. This was, she thought, a type of memory lapse common to New Yorkers.

"Cleo, you create," she declared briskly. "Do you think taking ayahuasca would enhance your painting?"

"I think I need my ego." Cleo laughed. "It's pretty much the only thing getting me to the canvas these days."

"Well, Frank says you're very talented," sniffed the turbaned food critic. "Perhaps your generation will restore the prominence of painting to the art world finally."

Cleo smiled graciously. Even in her writing, this critic had a way of giving compliments with an air of unwillingness, as though she had only a finite number and was never quite sure if now was the occasion to surrender one.

"Here's hoping," said Cleo.

"Not that Frank would be biased or anything," shot Zoe.

Cleo felt her face fall. Every time she met Zoe, she was left with the bruised feeling that the younger girl did not like her. Of course, this only made her more desperate for Zoe's good opinion, while uncomfortably aware that she was courting the approval of a sulky teenager. She had brought the tension up to Frank before, but he sidestepped the conflict with his usual light-footedness.

The food critic appeared to have lost interest in the conversation now that she was no longer speaking, and an awkward silence descended between Cleo, who was still straining to look unbothered, and Zoe, whose golden eyes were resting on her with predacious calm. Thankfully, Frank soon began calling Cleo's name from across the room.

"Cley, you've got to hear this story of Anders's!" he yelled, still mid-laugh. "You too, Zo!"

Frank had abandoned his top hat and jacket but left his napkin tucked into his shirt. His glasses were slightly askew, a telltale sign that he was already well on his way to being drunk. Zoe bounded over, leaving Cleo to follow behind her.

"You sit here, my bride," said Frank and pulled Cleo onto his lap.

"Okay, I start from the beginning," said Anders.

Zoe, for whom there was no available seat, hovered over Anders's shoulder. Anders was from Denmark and had worked for many years as Frank's art director before leaving to head the art department of a women's fashion magazine. Like Zoe, he was almost unfairly attractive, a former model in fact, but whereas Zoe seemed to radiate her own heat, Anders emanated a Nordic cool.

"So," said Anders, "I hurt my knee quite badly playing tennis."

"In a game I won, if I recall," said Frank.

"You only 'recall' the games you win," said Anders. "And it is not such a victory if your opponent is injured, is it? Anyway, I go home and the pain is really bad, quite unbearable. I remember that I have some leftover muscle relaxants from an injury years ago. They are expired, but I think, okay, I'll just try one. I take it, forget all about it, spend the afternoon on the roof with friends drinking beers, maybe a bottle of rosé. I realize I need to go the bathroom, so I get in the elevator and press my floor. At that time, I lived in an apartment where the elevator opened right into—"

"Great apartment," said Frank.

"Yes, it was very nice," said Anders. "Now suddenly I realize—"

"What happened to it again?" asked Frank.

Anders gave a distracted wave of his hands.

"Christine kept it after we called it quits, you know this. She still lives there with her son."

"That bitch," said Frank.

"Frank," said Cleo.

"Cleo," said Frank. "You didn't know this woman. Cut her open, and instead of a heart you'd find an abacus."

"You still shouldn't call—," said Cleo.

"Would you rather I call her a cunt?"

"I'd rather you didn't call her anything."

"What's the plural of abacus, anyway?" said Frank. "Abaci?"

"It's not," said Zoe confidently.

Cleo doubted that Zoe had ever seen an abacus.

"The elevator goes down," continued Anders. "The doors open, and I realize I cannot move. I am fucking paralyzed. If I let go of the rail, I will topple over like a tree."

"Been there." Frank nodded. "Two tabs of acid on a farm upstate when I was sixteen. Ended up lying in a pig trough the whole night."

"What did you do?" asked Zoe.

"Nothing," Frank said. "I couldn't get out of the trough."

"Not *you*," said Zoe.

"I could do nothing either!" said Anders. "I waited, hoping to regain movement soon, and eventually the elevator was called to another floor. The doors open, and a young family is standing in their apartment looking at me. I forgot to mention I am wearing only my tennis shorts, no shirt, no shoes, and cannot even open my mouth to beg an apology."

"Hot," said Zoe.

"Don't even think about it," said Frank.

"I'm standing there staring like a big slobbering Viking as they hide in the corner of the elevator," said Anders. "They are terrified of me!"

Frank laughed and reached behind Cleo to grab one of the profiteroles Santiago was parading around the room while singing "That's Amore."

"Eventually I make it back to the roof, and everyone is asking where I've been," Anders continued. "I explain the situation to them, how at last I crawled on my belly from the elevator to the bathroom, propped myself up on the towel rack to pee, which, as you can imagine, was not so successful. And do you know what they say? 'Hey man, that sounds amazing! Do you have more?' I'm telling you, in this moment I realize I will never understand Americans."

Zoe, tired of standing, or perhaps of not being the center of attention, squeezed beside Anders on the narrow set of apple boxes he was perched on, an act that would have been difficult had Zoe not been slight as a fawn. Anders smiled, revealing a mouth of gappy, uneven teeth, and the perfect symmetry of his face was momentarily shattered.

"Ah yes, Americans are all addicted to pills," said Frank. "I've heard this one before."

Zoe ruffled Anders's blond hair. Cleo wondered if they were going to sleep together, or possibly already had. This wasn't hard to imagine, since Anders had slept with everyone—including Cleo.

"I am not saying they are all drug addicts," Anders said. "I am merely pointing out that there is a cultural difference in terms of attitudes toward self-medication. Back me up here, Cleo."

It happened right after she met Frank, when she still thought she'd be leaving the country in a few months, following a party with an open, and subsequently lethal, bar. After a brief, unsatisfying fuck on his Chesterfield sofa, Anders had casually dismissed her. *I'm sure you'd rather go sleep in your own bed?*

"Anders thinks everyone in America is taking something," said Frank.

"The booming pharmaceutical industry here speaks for itself," said Anders.

Everything Cleo needed to know about lust and its humiliation, she learned in the moment she found herself lurching home from Anders's apartment with his semen still coating her stomach. Neither of them had ever told Frank.

"Okay, okay, let's keep the cultural criticism to a minimum," said Frank. "Since Cleo is just about to become one of us."

"What?" Cleo snapped back to the conversation at the sound of her name.

"You're becoming an American," said Zoe pointedly. "Right? That's what all this is for?"

She twirled her long finger around the room.

"Yes. I mean, no—," stumbled Cleo.

"You have to apply to be a permanent resident first," jumped in Anders. "Is what she means." He gave her a reassuring look.

"First comes love, then comes marriage, then comes a green card application and a shitload of paperwork," Frank sang.

The hem of Cleo's dress had flipped over her knee. She glanced down to smooth it and noticed, for the first time, a tiny silken tag on the inseam. Written in feminine cursive was one word: "Intimates." So it was a nightgown. She had worn a nightgown to her wedding. Slowly, Cleo bowed her head.

"Just never lose your accent," Zoe said, wrapping her arm around Anders's waist to further secure her seat. "British accents are so hard to get right. My voice coach says I sound cockney."

"I never lost mine," said Anders. "Unfortunately."

"Yeah, you still sound like the Terminator." Frank laughed.

"He was Austrian, you idiot," Anders said.

Cleo looked up at the sound of her name being called from across the room. She twisted around to see Audrey's face peeking from the bathroom door, mouthing *Help*. Cleo got up to excuse herself and gave Frank a peck on the lips. Another whiff of wine.

"Don't forget to drink water," she said.

Audrey was leaning over the sink when she entered, scrubbing fero-ciously at a red wine stain on the front of her shirt. It seemed a futile case until Audrey remembered that the trick to red wine stains was to pour white wine on them, something about neutralization. Cleo ran to the kitchen, returned with a bottle of pinot grigio from the fridge, and, at Audrey's instruction, proceeded to slosh it over Audrey's chest while she stood in the bathtub, gasping for breath.

"Shit, I'm soaked. Is it out?"

Cleo looked at Audrey's shirt, which had turned a urine shade of yellow, the red blemish unaltered at its center. Audrey pulled it off her body with a wet suck to inspect. They exchanged a long look, then exploded into laughter. Audrey stripped the shirt off and stood in her bra.

"Do you think I can just wear this?"

"Wait," said Cleo, hopping out of the tub and opening the laundry hamper. She pulled out a dress shirt that looked clean enough and offered it to Audrey. It was long enough to be a dress on her. She cinched it at the waist with her belt, then inspected herself in the mirror.

"Not bad." She turned up the collar. "Anyway, the only outfit anyone will remember is yours."

Cleo sat down on the cool lip of the tub with her knees together. Her hair made a curtain around her downturned face. "Audrey," she whispered. "Does it look like I'm wearing a nightgown?"

Audrey turned around and kneeled in front of her. "That's a really weird question, Cley," she said. "Since you look like a fucking angel."

Audrey pulled back the curtain of hair and kissed her on the cheek, then returned to the mirror to fix her eyeliner with the tip of her finger.

"Anders is like serial-killer handsome," Audrey's reflection said. Cleo nodded slowly, trying to keep her face neutral. "Did I ever tell you about the time we hooked up?"

"You did?"

Cleo was surprised to feel a pang of jealousy shoot through her.

"Ages ago," said Audrey. "It was like a chest of drawers with the little key sticking out falling on me."

Cleo could feel her face begin to flush with shame. But no, it was something else, something lighter, warmer. It was laughter.

"And he tried to stick it in, you know, the back," said Audrey.

"No!"

Both girls were laughing. Audrey leaned against the sink to catch her breath. "Maybe that's why he never called me." She sighed.

"You think?"

"If I was into anal," she said, "my whole life could be different."

Dessert had been laid out while they were in the bathroom. As well as the tower of profiteroles, there were silver trays of strawberries dipped in white chocolate, dishes of red-and-gold Rainier cherries, bowls of whipped cream and warm dulce de leche, pots of pink sugared almonds, and a box of chocolate cigars. The guests barely touched any of it. Cleo suspected there was enough cocaine circulating that half of them had no appetite at all. She took a little comfort in the thought that the cake she'd secretly pined for—a three-tier buttercream with scalloped icing, bands of white satin ribbon, and a cascade of frosted pink roses—would have gone unappreciated as well.

Santiago clinked his glass with a spoon and called for quiet. He was balancing precariously on a milk crate, enveloping the room with a smile.

"Speech!" one of the guests smoking at the window yelled. "Shut up for the speech!"

Someone moved to turn down the music, and the chatter quieted in tandem, as though the volume dial controlled the entire room.

"I am not good with words," Santiago began, tapping the spoon against his thigh nervously. "I express my feelings through my food. But I wanted to say something to commemorate this beautiful occasion between two dear friends, one old, one new."

"You mean one old, one young!" someone yelled to a sprinkling of cheers.

"But both young in spirit," Santiago demurred. "Cleo and Frank, you two met in this very home—or, as I understand, my elevator. Now I see you both sitting here, so happy and in love, surrounded by friends, and I hope you do not mind if I permit myself a little pride of the match-maker. And so I offer you these lines from *Don Quixote* that are much loved in my home country: 'El amor mira con unos antojos que hacen parecer oro al cobre, á la probreza riqueza, y á las lagañas perlas.'"

Santiago looked around expectantly to a vague murmur of approval. "Ah, I see I have to translate for you gringos. It means (Love looks through spectacles that make copper look like gold, poverty like riches, and tears like pearls.) He turned back to Cleo and Frank with a warm smile. "But, of course, in my eye you are both already gold."

The room erupted into cheers and a clatter of cutlery on glass.

"Now," Santiago said, beaming, "let's get drunk and dance!"

They moved the furniture to the walls, piling plates of half-eaten food and stubbed cigarettes onto the dining table. The sound of a jangling Brazilian band, hectic and happy, filled the room. One of Cleo's friends, a Batsheva-trained dancer turned babysitter, performed a gymnastic sequence of moves that resulted in the upturning of several jars of peonies and a French make-up artist getting kicked in the face. Empty bottles piled up on the kitchen counter, the table, the windowsills. Everyone wanted to put the next song on.

Cleo was dancing with loose-limbed abandon with Quentin when Frank caught her mid-spin and led her down the hallway, away from the guests, into Santiago's bedroom. The bed was covered in gifts. He closed the door behind them.

"I've barely seen you," he said, drawing her toward him.

They kissed each other deeply, eagerly. Outside, they could hear people laughing. Someone changed the song, and the sound of an old soul track slid under the door, the familiar guitar riff filling the room. Frank took her in his arms and guided her around the bed. He was a surprisingly smooth dancer, with a confidence that came with age. It was one of the things she'd been most happy to learn about him.

"First dance." Frank was laughing. "First married dance."

He dipped her backward, low to the ground, and her heart seized. He was drunk. He would drop her. But he pulled her back up and pinned her to him, slowly swinging her hips in time to his. Then he was sliding down the straps of her dress one by one. She stood in a puddle of blue silk on the floor. She was wearing white lace underwear with a tiny pink rosette at the center, her only concession to traditional wedding attire.

31

He stepped back to admire her. She felt very young, very beautiful. To delight in another, to be delighted in turn by them, that was what she had always wanted. Frank pulled her forward and kissed her ears, her neck, her clavicle, her nipples. He knelt to kiss her rib cage, her belly button, her hips.

"You taste," he said, his mouth filled with her skin, "delicious."

He picked her up and sat her on the dresser. Cleo rested her head against the mirror. Across from her the window framed a lavender square of sky through the window. He nudged her legs apart and knelt before her. Very tenderly, he slid her underwear to the side and pulled her toward his mouth. Her hands were in his hair, cupping the back of his head. Frank's tongue was like a little flame. Cleo turned her eyes to the ceiling and exhaled. Then Frank slid his fingers inside her, moving them slowly while the flame of his tongue licked her, and there was only warmth, no more thought. She pushed her knuckles into her mouth. *Too much.* She threw her head back with a sharp cry.

Frank's head bobbed back into view. His eyes were darting around her head.

"Are you okay?"

Cleo turned to see what he was looking at. It was a slim crack in the center of the mirror. Dangling from the fissure was a single strand of her blond hair. She touched her fingertips to the back of her head.

"Is it bleeding?" he asked.

"I don't think so," she said. "I barely felt it."

Frank smiled.

"Well, you were otherwise occupied."

He went to inspect her head and kissed her gently on her crown.

"What do we tell Santiago?" she asked.

"He won't notice," said Frank confidently. "Come on." He lifted her off the dresser and handed her the dress from the floor. "Flee the scene of the crime."

They left the bedroom to find Quentin languishing against the wall outside. He had a gift-wrapped box in his hands.

"I know," he said, "what you two were doing."

"You have her heart," Frank said, and laughed. "Let me have her body."

"Don't be vulgar," said Quentin. "Want to open your wedding present?"

Cleo untied the grosgrain ribbons and slid off the box's lid, pulling away fluttering layers of tissue paper. Inside was a Fabergé egg. It was the cream and powder blue of Michelangelo's painted skies, encased in a gold lattice studded with diamonds. Cleo carefully pulled it out of its box; it stood on four scrolled golden legs like a miniature carriage and felt surprisingly heavy in her hands.

"It's so beautiful," she breathed. "Oh, Quentin."

"It's not a real one," said Quentin quickly. "From imperial Russia or anything. Those are like three million dollars. But this is from the same company. And, well, I thought you'd like it."

Frank put his arm around Quentin's shoulders and squeezed. "It's great," he said. "So Cleo."

"There's more," said Quentin. "When the first egg was given to the Russian royal family, it had a surprise inside. A golden yolk, and inside that was a golden hen, and inside that was a tiny crown. Every egg is meant to have a surprise inside. So . . . open it."

At the top of the orb was a gold clasp holding each side of the lattice together. Cleo clicked it, and the egg sprang open. Inside was a slim gold pedestal protruding from a sky-blue floor. It held a tiny metal chest encrusted with jewels.

"Open that too," said Quentin.

Cleo lifted the chest's lid with her fingertip. Inside was a vial of white powder. Frank exploded into laughter.

"I'm guessing this is the part of the present that's for Frank," said Cleo.

"For both of you," said Quentin. "And me."

"Thank you," Cleo said, clicking the egg shut and kissing Quentin's cheek. "It's my new favorite thing."

She went to put it on Santiago's bed, but Quentin grabbed her arm and pulled her toward the bathroom.

"No, no," he said. "You're coming in here with me."

Cleo handed the egg off to Frank with a weary smile. Clearly, she was destined to spend most of her wedding in the bathroom.

"I'll entertain the rabble," said Frank. "Go."

Quentin pulled her after him and closed the door. He removed his own stash and took out his keys.

"I would have married you, you know." He held a key up to his nostril and sniffed hard. "If you needed me to."

"I do love him." Her voice was sharper than she'd intended. "It's not just the visa."

"I know, I know," Quentin said. "It's just so weird that you're actually married."

Cleo was peering into the mirror, teasing her hair into a braid, mostly to give her hands something to do. She touched the back of her skull gingerly. There was the tender spot where her head had collided with the glass. Quentin offered her the key, but she shook her head. He shrugged and inhaled it himself.

"There are worse reasons to marry someone," said Cleo.

"There are better ones," said Quentin, rubbing his gums with his finger.

"And how would you know?" Cleo snapped.

"Hey." Quentin came and stood behind her. He wrapped his arms around her waist and perched his chin on her shoulder. "Calm down. No one thinks you did anything wrong. I know you love each other. I'll just always love you best, that's all."

"I know," said Cleo. "Wipe your nose."

Quentin grabbed some toilet paper and blew into it, inspecting the contents before throwing it in the wastebasket.

"I definitely love you more than Johnny loves me," he said. His voice was hard and bright. "I think he's stealing from me. Well, I think he's stealing my vitamins. I'm not kidding! Hundreds of dollars' worth of them. But when I asked him about it, he went crazy and claimed I must have taken them all and forgotten. Who the fuck takes that many vitamins and forgets about it? He didn't even leave me my magnesium, which you *know* I need to stay regular."

"That's terrible," said Cleo, suppressing a smile. "Magnesium is . . . Well it's crucial, really. Essential."

"At least you know Frank will never steal your shit," said Quentin. He darted his eyes up and down her. "Not that you have much to steal."

"You know, I wish he'd put that in his vows," said Cleo, deflecting the insult before it could sink in. "'I promise to love you, protect you, and never steal your worthless shit.'"

"Or hold your hand to a burning stove," said Quentin. "Like my dad did to my mom."

Quentin had a knack for tipping a conversation from light to dark, like snapping off a light.

"He really did that?" asked Cleo.

He was looking down. His long eyelashes cast feathery shadows over his cheeks.

"Poland." Quentin shrugged by way of explanation.

"I didn't know," said Cleo.

"Why would you?" He looked up, his face suddenly alive with possibility. "*Now* will you do a line with me?"

Cleo rolled her eyes and relented with the slightest nod of her head.

"You do look beautiful," he said as she knelt beside him over the toilet seat. "Like a child bride."

Outside the bathroom, a group was gathering around the front door, scuffling to find their shoes and refill their glasses. The bowls of cream and dulce de leche were scarred with cigarettes stubs. Zoe lay passed out on the sofa with Frank's tuxedo jacket over her.

"There you are." Frank came up behind her. He was rubbing his eye with his knuckle, back and forth, like a sleepy child. "We're going up to the roof to do fireworks. Wedding fireworks."

"What's the difference?" Cleo asked, but Frank was already disappearing up the stairwell.

Up on the roof the winking skyline of Manhattan sprawled before them against a velvet black sky.

"I had some fireworks left over from the long weekend," Santiago said, unstacking the neon packages. "But I got a few new ones for the occasion."

Memorial Day. It felt like a long time ago now, but in fact it was only a few weeks. Cleo's student visa was up at the end of the month, and the company she'd been freelancing for as a textile designer couldn't afford to sponsor her. As a last hurrah, she'd presumed, Frank had taken her to his rarely used cabin upstate. Since neither of them could drive or were particularly domestic, it was three days of unmade beds, cereal for dinner, and pure, private bliss.

Frank moved to the far side of the roof and attempted to arrange a firework, propping it between two wine bottles. He lurched forward, sending the bottles scattering around his feet.

"Hey, man," Santiago said, coming up behind to steady him. "Why don't you let me do this. You go watch with Cleo."

"Who has a lighter?" Frank yelled, ignoring him. He slapped the pockets of his trousers. Someone tossed him one, but it went wide, sailing over the side of the roof into the darkness beyond. Anders appeared through the doorway and, exchanging a long look with Santiago, managed to guide Frank back to where a crowd of guests had gathered to watch. Cleo took his hand.

It was on the train home from Hudson that he'd asked her. She was drifting in and out of sleep on his shoulder, his cheek pressed against the crown of her head. *Cleo, my Cleo.* A black ribbon of river rushed beside them, barely distinguishable from the dark fields and trees beyond. *What would you think?* She could see the chalky reflection of Frank's face glowing in the window. He looked like a saint. *What would you think of us getting married?*

Santiago yelled for everyone to stand back as he and Anders lit the first fireworks. Bright flumes of light shot up behind them, suspended momentarily in the shape of stars. The sky crackled with light. Suddenly Frank shook his hand free of hers and darted forward across the roof, bent at the waist. He lunged for a rocket and lit it straight from his hand, sending it off at an angle that narrowly missed Anders's shoulder.

"What the fuck?" she could hear Anders yelling as Frank ran back.

He took her hand again and squeezed it hard. Sparks showered down on them. The fireworks gained momentum, illuminating the faces of the crowd on the roof in flashes. Cleo watched Frank's profile in the light. *Boom, boom, boom.* He was staring up ahead, jaw set, eyes wet and reflective.

She had not told Quentin what Frank's actual vow was. He'd surprised her by requesting to say something at the end of the ceremony, after the usual script had been read. He was noticeably nervous, his usual gregariousness gone. When he finally did speak, it was a single sentence. *When the darkest part of you meets the darkest part of me, it creates light.*

CHAPTER THREE

July

Less than a month after Cleo and Frank's wedding, Quentin and Johnny broke up. Cleo had stopped spending all her free time with Quentin, which meant he suddenly had a lot of extra energy to focus on Johnny—and find him wanting. Johnny, it turned out, was just another Irish Catholic queen with a drinking problem. He had Republican parents that he secretly adored, and the kind of body hair that could be described as a pelt. Quentin was better off without him.

Now that Johnny was gone and Cleo was always busy with Frank, Quentin had time to do whatever he wanted, like stay up all night watching anime, or chain-smoke in bed, or go to invite-only orgies—which was exactly the plan for that night. The invitation had been slipped inside his locker at the gym: "We Want You. Private Event. Email for Details." He'd heard about these parties before, run by an underground network of gays whose mission was to bring back pre-AIDS-era group sex in safe yet glamorous environments. This was his first invitation, and the knowledge that he had been watched, been chosen, sent a ripple of pleasure through him.

Johnny would never have allowed this. He was too staid, too judgmental. Quentin had only ever meant to sleep with him once or twice anyway, but Johnny had ingratiated himself into Quentin's life with his aggressive helpfulness. For Quentin's French Revolution–themed birthday party, for instance, Johnny bought an antique French cookbook and offered to make Quentin any cake he liked. Quentin picked a pear tart comprised of hundreds of individually folded and glazed pastry petals, not because he particularly liked pear tarts but because it had looked the most labor-intensive. Johnny had made it for him without complaint, and when Quentin stood over the amber glow of his twenty-six birthday candles, staring down at those hundreds of individually folded and glazed pastry petals, he felt certain that the tart was evidence of a love so pure, so dutiful, that he would never find its equal.

But ever since admitting to Cleo that Johnny was stealing from him, he'd become increasingly suspicious that perhaps it was he, not Johnny, who was being taken advantage of. It had all come to a head a few days earlier when Quentin, who liked to keep his large brownstone apartment at a frigid sixty-five degrees during the summer months, went to put on his favorite orange featherweight cashmere sweater. After searching in vain, he'd traipsed downstairs to find Johnny wearing it.

"That's my sweater," he said.

"So?"

"You know it's my favorite. I got it at the Barneys Warehouse sale with Cleo."

Johnny rolled his eyes. "You're a little obsessed, dear."

"With Barney's?"

"With Cleo."

Quentin exhaled a soft snort caught somewhere between disdain and embarrassment. "She's my best friend."

"Shouldn't that be me?" asked Johnny.

He took a bite of Quentin's organic chocolate cereal from Quentin's ceramic bowl. A trickle of brown milk dribbled from his chin down the front of Quentin's sweater. Johnny licked his fingers and stabbed at the stain. Quentin flinched. Johnny's finger had only succeeded in grinding the milk further into the fibers of the fabric. A faint brown drip was still noticeable against the orange cashmere. Quentin could feel heat building behind his eyes.

"Take it off," he said.

"What?" Johnny laughed. "No."

Quentin raised his trembling hands to his temples.

"TAKE IT OFF!" he screamed.

Johnny's mouth momentarily hung open. Brown flecks of chocolate had built up at the corners. He leaped up and ripped the sweater off to reveal his soft, freckled belly beneath.

"Jesus, Quentin!" He hurled the orange blur toward him. "It's just *stuff*. Does it matter? Does it make you happy?"

"It doesn't make me *un*happy," said Quentin.

"Things are not people, Quentin," said Johnny with the smug satisfaction of the truly obtuse.

"*Things* don't treat me like an idiot," said Quentin. "*Things* don't steal my identity."

"*Steal your identity?*" Johnny clutched his bare chest and cast his eyes beseechingly around the room, as if performing for a daytime talk show audience. "Did Cleo tell you that?"

She hadn't, in fact—she had always been diplomatically tight-lipped on the subject of Johnny—but it felt satisfying to make Johnny think she had.

"She's just trying to protect me," said Quentin primly. "That's what *best* friends do."

Johnny pinched his face into an unattractive scowl.

"British bitch," he sneered.

"Would you like her better if she was from Ohio like you?" snapped Quentin.

"For the one hundredth time, Quentin, Cincinnati is one of the most *European* cities in America."

Quentin could not contain his scoff.

"See!" Johnny exclaimed. "You're a snob, just like her. The two of you left me alone for like an *hour* at her wedding. It's obvious she doesn't think I'm good enough for you."

"Maybe that's because you're not," said Quentin.

Johnny gasped dramatically. "All I ever did was love you," he said. "You're just too fucked up to know what that feels like."

"Maybe," said Quentin. He stooped to pick up the sweater and draped it over his shoulder, gathering all his pride with it. "But I'll settle for knowing what Italian cashmere feels like."

Quentin was proud of this line, which he thought sounded like something out a movie, striking just the right timbre between resignation and hope. He was proud of it right up until Johnny took a step toward him and smacked him square across the jaw. It felt like a firework going off in his face.

"You and her deserve each other," he said.

Ordinarily, Quentin would have scornfully corrected him (you and *she* deserve!), but he was too stunned to say anything as Johnny proceeded to storm, still shirtless, out of the house. At the sound of the door slamming, Quentin surprised himself by bursting into tears. He cradled the side of his face with one hand and waited for them to pass. When they didn't, he called Cleo.

Within half an hour, she was in his kitchen. She was wearing a traditional Mexican embroidered dress, her hair pulled into two long fishtail braids down her back and tied with white ribbons. He found her style too bohemian for his taste, but he appreciated that she always made an effort with her appearance. She put a bottle of his favorite Japanese soda and a packet of Advil on the kitchen table in front of him, inspecting his face with a look of concern.

"You're bruising," she said. "What happened?"

"He was wearing my sweater," said Quentin sulkily. "And he's a psychopath."

"Do you have any frozen peas?"

She opened the freezer door to reveal a large frosted bottle of vodka and three cartons of Polish cigarettes. She raised an eyebrow at Quentin. He shrugged.

"Keeps them fresh."

Cleo removed the bottle and wrapped it in a dish towel. She sat down across from him and held it gingerly to his jaw. His eyes would not stop leaking.

"Hurts?" she asked.

Quentin shook his head and wiped his face roughly with the back of his palm.

"I don't know why I'm—" He stopped himself and rubbed his hands on his pants. He tried to laugh, but it escaped from his throat as a scrap of sob.

"It's just tender," said Cleo, cupping his cheek with her palm. "He got your tender part, is all."

He bowed his head and pressed his forehead to hers. He was about to tell her that all of him was the tender part when her phone buzzed and she pulled away.

"I'll tell Frank to meet us here, shall I?" she said.

Quentin felt a jolt of irritation.

"Or you could not?"

"Quentin." She put on her stern maternal voice. "You know how much he works, and the weekends are our only real time together. Please don't be difficult about this."

"Can't you just bail?" whined Quentin. "You bail on things all the time. It's one of your greatest attributes."

"But I don't want to. I was painting all morning, and now I want to see my husband."

"You can just call him Frank. I hate all this 'my husband' crap."

"But he is my husband!"

"Only because you needed a visa."

"For the one hundredth time, it is *not* just a visa marriage." She exhaled wearily. "Why are you acting like this? You like Frank, remember? He makes me happier than anyone I've ever known . . ."

Cleo launched into a monologue about her and Frank's marital bliss, but Quentin had lost interest. Quentin did like Frank—he was always down to party, and unlike the litter of unwashed skateboarders and street artists Cleo usually dated, he had some money at least—but he was not Cleo's person. Quentin was. Quentin suspected deep down that he and Cleo would end up together, not romantically of course, but as true soul mates, growing old together in some crumbling town house uptown surrounded by pedigreed dogs and vintage furs. Frank was just a brief inter-lude into the tropes of traditional heterosexuality for Cleo. He and Cleo belonged together, were more like family to each other than either of their real families ever had been. They were practically sisters.

". . . I've even gone off my antidepressants," Cleo was saying.

Quentin snapped back to attention.

"Babe, no. That is *not* a good idea for you. Remember sad Cleo of yesteryear? No one needs her to make a comeback."

"That was just because I was lonely and, you know, all the stuff with my mum. My life's really different now. I have Frank, I have a proper home—"

"His home."

"*Our* home. I just think I'm a lot more set up to be happy now. I know I am."

Quentin felt a wave of concern, followed by a riptide of apathy. In the end, she was going to do whatever she wanted to do.

"It's your life." He shrugged. "Just let me ask you one question. And you have to answer honestly." He looked deep into her eyes. "When was the last time you were with a straight man, I'm talking *any* straight man, and he said something more interesting than what you were already thinking?"

Cleo laughed and turned away.

"I'll tell Frank to bring us lunch," she said.

"I'll take that as a never."

By the time Frank arrived, loaded with bags of sushi takeout, Quentin's chin had turned a mottled purple and was producing a dull, aching throb. Cleo ran to greet Frank as if he were a soldier returning from war with spoils, fussing over the plastic containers of miso soup, seaweed salad, and rice.

"At least now you can say you've taken a punch standing," said Frank. "That's more than I can say."

Quentin flicked his eyes up and down Frank.

"Why is that not surprising," he said. "Remind me why you're here again?"

Cleo gave him an imploring look.

"Hey, I was worried about you," said Frank, removing his hand from Cleo. "Anyway, it might be good to have a man around, you know, in case he comes back."

"In my experience, having a man around is usually the problem," said Quentin.

Frank laughed. "No disagreements here."

But when Johnny did return later that evening, Quentin was glad to have Frank there. They were watching one of Quentin's favorite documentaries, *Princess Diana: Her Life in Jewels*, while drinking screwdrivers with the now warm vodka when they heard the front door open. Johnny yelled Quentin's name. His voice sounded thick and muffled. Cleo put her hand on Quentin's leg and motioned for him not to move. Frank stood up and went to the front room. Quentin could hear them murmuring, then Johnny's voice growing louder, demanding to see him. Quentin shook Cleo off and moved closer to the front hall.

"He doesn't want to see *me*?" Johnny was slurring. "I don't want to see *him*."

"All right," said Frank, ushering him toward the door. "Why don't you come back when you've sobered up."

"You know he thinks he's a woman, right?" Johnny continued. "All his dresses . . ." Johnny started cackling. "He's never going to meet someone better than me."

Beyond the front door, Quentin could hear a siren's wail passing. The thought occurred to him that if you listened hard enough in New York, you could always hear a siren. Someone, somewhere, was always getting hurt.

"All right, I'm going," said Johnny.

Quentin peered out of the living room into the hallway. Johnny was standing on the top step of the stoop, silhouetted by the yellow streetlamp. He turned to go, then changed his mind and wobbled to face Frank again.

"Gay men want to date *men*," he said. "That's the *reality*."

"Enough," said Frank. "Go sleep it off."

"I *see* you, Quentin!" Johnny yelled past Frank's shoulder. "Little trans freak!"

Frank shut the door and stood with his back to Quentin. Johnny was still yelling something about reality on the street outside. Quentin watched Frank's back. What was he thinking? Was he judging him? Pitying him? He probably thought he was just another fucked-up fag with a closetful of dresses. He must think he was pathetic. Frank turned and caught his eye. He walked over and squeezed Quentin's shoulder.

"I've gotta say," Frank said, "I liked him more when I knew him less."

Quentin had not spoken to Johnny since, but he couldn't stop thinking about what he'd said. What did *reality* have to do with anything anyway? Quentin hated reality. Reality was sweaty and ugly. It was deodorant stains on black clothing and cold sore cream and utility bills. It was fake girlfriends and formal dinners in ill-fitting suits. It was his father lecturing him in broken English about being a man. It was all of Poland, that rundown junk shop of a country, with its stray dogs and secret forests where men fucked each other in the dark and then went home to their wives. No, Quentin wanted *fantasy*, which was exactly why he was going to the orgy that night.

The night could not come fast enough. The setting sun cast a golden light over the buildings as Quentin walked his dachshund, Lulu, around his neighborhood. It was the hour of evening in which the shops were still open but the bars and restaurants were already beginning to fill, and an air of both industry and frivolity permeated the streets. He let himself into his apartment and poured dog food into a bowl, thinking about who he could call.

Not his mother, who was snorkeling with her new boyfriend on a private island where, she'd told him delightedly, cell phones weren't allowed. He tried his father's number, but his phone went straight to voicemail; it was already past midnight in Warsaw. He tried Cleo again. No answer. He thought about calling Johnny. Instead, he opened his inbox and scrolled down to the email with the address for the orgy, rereading it again for any clues, but the information was the same, of course. Then he tried his drug dealer, who picked up on the second ring. He ordered his usual and perched on the windowsill to light another cigarette. The sky outside was turning a dark, bruised blue.

The address given was in a part of Brooklyn he'd never been to before. The only nonresidential building was a laundromat a few doors down. Its lights had been left on for the night, illuminating its checkered vinyl floor and rows of silver washing machines.

He'd made himself a couple of vodka sodas before he left, too strong, he realized now as he shook his head. It felt like a tank of water being sloshed from side to side. He'd decided not to eat that day, which might have been a mistake. Stepping into the faint halo of light cast by the laundromat's window, he pulled out the vial from his jacket pocket and inspected it. It was already half empty. He should have brought two with him, he thought with irritation, while tapping two small bumps onto the back of his hand. It was his least favorite way of doing coke, messy and inefficient, but he wanted to be quick. He felt better almost instantly, that sharp, bitter clarity shifting his mind into focus again, giving him purpose.

He hadn't told anyone he was coming here. By the time Cleo called him back, he was already in the cab, and he didn't want to be talked out of it. He suspected that even girls like her, the socially liberal, sexually adventurous types, were deep down a tiny bit disgusted by what men did together. He couldn't imagine having the kind of frank discussions with her that other girlfriends had with each other over brunch, giggling about penis size and elusive orgasms. *And then I let him piss in my mouth while his power bottom boyfriend watched! Another round of mimosas!*

He'd seen it once, the way Cleo recoiled when he'd told her about the bathhouses he'd gone to before he met Johnny. They were in the back of a cab hurtling from one party to another; he'd taken so much ketamine he could barely lift his head—*like a baby, like a baby*, he'd kept saying. As he babbled on to her about what he'd asked those men to do to him, what he'd done to them, he saw, as if from a great distance, Cleo turn her face slowly, slowly toward the window, leaving him just a sliver of her profile, queenly and remote, focusing her eyes on the wet glow of the traffic lights beyond, and a shame—he could almost taste it now, along with the drip of the coke—a terrible bitter shame had filled him. *Enough now, enough.*

He rang the doorbell and was buzzed into a dark entrance hall where a bald man wearing a leather loincloth and spiked dog collar sat on a stool, guarding a second door.

"Name?" he asked and scanned his list to confirm. "Proof of negative?"

Quentin removed a piece of paper. He had been tested earlier that week in preparation and was amazed by how relieved he'd felt to get the negative result. He used condoms, but there had been a couple of times with Johnny that they'd forgone them. There was nothing like taking an HIV test to immediately convince yourself that you had it. The bald man looked it over and nodded.

"Check all clothing and belongings before entering. There are no cell phones inside."

Quentin laughed, but the man looked back at him blankly, waiting.

"Are you serious? Take my clothes off here?"

Quentin thought about turning around, but it seemed like such a waste, after the hours of expectation, plus the cab ride and drug money, not to at least see what was inside. He removed his shirt, then knelt to unbuckle his gladiator sandals. With some difficulty he managed to shed his leather shorts. He folded it all as neatly as he could and passed it to the doorman.

"These are a collector's piece," Quentin said. "They're worth more than you."

"Underwear too," said the bald man.

Quentin pinched the bridge of his nose, took a deep breath, and pulled down his underwear. In return the man handed him a spiral plastic bracelet with a round number tag on it, not unlike the kind given at public swimming pools.

"What's next?" Quentin asked. "A full cavity search?"

"You can get that inside," he said. "Just don't let anyone take the bracelet."

"This fabulous thing?" said Quentin. "I wouldn't dream of it."

The man shifted in his seat to indicate Quentin should pass. He opened the door and entered a long, narrow corridor leading to another door, behind which he could hear the insistent, bludgeoning beat of techno music and the dark ripple of men's voices. He would have loved another bump, a little jolt to get him through the door, but of course the drugs were with his clothes. Naked but for his yellow bracelet, Quentin felt exposed in a way that was deeply unerotic. In fact, he thought, the whole experience thus far had been about as sexy as a prison check-in.

He pushed the door open and walked into what looked like a large living room. A glow-in-the-dark mural depicting muscular Greek bathers covered the entirety of one of the walls. Fake stone fountains of young cherubs pissing water dotted the space. Strobe lights flashed overhead. In front of a makeshift DJ booth, behind which an oiled man sporting a ginormous set of ram horns was swaying, a small crowd of naked men danced. The whole place felt cheap; they'd striven for Grecian fantasy and ended up with Greek restaurant.

Quentin wandered around the periphery of the room, where black curtains partitioned off smaller, private areas. He peered through the gap between one and saw a pile of men, five, maybe six, fucking each other. It reminded him of the inside of a beehive, all that swarming activity. Peering into the next area, he locked eyes with a thick-necked man fiercely pumping at a hooded figure beneath him on all fours. He held Quentin's gaze for a long, ferocious moment before rolling his eyes back into his head.

Quentin was just wondering if he should leave—he didn't feel nearly uninhibited enough to join the dance floor, let alone one of the private areas—when he saw a tall boy moving with great speed and deliberateness toward him. He was smiling in a way that seemed to suggest he had been expecting Quentin.

"Zdravstvuyte," he said, putting a hand lightly on Quentin's shoulder.

Quentin stared back at him mutely. He was very striking, with a freshly shaved head that gave his skull a vulnerable, newborn look. His face was full of contradictions; pale, sensitive eyes set above a crooked boxer's nose, feminine bow lips and a strong, square chin. Quentin let his gaze drift down his sinuous torso to his long straight cock, nestled in a bed of dark hair.

"Are you the one who put the note in my locker?" Quentin asked, feeling ridiculous.

"Note?" The boy's smile faded into confusion. "I'm sorry, no. It's just that I was certain you were Russian."

"No," said Quentin. Then, sensing that he was disappointing him, he added. "Polish. I'm Polish originally."

"Ah!" The boy's face lit back up. "That is why then."

"Why did you think I was Russian?"

The boy flicked his eyes lightly up and down Quentin.

"Your eyebrows," he said and laughed.

It was a glinting, surprising sound, like water springing suddenly from a tap that appears dry. Quentin's eyebrows were, in fact, often commented upon. Velvety and dark, with long, thick eyelashes to match, they were one of the few benefits he could think of from being Eastern European.

"I'm sorry I'm not Russian," Quentin said, desperately thinking of something to say.

"Polish is better," the boy said and shrugged. "You have less problems."

He grabbed Quentin's hand in his and shook it. His hand was both soft and rough, like a cat's tongue. Quentin could feel his own cock stir at the touch of him.

"I'm Alex," the boy said.

"Quentin. Can I get you a drink?" he asked.

"Yes," the boy said, still smiling. "And I get you one also. I hear they're free."

Alex guided Quentin to the bar, which was a piece of plywood on two crates, behind which another impossibly buff man, this one wearing antlers, was serving drinks in little plastic cups.

"It's a dry bar, boys," he yelled across the table. "You want a soda?"

Quentin and Alex looked at each other.

"I know somewhere very cool we can go if you like," Alex said. "Just across the bridge."

Back outside it was like being exiled from Eden; both were suddenly aware of their nudity. They reclaimed their clothes from the bald man, who took their bracelets with the same blank inscrutability as before, and dressed quickly in the hallway. Quentin watched Alex out of the corner of his eye. His clothes were very simple, a white T-shirt, loose jeans, sneakers, and a faded denim jacket. They seemed almost deliberately chosen to reveal as little as possible about the wearer. Once fully clothed, they both stared at each other, as if for the first time.

Alex laughed. "You are dressed for a different party."

The bar Alex took him to on the Lower East Side had no sign and was at the bottom of a cracked, unlit stairwell that no longer looked in use.

"Careful," Alex said, turning to offer his hand.

Inside, the space was small and cavelike, diffuse red light pooling on the sticky mahogany bar top and smudged mirror behind. Arranged on the shelves above the glowing liquor bottles was a collection of samovars. Squat round tables and spindly wooden chairs faced a slightly elevated stage. Men sat slumped around the tables, and Quentin had the sensation that they never left, were as permanent to the place as the chairs and the samovars. Alex greeted the elderly bartender and chatted easily in Russian while he poured three tumblers of vodka.

"Nostrovia!" they said.

Each downed his glass in one long, luxuriating gulp, gesturing for Quentin to do the same. The bartender was already refilling his and Alex's drinks as Quentin choked down his.

"Another," said Alex. He affected his thickest Slavic accent. "Tonight, you drink like Russian."

"I have to go to the bathroom," said Quentin.

"Okay. Hurry, there is also a performance starting now."

In the bathroom Quentin tapped the remainder of the vial onto the metal toilet paper dispenser, an object seemingly designed for this very activity, and slid out his credit card. There was enough for two short but decently plump lines, not ideal but enough to form a break in the clouds of vodka already overcasting his mind. He took a short straw out of his wallet and snorted the first line. Delicious. He briefly considered saving the second line for later, then immediately hoovered it up through the other nostril.

When he reappeared, the performance had started. On the stage, in a silver pool of light, a woman was singing. She was sinuously thin in a strappy gold dress plunging low between her small breasts. Her bony knees and ankles protruded from beneath a pair of fishnet stockings. Alex gestured for them to take a seat at one of the tables closest to the stage and brought a carafe of vodka and two tumblers from the bar. Spotting him, the singer blew a kiss in his direction. He nodded and covered his heart with his palm. She cast her long, dark eyelashes down and swayed slightly from side to side, singing in a low voice that sounded like a needle ripping through silk.

Alex poured each of them another glass and downed his in one smooth, practiced movement. Quentin drank his down too as Alex nodded approvingly. At this distance, Quentin could see that the singer's complexion, despite the white powder she'd caked on, was the sour color of white wine. Along her chin the dark shadow of stubble was beginning to show, and Quentin felt, in spite of himself, a shiver of horror. Not being able to pass, that was his greatest fear.

They sat drinking without speaking as the singer performed. She swayed and the men swayed too, mirroring her, and soon the room was swaying, the walls and the floor and the little army of samovars, and Quentin had the sensation that they were all being pulled, back and forth, by that constant rocking motion of the singer's hips. He wondered what Cleo would think if she could see him here. She would never find herself in a place like this with a person like Alex—itinerant, mysterious, perhaps a little dangerous. Or maybe at one point she would have, but not now, not after meeting Frank. Her marriage had given her access to a world he would never know. She would not admit it, perhaps would never consciously know it, but she had left him behind. She had become acceptable.

Finally the singer spoke softly into the microphone and pressed her palms together. Quentin understood that it was her final song. As the first notes played, a murmur of recognition rippled through the bar, and the men began to clap steadily in time.

"Ah!" Alex said, clapping too. "This is very famous Russian song. From the gypsies."

"What's she saying?" asked Quentin.

"Let me see." Alex craned his neck forward to listen more carefully. "She sings now, 'we were riding *troika*'—I don't know how to translate that, a carriage maybe—'with bells jingling. Far away were the'—how would you say—'shining lights. How I wish that I could follow, to lift the sadness from my life' . . . It doesn't sound so good translated."

"Sounds very Russian," said Quentin.

"Yes, it is beautiful and sad like Russia," said Alex, staring ahead at the shining figure on stage. "She sings well."

"And her? Do you think she is beautiful and sad?" asked Quentin.

"Of course," said Alex. "Don't you?"

"You're not some kind of tranny chaser, are you?"

Alex turned in his seat to face him.

"I've never heard that expression," he said. "But no. When I first came here there was someone like her, not her but like her, who became like a mother to me. You don't find her beautiful?"

"I have nicer dresses," said Quentin.

Alex laughed and poured out the last of the vodka.

"Then maybe you should be up there," Alex said.

Quentin tilted his head back to drain his glass. A cloud of red light spun around his head.

"I should have been a girl," he said. "That's what I should have been. I should have been born a girl."

———

Outside the cool air licked his skin. They took a taxi back to Quentin's, and he was relieved to see through the window dark figures still smoking outside bars. He hated being the last one to go home. They pulled up in front of his building and he paid for the cab, blindly pulling bills from his wallet.

"You are rich," said Alex quietly as Quentin opened the front door.

"My grandmother," he said, dropping his keys and wallet onto the hallway floor.

"Me, I am very poor," Alex said.

"Want a drink?" Quentin said, leading him through to the kitchen.

Lulu ran at them as they entered, yelping in happy relief to have Quentin returned to her.

"Is just like you!" Alex laughed, picking her up to let her sniff his face. "You are twins."

He put her down and she skittered at their heels. Quentin tried to push her away with his foot but lost his balance, stumbling against the counter.

"You have some vodka?" Alex asked.

"Of course. There's soda water and I think—"

"Just the vodka," said Alex. "As long as it's cold."

"I have this too," said Quentin, removing his other two vials from their hiding place inside the cutlery drawer. "If you want."

Alex's eyes snapped toward his outstretched hand. In the kitchen light Quentin could see they were eerily pale, with glossy black pupils the size of dimes.

"And ice?" Alex asked quietly.

"Um, sure." Quentin turned toward the freezer, but Alex grabbed his forearm.

"No," he said impatiently. "*Ice*. Crystal."

Quentin looked at him in alarm.

"You mean *meth*? God, no."

"Have you tried it?" asked Alex, dropping his arm.

"Well, no," said Quentin. "But why do that when you can do this?"

"Because is like this," said Alex, nodding toward the vials. "Times everything."

Quentin looked at him skeptically. He'd seen what happened to men who got hooked on crystal. Their faces ended up looking like one of Lulu's chew toys.

"It's really that good?" he asked.

"In Russia we have a saying. 'If you are going to drown, drown in deep water.'"

Quentin shook his head, unsure what that meant.

"Okay." Alex smiled his sharp-toothed smile. "Tonight, we do it your way."

Then he dropped to his knees, as though offering himself as a gift at Quentin's feet.

An hour later, and Quentin was teetering around the living room in thigh-high boots and a silk slip dress, singing along to a glittering disco track while Alex watched from the floor. Strewn around them were half the contents of Quentin's secret wardrobe: an assortment of plunging satin and velvet dresses, mismatched stiletto heels, and real hair wigs. Alex was lopsidedly wearing a platinum-blond bob and cutting them more lines on a plate, laughing as Quentin attempted to dance on top of the plump sofa, his ankles buckling beneath him. Quentin dropped to his knees, still singing, and shimmied his dress up to reveal the strip of thigh between the top of his boots and his boxer briefs. He felt lithe and sexy, feminine and free. Alex grabbed his wrist and tugged him, a tumble of legs and heels, down to the floor.

He pulled the wig from his head and rolled on top of Quentin, so they were face to face, his hands on either side of Quentin's head. Alex was breathing hard; Quentin could see white clumps of powder clinging to his nostril hairs as he exhaled. Quentin turned his face to the side and threw his arms above his head. He didn't want to see anymore, he just wanted to feel and be felt, texture on texture. Alex reached a hand down and worked Quentin's legs apart, sliding the dress up his thighs. He yanked down Quentin's underwear and slipped a hand between his buttocks to caress him, circling with the tips of two fingers, working him open.

"Your pussy is so wet," Alex murmured into the air above Quentin's face.

"It is?" said Quentin. He had meant it to sound teasing, but instead the question came out as genuine, his voice earnestly high-pitched.

"Mm," Alex said. "It's hungry for me." He fumbled to unbutton his jeans and released his cock between Quentin's legs. He held himself straight as he began to push inside Quentin.

"Wait," said Quentin, louder than he'd intended. He brought his hands to Alex's chest. "I need something. There's olive oil in the kitchen."

"No, no," murmured Alex, taking Quentin's arms and pinning them back above his head. "Girls don't need that stuff. You're wet, you're wet already for me."

He let Alex spit on his palm and push inside him, and the pain mingled with that word, *girl*.

———

Quentin woke on his back with the light in his eyes. They had made a bed on the living room floor using the sofa cushions and two of Quentin's fur coats. They were both naked, Alex's back curved to Quentin's side. Quentin turned and very gently cupped the back of Alex's head with his hand. Alex stirred immediately, turning onto his back and shielding his eyes with the crook of his arm. A sunbeam striped his face.

"Did we sleep?" he asked.

"A little," said Quentin.

"Water," he said.

Alex stood up stiffly, scooping his underwear off the floor with his foot and flicking it into his hand. He pulled it on and walked to the kitchen. Quentin balanced himself on his elbows and watched Alex turn the tap on, leaning to drink straight from the faucet like a cat. He splashed the water over his face and neck.

Alex returned from the kitchen and began plucking his clothes from the pile on the floor without looking at Quentin.

"You have to go?" Quentin asked.

"Yes, I should work today."

Quentin stood up and cast around for his own underwear. As he slid them on, the day, with its acid-mouthed hangover and hollow come-down, felt like an unbearable debt to pay. He moved behind Alex and rested his cheek against the back of his shoulder, feeling the rough denim of his jacket against his skin.

"You could stay," he said into Alex's back. "If you want. Stay."

Alex turned to face him with a puzzled, searching look. He said nothing.

"I'll walk you out," Quentin said. "Let me get dressed."

He retreated upstairs to his bedroom and stood uncertainly in front of the clothes that still remained in his wardrobe. He pulled on a pair of basketball shorts and an old T-shirt of Johnny's, then went back downstairs. Alex had his shoes on and was standing in front of the dining table, looking intently at a pile of euros.

"Do you need these?" Alex said, turning to Quentin. "I can exchange for dollars."

"Seriously? I think you're selling yourself a bit short." Quentin tried to force a laugh. "That will only be about sixty."

"It's not *for* anything," Alex said. "Is just a gift. You don't need it. See—" he stooped to pick up a note that had fallen to the floor under the table. "You leave it lying around like nothing."

"Fine, take it," Quentin said, feeling ashamed for them both. "You're right, it is nothing. Let's go."

He followed Alex down the hall, watching the soft blank square of his neck above his jacket move. They reached the door, and Quentin picked up the wallet and keys he'd dropped the night before. He tried to smile. His face felt like a new, more fragile thing.

They walked together as far as the corner and said goodbye without touching. Quentin headed in the opposite direction and sat on a stoop to light a cigarette. He could feel people staring at him as they bounced by on their morning jogs or shepherded their children to the playground down the block. He didn't care. He would go home soon and get Lulu, take her for a walk. Maybe buy some flowers at the farmer's market. He looked down at his phone. Cleo was calling. The day, after all, was just beginning.

CHAPTER FOUR

Early August

F rank was having a long day. Not only had his new client, the second largest rum manufacturer in South America, asked for yet *another* edit of a fifteen-second TV spot that should have been wrapped and delivered weeks ago, but this particular spot was from a shoot they'd relocated to Buenos Aires, which meant that Frank had not been able to attend, despite having promised the client he'd oversee all shoots *personally*, because it had coincided with the week he married Cleo, and the footage that he now found himself looking at from the shoot that he had not actually been present at but must now pretend he had overseen was, to Frank's eye, tainted, no, *blighted*, by the presence of an extra so colossally miscast that Frank had to question whether he was surrounded by incompetents, or if someone on his staff was indeed out to fuck him. He was also hungover. Painfully, royally hungover.

"There," Frank said, jabbing a finger at the large screen silhouetting him and the editor, a pasty guy he thought might be called Joe. "Right. There. Am I the only one who sees this large, shirtless white guy in the frame? Tell me, seriously, can you not see him?"

"Oh yeah," said the editor, cracking his knuckles with such obvious satisfaction that Frank had to restrain himself from reaching over and snapping his fingers like breadsticks. "What's he doing there?"

"What he's doing there," Frank said with slow deliberateness, "is messing up the shot. What he's doing there is interrupting a carefully choreographed milieu of young, genetically blessed Argentines—who are each, incidentally, being paid union rates—with his, his . . . I don't even know what you call this. Porcine! His porcine appearance."

"Maybe he's meant to be adding some, you know, like, reality to the scene?"

Frank gave the editor a murderous look. They'd shot in Argentina for the better production value, though any sign of authentic South American culture had been scourged from the product itself (the company was trying to disassociate itself from the Latin market). The spot featured a suburban yet improbably good-looking white guy sitting alone in a bar. He orders a drink—a glinting, jewel-like glass of rum— tosses it back, and is suddenly transported to a tropical beach. A crowd of attractive revelers (tanned, but in a familiar European-looking way) gather around him. As one taut, bikini-clad girl passes him another drink, an airplane garishly emblazoned with the brand logo pulls a banner declaring "There's a party somewhere. Find it" across the empty blue sky.

The irony that Frank should have to work on this particular ad while feeling as he did, like his brain was a cotton ball soaked in rubbing alcohol slowly drying in the sun, was not lost on him. He'd gone to meet Anders after work the night before with the innocent enough intention of watching highlights from that day's Premier League game. Anders was already there when he arrived, recounting last night's sexual exploits to the bartender.

"I'm telling you," he said, signaling for the bartender to bring Frank the same dark lager he was drinking, "if the genders had been reversed, it would have been sexual assault."

"So you're saying you didn't get hard?" Frank mounted a barstool and looked at Anders over his glasses.

"Well." Anders ran his hands through his sandy hair and offered his gap-toothed smile. "I did not want to offend her. But she was certainly the aggressor. Much too aggressive for me, in fact."

"You're lucky Cleo's not here," Frank said, taking a thirsty gulp from the pint glass that had appeared before him. "That comment would definitely incur a feminist outcry."

"Perhaps," said Anders vaguely, turning back to the glow of the screen. "Ah, did you see that pass? Beautiful!"

"I'm only drinking beer tonight, by the way," said Frank, taking another deep sip. "Sólo beer."

Anders raised a white-blond eyebrow. "Did Cleo decide that for you?"

Frank had noticed that Anders was unusually tight-lipped on the subject of Cleo. He wondered if Anders was jealous of her. He and Anders had a decades-long friendship that was both deepened and threatened by an intense rivalry. When Anders split from his ex-girlfriend Christine, it was Frank whose couch he slept on for weeks while he looked for a new place. Neither of them had been in a serious relationship for years— they were each the other's emergency contacts, for Christ's sake—so it must have been disconcerting for Anders to watch Frank go from being single to married in only a few months.

Or perhaps, Frank thought, Anders was jealous of *him*. Who wouldn't want to be with someone like Cleo, so thoughtful and special and beautiful, after the parade of dull models Anders had dated since Christine? Either way, the thought that he had something Anders wanted gave Frank an inner glow of satisfaction.

"So you want me to crop the shot?" asked the editor. "Even though that means we'll lose the parakeet in the branch over there?"

Frank refocused his eyes on the screen, staring at the god-awful tagline hanging like a divine verdict in the sky. The whole thing was, of course, unadulterated shit. What had started out as an ad that was going to subvert the standards of alcohol advertising had become an ad that was playing *off* the standards of alcohol advertising, and had now devolved to an ad that was just trying to *meet* the standards of alcohol advertising.

"Yes," said Frank, cracking open his third Diet Coke of the day. "That's what I want you to do, Joe."

"Dude, my name's Myke," said Joe. "With a y."

"Not until you get that shirtless asshole out of my shot, it's not," said Frank.

Frank wasn't surprised at how the ad had turned out, but at heart he was still a bit of an idealist. He'd skipped college and started as a copywriter at eighteen, coming of age at a time when it was still possible to make work that felt, somehow, important. He had a gift for storytelling and a strong visual eye; he'd had ambitions to write and direct movies, but the family money his mother had lived lavishly on for years had dried up, and advertising was the more dependable bet. He'd earned awards and bought his own apartment in his early thirties, but he had not forgotten what his former boss, an icon who'd been one of the creatives behind Nike's "Just Do It" campaign, had slurred to him at his retirement party. *If you want to make good art, don't go into advertising. And if you want to make good advertising, don't stay in America.*

"Frank?" His assistant Jacky's head appeared in the doorway. "I've got Zoe on hold in your office."

Jacky was a Queens native with a cotton-candy puff of dyed blond hair and navy-blue eyeliner that Frank was sure was tattooed on. In the fifteen years she'd been his assistant she'd never forgotten an appointment, never given out information on Frank to prying parties, and only once called in sick, with appendicitis.

"Why didn't she call my cell?"

"She says you never answer her."

"There's a reason for that." Frank wheeled his chair toward Jacky and took her hand, propelling himself in a seated pirouette beneath her. Jacky gave him a knowing smile.

"Family's family, hon. She says it's important."

"Everything's important with Zoe," said Frank. "She's an actress."

Zoe was the result of what his mother claimed was a surprise pregnancy in her early forties, but which Frank suspected was a last-ditch effort to create a shared interest with her second husband, Lionel. Lionel was a striking African-American midwesterner with a moderately successful real estate business and a talent for squash. He was also the first man to not let Frank's mother walk all over him, a fact Frank acknowledged with grudging respect. Frank's mother had divorced his father when Frank was two, prompting his father to move back to Italy and start a new family with a wife who, presumably, didn't leave knives in his bed when he stayed out too late.

"What are you going to do by the time I get back?" Frank turned to the editor, who was looking dejectedly at the screen.

"Take the shirtless asshole out of the shot," he said in a low monotone.

Frank laughed and slapped him on the back.

"That's the spirit." He gave him a little wink. "Myke with a y."

Frank followed Jacky out into the white light of the hallway. Honestly, he was grateful to Zoe for the excuse to leave the soporific editing suite. He'd rather speak to her than any other member of his family.

"Just think, hon," said Jacky, with her usual knack for reading his thoughts, "it could be your mother."

Lionel and his mother had raised Zoe in Manhattan, then enrolled her in boarding school after they moved to Colorado to open a luxury ski clothing store. Frank's mother loved skiing; he'd grown up accompanying her on ski trips to the Alps and Aspen. She came from money and had a regal disposition on and off the slopes. Her long nose and arched white forehead lent her the imperious look of Russian wolfhound. But she was young when she had Frank, and treated him more as a companion than a son.

Growing up, he'd often had dinner with her at restaurants near their apartment on the Upper East Side; she'd order them escargot, truffle salad, or steak tartare, dishes not particularly suited to the indelicate palate of a child, and talk about her life in the same frank manner she would to any adult. *Oh, men are afraid of women my age. They think any woman over thirty's got a bear trap instead of a cooch!* Occasionally they'd steal the cutlery, just for the hell of it, laughing as they pushed past the doors hand in hand, butter knives sliding down his trouser legs. Even now, when he thinks of his mother's laugh, he can hear the jangling sound of silverware on the sidewalk.

"Little Z," he said, picking up the phone. He looked out the window at the pleasant bustle of Madison Square Park below. "What have I told you about grown-ups with jobs?"

"Fraaaaaank." Zoe's voice was high and keening.

"Zoooooooo," Frank echoed, elaborately miming tying a noose around his neck for the benefit of Jacky, who was lingering in the doorway to ensure he'd answered. Jacky shook her head, but her eyes were smiling with the good humor that had allowed her to tolerate Frank's antics for over a decade. Frank noticed she'd left a bottle of water and two Advil by the phone.

"It's not funny!" Zoe's voice wailed in his ear. "I'm at Beth Israel. I had a seizure at the theater, and the stage manager took me here. I'm meant to be getting a brain scan, but they want to put this weird glue in my hair." She raised her voice, presumably for the benefit of some harried medical personnel within earshot. "*Which is never going to happen!* Can you come down here? I'm freaking out."

Zoe had been diagnosed with epilepsy at boarding school after having a seizure while drunkenly breaking into a boy's dorm room. It was Frank who had gone to the family weekends at the wilderness program (or "not-a-rehab," as his mother referred to it) she'd spent her last semester of high school in, and it was Frank who'd taken over Zoe's Tisch tuition and rent her sophomore year, when his mother's ski business failed to produce profits.

He had even given Zoe a monthly allowance so she could focus on rehearsals for Tisch's production of *Antigone* that summer, but he had stopped that once he and Cleo decided to get married. There were only so many wayward young female artists a man could support at once. But he never stopped worrying about Zoe, and he would still do anything, go anywhere, to make sure no one touched a hair on her head without her permission.

"I'll be there," said Frank. "Give me fifteen minutes."

He lunged for his bag on the white leather sofa, inadvertently pulling the phone and a pile of papers off his desk.

"I got it!" yelled Jacky from the hallway.

The rush of the elevator sent a wave of nausea through him. He slid on his sunglasses and tried to breathe deeply, resting his head against the cool steel of the walls as they stopped at floors 24, now 19, now 11 . . . God, he was getting old. When he was Cleo's age, he'd been able to stay out all night before work, even squeezing in time for the gym at lunch. Now, if he hadn't known he was hungover, he would have thought he was dying.

He and Anders had downed a few more beers and finished the highlights, which ended on a high note with a gorgeous goal from twenty-five yards out. The celebratory spirit carried Frank all the way to the basement bar of a restaurant downtown, where Anders knew someone doing something with some magazine. He was downstairs at the bar, the music pulsing around him, and Anders was passing him a shot. Then he was talking to the DJ and buying another round for him, for Anders, for a guy wearing a bolo tie, for anyone. He was in the bathroom cutting lines on the sink with two girls both called Sara who thought everything he said was hilarious. He was on the dance floor again and a song he knew was playing and he was feeling fine, fine, fine. He was crushed in a cab with five other people going to he wasn't sure where. *There's a party somewhere. Find it.* Then he was in his hallway, standing in front of his apartment door, trying to work out how to get the key into the lock when there was one hole, three keys, and he was seeing double.

When Frank finally managed to open the door, he'd found Cleo sitting in the darkness, staring at the front door. The only concession she made to his entrance was to close her eyes against the bar of yellow light from the hallway that fell across her face. The thought of her silently listening to him scrabble to get the keys in the lock sent a pulse of humiliation through him. He closed the door behind him with pointless care, as though still trying not to wake her. When he turned, her stare was so direct it startled him. *Why do you do this to yourself?*

The truth was, he had no more idea why he drank than why his heart pumped blood or his lungs absorbed oxygen. It just happened. There was no language to explain that, so he had simply stepped around her, leaving her sitting in the dark, and fallen blindly into bed. When he woke up that morning, she was already gone.

In the taxi on the way to the hospital Frank rolled down the window, trying to cool down, and took out his phone. He sat with his thumb hovering over Cleo's contact for five blocks. When he finally did call, asking her to come meet him there, nothing in her tone of voice revealed either warmth or coolness. Listening to her was like trying to test the temperature of bathwater with biohazard gloves on.

Frank made his way up to the radiology department through the steel swinging doors and found Zoe curled in the waiting area, flicking dispassionately through the *New Yorker*. She was wearing her usual nouveau bohemian attire of a tiny leopard-print dress, espadrilles, and giant hoop earrings. A passing internist did a double take as Zoe unfolded her legs from beneath her. Frank resisted the urge, as he always did, to bark at her to cover up. He was not her father, after all.

"You're here!" Zoe leaped from the sofa and launched herself onto Frank for a hug. Her bracelets jangled around his ears.

"You okay?" he asked, patting her shoulders, her face, her hair. "Not hurt?"

Zoe smiled. "Yeah, I'm all right. Better now you're here."

"Cleo's coming too."

Zoe's nostrils flared in a familiar motion of frustration. She had an open, leonine face and bronze-flecked eyes that had a light of their own. Her beauty was a mild source of concern for Frank, stemming from an inchoate sense that every really attractive woman he knew was secretly deeply unhappy.

"Why is *she* coming?"

"Because she's family now," he said. "Don't be like that, Zo."

"Whatever," said Zoe.

Frank was baffled by Zoe's hostility toward Cleo. It had seemed a given to him that she would adore having Cleo as an older sister, especially as the two women were so similar: opinionated, creative, and youthfully, irrepressibly irreverent. Zoe was probably just intimidated; Frank knew she'd get over it and love Cleo soon enough. Everyone else did.

Zoe threw herself back onto the waiting room chair and stared dolefully ahead, occasionally emitting a dramatic sigh. Moments later a nurse with floppy brown hair appeared beside them, clutching a clipboard.

"Well, you seem recovered," he said.

"This is my big brother," said Zoe, tilting her chin toward Frank.

Frank saw the familiar flicker of surprise that crossed the nurse's face. He had been expecting a caramel-skinned *brother* brother, not a bespectacled, vaguely Jewish-looking white guy.

"Frank, will you ask them why I have to do this stupid test?" Zoe whined.

"Don't worry, we'll get all the information," said Frank, checking his phone to see if Cleo had texted how far away she was. "I'm sure it's the best thing for you."

"It is." The nurse nodded eagerly. "It's called an electroencephalogram, or EEG, and it allows us to see the activity in your brain using electrodes placed around the head. We map it on a computer, and then we will hopefully be able to figure out what's causing your seizures."

"They have to put fucking glue in my hair," said Zoe.

"Yes," the nurse said with a look of such genuine concern that Frank wondered how long he could possibly last in this job. "We use a pretty strong adhesive on the scalp to make sure the electrodes stay put. But it comes out in a couple of washes, or so I've heard from other patients."

"Yeah, *white* patients maybe," said Zoe, shaking her head of thick curls. "Do you have any idea how hard this is to maintain?"

Frank put his arm around her narrow shoulders and kissed the top of her head. "Is that really the only way?" he asked.

"Oh, there's another way," said the nurse brightly, handing him the clipboard. "We just don't know it yet."

By the time Cleo arrived, Zoe was settled on a hospital bed like a supine Medusa, a dozen electrodes sprouting in coils from her head. The nurse had used something called an abrasion gel to exfoliate her scalp before attaching the discs, a process that looked to Frank about as comfortable as having your skull massaged by a belt sander. Zoe had gripped his hand through the whole process, her face flickering from resignation to pure rage.

Frank saw Cleo before she saw him. She stood for a moment, anxiously looking up and down the hall. He was struck, once again, by how young she was. She still looked like somebody's daughter. She caught sight of them and rushed over. Frank remained seated sheepishly. He tried to catch her eye, but her attention was on Zoe. He searched her face for traces of anger or disappointment, but it was calm. Cleo leaned down to greet Zoe, her hair falling forward in a golden curtain that left Frank offstage.

Maybe it was the sensation of relief, then unease, he felt seeing Cleo, but he was reminded of being with his mother. This shame was how he used to feel when she arrived to pick him up from school. She was always late, always annoyed, as though his life was something he'd conceived of to inconvenience her. She did not greet him with hugs or questions about his day as the other mothers and nannies did. It was only when they returned home and the first cubes of ice were in the glass and doused with gin, once she'd sent him to light her cigarette on the stove and carry it to her, that she'd finally listen to his stories about his day, her whole face softening as the gin made its way into her bloodstream.

"Only you could make a hospital gown look so good," Cleo said. She offered Zoe a tissue for the tear that was sliding down her cheek.

"I'm fine," Zoe said, ignoring it.

Had Zoe been crying before Cleo arrived? Frank had been trying not to make her feel worse by staring at her. He was so bad at this stuff.

"I brought you a couple of scarves so we can wrap your hair up afterward," said Cleo. "And I picked up a bottle of witch hazel. I read it will get the glue out gently."

Frank had never particularly prized kindness in people. His mother hadn't taught him to, he supposed. He'd always been drawn to characters, people with talent or ambition or a taste for fun. The kind of people who, like Frank, tended to put themselves first. Even with Cleo, it was her intelligence and sexual charge he'd been drawn to; he'd never once considered whether she was a good person. Now, watching her pull scarves from her bag like a magician flourishing handkerchiefs from a hat, he realized he'd been wrong. Fun was fine when you were young, but as you got older it was kindness that counted, kindness that showed up.

"They're just old samples I did for work," Cleo said.

"You still working with that brand?" asked Zoe.

Cleo shook her head. "I'm focusing more on my own painting."

"Nice for you," said Zoe.

Frank wasn't certain, but he thought he saw Cleo flinch. Zoe turned to address Frank. "By the way," she said, "you'll be pleased to hear I got a new job. It's this boutique on Christopher Street."

"The bougie end near Citarella, or the part with all the gay sex shops?" asked Frank.

"Bougie," said Zoe. "I started last week."

"That's great," said Frank. "Did you find it through one of your school friends?"

"I met the owner at an after-party." Zoe shrugged.

Frank rolled his eyes at Cleo. Like brother, like sister, he supposed. Cleo lifted her hands and let the colorful bolts of fabric run through them. One was painted with blossoming branches in the style of Japanese ink drawings, another with abstract shapes in electric blue, and the last with crinkly blood-red flowers splashed with shadows. Frank kept trying to catch Cleo's eye between the swathes of fabric, but her face was obscured from view. He would have preferred if she was overtly angry with him, at least then he would have known how she felt.

"The poppies," said Zoe. "I suit red."

"You can keep any you like," said Cleo.

"Thanks," said Zoe. "Really."

And a momentary peace was brokered. The nurse reappeared through the partition.

"Looks like we're having a party in here," he said.

"Hi, I'm the sister-in-law," said Cleo, reaching over to shake his hand.

"How lucky am I?" The nurse beamed. "Two beautiful women here in one day. You two could be models."

"Well, Zoe could," said Cleo.

"Not after what you did to my hair," said Zoe.

"Are we going to talk to an actual doctor any time soon?" asked Frank.

"After the test we'll have a specialist walk you through the results. Once we've done all the hard stuff." The nurse winked at Zoe. "You guys can relax and chat for the first half or so, but Zoe, I'm going to ask you not to move. And then we'll do about fifteen minutes of silence to monitor you in a rested state. Sound like a plan?"

Cleo and Frank sat either side of Zoe as the nurse turned on the monitor. Squiggly red lines began to dance across the screen.

"That's your brain activity," said the nurse. "Pretty neat, huh?"

"Sure," said Zoe. "Want to swap places?"

"Oh, when I was training, I went through worse than this," he said. He leaned toward her conspiratorially. "We used to practice enemas on each other."

Cleo tried to contain a laugh by holding a scarf up to her mouth but ended up snorting loudly into it. Zoe grinned up at the nurse.

"Sounds sexy," she said, poking the pink tip of her tongue between her front teeth.

"You two are fucking incorrigible," said Frank.

The nurse pulled the curtain around them again, and they sat for a moment listening to the beep of the monitor. Frank checked his watch; it was already past four.

"Well, I'm not going back to work today," he said, putting his feet up on the side of Zoe's bed.

"Me neither," said Zoe. "Let's go get a drink after this, make an afternoon of it."

"Absolutely not," said Frank, bolting back up in his seat. "I'm sure that's what got you here. Is that what you were doing last night?"

"I was kidding!"

"Were you?"

"I didn't drink that much," said Zoe, staring straight toward the ceiling. "I felt fine when I went to rehearsal."

"You had the seizure at the theater?" asked Cleo.

"Were you with that roommate of yours?" asked Frank. "The one that hangs out with the drug addicts?"

Frank had gotten a weird feeling from that girl when he helped move Zoe into the apartment. She had a pet rat, which pretty much said it all.

"She works at a needle exchange," said Zoe. "That's a bit different."

Frank made a noise to illustrate that to him, it was not.

"Anyway, it was horrible," continued Zoe. "I pulled down the whole backdrop of Antigone's cave."

"Antigone's suffered worse," murmured Cleo.

"The stage manager brought me here afterward," said Zoe. "I told him I'd call you." Zoe picked ruefully at her hospital gown. "I bet my understudy is *thrilled*. She's been dying for the part."

"You brought this on yourself, Zo," Frank said. "You know you shouldn't drink on your medication."

The squiggly lines on the monitor next to her were beginning to move faster.

"Ignore him," Cleo said. "He's just being a man about it."

She rubbed Zoe's arm soothingly. Zoe, however, was not going to side with Cleo over Frank. She pulled her arm away.

"You're the one who married him," she said. Then, unable to resist getting a dig in at Frank too, she added, "Although god knows why."

"For a visa," said Frank. "You know that, Zo."

He shouldn't blame Cleo, really, for trying to bond with Zoe, but it bothered him always having to be the bad guy. Plus, he was sick of "man" being used as a synonym for "asshole." To his gratification, he saw Cleo's eyes snap up with surprise.

"That's not fair," she said softly.

"But *you*," he said, turning to Zoe. "My ungrateful little parasite. I just want you to take care of yourself."

"I know," Zoe said, patting him on the cheek. "Now stop making me move, you heard the male nurse."

"You can just call him a nurse," said Cleo.

Frank smiled in spite of himself; he knew Cleo wouldn't let that one pass. They fell back into silence, the incessant beep of the monitor keeping time.

"Okay, no drinks," said Zoe eventually. "Movie? It's too hot to be outside anyway. There was something on at IFC I wanted to see."

"God, I haven't been there since . . . ," said Frank. "You remember, Cley?"

"I remember," said Cleo.

"What?" said Zoe.

"I guess it would have been our first official date," Cleo said. She was looking at Zoe, but she was speaking to him. "Not that we ever really dated in the traditional sense."

"We mostly just fucked," said Frank.

"Gross," said Zoe.

"But accurate," said Cleo, giving Frank the smallest corner of her smile. "We went to see a film by that Norwegian director. What's his name? Always very depressing?"

"I know the one," said Zoe. "The Norwegians are so dark."

"What about Bergman?" said Frank.

"Swedish," said Cleo and Zoe in unison.

"Anyway, Bergman's depressing too," said Zoe. "You know the divorce rate in Sweden doubled after *Scenes from a Marriage* came out?"

This fact hung in the air for a beat.

"Anyway," said Frank, steering the conversation away from divorce and back to the memory he wanted Cleo to have, "it was in the middle of that massive snowstorm."

It was the last storm of the winter, midway through March, which heaped five feet of snow onto the city and swathed it in a silence Frank had never before witnessed. There was something miraculous about meeting each other at the empty cinema, which was improbably still open, the two of them sitting alone in the dark, the smell of damp wool and melted butter curling around them. Afterward, they'd walked blindly through swirling white streets, the occasional headlamps of a car crawling past illuminating their path. There were no cabs, so they'd ducked into an Italian bakery on Bleecker Street that was still open. Cleo ordered a Venetian-style hot chocolate that was thicker than syrup and burned the skin off the roof of her mouth.

"We went to this bakery," said Cleo. "And immediately started arguing."

"I think you mean passionately discussing the movie's cinematic merits," said Frank.

"I thought the lead actress was terrible," said Zoe.

"Well, our impassioned discussion was about the father's choice to feed himself first when he had risked his life to get the family a meal during the war," said Frank.

"Frank was actually defending him," said Cleo.

"You said," Frank said, holding Cleo's eyes, "that I empathized with the father because I've always put my own needs first."

Cleo was the first woman who could actually turn him on by criticizing him. She was smart about it, insightful in a way that made him feel defenseless but *seen,* really considered, for the first time in his life.

"That's kind of harsh," said Zoe.

"This was before she knew everything I do for *you,*" he said.

"He stood up, grabbed my hot chocolate, and walked out of the bakery," said Cleo. "He even left his jacket. I thought he was storming out in a rage, but when I looked up, he was standing outside, holding my cup out to catch the snow."

"Why?" asked Zoe, stifling a yawn.

"To cool it down," said Cleo.

"To make her laugh," said Frank.

It felt almost impossible to imagine the severity of the cold now during the heat of August, the same way it's impossible to think of being hungry when one is full. Frank tried to remember the shallow clouds of smoke his breath made and the feel of heavy snowflakes sinking through the thin skin of his shirt. What he could recall with absolute clarity was the way Cleo had looked sitting in the window, her lovely shining face and honey hair. Everything about her was golden then, the stack of gold rings she was always leaving by his sink, the first surprise of her light, silky pubic hair. She even smelled like honey, some cream she was always lathering herself with, complaining that her skin was too sensitive for the harsh New York winters.

"Can we talk about me again now?" asked Zoe.

But Frank was looking at Cleo. She held his stare. She smiled, and he was forgiven for last night. She *was* sensitive, he knew that, but she was tough too. He'd yelled to her from the street outside, but she hadn't heard. *Happy?* That was what he'd been calling through the window, through the swirling snow. *Have I made you happy now?*

CHAPTER FIVE

Late August

The Climaxing to Consciousness group met every Friday in a hot-yoga studio on Canal Street above a store advertising $10 aura readings. Zoe had been persuaded to come by her roommate, Tali, who had hair the color of Windex spray and said things like "Your pussy is your power." She had agreed solely because the class was free, which meant it was the only thing she could afford to do that night.

Until that week, she had been making just enough money as the sole employee of a women's boutique on Christopher Street. It was a tiny velvet box of a store, owned by a stylist with family money and a fairly obvious drug problem to whom Zoe had lent a tampon at an after-party (she'd used the applicator as a coke straw). The clothing sold there catered to the tastes of a particular type of West Village woman, one both wealthy and vaguely bohemian, who worked as . . . Well, Zoe wasn't quite sure, but in some career path that meant she was free to shop during the weekday.

Zoe had been instructed to sit in the window and look pretty to attract foot traffic, which suited her inner exhibitionist well. Despite this robust marketing plan, the store was often empty for hours at a time, leaving her free to practice her lines uninhibited. And, since it remained closed between her shifts, Zoe decided that she was free to borrow the clothes with impunity, as long as she was careful not to spill on them, a plan that nipped her own nascent shopping habit in the bud. Best of all, she was paid under the table in cash, which meant she had even been managing to save a tiny bit of money for the first time in her life.

But then she got the medical bill. She'd opened the envelope from Beth Israel carelessly enough, not anticipating that it contained the financial equivalent of a dick slap. Within it she found outlined in clinical detail the substantial costs of the brain scan she'd had at the hospital with Cleo and Frank. She had health insurance (paid for by Frank, of course), but that only brought the remaining payment down to just over $1,000. Her options for getting funds fast were limited. Since the wedding, Frank had made it clear that the Brother Bank was officially closed. Going to her parents would require telling them that she'd had the seizure in the first place. She had no choice but to pay the bill, and in doing so wiped out her entire measly savings in one go.

And so, her Friday-night plans had been reduced from dinner at Indochine with her Tisch friends to attending a free sex-positive meetup with her slightly unhinged roommate. At nineteen, Zoe was substantially younger than most of the men and women settling into a semicircle on the wooden floor when she arrived. She thought that, if asked to describe the group afterward, she would sum it up by saying there were *two* people present wearing, for no functional purpose, leg warmers. One pair belonged to the man who was now standing in front of them, slapping his large palms together and asking everyone to take a comfortable cross-legged position.

Zoe sat down next to Tali and studied the group more carefully. She counted two tie-dyed T-shirts (one emblazoned with the slogan "The Motion Is the Lotion"), a handful of newsboy caps and fedoras, one white woman wearing a bindi, and an assortment of crystal pendants. The only other person near Zoe's age was a girl sitting directly across from her in a deep V-neck T-shirt that barely contained her pushed-up cleavage. She had a pretty, slightly sulky face that reminded Zoe of a French bulldog.

"Welcome, guys," said Leg Warmers. "As most of you know, I'm Kyle. And how are we all feeling tonight?"

"Fucking fantastic, Kyle!" yelled one woman—the bindi wearer—and the group whooped in agreement.

"Glad to hear it," he said, beaming. "Now before we get started, do we have any new members tonight?"

Several people tentatively raised their hands, including Zoe and the busty girl across from her. Zoe felt the group's attention shift to her, and the warm sensation of being witnessed, and inevitably admired, rushed through her.

"Welcome," said Kyle. "No need to be nervous. We're all a bunch of weirdos in here, but the good kind, I promise. Now, hopefully you already know a little bit about Climaxing to Consciousness and what we do here."

Nevertheless, Kyle launched into a detailed explanation of the practice. Zoe felt her face grow hot as he described how a "stimulator" would stroke the clitoris of the receiver in an attempt to bring her to a higher plane of consciousness. According to Kyle, there were three physical stages: the caressing of the receiver's inner thighs, the application of pressure to the upper left quadrant of her clitoris, and the grounding of the groin area with a flat palm after orgasm had been achieved.

"Upper left, guys!" repeated Kyle. "That's the sweet spot. Now, any questions?"

He smiled enthusiastically around the room. Zoe, who felt she was grounded enough already, looked toward the door longingly.

"Nope? Well, tonight's group is just about getting to know each other," said Kyle. "We'll be re-creating the stages of the physical meditation *verbally* through some fun word games and exercises." He winked at the group. "So sorry, none of you will be taking off your pants tonight."

Several people mock-groaned or whooped, followed by a smattering of applause. Zoe checked her phone; she had been there less than ten minutes. For the first exercise, Kyle asked the group to go around the semi-circle, each person shouting out how they felt in that moment. *Excited! Nervous! Horny! Ready to do this! Grateful! Loved up! Motivated! Sexy as hell!*

"Broke," said Zoe when it came to her turn.

"Sorry, was that 'broken'?" asked Kyle.

She repeated her word.

"That's great, Zoe," said Kyle. "Although I think we'd call that more of a state than an emotion."

"It's a pretty emotional state when you're in it," said Zoe.

Tali glanced sideways at her disapprovingly, but the other girl, the pretty bulldog, met her eyes and smirked. Zoe had always been good at connecting with one other person in a group this way. "Connection through rejection" or "bad-behavior bonding" was what her counselor at the therapeutic boarding school she'd been sent to called it.

"All right." Kyle rubbed his hands nervously. "Onwards and inwards."

For the next game, individuals could volunteer to sit on a stool at the center of the room known as the "hot seat" while the group called out personal questions to them. Zoe learned that Sandra the bindi wearer was a life coach who enjoyed masturbation in the bath, newcomer Ralph's biggest turn-on in a woman was kindness and a willingness to try anal, and that Kyle—who abashedly agreed to take a turn in the hot seat at the group's request—was a polyamorous vegan who loved cooking for his mother. Zoe caught Tali's eye and mouthed *I hate you* to her before turning back to the group with a tight-lipped smile.

Next, Kyle asked them to lie on the floor and relax their bodies as much as possible. Zoe checked her phone again; some friends were meeting for drinks at the opening of a new bar in the East Village. All of life, it seemed, was happening outside that room.

"I want you all to close your eyes and imagine a moment in which you were really vulnerable," said Kyle, dimming the lights.

Zoe would do nothing of the sort. She stared at the ceiling and tried to think, instead, of how she could make money quickly and without effort. But the thought, the one she'd been so carefully not thinking about, bullied its way to the front of her mind. She was fifteen years old, and she was in love. He was in the grade above her at her first boarding school, a guitarist in the school jazz band. He kissed her at the Halloween party—he was dressed as a strip of bacon, she a sexy mouse—then took her to a grassy knoll behind the science building. They had sex in the wet grass with their costumes scrunched to their waists. And that was it. He became the hook upon which she hung her whole self.

"How did that moment make you feel?" whispered Kyle. "Scared? Exhilarated? Angry? Really sink into that feeling."

Just the thought of him was a kind of warmth, a blush from the inside out. In class, she would ignore whatever lesson was happening and turn into herself to relive every moment of that night. He was kind but indifferent toward her when she showed up to his band practices or orchestrated ways for them to bump into each other between classes. She couldn't stand, or understand, his passivity. They had found this incredible thing together. Why didn't he want to do it again and again and again?

The following weekend, exhausted by her own disappointment, she decided to try getting drunk. She and a friend waited outside the liquor store in town until they found a man willing to buy them a bottle of vodka, then sat on a bench with a carton of orange juice taking turns slugging one, then the other, until they'd finished both. An hour later it had seemed like an amazing idea to break into his dorm room and surprise him. It would be adventurous, romantic. She wanted to lie next to him, to cradle his head on her chest and comb his hair with her fingers. She was scrambling through his window, too drunk to even remember the act afterward, when she'd collapsed onto his dorm room floor in her first seizure.

"Now imagine a moment in which you felt safe and loved," said Kyle.

But she was already too deep inside the memory to leave now. Coming back to consciousness after seizing was like smashing through a pane of glass. She remembered opening her eyes to the school nurse's round white face. She'd had no idea where she was. It was when the nurse helped her to her feet that she felt the wet cling of her skirt to her thighs. There was a dark patch on the carpet. The shame she'd felt, such shame. So physical that even now it brought her hands involuntarily to her face.

"Now imagine a moment in which you made someone else feel safe and loved," said Kyle.

She'd read afterward that it was common during grand mal seizures and had lived in terror of it happening to her again, but so far it had only been that first time. In the weeks after, she'd watched video after video of people thrashing on the ground, heads whipping from side to side as though trying to break free from their bodies. It was an act of violence to herself to watch them. *He* had seen her like that. Had anyone in this room ever been vulnerable like that? Had anyone in the history of the world ever been humiliated like that?

"I feel the healing energy in this room," said Kyle. "I feel it."

After they'd stretched and sat up, Kyle told them they would be working in couples for the final exercise. Zoe was relieved to be paired with the girl who'd seemed amused by her earlier. Kyle instructed them to press their palms to their partner's and make short, declarative statements about themselves starting with "I am" and "I am not."

Zoe pushed her palms to the girl's, who introduced herself as Portia. Up close she was more sultry than pretty, with a slightly upturned nose and full, pillowy lips colored a dark plum. She had a diamond stud in her cheek where a dimple might have been. They eyed each other shyly.

"Go on, girls," said Kyle. "*I am* . . ."

"I am thinking this is a load of horseshit," muttered Portia as Kyle retreated, rolling her dark eyes around the studio.

"I am not disagreeing with you," replied Zoe.

"I am only here because my psychiatrist suggested it."

"I am not here because I want to be," said Zoe. "My crazy roommate convinced me."

"I *am* ready to start drinking heavily." Portia grinned.

Zoe laughed. "I am not opposed."

Accelerated intimacy, that's what Zoe was good at. She'd learned early that it was quicker to bond with another person over what you didn't like than what you did, and that the easiest way to feel close to someone was to do something transgressive together. That's why smokers always made friends. Her counselor after the seizure incident had suggested that this was part of what got Zoe into trouble, but Zoe still didn't see it as problematic behavior. So far it had always worked for her. Tali, who had looked over when they started laughing, frowned at Zoe from across the room.

"Why'd your psychiatrist think you need this?" Zoe whispered, leaning closer.

"Because I like my job. And he's a prudish piece of shit. It was either this or SLAA." Zoe cocked her head. "Sex and Love Addicts Anonymous," Portia explained.

"Oh right. My mom's in the other one."

"AA? Mine too." Portia rolled her eyes. "Or she *was*."

"So, what's your job?"

"I'm a Sugar Baby," she said proudly. "I'm on this website called Daddy Dearest that pairs 'gentlemen of a certain means'"—she pulled her palms from Zoe's and curled her long lilac nails into air quotes—"with girls like me. You have to be in college or have graduated to be a Baby. They just have to be rich. It's men who want attractive but, like, educated girls to take to work functions and business meetings and such."

"Do you . . ."

"Sleep with them?" Portia said brightly. "That's between you and your Daddies. But if you want to arrange something with them . . . Well, I paid off my college loans and bought a Honda Accord off that shit."

Zoe didn't know what a Honda Accord looked like, but the loans part was impressive.

"And you just have to be in college?"

"And hot," Portia said, her cheek diamond winking. "Which, girl, you are. Anyway, if you're really broke like you said, you should try it. They go mad for ethnic girls on there too."

Zoe decided to let this comment go.

"I think I'll ask my brother to help me out," she said. "But that's really cool about your car and everything."

She knew Frank was already being generous by covering her rent and tuition. It was her mother's fault, really, that she was in this mess. Her mother had always been careless with money, in the way that people raised with a lot of it often are. She should never have started that luxury ski rental business, taking Zoe's poor father along for the ride. It seemed to Zoe that she was the only person in her friend group at NYU who didn't have parents providing her with endless funds for dinners and nights out—everything that made living in New York actually fun.

"Look, I'll give you this." Portia turned to rummage through her Louis Vuitton bag and produced a business card. "I'm stopping soon, so I'm not saying it to promote their shit or anything. One of my Daddies wants me all to himself, so he's hooked me up with this swank office management job. I'm making money, honey!" She snapped her fingers and wiggled cross-legged on the floor.

Zoe laughed and took the card. It was thick, matte black, with Portia's name and the words "Sugar Baby" scrawled in hot pink above the website address. On the flip side was a silhouette of a woman. She could have been anyone.

To close the session, the group joined hands and chanted a series of long "oms" with their eyes shut. After a few minutes Zoe could no longer hear where her voice ended and the others' began; she could feel all the human noise in the room humming in her own throat. Maybe, she thought, this was what an orgasm with another person felt like, not knowing where they end and you begin.

The truth was she had never had one—not with anyone, not even with herself. Maybe she was a late bloomer, but she had never tried when she was young. She lost her virginity before she had really gotten to know her own body. She had tried to touch herself a few times after the seizure incident, but she had mostly felt uncomfortable and numb down there, so she had quickly given up. Sex since had been about validation and power for her, rarely physical pleasure. She felt no closer to having an orgasm with a man inside her than she did riding the subway. Her body, she had decided, was defective. She couldn't even drink alcohol like a normal person, let alone come like one. All her body knew how to do well was betray her.

The chanting grew quieter until they were silent. Kyle struck a single gong, and the people either side of her released her hands. When she opened her eyes again, she was surprised to find herself blinking back tears. She tried to make her way quickly toward the bathroom, but Kyle intercepted her.

"I'm so glad you came tonight, Zoe," he said. "I get the sense you might still be a little confused about what we do here, so I was wondering if I could tell you a quick story?" Zoe nodded unwillingly. "Great! One day, out of the blue, a guy falls into a deep hole. 'Help, help!' he yells, but no one comes. Eventually a rabbi walks by. He lowers a Torah down and tells him to pray to find a way out."

Zoe looked toward Tali in the hopes that she would help *her* find a way out, but she was talking animatedly with a woman Zoe had earlier heard claim to have given birth in silence.

"Next, a priest walks past and gives him a Bible. Again, no result. A psychiatrist tells him he's stuck because he's depressed and throws down some pills. No dice. A nihilist tells him to imagine the hole doesn't exist, but that doesn't work either. A politician, an intellectual, and a bunch of others try, but nothing works. Then a spiritualist, a wise man really, comes to the edge of the hole. He looks down at the man at the bottom and jumps right in with him. And that's what this meditation is about, Zoe—someone getting in the hole with you."

Kyle smiled expectantly at her.

"But how do they get out of the hole?" asked Zoe.

"Exactly," said Kyle.

"But there are two people stuck in the hole now," said Zoe.

Kyle squeezed her arm

"Hope to see you next week," he said before walking away.

Zoe looked toward the door just as Portia was leaving. She caught Zoe's eye, slapped her ass, and mouthed something at her. It was *money, honey*.

———

Buoyed by the conversation with Portia and unable to bear the idea of a Friday night in which the highlight was hearing about Kyle's polyamory, Zoe left Tali and found herself walking north toward the bar her friends had texted about, just for the company, she told herself; she wouldn't spend any money.

It was one of those late-summer nights where the air felt like bathwater and the potential for sex was everywhere. Zoe had rubbed herself with an expensive moisturizer before leaving the house, and the perfume of it rose off her skin as she walked. She took off the plaid shirt she'd been wearing and tied it around her waist. Now, she was as close to naked as she could reasonably be, in a white minidress so tight you could practically see her heartbeat. She'd borrowed it from the Christopher Street boutique, of course, delighting in how it set off the tan she's been perfecting all summer. A busboy clearing tables outside a seafood restaurant actually set down his plates so he could watch her walk by unencumbered. She popped in her headphones and added a little bounce to her step as she passed. God, she loved the last days of summer in the city.

Zoe arrived at the packed place on Avenue B and flashed her fake ID at the doorman with a familiar flurry of nerves. He was a big thick-necked white guy, his bald head dotted with beads of perspiration.

"Hold on, let me take a look at that."

He grabbed the ID card and flicked his eyes up and down her, lingering for a moment on the swell of her chest.

"So you're from Delaware?" he asked. "Which part?"

Zoe's mind went blank. She had never been to Delaware. She'd bought the ID for forty bucks from the cousin of some guy in her freshman dorm. She pushed back her shoulders and smiled her brightest smile. "The windy part?"

He held her gaze, then exploded into laughter.

"All right," he said. "You can go in."

He pinched her waist as she passed. "Come back out and see me, will you?" he murmured.

She smiled at him again, this time less brightly. She loved the atten-tion, but she knew it was a tightrope walk.

Inside, there was no sign of her friends. She pushed her way through the crowd to the back of the bar. A piece of paper taped to the bathroom doors read GUYS, DO YOUR DRUGS OUTSIDE. SOME PEOPLE ACTUALLY NEED TO PEE. No one seemed to have taken much notice, however, and the usual carousel of giggling groups of girls and twitchy guys tumbled in and out. She took a place in line and checked her phone. At least it was something to do, since she couldn't afford to buy drinks.

The bathroom door swung open again, and out tripped Cleo with her Asian friend, who Zoe had met at the wedding, though she could not remember her name. She had a terrible memory, which for an actor was a problem. She knew it was because of her seizures. Cleo's friend was wearing tiny denim shorts that showed off her tattooed legs, and instinctively, Zoe looked down at her own to see whose were skinnier.

"Baby Zoe!" cried Cleo and flung her warm arms around her neck. "What are you doing here? You know Audrey, right?"

"It's hot as fuck in here," said Audrey, ignoring the introduction. She mimed smoking a cigarette and pointed to the door. Cleo crinkled her eyes at Zoe and squeezed her elbow.

"Come with us?" she asked.

Zoe knew Cleo was trying to be kind, but her continual attempts at friendship irritated her. It was easy to be generous when you had someone paying for everything. With no friends in sight, however, Zoe didn't exactly have another option.

"I'm leaving soon anyway," she mumbled, following them out.

Outside offered little relief from the heat. Cleo removed a wooden fan from her purse and lifted up her long hair to cool the back of her neck with it. She handed it to Zoe to try, then produced a pack of cigarettes. Zoe carefully avoided the hungry stare of the door guy as she fanned herself. Cleo passed Audrey a cigarette, then pursed one between her lips.

"Can I have one?" Zoe asked.

Cleo raised her eyebrow. "Frank would kill me."

"I won't tell," said Zoe. "Swear."

Cleo relented and offered her the pack.

"They're so skinny," Zoe said, lighting one with feigned casualness. She was not really a smoker; she just hated to be left out.

"Cleo's too chic to smoke anything but slims," said Audrey.

"Chic as can be," deadpanned Cleo. "That's me."

"Where's my brother anyway?" asked Zoe.

"Overnight shoot," said Cleo. "He works so hard."

"Well, someone's gotta," said Zoe before she could stop herself.

She saw Cleo flinch, ever so slightly, then set her face back in a mask of calm.

"Oh god, hide me," said Audrey suddenly, pulling Zoe in front of her. "It's that guy from the restaurant."

"The one with the nipple thing?" asked Cleo, craning around. "What happened to him?"

"He just left, phew." Audrey unclasped Zoe. "First of all, he couldn't make me come."

Zoe was amazed to hear anyone talk so freely about this, but she tried not to show it.

"Also," continued Audrey, "he called me sexy."

"Isn't that a good thing?" asked Zoe.

"Not as an adjective, as a proper noun. As in 'Sit tight, sexy,' or 'What are you ordering, sexy?'"

"Got it," said Zoe. "Gross."

"Plus, he's hunted actual animals," Audrey continued. "And had shoe trees in all his shoes, even the sneakers. Like a psychopath."

"Shoe trees?" gasped Cleo. "And they let him work around *food*?"

"Stop laughing at me," said Audrey. "That is definitely an undiagnosed symptom of mental illness."

Zoe, who was always game for this tenor of conversation, gave Audrey a look of collusion.

"It's definitely psychotic," she said. "You're lucky he didn't murder you."

"*Right*?" said Audrey, grabbing Zoe's arm. "You're fun. Cleo, she's fun. How old are you again?"

"Nineteen," said Zoe. "And a half," she added quickly.

"Oh my god I *hate* you," said Audrey. "Come on, let's go fishing."

"Fishing?"

"I stand at one end of the bar and Cley stands at the other, and we both look sort of dopey and lost until some guy offers to buy one of us a drink. We order two, letting him think one's for him, then hightail it out of there and drink both ourselves."

"Truly the only sport we're good at." Cleo laughed.

"Except we've stopped playing since you met Frank," shot Audrey.

"Because he pays for our drinks," replied Cleo.

"That's true," demurred Audrey. She nudged Zoe's shoulder. "You have one generous brother, girl."

Zoe thought with a pang about the medical bill. Not quite generous enough, she thought. "You know what?" she said. "I'm gonna head out. It's late, and . . . Yeah, I'm gonna go."

She dropped the cigarette to the sidewalk and stomped the embers out with the heel of her high-tops. When she looked up, she found a look of genuine disappointment on Cleo's face.

"Oh, don't go," said Cleo. "I never get to see you without Frank. And I was hoping—"

"I'm out," Zoe interrupted with a shrug. "Good luck with the fishing."

She walked away without letting Cleo finish. It was rude, she knew, and probably undeserved, but the thought of her overdrawn bank balance had sapped her of the energy to play nice. She strode back past the bar entrance and felt a pull on the back of her dress. She expected to turn to see Cleo, but instead found the door guy towering over her. This close, she could see the blocked pores on the end of his nose, the film of sweat covering his forehead.

"Heading home already?" he asked

Zoe yanked down the hem of her dress, which had ridden up when he tugged it.

"Yup," she said.

"I know you ain't gonna do me like that after I let you in with that dodgy ID."

Zoe gave him a tight-lipped smile and shrugged to indicate she had nothing to say to this. She turned to carry on walking.

"At least give me your number," he said.

"I don't think so," she said over her shoulder.

He walked in step with her as she continued down the block. She would have dashed across the street away from him, but they were blocked in by traffic.

"Don't you have to watch the door?" she asked.

She had been aiming for playful, but the question had come out more forceful than she'd intended.

"Oh, it's like that? You think you're too good for someone who does the door?"

There it was. The shift from admiring to aggressive; Zoe knew it well. She stopped so he could not keep walking with her. The other end of this block was quiet, and she didn't want to go any farther with this man.

"I'm just not . . . dating right now," she said weakly.

He stepped so his face was inches from hers and lowered his voice.

"Who said anything about dating?" he murmured.

He looked pointedly down the front of her dress. Zoe felt a hot flush of shame heat her cheeks. What was it about her that made her look like she wanted this? She suddenly hated this tiny white dress. She hated that her cleavage and legs were on full display—the very things she had initially loved about it. She wanted to throw her shirt back on and skulk home unnoticed. She wanted to disappear. The door guy was about to say some new, probably disgusting thing when she heard her name.

"Zo! Zo! Is this guy bothering you?"

Cleo and Audrey were trotting down the street after her, arm in arm.

"Dude, can you step away from her?" said Audrey. "Invasive, much?"

"We're just talking," he said, opening his palms.

Audrey grabbed Zoe's arm and pulled her toward them. "Do you know how old she is?"

"She's *twenty-one*," muttered Cleo between her teeth. "The legal age. Remember?"

"Oh, right," said Audrey quickly. "But, like, a young twenty-one."

"Exactly," said Cleo, turning back to the door guy. "Which I'm guessing you're not."

"And by the way, we know the owner," added Audrey. "So . . . yeah, don't mess with us."

The door guy lit a cigarette and inhaled, laughing softly to himself as smoke escaped his mouth. He looked Zoe in the eye and flicked his tongue up against his top lip.

"You know where to find me," he said.

"Gross," Audrey mumbled under her breath.

Zoe was relieved not to have to deliver a suitably outraged response to this, since the two girls were shepherding her back up the street toward the bar. Cleo paused in the entranceway and turned to Audrey.

"We know the owner?" she asked. "Who is it?"

"No idea," said Audrey. "But we *could*, you know?"

They looked at each other and laughed. Cleo turned to Zoe, her face serious again. "You okay, Zo? You want us to get you a cab home?"

She considered it. The thought of being alone in her apartment suddenly seemed incredibly unappealing. She realized, to her surprise, that she wanted to stay.

"Absolutely not," said Audrey, answering for her. "Taking a dress like that home before eleven? We simply won't allow it."

"Come dance with us," said Cleo in a singsong. "You might actually have fun."

In spite of herself, Zoe smiled. It really was a fabulous dress, despite the trouble it was causing her.

"But I don't have any money," she said.

"We can fish!" said Audrey brightly.

"We don't need to fish." Cleo grinned and shook her bag. "I have Frank's credit card."

Zoe thought about saying something cutting to this, then let it go. At least she could get some free drinks out of it. Audrey whooped and threw her arms around each of their necks as they made their way toward the bar.

"Do you know what this is, ladies?" she yelled over the music. "It's a motherfucking girls' night out!"

Zoe never did find her friends that night, but it didn't matter. The next few hours were a joyful swirl of drinking and dancing. To her surprise, she loved being in the protective sphere of the older girls, who laughingly eschewed the clumsy advances of any man who tried to talk to them and protected her in a sandwich of their bodies.

She had never had a group of close female friends. She usually had one person she was close to, a sidekick really, on rotation. These tended to be introverted, mousy girls with dreams of social greatness, who inevitably idol-worshipped Zoe. She knew that she was prettier than most girls and had accepted some time ago that the price of beauty was that she would always be a little bit lonely. It didn't seem like the worst deal to her. But now, in the warm fold of Cleo and Audrey's attention, she wondered if she had been missing out.

At 2:00 a.m. the night peaked, and the trio decided to head back to Cleo and Frank's place. Zoe was sitting with Audrey on the large fire escape learning how to roll the perfect joint when Cleo clambered out, her arms laden with colorful Popsicles.

"I raided the freezer," she said. "It's too hot to eat anything else."

"Amen," said Audrey, expertly licking the rolling paper. She pinched the tip and shook down the blunt into a smooth, plump cylinder.

Across the street below, a trio of finance-looking guys in rolled shirtsleeves stopped to stare up at them, nudging each other.

Wow ladies, looking good! Where's the party tonight? You wanna let us up?

"Sure!" yelled Audrey. "But you have to guess the password first!"
The men started laughing.

Open sesame! Abracadabra!

"Sorry, fuckers," yelled Audrey. "Keep it moving."

The men waited to see if she was joking. Once it was clear she was not, one of them shook his fist over his crotch at them as they wandered away.

"Charming," said Cleo.

Zoe laughed. "So what was the password?"

Audrey lit the joint and took a deep pull. "Get-the-Fuck-Away-from-Me-You-Rich-White-Cunts," she said on the exhale.

"You know, I think that was their next guess," said Cleo.

Audrey shook her head. "White men in this country think they can do anything they like."

"Now would probably be a good time to tell you Audrey hates white people," said Cleo.

"Mostly just the men," said Audrey. "But yeah, they all have the potential to be assholes."

"I feel you, girl," said Zoe, then looked to Cleo quickly to make sure she wasn't offended.

Cleo raised her hands in surrender. "No disagreements."

"I don't think white women like me much," said Zoe. She stopped to think about this. "Or any women, for that matter."

"At least all men seem to like you," said Audrey. Cleo looked at her disapprovingly. "I'm kidding!" she added. "Kind of."

"You really think women don't like you?" asked Cleo.

"I don't know," Zoe said quickly. "I'm generalizing. In my psych class we read this study that said what men feared most was pity, and what women feared most was envy. And it resonated with me. For a guy envy can be empowering, but for a girl it just means you're going to get attacked or excluded."

Zoe looked furtively at the others' faces. She felt as though she had just exposed some hidden part of herself to them, a truth she had always felt but never articulated, and was afraid they might call her arrogant or delusional. But they were both nodding.

"I get that," said Audrey. "That's why girls always bounce back compliments. Like, if you say you like my hair, then I have to be all, no it's so gross and lank, *your* hair is amazing!"

Cleo laughed. "But if you tell a man he has nice hair," she said, "he's like, thanks, *and* my cock is huge."

Audrey unpeeled a grape Popsicle from its plastic wrapper and began scraping the freezer frost from it with her finger. "I understand why men fear pity, though. My dad's like that, always has to be so tough and strong. It's hard for Asian men in this country. They're really emasculated here, which is crazy because Korean men are actually super macho."

"They are?" asked Zoe.

"Oh yeah. Have you ever been with one?"

Zoe and Cleo shook their heads.

"You're missing out," she said. "They're like sexy seals, all smooth and hairless."

The three of them shrieked with laughter.

"But that guy from the bar was white," said Zoe, taking the joint. "And you slept with him."

"It's true." Audrey nodded. "What can I say? The colonialists got to me. I even fucked Anders, the original Aryan asshole."

Zoe dipped her head. She had drunkenly made out with Anders after Cleo and Frank's wedding, though she knew better than to tell anyone. Frank would kill her, and anyway, she had felt weird about it afterward. He was older than Frank, who was already pretty old. When she looked up, she noticed that Cleo seemed to be flustered by this information too.

"Did I ever tell you about the time a Hare Krishna flashed me on the subway?" said Cleo, clearly anxious to change the subject. "Just lifted up his robe. Never broke eye contact."

Zoe shuddered dramatically. She told them about the janitor at her boarding school who used to bet the girls that he could guess the color of their underwear. If he was right, they had to give him the pair.

"He was Irish," she said. "So he would be like—" She affected a near-perfect Irish accent. "'What color are your knickers, girlies?'"

Audrey made a noise that registered both delight and disgust.

"But why would you agree to those terms?"

"Because, get this, he was also our weed dealer," said Zoe.

They all laughed again.

"I gave my coke dealer a blow job once," said Audrey when she'd caught her breath.

Cleo covered her mouth as if aghast. Zoe, who was genuinely shocked, tried to look unfazed. Audrey shrugged.

"Not for trade or anything. He was just hot."

Zoe snorted with laughter. There was something so freeing about talking to the older girls like this. They weren't surprised by anything. They didn't judge her, and they weren't jealous of her. They treated her as one of them.

"Guys, what do you think this means?" Zoe asked them, and recounted the story Kyle had told her about the man falling into the hole.

"And that's the end?" asked Audrey. "There's just two people in the hole now?"

"Apparently," said Zoe.

"I'm too high to figure this out," said Audrey. "Do they have sex in the hole?"

Zoe giggled. "I don't think so."

"The hole is loneliness," said Cleo quietly.

"Why's that?" said Audrey.

"You can't stand above someone and tell them to get out of it," she said. "Or teach or preach it out of them. You have to be in it with them."

"You really think that's it?" said Zoe.

"That's why it's a riddle," said Cleo. "Someone else being in the hole with you means you're no longer in the hole."

"That's deep, Cley," said Audrey. "But I still suspect they have sex." She stood up and clambered back through the window. "I'm gonna try to pee standing up like a dude!" she yelled over her shoulder.

Cleo met Zoe's eye and laughed.

"Is that how you feel with Frank?" asked Zoe. "Like someone's in the hole with you?"

Cleo looked out over the unlit buildings. The street below them was quiet and empty. It felt as if they were the only people still awake in the whole city.

"Sometimes," she said. She paused to think some more. "And sometimes . . . Frank is the hole."

Zoe looked at Cleo, and just for a moment, she saw her sadness. Something about her eyes, the slight downturn of her mouth when she thought no one was watching. She looked like the loneliest girl in the world.

"Sorry I haven't been that nice to you," she said quietly.

Cleo looked back at her and smiled faintly. Zoe thought she might try to pretend not to have noticed, but when she did speak, her voice was direct.

"Thank you for apologizing," she said.

"I was protective of Frank, I guess," Zoe said. ". . . And an idiot."

Cleo shook her head softly. "You're not an idiot, Zoe," she said. "You're lovely."

Zoe wanted to hug her, but felt that would be awkward, so she reached over and put her hand on top of Cleo's. This was also awkward, she realized afterward, but less so. Then Cleo did something Zoe didn't expect; she lifted her hand and kissed the center of her palm. Zoe had never been kissed there by anyone. It was so tender, she thought. The tenderest part of her. Cleo released her hand and placed it gently back down between them.

"I'm exhausted," she said. "Shall we sleep a little?"

They left the Popsicles melting on the balcony and clambered back through the window. Zoe and Audrey could have slept on the sofas, but Cleo insisted they all get in her and Frank's bed. Zoe was squeezed in the middle, curled between Cleo's back and Audrey's shoulder. She'd never slept so well.

CHAPTER SIX

Early September

They were on the subway hurtling north toward Grand Central, where Cleo and Frank had arranged to meet her father and step-mother for lunch. It was midday on a weekday, and the subway car was cool and quiet after the din of the street. An elderly man rattling a coffee cup of coins shuffled past them.

"Who will help me?" he repeated in a high, querulous voice.

Frank dropped a crumpled dollar in his cup, then turned back to Cleo.

"So, what are their names again?" he asked.

"You can just call them Peter and Miriam, that's what I do."

"Not Dad?"

She shook her head.

"He's my father, but he's not my dad, you know?"

Frank nodded. He did.

"Peter calls her Mimi, which I think is—" Cleo mimed sticking her fingers down her throat.

Peter and Miriam were only passing through town for a couple of hours and had asked Cleo to meet them in midtown before they took a train up to New Haven, where Miriam, a healer and psychologist, was leading an inner child workshop as part of some corporate retreat.

It was Frank who had suggested they go to Grand Central Oyster Bar and insisted on taking a long lunch so he could join. He privately thought it was absurd that they couldn't spare more than a few hours for Cleo, but he recognized that each family functioned with its own impenetrable logic, so he resisted the urge to say anything. By contrast, Cleo was surprised that they had made arrangements to see her at all. Most of the time her father was so wrapped up in his new family, he didn't seem to remember he had a daughter at all.

"Our stop's next," Frank said. "Anything else I should know?"

"Let me think," she said. "Peter *says* Humphrey is his son, but he's not really. He was eight when my dad met Miriam, but he adopted him later. Humphrey won't be there, but you'll hear about him. He's going to Cambridge next year and is amazing at sport. Everyone just *loves* Humphrey."

She rolled her eyes and attempted a smile. Frank recognized within the forced casualness of the gesture a familiar attempt to dismiss years of resentment and hurt. He took her hand and looked earnestly into her eyes.

"I just have one question," he said. "What kind of a person looks at a newborn baby and names him . . . Humphrey?"

Cleo laughed and shook her head.

"You haven't met Miriam," she said.

Cleo and Frank climbed the stairs from the subway's fetid platform and emerged into the airy expanse of the station's main concourse. They looked up at its famed celestial mural and smiled at each other in wordless recognition of their good fortune to live in this city. For even the most jaded New Yorker, it is hard to stand beneath the soaring robin's-egg-blue ceiling of Grand Central, to tilt one's face toward the golden constellations inscribed upon its vaulted dome, without feeling a tug of awe. On top of the information booth, the golden clock that had borne witness to so many millions of reunions and departures glowed warmly. Beside it, dressed in a tuxedo and a frothy white dress, a Japanese bride and groom were having their photos taken.

"You know," said Frank. "We don't have a single picture from our wedding."

"Except the aura photos," said Cleo.

"True." He nodded. "You ever wish we'd done something like that?"

He gestured toward the couple. The groom had picked up the bride and was carrying her in his arms like an unwieldy baby, her voluminous tulle skirts partially eclipsing his face. Clenched between his teeth was a single red rose.

"I wouldn't change a thing about what we did," said Cleo.

Frank took her hand. "Me neither. But I was thinking we should do *one* traditional thing."

"What?"

"Take a little honeymoon. You and me sunbathing in the South of France . . . What do you think?"

Cleo did a little skip beside him, swinging his hand in hers.

"I think, *c'est cool mais c'est fous!*" she said, and beamed at him.

The Oyster Bar was located on the lower level of the station, down two sets of wide marble steps. To reach it, they had to cross the whispering galley, a swooping archway of interlocking terra-cotta tiles meticulously laid in a herringbone pattern.

"Do you know about this?" asked Frank.

Cleo shook her head.

"If we stand in opposite corners, and I whisper something into the wall, you'll be able to hear it. Something about the acoustics of the architecture means it carries. You wanna try it?"

They each went to a separate corner and leaned their bodies against the cool cavernous walls. The sounds of the station echoed around them. Frank was just about to whisper to Cleo that he loved her when he heard her voice reverberating through the tiles next to his ear.

"I haven't told them we got married," she whispered.

"You didn't?" he whispered back.

"So don't mention the wedding," she whispered.

Frank turned to look at Cleo, whose back was still to him. She was wearing a long lemon silk dress that made her look like a bar of sunshine. He was crossing the walkway to speak to her when they heard the sound of Cleo's name being called. Peter and Miriam were standing in front of the restaurant, waving at them.

"I told them we live together," said Cleo hurriedly. "But that's it."

"Whatever you say," said Frank.

Cleo's father was a large strawberry-blond man with the same pale eyes and slightly distrustful expression as his daughter. He was wearing a faded polo shirt and cargo shorts, from which his thick arms and legs sprouted like cactus limbs covered in a thin layer of blond fuzz. His dense, weathered body suggested a life of hard physical labor, though this impression was offset by a delicate silver thumb ring and a collection of gemstone bracelets tied around each wrist.

Miriam was also wearing an assortment of silver and turquoise jewelry, which included a chunky, veined ring on each finger and an old-fashioned clock dangling from a chain around her neck. She was an attractive woman in her mid-fifties with long mahogany-brown hair streaked with gray. Tied around her head was a teal headscarf the same color as the loose linen tunic she wore. Both she and Peter were wearing matching Teva sandals, hers in aqua, his in black. The nails on Miriam's hand, when she waved, flashed green.

"Oh yeah," Cleo muttered as they made their way toward them. "Miriam's obsessed with the color turquoise."

"We were worried you wouldn't recognize us," said her father when they reached them.

"Why wouldn't I recognize you?"

"Oh, you know," he said. "It's been a few years."

"You look the same," Cleo said. "You look good." She gave each of them a stiff hug. "This is Frank," she said.

Frank instantly swooped in to pump Peter's meaty hand in his own. He attempted to give Miriam a kiss on each cheek the European way, but she resisted, and he ended up smooshing his face messily into hers and then breaking away.

"Awesome to meet you guys," he said.

Awesome was a not a word he generally used, given that he was a man in his forties and not a college frat boy, but he had been thrown off by the bungled double kiss and was now in a tailspin of social unease. He resorted to grinning manically at them and rubbing his palms together like some kind of cartoon villain. Cleo, on the other hand, could feel herself physically shrinking in their presence. She made a conscious effort to push her shoulders back and meet Miriam's eyes, which were regarding Frank with bemusement.

"You're very American, aren't you," said Miriam.

"I'm not sure that's a compliment," said Frank, widening his grin into an even gummier grimace.

"He's from New York," said Cleo defensively. "That's just how they sound."

"Oh, I love it, darling," trilled Miriam. "Everyone keeps telling us to 'Have a great day.'" Here she affected an obscenely nasal American accent. "They're all so friendly, aren't they?"

"I dig your, um, green thing," said Frank. "Very cool."

"Turquoise represents coming into one's own power," declared Miriam. "It's a little more than *cool*."

"I'm hungry," said Peter. "Let's go in."

The subterranean Oyster Bar could have been in any season of any year. It was untouched by time or sunlight. The same curved ceilings as the whispering gallery outside continued within, the sweeping contours of the tiles creating the sensation of being inside a brick oven. Low chandeliers in the shape of ship's wheels shone their buttery light on the gleaming stainless steel and Formica counters, around which stood rows of vinyl swiveling stools. The group decided to sit at a table rather than the bar and were led to a separate section with red-and-white-checkered tablecloths and stiff white napkins that glowed amber in the light.

"What a funny place," said Miriam as she took a seat.

"It's a New York institution," said Frank. "Freshest oysters in the city. My mom used to take me here when I was a kid."

"That must have been some time ago," said Miriam lightly. "You're quite a bit older than Cleo, no?"

"Now, now," said Peter. "Let's order first before we begin the inquisition."

Cleo usually found a private pleasure in watching strangers try to decipher her relationship with Frank. They both looked young for their age; people tended to place her in the twilight of her teenage years, him in his mid-thirties. Was he a father? A family friend? *No*, she'd imagine whispering to them. *I fuck him.* But now, in front of her actual father, she felt only a hot sense of shame.

"Drinks?"

A server with the long face of a retired racehorse appeared before them. Both Cleo and her father ordered iced teas, Miriam requested hot water with lemon, and Frank asked for a Tom Collins. He had been hoping to slip this order in with as little fuss as possible, but Miriam was on him in seconds.

"Is that like an Arnold Palmer?" she asked.

"Kind of," he said, busying himself with his napkin.

"Is Bombay Sapphire okay for you, sir?" asked the waiter.

"Sure, sure," he said.

Frank gave the server a meaningful look, which he hoped would convey his disappointment in him, but he merely turned on his heel with a curt head nod.

"Drinking at lunch on a weekday!" exclaimed Miriam. "How very urbane."

Cleo could feel her cheeks burning. She took a large gulp of ice water. Frank, who had been momentarily embarrassed, now made the conscious decision not to care what she thought. There was no way he was getting through this lunch without a drink.

"Do they serve bread in this place?" Peter asked, looking around the room testily.

"I'm sure they do, sweetheart," soothed Miriam. "This is a New York institution, after all."

Miriam covered Peter's hand with hers. Cleo shot up in her chair. "I can go ask for some," she said.

"Nonsense," growled her father. "Sit down."

She sank back into her seat. Even after all these years, she could not disobey her father. To Frank, her father seemed like some kind of grumpy grizzly bear who was being subjected to the equivalent of a teddy bear's picnic.

"Oh, Cleo," cooed Miriam. "Humphrey sends his love. You know he's starting Cambridge next month?"

"He's a hardworking lad, that one," said Peter.

"Hopefully it means he'll finally be rid of that horrible girlfriend of his," said Miriam. "He keeps trying to break up with her, but every time he does, she cries, and he just can't go through with it, poor thing."

"Maybe he doesn't really want to break up with her," said Cleo.

"He most certainly does," said Miriam. "She's absolutely ghastly, as I keep reminding him. He's just too *nice*, that's his problem."

"Sounds like he needs to grow a pair," said Frank.

Miriam inhaled sharply as if she'd been struck.

"Humphrey's a very sensitive boy," she said. "Exceptional in many ways. There's certainly nothing wrong with Humphrey."

"The boy's a red belt in martial arts," said Peter.

"I was just kidding," said Frank.

"He was just kidding," said Cleo.

"Where's that bread?" said Peter.

Frank glanced at Cleo, who had reverted back to staring at her lap. It was up to him to make nice, he gathered.

"So," he said. "Cley mentioned you're leading some kind of work-shop for children?"

Miriam tipped her head back and laughed with an abandon that rang entirely false.

"I run workshops for healing your *inner child*. It's a little different." She turned to Peter, still giggling. "Did you hear that, Pete?"

Peter grunted an acknowledgment. He was distracted by a bountiful breadbasket winding its ways toward them, along with the tray of drinks. The server was still relinquishing his load when Peter snapped off a bread-stick and speared it into the pat of butter.

"We just led a workshop for a tech start-up in San Francisco, and now we're heading to New Haven. In fact, I've toured it all over the world. Last month we were in China!"

"That's amazing," said Cleo.

Frank noticed that Cleo looked anything but amazed by this. In fact, she looked deeply depressed. He took a long pull from his drink.

"You do the workshops together?" he asked.

"Mimi's the brains behind the whole operation," said Peter, demolishing a bread roll. "Now I'm retired, I can travel with her."

"You're like my groupie, aren't you, darling?" said Miriam.

The breadstick Cleo was holding snapped between her fingers.

"Let's order food, since you're so hungry, Peter," said Frank. He beckoned over the long-faced waiter. "A dozen oysters and a couple of the lobster seafood platters for the table. How does that sound?"

"Perfect," said Cleo, inwardly relishing the fact that for once her father was not the head of the table. Frank was more successful than he had ever been.

"And guys, this is on me," added Frank. "So please order whatever you want."

"No, we couldn't possibly," said Peter.

"I insist," said Frank.

"Absolutely not," said Peter.

"That's very generous of you, Frank," said Miriam. "Thank you."

"Mm," said Peter sullenly.

"Frank has his own advertising agency," said Cleo. "He's the creative director."

"Is that so?" said Peter.

"I work with a *lot* of media people myself," said Miriam.

"It's just a little firm," said Frank. "But we're growing fast."

"He won a big award at the Cannes Advertising Festival last year," said Cleo.

Neither Peter nor Miriam responded to this. Despite the earlier promise of an inquisition, Frank noted, they both seemed remarkably incurious about him or Cleo.

"And what did you do before you retired, Peter?" he asked.

"I was an engineer," he said. "Construction mostly."

"That's how he met my mum," Cleo said. "She was an architect."

"A very fine one too," said Peter.

"But now he's terribly helpful to *me*, aren't you darling?" said Miriam.

"I try to be," he said.

"Not to mention hundreds of people in need of a safe space to heal," added Miriam.

Peter looked at her with shy pride. "Tell them what that Chinese busi-nessman said to you, Mimi."

"Oh, they don't want to hear about that." Miriam raised her eyebrows at Cleo and Frank expectantly. Clearly, they were required to rebut. Cleo stayed steadfastly silent.

"Sure we do," said Frank.

"If you insist, then," said Miriam. "Really, what we were looking at in China were the ramifications of the one-child policy. There's this entire generation of adults who all grew up only children, what has now been dubbed the 'lonely generation.' Many psychological studies show that only children exhibit higher degrees of selfishness, pessimism, and risk aversion than children with siblings. No offense, Cleo," she added, looking pointedly at her across the table.

"Humphrey's an only child too," said Cleo.

"He's a little different," she snipped. "*Anyway*, this can really affect them as adults when they enter a work environment and are expected to be part of a team. So, my role is to come in and help corporations really *look* at how their employees' childhoods are affecting their daily produc-tivity by doing these interactive multi-day workshops where I really get *in*to those early childhood wounds and start to heal them from the inside out."

"Tell them what the man said," repeated Peter.

"Well, at the end of this workshop, the CEO of the company comes up to me—and I'm telling you this man is richer than God—and do you know what he says? 'Miriam,' he says, 'I have traveled all over the world meeting some of the world's most influential thought leaders, I've even met the Dalai Lama, for Christ's sake, but *you* have changed my life more than anyone I've ever met. Miriam,' he said, 'you are the first real genius I've ever met.'"

She paused to look first Frank and then Cleo in the eyes to ensure that they could feel the impact of her words.

"And do you know what I said to him? I said, Liu—that was his name, Liu—I'm no genius. I'm no world leader. I am merely a humble fellow traveler. And I am so honored to be on this journey *with* you."

"They've invited her back twice next year," said Peter.

Frank was afraid to look at Cleo in case he burst out laughing. Cleo, on the other hand, was having a fantasy of reaching across the table and delivering Miriam a sharp slap to the face. But if her childhood had taught her anything, it was to do the opposite of what she felt. "Sounds like they're lucky to have you," she said.

"It was the best thing we ever did," nodded Peter.

"*I'm* the lucky one," said Miriam, fanning her face with her hand. "To be given the opportunity to freely help another human being."

"So these workshops are free?" said Frank.

"Well, no," she said. "But it's not about the money."

"How much do they cost, then?"

"Their value can't really be quantified in money."

"They're very expensive," said Peter. "But worth it."

"Peter," said Miriam, shushing him. "We give a lot more than we receive."

"We get a lot out of them too," said Peter. "This time we got to travel all around northern China. We went to the Great Wall of China."

"Now that was sensational," agreed Miriam.

"*That* was the best thing we ever did," said Peter.

"I'm afraid New Haven may be a bit of a disappointment after all that," said Frank.

"Oh, we're simple people really," said Miriam. "New York, for instance, is too much for us. We've only been here a few days, and we're already gagging to leave."

Cleo's eyes shot up from the napkin she had been playing with. "Few days? I thought you were only in town for a couple of hours before your train?"

"We decided to come a little earlier to see the sights," said Miriam. "Sorry we didn't tell you, darling, but it's all been very last minute, and we really needed some time to ourselves to decompress between workshops. Holding that space for everyone is exhausting work."

Cleo looked at her father, who had visibly colored.

"You didn't say anything," she said to him.

"Miriam's right," he stammered. "It was very last-minute."

Cleo's face hardened. She should have known there was no end to the ways in which her father could disappoint her. Frank gave her leg a sympathetic squeeze under the table.

"So, what did you think, Peter?" she asked. "Of New York?"

"I don't know how you two can live here," said Miriam. "The noise! And it's filthy. I saw an actual *rat* yesterday."

"It's a fine city," Peter said. "Very fine. But it's not for everyone."

"My mom always used to say, don't fuck anyone who doesn't love Manhattan," said Frank.

"Well, let's not be vulgar," said Miriam.

"At least she has an opinion," said Cleo, glancing at her father.

Miriam, catching this, gave the table a light slap of her turquoise-manicured hand.

"So *true*," she said. "Opinionated women just aren't celebrated enough, are they, Cleo?"

"And some a little too much," said Cleo.

"Ah! Here's our food!" said Frank.

Two burgeoning silver platters of seafood on ice were placed ceremonially before them. The ruby-red lobsters sat at the center, their shells cracked open to reveal the plump flesh within. Nestled around them were fresh shucked oysters, chubby pink prawns, green-lipped mussels, and clams the size of a human palm. Flimsy white paper cups of tartar sauce and thick slices of lemon finished the impressive display.

Frank emptied his glass and passed it back to the server.

"I'll have another," he said, then turned to the table. "Let's feast!"

Miriam continued to do most of the talking while they ate. She had been asked to contribute to a psychological study on childhood trauma and masturbation and was regaling them with the story of her own first orgasm, which she achieved at the precocious age of four and a half. Frank marveled that neither she nor Peter asked a single question about Cleo the entire time. Not about where she lived, how they'd met, who her friends were, what she was painting, or any other facet of her life in New York. Finally the abundant platters were reduced to a collection of scraped-out shells floating in melting pools of ice and whisked away.

"Do you have any baby pictures of Cleo?" Frank asked. "I'd love to see them."

"Do you know something, darling?" said Miriam. "We don't."

"I didn't think . . ." began Peter.

"We should have brought some photos of Cleo's paintings," said Frank. "She's so talented."

"How old were you when I met you, Cleo?" asked Miriam, ignoring this.

"Fourteen," she said.

"So Humphrey must have been eight," she said. "God, he was precious."

"Cleo was a beautiful child," ventured Peter. "Hair like spun gold."

"Oh yes, she *was* a beauty," said Miriam. "Until that ugly tomboy phase. Can you believe it, Cleo, I still see some of those skater boys you used to hang around with in town? I call them boys, but they must be men now. What was the one you were so fond of with the funny name? Ragamuffin? He works at the Café Nero now."

"Ragdoll," said Cleo. "His name was Ragdoll."

"Oh yes, that's much more sensible."

Miriam raised an eyebrow at Frank in wry collusion. He looked away from her to Cleo, who was staring blankly at the checkered tabletop.

"Was this in London?" he asked.

"Miriam and I live in Bristol," Peter said. "Cleo spent a year with us while her mother was ill."

Frank glanced to Cleo again, but she was no longer at the table. She was back in Bristol, back to being fourteen. It was the first time her mother had been put in psychiatric care, but it would not be the last. Ragdoll was older, eighteen maybe, named for the loose-limbed way he fell off the skateboard. She had been ice-skating with some of the girls from her new school when he saw her. She was spinning in a slow orbit, arms outstretched, when he leaned across the partition and caught her wrist, pulling her toward him. None of the other girls could believe it, that she went with him so easily. But she was not like them. She was unmothered, unmoored. He took her under the overpass, where the boys carved and swooped on their boards in the gathering gloom, and later to a council flat with a single mattress on the floor. She lost her virginity to him that first night. Afterward, he had peeled the condom off and disposed of it in an empty pizza box. When she came home, no one asked where she had been. No one asked her that night, or any other night she spent in that house.

"I didn't know you lived there," said Frank.

"That's not surprising," said Miriam. "You hardly know each other!"

"We know the things that matter," said Cleo.

"What Miriam's saying is we just don't want either of you to rush into anything," said Peter. "You're so young, Cleo, there's no rush."

"Please don't speak for me, darling," said Miriam. "But you're right, Cleo is certainly very . . . young."

"And how long did you two wait after you and Mum divorced?" said Cleo. "Five minutes?"

"Don't be hyperbolic, Cleo," said Miriam. "You're not an American."

Peter's face reddened with discomfort. He looked down at his fists, which were balled on the table like two mounds of mincemeat.

"It was a different situation," he said gruffly. "One you couldn't have understood at your age. Wasn't your *business* to understand."

"You're right," said Cleo. "Why on earth would who my father marries be any of my business?"

"Cleo's anger is quite natural and healthy," said Miriam, turning to Frank. "Haven't we always said that, Pete?"

"I am *not* angry," said Cleo.

"We're just saying it would be perfectly acceptable if you were, sweetheart."

"You didn't even invite me to your wedding."

"That was ten years ago," said Peter.

"Yes, don't hold a grudge," said Miriam. "It will give you wrinkles."

"I was your *child*," said Cleo.

"I didn't want to upset you and your mother," said Peter. "I was trying to protect her. Protect you."

"You did a great job of that," said Cleo. "Five stars, Peter."

"Your father has always put others first," said Miriam.

"She wasn't *well*, Cleo," Peter said. "Nothing either you or I did could change that."

"Well, guess what?" said Cleo, her face flushed. "I didn't invite you to mine either."

"Cleo, I don't think—" said Frank.

"We got married," she said. "In June."

The server reappeared with his long, mournful face. "And how was everything today?" he asked.

"We'll just take the check," said Frank.

"Can I interest you in any dessert?"

"No!" said Frank, practically shoving him away from the table.

"Well, congratulations are in order!" said Miriam, turning to them with a bright smile that did not reach her eyes.

Peter's face was a deep, stormy red. "I don't want to talk about this," he said.

"*No*, darling," said Miriam, in the tone of a mother scolding a petulant child. "It's not good for Cleo to bottle all of this up. Talking is healing—"

"My mom never talked to me about anything real," said Frank. "Including who my dad was!"

Miriam gave him a perturbed look. She clearly hated to be interrupted.

"Well, *Cleo's* mother," she said, "as she probably told you, Frank, was a deeply troubled woman. Unwell in mind and spirit."

Cleo, in fact, had never spoken to him about her mother in any depth. She had told him the first night they met that she died when she was in her last year of college, and that was the most he ever got out of her.

"Don't talk about my mother," said Cleo.

"It was upsetting for all of us," said Miriam.

"Don't talk about my mother," repeated Cleo.

"Suicide," said Miriam, sucking in her breath as though the word was something sour she had bitten into, "is a family disease."

Cleo could feel her entire face vibrating. She wanted to leave, but she knew she wouldn't. Soon the blackness would come, and she would feel nothing.

Frank looked at Cleo, whose face was blanched except for a single high red dot on each cheekbone. He could sense, beneath the still surface of her, a great roiling of feeling. But she did not move, did not even flinch. She reminded him of some great, noble boxer standing dazed after what should have been a knockout blow. He sprang up from his chair.

"I'm sorry, but this is bullshit," he said. "Cleo, you don't deserve this shit."

"This language!" said Miriam. "Americans can be *so* coarse."

Peter stayed silent, his head hanging heavily between his thick shoulders. Frank turned to Cleo and offered his hand. Slowly, with great dignity, she rose to stand beside him.

"We're leaving," she said.

She walked out of the restaurant with Frank following behind her. Suddenly, he turned back and took out his wallet. He strode back to the table and placed two $100 bills on its surface in front of Peter.

"The best thing you ever did," he said, "was Cleo."

CHAPTER SEVEN

Late September

I t had been the perfect honeymoon, until Frank decided to take the bet. He was balanced barefoot on the hotel balcony, preparing to jump from its height into the pool below, while Cleo watched the silhouette of his back and seethed. The night had turned cool, but Frank had stripped to only his linen suit trousers, held at the waist with the brown alligator belt she had bought him earlier that week from the market in Nice. He hovered on the bottom rung of the railing and stretched out his arms like a tightrope walker readying himself for a trick.

"How much did we say?" he yelled.

"One grand!" a man's voice answered from below.

Frank laughed.

"That it?"

"Two if she dives with you!"

Cleo shifted in the wicker armchair. Behind her she could hear the low hum of the last diners on the restaurant's terrace below, and beyond that the cicadas in the lavender banks sloping down to Cannes, and beyond that the vineyard dogs barking in their nighttime cages, and beyond that the sea, where every animal was free.

"She wouldn't," said Frank.

But when he turned to face her, she knew his expression even in the shadows, the look that was half question, half dare. Cleo looked at the ashtray she'd been turning in her hands. Gold and scalloped, it was at odds with the spartan look of the room. Frank liked to joke that this hotel charged a king's ransom to live like a monk, but it was he who'd suggested they stay here. Cleo loved the simplicity of the room, as he knew she would, the stone floors that stayed cold underfoot all day, the low wooden bed and sun-bleached mosquito net knotted above the bed like a beehive.

Europe's most celebrated artists had stayed in this hotel, paying for their pleasures with their work. A large Calder mobile swung in the breeze at the head of the swimming pool. There was a Fernand Léger mural on one side of the restaurant courtyard, and a César Baldaccini sculpture standing guard at its entrance. In Cleo and Frank's bedroom, a pencil sketch of the Virgin Mary by Matisse hung unassumingly above the bed.

"One and a half grand!" called the voice downstairs. "But you've got to bull's-eye through the swan. Last offer."

"The swan?" Frank shouted. "You're kidding! It's child-sized!"

The swan was Cleo's ride of choice. Frank had returned from the tabac that morning with a shopping bag of pool toys that included a grinning dolphin, a crocodile bed, a flotation ring with a swan's head and wings, and a surrealistic giant lobster claw. Cleo and Frank had made a game of racing them while the other guests lay sunning themselves like lizards around the pool.

"Frank, please," said Cleo quietly to his back.

"Cleo has an objection!" Frank said, laughing, to the voice below.

"Don't wimp out now, brother!" The voice was taunting. "It's only one floor. Well, two . . . You can make it."

"Please don't," said Cleo. "For me."

Frank looked back at Cleo. She held his gaze. He smiled.

"Fuck it!" he yelled and turned back to the voice below. He clambered over the railings and held himself steady with two hands behind him. "One and a half grand! A down payment on my head surgery!"

"We're in Europe!" the voice yelled. "It's free!"

It took Cleo less than ten seconds to walk to the door and slam it behind her. It took her another thirty to realize he was not coming after her. She stood in the hallway, still holding the ashtray, and listened for the splash, but she heard nothing. She would not turn back now. Carefully, she carried herself down the stairs and through the courtyard below. She paused again in front of the wooden door that led outside. Suddenly it opened, revealing one of the pair of retired headmistresses who had introduced themselves to Cleo and Frank a few days earlier by the pool.

"Hello, dear. Heading out?"

It was the beginning of the off-season, and the handful of remaining guests at the hotel had formed a temporary community, chatting to each other over their cantaloupe and coffee in the mornings, taking up the same positions around the pool each day. Cleo and Frank suspected that the headmistresses were covertly a couple and enjoyed watching them sit under the shade of the Cyprus trees, playing cards. They both adored Frank, who flirted with them shamelessly and always offered them a glass from the bottles of chilled white wine he ordered a steady supply of by the pool.

"Here, let me help you." Cleo rushed to hold open the heavy door.

"Hard to get fruit at this time of night," the headmistress said. She lifted up a mesh bag of oranges. "At my age, you need a lot of it. Keeps you regular."

She walked past, then turned and held Cleo's arm with a firmness that surprised her.

"You're very lovely, you know," she said. "You must enjoy it while you can. You think it will last forever, but it won't."

The older woman patted her elbow matter-of-factly and walked on. Cleo took a breath and passed through the wooden door into the square outside, where men were playing boules on a patch of red earth. The café across the square glowed like a paper lantern. Clusters of people sat round little wooden tables outside, releasing bubbles of conversation and laughter that popped against Cleo's skin. She turned away and walked up the quiet cobbled street that led to the top of the town.

She told herself she'd turn around after every step, but she did not slow her pace as she clambered past the dark shops full of garish tourist art, the closed tabacs and patisseries. At the top, she could see the high medieval stone wall that encircled the town, originally built to keep out intruders, but now a viewing platform for visitors to overlook the bright lights of Cannes and the Cap d'Antibes below.

Cleo tucked the ashtray under her arm and checked the pockets of her skirt. One held her cigarettes and a lighter; the other, two large bills Frank had given her that morning for souvenirs. Everything she needed. She took a seat outside a half-empty café across from the dark church and shuttered ice cream shop. Peering through the window of the café, where a handful of men sat huddled in the green glow of a soccer game on the television, she caught the waiter's eye. He peeled himself away from the others with the disgruntled look of someone who believed his work was finished for the night.

"Un verre de malbec, s'il vous plait," Cleo said, pleased to have pronounced the words smoothly for once.

"We don't have malbec," he said.

He had a nose like a fishhook and tiny pink ears the size of clamshells.

"Oh, I see." Cleo was flustered out of her French. "Anything red is fine." Her face tightened into an ingratiating smile.

The waiter nodded and stalked back inside. Why did she feel the need to make everyone, even this waiter, like her? What a thing it must be to be indifferent to indifference.

A group of teenagers had gathered by the locked gates of the church, leaning against their mopeds and smoking aimlessly. Cleo recognized some of them from the hotel. They were the brown-armed girls who carried towels to the pool, the young waiters who served her and Frank at dinner. Cleo felt uncomfortable in their presence, aware that she was not much older than them. Frank joked and bantered with all the staff unselfconsciously, distributing compliments and palmfuls of euros liberally. Meanwhile, Cleo kept her eyes downcast when the eager waiters reached across her to clear the plates, pretending not to see their admiring glances. Free now of their starched white shirts and ties, they appeared to Cleo to be even more robustly youthful and male. She watched as they bent toward the girls, teasing and pulling away, that familiar dance of shyness and desire.

The waiter returned carrying a small carafe, a glass, and an ashtray.

"It's okay, I brought my own." Cleo held up the white-and-gold ashtray she had inexplicably brought from the hotel. Out came her inexhaustible smile. The waiter said nothing, returning to the football game with, Cleo was sure, even more disdain for the tourists he must serve all summer with their strange customs and sunburns and complete ignorance of wine. Bringing one's own ashtray was the kind of nonsensical joke Frank would have liked, though he was more in the habit of taking things from the places they went. Often they'd leave a restaurant and Frank would slip open his pocket to reveal a salt shaker, teaspoon, or candleholder with a grin.

"Memento," he'd say.

"Loot," Cleo replied, but she always laughed. It was freeing to be with someone who wasn't afraid of breaking the rules.

Cleo took a deep sip of her wine, then another. She had not yet managed the art of being alone in public unselfconsciously, of feeling that she could watch rather than be watched. She'd tried to explain this to Frank, that life in public for her happened from the outside in.

"You should enjoy the fact that people admire you," he'd said. "You'll miss it when you're my age, trust me."

The American man at dinner had noticed her. Frank and Cleo were sitting at one of the courtyard tables by the wall where the ivy and bougainvillea grew thickest, when he had insinuated himself into their conversation through some shared acquaintance with Frank in New York. Frank didn't mind, he liked a drinking partner, but Cleo had felt from the moment he leaned down and shook her hand that he was there for her.

He'd turned to talk to Frank, but he watched her with the side of his head like a seagull. He was handsome and southern, with a mahogany tan and a cream Panama hat, white teeth clinking against his glass. Frank was from Manhattan, but this man was what Cleo thought of as a real American, the kind who grew up going to the big game and having sex with girls in the back of cars. Neither Frank nor Cleo could drive.

"Cleo's the Francophile," Frank had said over dinner. "Did her thesis on Soutine. His meat paintings. Genius stuff."

"So, you're smart," said the American. "Lots of pretty girls out there, but you're smart too. That your thing?"

He stubbed out his cigarette and looked her square in the face for the first time.

"I don't think I have a thing," said Cleo.

"Sure you do," said the American. "Everyone does."

"Cleo's like a cat," said Frank. "She can touch you, but you can't touch her. That's her thing."

"I think that's a British thing." The American laughed, pouring them another round from the bottle Frank had ordered. Cleo stuck her hand over her glass. "No more? Okay. What's the saying? Only show affection to dogs and horses? Stiff upper lip and all that crap."

"Actually, we're the most sexually active country in Europe," said Cleo. She nodded toward a middle-aged French couple fondling each other over their soufflé at the next table. "Even more than here. If you can believe."

"I sure can," the American said. "It's the polite ones you gotta watch out for."

Frank's glasses flashed in the candlelight.

"So, what's my thing?" Frank asked.

"Yours is easy," said the American. "You have to win."

"Everyone likes to win," said Frank. "That can't be my thing."

"Not like to," said the American. "Have to. *Need* to. I know your agency. How many Lions did you win at Cannes this year?"

"One gold, two bronze," Frank said with evident pride.

"See?" said the American.

Frank was smiling down at his hands in blissful recollection of this triumph. The American lit another cigarette and barely perceptibly winked at Cleo.

"What's your thing?" asked Frank.

"You tell me," the American said.

"You're the expert," said Frank.

"Well, I—" began the American.

"You want," said Cleo, "what other people have."

The American barked a laugh.

"You're not wrong, honey," he said. "But you're also only half right. I want what other people have, sure, but I also don't want what *I* have." Frank shrugged. "That's just the human condition."

"You don't want what you have?" asked Cleo.

"I want *more* than what I have," said Frank. He began counting on his fingers. "Two gold lions, two agencies . . ."

"Two wives?" said Cleo.

"Only if it was two of you," said Frank quickly.

"Nice save." The American laughed and slapped Frank's back. He stretched his arms behind his head. "Here's the thing. We want because we're *wanting*. Both senses of the word. The lacking and the longing, all rolled into one. The more you find yourself wanting, the more you want."

"So you're a philosopher," said Cleo.

"And you're smarter than you look," said the American.

"People only ever say that to women," said Cleo.

"What am I?" asked Frank. "The court jester?"

The more the two men drank, the more competitive they became. Cleo watched them and wondered what ancient belief was at play that, despite their lives of great abundance, they felt there could never be enough for them both. The American bragged about the business school he'd attended in Beijing. Frank countered, triumphantly, that he'd never been to college. Cleo leaned drowsily back in her chair, forgotten. Now they were on the topic of high school accolades. The American had, appropriately enough, been something called an All-American. Frank revealed he'd been a competitive springboard diver, breaking state records in the ten-meter.

"I've got to see this," the American said.

Cleo slid a cigarette from her pack, and he leaned to light it for her. They smiled at each other over the burst of flame.

"Well, it was a long time ago," Frank said.

He picked up a cigarette and put it between his lips the wrong way.

"Hey." Cleo reached to turn it around for him. "You don't smoke, remember?"

"You two chimneys are leaving me out."

"Back to the diving," the American said.

———

The sullen waiter from the café returned, eyeing Cleo's empty glass.

"Finished?"

"I'll have another."

A bell tolled steadily from the church's clock tower. It was 11:00 p.m. The day before, Cleo had left Frank pacing their room, arguing with his art director in New York about a new hire, and walked to Matisse's chapel. From the outside, it was simple as a sugar cube. Inside, it was like stepping into the center of a jewel. Stained glass windows splashed the white walls with colorful light. Matisse had used only three colors in the windows: green for the plants, yellow for the sun, and blue for the sky, the sea, and the Madonna. He considered it his masterpiece.

Her mother would have loved the architecture of the cathedral. She always said that a building should be two parts contentment, one part desire. Cleo had never understood what that meant, but now the phrase returned to her like a prophesy. *Two parts contentment, one part desire.* It seemed a good formula for living, though one she had not mastered yet. Her mother certainly never did.

Frank had not pressed her on the subject of her mother's suicide, but he had taken to anxiously hovering in doorways, observing her as she read or watched television. He was looking for the cracks. She had been distant since they met her father, she knew. She had not wanted him to see her sadness, which was so ugly and so old. Grief wasn't linear, she knew, but she hated to feel the old sensations return. She felt sluggish, low, in a way that she had not since living in London. She'd considered going back on her antidepressants, but she still hoped it would pass. And she was mostly doing a good job of hiding it. She washed her hair and ate dessert and tried to laugh when everyone else laughed.

But Frank had noticed. It was he who suggested France, the home of her favorite artists, for their delayed honeymoon. He was trying to cheer her up. And now that she was here, on this beautiful night in this beautiful country, she did not want to think about her mother or her sadness or Frank's drinking. She did not want to think of anything at all. The waiter refilled her glass, and she drained half of it in one gulp. She felt buoyed by the wine, beginning to enjoy herself. With the end of her cigarette she pushed the ash to the outer circumference of the white bowl. She looked up to see one of the teenage boys from the church walking toward her with the loose-hipped, swaggering posture of someone who knows he is being watched. The girls had disappeared, and only two other boys remained, regarding her with steady watchfulness as their friend approached.

"Avez-vous du feu?" he asked

He reached her table and pointed at the lighter. She nodded.

"Parlez-vous français?" he said. "You speak French?"

"Un peu," she answered, the pronunciation of even these small words reducing her to bashfulness. "And you? English?"

"I learn in school."

"Your accent sounds pretty good."

"No," he said, blowing smoke from his nostrils. "Is not."

His nose was square and blunt but his eyes were velvety brown, with long, thick eyelashes.

"I see you at the hotel," the boy said. "You wear a, how do you say, yellow . . ."

He circled his hands over his chest and exploded into laughter, doubling over and staring back at his two friends. They waved from their mopeds and yelled something in French that Cleo could not catch. They were still children, Cleo realized. She suddenly felt very old, when what she wanted was to feel the opposite.

"Right. Well, have a good night," she said.

She rose partially from her chair and looked around as if to catch the waiter's attention.

"No, no." He shook his hands out, releasing the imaginary flesh they held, and gave her a look of exaggerated contrition. "I'm stupid. My friend ask me to tell you that you are *trop belle*. Beautiful. Understand?"

She stared at him. A breeze hurdled the stone wall, sending the trees into a rustle of applause. Lavender, earth, a faint tang of salt.

"You come to a disco with us?"

"No." She stood up, brushed the ash off her skirt. "Where is it?"

"Not far," he said. "A stone's throw."

Cleo laughed.

She left a note on the table, too much, but she could not wait, she was being carried on the breeze away from the café to the church, where the boy's incredulous friends stood waiting, onto the back of a bike that shuddered to life beneath her, then zipped her down one cobbled street after another, out of the lights of the town and into the blue-black night. The ashtray lay forgotten on the table.

On the back of the bike, the world softened and smeared. She stretched her arms out either side of her and grabbed palms full of solid air. The night was a thousand black butterfly wings beating against her skin. Cleo understood why bikes were so often described as freedom; not for their ability to take you elsewhere, but for the way they transformed the place you already were.

They raced toward the lights at the foot of the hill and pulled up in front of an aging bar on the corner of a quiet residential street. A neon martini glass blinked blue, pink, blue, pink in the window. The boy jumped off and held his hand out for her to dismount. When she stood, she shook all over as though an engine was still revving inside her.

The bar had been turned into a makeshift club with the help of some loudspeakers, a spluttering smoke machine, and a disco ball that turned lazily overhead. Lozenges of silver light spun over the arms and faces of the bodies within. It was packed with mostly locals, teenagers who worked at the nearby hotels, busty women who ran the tabacs and patisseries in town, a couple of old fishermen types slouched over the bar, their white undershirts glowing against brown, sagging skin. The speakers were blaring the kind of music Cleo listened to as a teenager.

The boy brought his thumb to his lips and poured imaginary liquid down his throat, pulling her toward the bar. He squeezed her to the front and caught the eye of the bartender, who had unbuttoned his shirt to reveal a full-chest tattoo of a hawk holding a herring between its talons.

"Let me," she said, reaching into her pocket for the remaining note.

"No." He batted her hands away. "You're guest."

The drinks came in two tall frosted glasses with umbrellas and mara-schino cherries stuck on the top. They seemed laughably juvenile to Cleo, who would have preferred a glass of wine or a beer. The cherry left a red stain like a bloody footprint on the cap of white froth. She pulled a sip through her straw. It tasted of coconut and cane sugar and soap.

"Good, no?" he said, puckering his face in barely concealed revulsion as he swallowed his own large gulp.

It occurred to her that he had ordered them for her benefit. They were probably the most expensive thing on the menu.

"Delicious," she said.

She let him circle her in his arms and pull her forward into the crowd of bodies. His friends were already on the dance floor, crushing them-selves against two long-haired girls, smooth and lithe as eels in tight spandex tops and skirts. Cleo stood, suddenly shy and stiff, against the body of the boy. She wished Quentin or Audrey were with her. They would know exactly what to do. The boy grabbed her waist and moved her side to side, matching the sway of her hips with his own. The music filled the room like water, seeping into every corner. She turned around and round, sloshing her drink over her wrist. The boy took her arm and slid his tongue from her elbow to the tips of her fingers, pulling them from his mouth with a wet pop. Cleo threw her head back in a silent laugh. He pulled her closer again.

"This song is cool!" the boy said.

"I'm married!" Cleo said.

"I don't hear you!" he said.

"Married to a man!" she said. "Twice your age!"

But the boy just laughed and pointed to his ears.

In spite of the taste, they both finished their drinks quickly. Cleo went to the bar and bought them another round. The second tasted better than the first. A song they all knew came on, and they threw their arms over each other's shoulders and screamed the words, turning in a clumsy circle. She was spinning out, unraveling like the ribbons of a maypole, caught by no one. One of the long-haired girls lit a joint and passed it around the group. Cleo waved her hands no. With one surprisingly forceful movement, the girl leaned forward and cupped the nape of her neck, pulling Cleo's mouth to hers. Cleo could see clumps of blue eye shadow in the creases of her eyelids, sparkling in the light. She was too stunned to stop her as the girl exhaled into her mouth, filling her throat with the thick smoke. She pulled away, coughing. The boys all laughed.

"Is okay," her boy said. He patted her on the back.

Cleo tried to smile but coughed again, a wave of nausea rising in her throat. The room carouseled. She stumbled toward the door into the cool outside, just in time to vomit onto the street, clasping the wall of the bar to steady herself. There had been a seismic shift; she had moved from inside to outside without knowing how. The boy came outside and looked at the vomit, which was the same frothy white of the coconut drink, then lit a cigarette.

"You feel better now," he said.

Cleo nodded and leaned her back against the bar window, wiping her damp forehead with her palm. She closed her eyes. A ballet of swans danced in front of her. The boy placed his hands on her shoulders. She saw Frank's body, a curved comma in the air. The boy peeled her hair from her neck. Frank was diving toward the heart of the swans. She opened her eyes. The neon martini sign splashed across the boy's face. Blue. Pink. Blue. Pink. He leaned toward her. Her mouth was sour from the vomit. Still, she could let him. It would be much easier to let him.

"Can you take me back?" she asked, turning her face away. "To the hotel?"

"Is early," the boy said, pecking the side of her neck.

"Please," she said. She pushed him gently back.

"S'il vous plait . . ." said the boy, mimicking her voice.

He grabbed for her waist again. His face was back in her neck. "Allez," he murmured.

Cleo shoved him away from her. The boy stumbled backward, gave her a long imperious look, then threw his cigarette into the road. The orange ember rolled in the breeze.

"Non." He shrugged.

"No?" Cleo repeated.

"You go," he said. "I don't."

Cleo stared at him. Then she turned and began walking along the quiet street, past the row of streetlamps casting their sulfurous pools of light, toward the main road. The boy yelled something after her in French she didn't understand. She stuck her middle finger in the air above her head and kept walking.

The exhilaration she felt in leaving quickly hardened to panic as she found herself trudging along the dark road that led back to the center of the town. What had taken minutes on the bike would take close to an hour on foot, she realized. The white balustrade glowed in the darkness. Along the side of the road, banks of lavender filled the air with their purple fragrance. A pair of headlights appeared ahead; Cleo steeled herself against its glare. Her heart hammered. It could be anyone. No one would know if they stopped and pulled her into the back. The car was just ahead. She clenched her fists and walked. An assault of bright lights, then darkness. It whipped past without slowing down.

Her breath was shallow. The lights from the top of town seemed no closer. It was interminable, unbearable. She thought about laying down amid the lavender to sleep until it was light. But it was chilly and damp in that part of the country at night; in the mornings the lemon trees' leaves were covered in cool drops of dew that burned away in the sun. Another car was winding toward her. A new thrum of fear in her chest. It slowed as it approached her. She was pinned in the twin beams of its headlights, rigid with fear. A dark head appeared from the back window.

Frank's curly hair was silhouetted against the purple hillside. Frank's voice was calling her name. And then she was running toward the lights, and the door was flinging open with the taxi still moving and Frank was stumbling out toward her, and she catapulted herself into his arms, and his lips were pressing hot and quick against her face, her ears, her hair, because it was a miracle, against all the odds he had found her here on this dark patch of road, and now everything else was forgotten, forgiven, all that mattered was that he was here, holding her close against his familiar chest, and she knew what it was to be a miracle.

Later, as they lay naked in each other's arms, the mosquito net breathing softly around them, Cleo turned to his profile.

"Frankenstein," she said, tracing his nose with her finger.

"Cleopatra," he said.

"Are you okay?"

"From the dive? Not a scratch."

"No, I meant . . . Generally."

He turned to face her.

"I'm just stressed about work. We're over budget for the year already, and I'm being forced to hire this new copywriter because she's a woman—"

"I wasn't asking about work."

"Then what?"

"Never mind."

She turned to flick off the bedside lamp.

"Why did you take that bet?" she asked in the darkness.

Frank pulled her closer.

"The story, Cley," he said. "It's a damn good story."

CHAPTER EIGHT

October

M iraculously, I have a new job. It's a freelance gig at an ad agency as a copywriter. My contract is for three months, with the option to extend. They call this "temp to perm." I love this phrase. Not only is it palindrome adjacent, it is extremely useful. All situations in life fall into one of these two categories. For example, the fact you are thirty-seven years old and currently live with your mother in New Jersey, I remind myself, is temp. But the shape of your chin is, sadly, perm.

★

Until recently I was living in LA, working in the writer's room of a show about a clairvoyant cat, but due to creative differences I made my departure. In fact, I was departed. The exact words they used were "invited to leave." Not even the cat saw it coming.

★

To hell with it. I'm relieved to leave LA, that sinkhole of creative ambition masquerading as an industry town. At least in Fair Lawn, New Jersey, the first question posed isn't always "TV or film?," like getting asked "Still or sparkling?" at a restaurant.

★

I'm being shown around the office by Jacky, the creative director's assistant. She's in her fifties, with a pouf of blond hair and large blue eyes, lined, disconcertingly, in more blue. Jacky is like a poodle in that her fluffy exterior belies a keen and cunning intelligence.

"No," she says when she sees where I'm sitting. "Nu-uh. We're not keeping you here." She leans over the desk and taps numbers into a phone with practiced efficiency. "Raoul? Hi hon, it's Jacky. I'm going to need you to help me move a new hire. We have her at the wrong desk. Yup, see you in a few. Thanks, gorgeous."

She hangs up and turns to me.

"Is there something wrong with this desk?" I ask.

"You're our only female writer," she says. "And an actual adult. You're not sitting in the boondocks with the interns."

★

The only object on my new desk when I arrive is a mug that says "Always do what you love." It goes straight into a drawer.

★

My mother is picking fresh mint from the garden for tea when I get home. Her mugs have different bird species painted onto them. Her favorite is the goldfinch. She gives me the red cardinal. She only gives the blackbird to people she doesn't like.

★

We kill an evening watching Sing Your Heart Out, a singing competition that seems to demand that the singers have endured a life hardship ranging from the very bad (a dead parent or leukemia) to the kind of sad (a dead grandparent or hoarding) to the really stretching it (a dead pet or mono). The contestants take turns tearfully recounting their stories in front of a wall advertising an energy drink.

"What song would you sing?" asks my mother.

"I don't know," I say. "Something about being a woman? You?"

"Oh, some sexy pop song," she says. "Really give 'em a show."

*

My mother's living room has two sofas, the eating couch and the visitor's couch. An essay I wrote about nature in the fifth grade hangs on the wall. She said she knew I was a sensitive child when she read the first line: "The park is a place of exquisite beauty and extreme danger."

*

I watch the car headlights stripe the ceiling and try to make a list of everything I want to do with the rest of my life. I get to number three, "Find my rollerblades," before the rain starts plucking at the roof and I give myself over to sleep.

*

One downside of my upgraded desk is that I now sit next to an editor named Myke. Myke is tall and sandy-haired with a pale, boneless face. He looks like soft serve. He has a miniature basketball hoop above his desk next to a picture of the Karate Kid.

"You meet the creative director yet?" he asks before asking my name.

"Not yet," I say.

"He's the best," he says. "He got drunk at our last holiday party and started giving out hundred-dollar bills. Last year we shot an air freshener ad in Tokyo and he bared his ass to the whole of Shibuya Crossing from a Starbucks window because he lost a bet. All these Japanese people were freaking out."

"And yet, amazingly, the glass ceiling still exists," I say.

Myke rolls his eyes and wheels his chair away from my desk. "It's not because he's a *man* he did that stuff," he says. "It's because he was *drunk*."

*

My brother Levi calls from upstate to tell me he got a new job at the hot food counter of the local supermarket. Levi plays experimental jazz and still lives in the same town he went to college in. It has a gas station and four churches. He shares a house with a litter of his bandmates and his girlfriend, who may or may not have been homeless before they got together. He told me that the only thing she owned when he met her was an industrial-grade hair dryer.

"Congratulations on your job at the food counter, Levi," I say.

"*Hot* food counter," he says.

★

Before I left LA, I started a script about two parasites, Scrip and Scrap, who live in a junk heap at the end of the world. When I close my eyes, I see colorful mountains of trash, skeletal sofas, strollers covered with moss, pigeon-winged books, twisted condom wrappers, crushed paint cans, smashed computers, moldy bedspreads, burned-out TV sets . . . It's a kid's show, I think. Or maybe a comedy. A kid's comedy. It's called *Human Garbage.*

★

I find Jacky making coffee in the office kitchen. She is dressed a bit like a Palm Springs realtor from the 1980s, all sunset hues and shoulder pads.

"So, where were you before this?" she asks. "Another agency?"

I tell her about the clairvoyant cat show, leaving out the part about my ignominious departure.

"My sister has three cats," says Jacky.

"Any of them clairvoyant?" I ask.

"Not that I know of." She laughs. "I don't get the appeal of any animal that shits in a box."

"More of a dog person?" I ask.

"Dolphin person," says Jacky.

★

The creative director comes by to introduce himself. His name's Frank. I once heard a man described as having so much sexual gravity, he could be his own planet. This is not exactly how I would describe Frank, but he does have a sort of electrical energy—jolty movements, a static shock of hair, and weird flashing eyes—that sends a current through his hand to mine.

"My mom's name is Eleanor too," he says and smiles. "But I'll try not to hold it against you."

★

Before she retired, my mother taught English at a high school for gifted children. Now she plays bridge with other women from her synagogue three nights a week and takes courses at the School of Professional Horticulture to improve her gardening. My mother is like a hummingbird in that if she stops moving, even for a moment, she will surely die.

★

My father lives in an assisted living facility for people with Alzheimer's not far from my mother's house. He was, up until a few years ago, a celebrated OB-GYN. My parents divorced when I was ten, and then my father moved in with a Brazilian dermatologist, who in turn left him for another woman. Despite all that, my mother still visits him once a week. We only ever refer to the place he lives in as That Home. Not to be mistaken with a home, which it isn't much of.

★

A Jewish gynecologist and a Brazilian dermatologist. There must be a joke in there somewhere, my mother likes to say.

★

"I heard something wonderful on the television today!"

My mother is calling to me from the kitchen table, where she is reading about different varieties of hydrangea. I come in and take soy milk from the fridge.

"Don't you want to know what it was?" she says.

"You can just tell me, Ma," I say. "You don't need an invitation."

"Bite my head off, why don't you," she says, passing me a mug. Sparrow. "Well, it's because of *you* I remembered it. It was on one of those daytime talk shows I never watch. A matchmaker came on to talk about dating in the digital age. And do you know what she tells her clients to say to themselves first thing every morning? 'Remember, you could fall in love today.' And I thought, I bet Eleanor would like that. I'm sure Eleanor would think that was just great." She beat the words out with her pencil. "You. Could. Fall. In. Love. Today."

"Why don't *you* fall in love today, Ma?" I say and accidentally slam the carton so hard it splats milk across the counter.

"Rag under the sink," she says and turns back to her book.

★

I must not forget to fill my mother's hummingbird feeder with nectar. Nectar, it turns out, is just boiled sugar and water.

★

I am lonely, of course. I'm so lonely I could make a map of my loneliness. In my mind it looks like South America, colossal, then petering out to a jagged little tip. Sometimes I'm so lonely I'm not even on that map. Sometimes I'm so lonely I'm the fucking Falklands.

★

"I'd throw myself off a bridge but I'm afraid of heights!" says one old woman to another as they carry their shopping bags home ahead of me.

★

I spend the morning working on subway ad taglines for a Swedish yogurt company.

I'm a dairy good idea.
I have culture!
Spoon me . . .
Then kill me.

★

Levi calls to tell me he's taken up whittling after reading an article declaring it the perfect antidote to the stresses and strains of modern life. I tell him I could use some whittling too.

"Hmm, how's work?" he asks, crunching on something loud down the phone.

"I'm a human pun machine," I say.

"Oxymoronic," he says, chomping away. "You can't be both human and a machine."

"I hope you're putting this streak of pedantry to use at the hot food counter," I say.

"You know what the best antidote for existential ennui is?" he asks.

"Tell me," I say.

"Physical pain."

★

Levi was born with the IQ of a genius, but I worry he's smoked so much weed he might be down to smart lab rat by now.

★

Myke insists on talking to me, despite having no verifiable interest in me as a person at all. I am playing a game with myself where I see how many questions I can ask him until he asks me one in return. So far, I'm at nine. It is like putting coins in a slot machine with no hope of ever getting a prize.

★

I'm in the office late when Frank walks by my desk.

"Still here?"

I tell him I'm waiting for my mother to finish her class at the Botanical Gardens so I can drive her back to Jersey.

"Ah, so you're a suburb kid," says Frank. "When I was in high school, they were always the craziest. Did you used to sneak into the city on the weekends too?"

Somehow it doesn't seem appropriate to tell him I spent my weekends with my forty-year-old boyfriend doing things like his laundry and helping edit his "memoir" about his nascent career as a race car driver. In fact, there's nothing about that situation that feels appropriate to tell anyone.

"Not really," I say.

"Ah, so you were a good egg," says Frank.

"More like a soft-boiled egg," I say.

"Soft-boiled, that's funny," he says. "What would that make me?" He starts to laugh. "A deviled egg," he says.

★

I'm still in the office when I see an email from Frank pop up on my screen.

I forgot to ask how it's going over there with Myke.

Oh, just fyne, I reply.

I can hear Frank laughing from my desk.

★

Everything about this tasteful Botanical Gardens gift shop makes me want to spend money. Would I ever use a pair of pruning shears in the shape of a pelican? Who's to say?

I find a tea towel that reads "You don't stop gardening because you get old, you get old because you stop gardening." This seems apt for my green-fingered and aphoristically inclined mother, so I buy it for her.

I'm making my way to the exit when I notice a Frisbee that says "You don't stop playing because you get old, you get old because you stop playing." Then I pass a mannequin wearing an apron embroidered with "You don't stop baking because you get old, you get old because you stop baking." Then I notice the sign by the bookshelf. "You don't stop reading because . . ."

When I tell my mother this on the drive home, she laughs so hard she upends the potted daffodils on her knee.

"You don't stop bullshitting because you get old," she says.
"You get old because life's bullshit," I say.

★

I've started seeing dead animals out of the corner of my eye. Some incidents of this are understandable, I think. A flattened leaf on the sidewalk does look like a dead mouse. An abandoned black sneaker trailing its laces is pretty much the same size as a rat. But it's the cow heads in trash cans and raccoon's bodies hanging stiff from trees that I'm having a harder time explaining. I google early signs of schizophrenia, mania, and psychosis.

"I think you need to wear your glasses more," says my mother. "At the bank the other day you read 'Free Checking' as 'Free Chicken.'"

★

I get assigned the copy for a new real estate development on the Upper East Side. It's designed to be a mini-metropolis. The brief says things like "This paragon of luxury living is a progressive mix of corporate and cutting-edge creative—*everything* a professional urbanite could need."

Frank is working on it with me. Since we're both vegetarian, we walk to the falafel place down the street together. We're meant to be talking about the 5.8 million square feet of commercial office space, but he's telling me about his childhood pets instead.

"My mom's cat Mooshi, now she was an asshole," he says. "Brigitte was a beautiful angel, a Persian, but they didn't get along. I was always calling family meetings to get them to figure it out, but eventually Brigitte disappeared."

"My first pet was a severed raven's wing," I tell him. "My mom let me keep it in the garden shed. I was only allowed to pet it if I wore latex gloves from my dad's practice."

"Your dad's a doctor?" asks Frank.

"Was," I say. "Anyway, when the wing fell apart I had a white feather called Spider that I kept in a matchbox filled with dead leaves.'

"He doesn't practice anymore?" asks Frank.

"Nope," I say. "One day I opened the matchbox and the feather was gone, just like that. I cried every day for a week."

"You should meet my wife," says Frank. "She does that too. Anthropomorphize."

★

For some reason, we have a stack of Rorschach test cards lying around the office. I am trying to psychoanalyze myself by keeping them face-down and turning them quickly over to judge my reaction when Frank walks past and laughs.

"Fourteen butterflies and a vagina," he says. "All you need to know."

★

I agree to go on a date with my mother's friend's broker's son. I've just poked myself in the eye with my mascara brush when my mother calls. She's spending the evening at That Home with my father. I can hear *Sing Your Heart Out* in the background.

"Don't do that thing you do tonight," says my mother.

"What thing?"

"You know."

"I don't know. That's why I asked."

"And remember to *suck in*."

"Bye, Ma."

"One last thing," she says. "You! Could! Fall! In! Love! Today!"

★

When I ask the broker's son what he does, he runs his palms down the shiny front of his shirt and says, "I make *money*."

In fact, he's in real estate. He tells me about a new building complex being built on Randall's Island. In what sounds like a win for the underdog to me, the mayor has sided with the current residents in a dispute over land rights.

"We're building the future," the broker's son says between mouth-fuls of crab cake. "And they want to cling to their rent-stabilized pasts."

I tell the broker's son that if I was mayor of New York, I'd implement a policy of public dismemberment for convicted rapists. It would be a penis guillotine built on the Brooklyn Bridge. I originally thought the severed penises would be nailed along the bridge next to their owner's mug shots, but now I think they should just be thrown to the crowd to be torn apart by angry hands. I'd be willing to guarantee that within a year the rate of violent sex crimes would drop by half, at least.

★

"That," says my mother the next day, after her friend calls to tell her what happened. "That is the thing that you do."

★

The couple next to me on the PATH train are both wearing leather jackets that reach their ankles. I wonder what came first, the jackets or the relationship.

"What was up with you this morning?" she says.

"I was just in a good mood," he says.

"That was you in a good mood?" she says. "It doesn't suit you at all."

★

Frank and I are walking back from the falafel place when he asks me how my date went. I try to give him the broad strokes, but it's too late, I find myself recounting my mayoral plans all over again.

"There'd be posters of me in the subway," I say. "Wearing a tuxedo and holding a severed penis like a microphone."

★

I will not say anything stupid for the rest of the day. If that means I do not say anything for the rest of the day, or every day thereafter, so be it.

★

I get an email from Frank. It says:
You could call it the guillo-peen.

★

On my father's birthday I bring him a book about the birds of New Jersey. I do my best watching him scrabble away at the wrapping paper like he has salad servers for hands, then give up and rip it off myself. I pass him the book; he wraps it around his shoe. Then we sit and watch *Sing Your Heart Out* until the TV is the only light in the room.

★

My father's illness is something I used to think was temp, but now I know is perm.

★

Frank and I have started an email chain filled with disturbing things we experience throughout our days. The idea behind it is that if one of us had to live it, the other should too. I guess that's friendship or something.
Blind woman tripping over the curb.
Baby rat dead on the subway tracks.
A condom, empty but seemingly used, outside Gray's Papaya.

★

"What are you smiling at?" asks my mother.
"Nothing," I say. "Email from someone at work."
"Is it a picture of a cat?" she asks. "The girls from synagogue are always sending me pictures of cats. What the heck do I want to look at cats for?"
"I think that just goes with the territory of being an older woman," I say.
"*Menopause* is the only thing that goes with the territory," she says. "Everything else is just marketing."

★

Frank wants to open an office in Paris. He's listening to tapes that will supposedly teach him French in a month. He says a couple of sentences to me that sound pretty good. They mean "Do you like vegetables?" and "Were you pretty as a child?"

*

Myke tells me Frank's wife is an artist from England. He tells me she is the fetal age of twenty-five. He tells me they got married in the summer and that she's come to the office once. He tells me she is *hot*.

*

"The one thing I will not tolerate is absolutely anything less than perfection," says the woman in black walking ahead of me down Fifth. Later on, I try repeating this to myself as I go about my day *The one thing I will not tolerate is absolutely anything less than perfection.* Nice try, I think.

*

Everyone I know is either more successful or more interesting than me. This realization is nothing new. In fact, it used to feel like everyone I *didn't* know was more successful and interesting than me too. I still remember the sensation of watching a talent show on TV as a child and realizing that the girl dancing was a whole year younger than me. She was wearing a red sequin dress and patent tap shoes. She looked like a ruby, a human jewel spinning across the stage. I was in my pajamas from T.J. Maxx eating cereal for dinner, already destined for a life of mediocrity. Why didn't I just pull myself together back then? I was five! I could have turned it around!

*

I meet Frank's friend Anders, who used to be the art director here before leaving for some big-shot title at a fashion magazine. What it's like to be a straight single man in your mid-forties at a place like that, I can only imagine. He is also almost insultingly handsome. When Frank introduces me, his gaze slides over me like he's scanning a news article he has realized too late is of no interest to him but must somehow finish.

*

I get an email from Frank. It's a video of Peruvian pan flutists playing "Hotel California" on the subway platform. Every time it comes to what should be the end of the song, it starts up again.

Lived this for fifteen minutes today, now you must too.

*

"You're smiling again," says my mother.

"Uh-huh," I say. "That happens sometimes."

"What are you smiling at?"

"Just work stuff."

"On the weekend? You think I was born yesterday. Who's the guy?"

"It's *work*, Ma."

"Okay, so you two work together. What's his name?"

"I don't want to talk about it."

"So there's something to talk about!"

Scientists discovering microscopic life on Mars sounded less triumphant.

"Nope. Nothing to talk about, Ma," I say.

"Ellie," she says more quietly. "I just like to hear about what makes you happy."

I look at her. She is getting smaller every year.

"Okay," I say. "Yes, we work together. His name's . . . Myke. With a 'y.' That's all you're getting."

"Myke with a 'y'!" She throws her hands in the air. "And *why* not? Myke. Myke! I like it. A mover and shaker called Myke!"

I walk out of the room as she begins miming maracas. Or should I say *myming*.

*

"So, what do people call you?" asks Jacky.

"What do you mean?" I ask.

"You have a nickname or something?"

"Well, my mother calls me Ellie," I say. "And I used to have this boyfriend who called me Nor, which I hated because I thought it made me sound like a Viking. But mostly people call me just Eleanor."

"What about Lee?" she asks. "Mind if I call you that?"

"Sure," I say.

"Suits you." She nods. "Kinda masculine."

★

My mother and I are planning to spend Thanksgiving at That Home with my father. There's no point traveling, and anyway, there's nowhere I can think to go. The wing of That Home my father lives in is called Memento Gardens, though I've heard the staff call it Memory Loss Gardens. Every time I think of that I want to grab my father's hand, douse the place in gasoline, throw a match over my shoulder, light a cigarette on the flames, and run and run with him without ever looking back.

★

"Do you know where I can buy weed?"

Frank and I are walking back from the falafel place. It's gotten cold all of a sudden.

"Whoa." He laughs. "Big plans for Thanksgiving?"

"Just family stuff," I say.

"Sounds like you feel about family stuff how I feel about family stuff," he says. "Sure, I can put you in touch with my dealer."

"I appreciate it."

"What are bosses for? But I should warn you. Don't go to his apartment."

"Why? Is he dangerous?"

"God no! He's a kitten. But he's a hoarder."

"I'm going to need more context."

"The context is that he doesn't throw anything away. Yellow newspapers to the fucking ceiling. He has, like, twelve old TV sets, none of which work. And once you're in there he'll want to show you everything. I got trapped looking at his collection of chipped old teapots for twenty minutes. Do yourself a favor and meet him on the street."

"Okay," I say. "Hoarder. Noted."

Frank gives me a sideways glance. "I can go with you if you like."

I try to suppress my smile. "Wouldn't that be a little inappropriate?"

"I think we passed appropriate about two blocks back."

"Two blocks and two months back," I say.

"No." Frank clutches my arm. "Have we only known each other that long?"

One month, three weeks, and five days.

"Round about," I say.

Frank says something, but a crowd of schoolchildren barrel between us as we turn the corner. He pivots to let them pass, and I miss the words.

★

Frank arranges for us to meet the dealer after work on a corner near Gramercy Park, the least suspicious of all the parks. As we walk up, I see a man wearing a T-shirt that reads "99% ANGEL" under a baseball jacket. He spots us and jogs over. He and Frank embrace. He puts his hand in Frank's pocket, and Frank puts his hand in his.

"Brother," he says.

"My man," says Frank. "How are we doing?"

"Blissful," he says. "You?"

Frank grins. "Haven't killed myself or anyone else today."

"This will help with that," he says, nodding toward Frank's pocket.

"This is my friend Eleanor," says Frank.

The dealer gives me his hand to shake.

"What's the other one percent?" I point toward his T-shirt.

He turns around and slides his jacket down his shoulders. The back of his T-shirt reads "1% ?"

"We've all got one percent question mark," he says, winking at Frank.

"I need to write that down," Frank says, laughing. "That's a tagline right there!"

My eye catches on something near the bushes by the railings of the park. It's partially covered by brown leaves, but it is unmistakably a dead piglet. Its little body is curved like a C. There's a red brand on its side. I can see the white hairs on its pale pink skin, its limp, dark trotters.

"Oh god," I say. "There's a dead piglet behind you."

"What the fuck?" The dealer spins around.

"Where? Where?" Frank is clutching my arm.

The dealer starts laughing. "You scared the shit out of me," he says.

He walks over to the railing and kicks it with his foot. I watch the piglet float into the air. It is a pink shopping bag. I stare at it. Red logo, black handles.

"Her mind," he says. He shakes his head at Frank as the pink bag lands softly between us. "That's a place I'd never want to go."

Frank puts a hand around my shoulder and squeezes as we walk away.

"His apartment," he whispers, "is a place we'd never want to go."

★

"Hair looks great," says the lady in line for coffee ahead of me into her phone. "But generally, I'm falling apart."

★

That Home has attempted to decorate. Drooping foil turkeys and pilgrim's hats line the walls. We find my father in the dining room, sitting alone at one of the tables by the window. He's wearing a thick woolen sweater with his hair combed back in two gentle curves around his ears. The collar of his shirt sticks up unevenly like a scruffy schoolboy's. He's staring ahead with that fearful-hopeful expression children get when their parents are late to pick them up.

"Hi, Pa," I say, leaning over to hug him.

His large hands roll around in his lap. He smiles down at them apologetically.

"We brought pie," says my mother, sliding it onto the table. "Pecan pie for our sweetie pie." She reaches down to untuck his collar. He tries to gently bat her away, then submits to this handling with a mournful look at the ceiling.

"Happy Thanksgiving," I say. "Remember how you used to cut the turkey wearing your lab coat?"

His face flares with recognition, then goes out like a match.

★

I pretend to have forgotten my phone in the car, then stand in the parking lot smoking the joint Frank rolled for me. After the first choking toke I get the hang of it and manage to get a few good hits, holding the smoke in my lungs and exhaling slowly. It tastes disgusting, like eating a tea bag. I spit onto the gravel and plow on.

★

Everything on my plate is beige except for a rosy streak of cranberry jelly. It is, however, delicious. No food has ever satisfied me so. If I could unhinge my jaw like a snake and eat the whole plate, I would. When I look up, my father is staring ahead of him, fork suspended, a silver streak of drool running down his chin.

"Dr. Rosenthal, are you finished?" A smiling nurse in peach scrubs leans over his tray. The fact she still calls him Doctor makes me want to clutch her hands and kiss her pink fingertips.

"You were certainly hungry," says my mother to me. "Didn't you eat breakfast?"

"I'm glad you enjoyed it," says the nurse, taking my tray.

I am trying to think of the right thing to say. It is on the tip of my tongue. The kind nurse has already turned away and is heading back to the kitchen when it comes to me. *Just what the doctor ordered.*

★

My mother and I walk to the car in silence.

"Well, I'm glad we went," she says as we pull out of the parking lot. "He seems good, don't you think?"

"Real good," I say, fumbling to plug in my seat belt. "Real, real good."

She narrows her eyes at me in the rearview mirror. I blink at her.

"Eleanor Louise Rosenthal," she says. "Are you high right now?"

I can't help it, I start to laugh.

"One percent question mark?" I say.

"What in God's name," she says. "Is this *Myke*'s influence? Is Myke a marijuana smoker?"

I roll down the window and laugh until I cry.

★

On Black Friday my mother drags me to the mall to shop the sales. She is specifically looking for a new towel rack, since our current one collapses if taxed with anything larger than a face flannel. We're wandering down the bathroom aisle of the home goods store.

"It has low self-esteem," says my mother, referring to the towel rack. "It doesn't believe in itself."

"Maybe it's just lazy?" I say.

I feel hungover from the weed and also all the beige food I consumed. Ahead of us, I watch a man carrying a boxed TV set over his head like a tiny coffin.

"You will learn, when you have your own children, not to use that word. When I was teaching, we were told that laziness in students is a *self-esteem* issue."

"I'm not going to have children, Ma."

"Mm, we'll see," she says. "You know who doesn't have esteem issues? Our dishwasher. It never shuts up! Have you noticed how it keeps making that whirring sound even after the cycle's over?"

"I'm not having children. And it's your dishwasher, Ma."

"What are you talking about?"

"It's *your* dishwasher. I didn't pay for it. Everything in that house is yours."

"Well, what's mine is yours, baby doll."

"No, Ma. What's mine is mine. What's yours is yours. That's the appropriate boundary between an adult woman and her mother."

"What are you getting so upset about?"

A girl wearing pajama pants under her long puffy jacket barges between us to snatch up a bath mat in the shape of a smiley face.

"I'm not going to live with you forever," I say. "I'm almost forty. It's pathetic. I should have my own household appliances with their own self-esteem issues."

"You're nowhere near forty, Eleanor, stop exaggerating. And I never said you were going to live with me forever. But since you are living with me right *now*, I thought you might enjoy being treated as a member of this household."

"This household? What household! It's just us, Ma. Levi doesn't even come visit. Pa might as well *be* a towel rack. It's just you and me, and then it's going to go back to being just you and just me."

"Don't talk that way about your father," says my mother.

"Are you kidding me? He *left* you, Ma. For a lesbian!"

"And so what?" she says. "All men leave! We outlive them anyway. I've got news for you, baby, in the end it's *always* just us."

"All men leave *you!*" I scream. "I still have a chance!"

"What exactly are you saying to me?" yells my mother.

"YOU CANNOT BE THE LOVE OF MY LIFE!"

A man wheeling an overflowing shopping cart appears at the end of the aisle, gives me a terrified look, and heads the opposite way. I hold on to the display towel rack and bow my head.

"I want more, Ma," I say. "Wouldn't you?"

★

My mother ignores me while we wait in the interminable checkout line. She ignores me when I point out that the line for "under 5 items" has been amended to "under 50 items" for Black Friday. She ignores me when I suggest going to the food court, where they have her favorite cinnamon buns, which are the size of her head and an entire day's worth of calories, and thus something she almost never allows herself to eat. She ignores me when I ask if she has any idea which of the three identical parking lots we parked in, though that one I think she may just not know.

★

We are almost out of the mall and home free when a woman intercepts us. Her face is caked in makeup the same color as my beige Thanksgiving meal. Her hair is slicked back into a bun so tight it forces her eyebrows into arches.

"Would you like to enjoy a free trial on our Rock and Recline Zero Gravity Massage Chairs?" she asks. I look into her eyes. Pure mania.

"We're okay," I say.

"But," she says, blocking our way with a ferocious smile, "it has six unique preset programs, five levels of speed and intensity, and two-stage zero-gravity positions inspired by NASA."

"We really don't—," I say, but she is already ushering my mother backward into one of the plush armchairs. My mother sinks down, stunned, her legs and arms encased in leather padding.

"Isn't that amazing?" beams the woman. "Here."

She takes the towel rack from me and guides me into the chair opposite my mother. There is no point in fighting. It feels like I am being eaten by the chair, rolled around on its leather tongue. It is not, I must admit, entirely unpleasant. The woman presses a remote, and pulsing waves of pressure flow up and down my back, arms, and legs. This, I imagine, is what it feels like to be digested.

"Relaxing, huh?" says the woman. "Now let's try the zero-gravity setting."

She presses the remote again, and our chairs lift from the floor with a crank, then begin gyrating back and forth on their stands. I am being pulsed, rocked, kneaded, and rolled. I have no idea where my body ends and the chair begins. I look at my mother. She is tiny, devoured by all that leather. She is looking at me. We rock toward and away from each other.

"Eleanor!" she calls over the vibrations of the chair.

"Ma!"

"I never wanted you to have less!" she says.

*

We put up the towel rack when we get home. Two mugs filled with tea balance on the edge of the tub. Goldfinch and kestrel.

"If you could have bought anything in that whole mall, what would you get?" I ask.

She closes her eyes and thinks. I watch a smile spread across her face.

"An electric can opener," she says.

Sometimes I worry my mother is shrinking in every way.

★

Since I am dateless and childless, it should be easy for me to spend my evenings writing my kids' comedy, *Human Garbage,* but it's not.

I open my browser and type "seeing dead animals" again. It does not appear to be an ailment others suffer from. I thought it was impossible in the internet age to find anything that made you truly unique, yet here I am. I go back to staring blankly at the screen. Somehow, I am still developing carpal tunnel.

★

Eventually I give in and search her name. It is a combination of letters so perfect it makes my teeth ache. I find a picture of her from an art show. She's standing in front of a splashy nude, looking seriously at the camera. Her hair is in a long fishtail braid. Her skin is the creamy color of whole milk. She's wearing cream too, a silk blouse tucked into a long, rippled skirt. Tiny gold rings in her ears. She is a pearl. A perfect pearl of a girl.

★

Okay, so I am not beautiful or blond or British. But I can make jokes, be nice to your mother, and give a decent blow job. That's what I got.

★

Jacky has invited me to lunch. When I swing by her desk, I notice a picture of her in the ocean with a dolphin either side of her, kissing her cheek. On her computer is a sticker that reads "Dolphins are a girl's best friend!"

"Are you married, Jacky?" I ask over lunch.

"No, hon," she says. "Running this place? When would I have had the time?"

"But." I look down. "Would you like to be?"

"Not my style." She smiles. "Move to Florida, that's the plan. Swim every day. Most of my people are down there now anyway." She leans toward me. "Why? Do you want to get married?"

"No." I shake my head. I am trying to find the words. Eventually I say, "You're so lucky you found dolphins, Jacky."

Jacky gives me a funny look. "You're lucky too," she says. "Frank tells me you're a great writer. You found the thing you love to do."

I think about the writer's room in LA. The jokes, the men, the sandwiches for every meal. I think about my evenings alone at my mother's house working on *Human Garbage*.

"Sometimes I hate the thing I love to do," I say.

*

"What we're looking for," says the real estate client, "is writing that makes you smile with your *mind*."

*

Frank tells me that in Poland they translated *The Flintstones* into rhyme, so it sounds like poetry.

*

Frank tells me there's nothing shameful about being creative for money. He tells me that John Lennon and Paul McCartney used to sit down together and say, "Let's write ourselves a new swimming pool."

*

Frank tells me the Nike slogan was inspired by the last words of a murderer in Utah. Moments before he was executed in 1977 by firing squad, he apparently turned to them and said, "Let's do it." I tell him, that sounds about right.

*

I tell Frank that in my experience, the better the headshot, the crazier the actor.

*

I tell Frank my favorite painting is Hans Holbein's portrait of Thomas Cromwell in the Frick. There's a patch of carpet in front of it that's grown bald from the thousands of feet that have stood before it. I tell him I think that's a good thing to hope for in life, for the carpet to grow thin before you.

★

Levi's girlfriend has up and gone. She met a Canadian Hell's Angel at a dive bar and took off, which is the kind of thing that happens in Levi's world.

"I should have known she wasn't right for me," Levi says. "When she designed our band flyer using Comic Sans."

★

My mother finds a dead hummingbird in the garden. This seems ominous. She carries it into the kitchen and lays it on the tea towel I gave her. Up close, it is remarkable. A feathered jewel. Its beak is the size of a needle. Its tiny black eyes are open and shine like onyx.

"Maybe I can stuff it and wear it as a pin?" she says brightly.

★

That old guy I dated in high school is dead now. I know this because I run into my former classmate, Candi Deschanel, outside Home Depot and she tells me, "That old guy you dated in high school is dead now."

Candi has a baby on her hip and two more children wrapped around her legs. I am carrying an extra-large bag of birdseed for my mother.

★

Later, I look up his name. There's a short obituary online written by his family. It was a lawn mower accident. They are not as uncommon as you'd think, the obituary takes care to point out.

★

A race car driver killed by his lawn mower. There must be a joke in there somewhere.

*

The pair of high school students next to me on this PATH train know so much more about life than I do.

"I was trying to be, like, hyper-rational," says the first girl. "And explain to him that he can't treat me this way."

"That's smart," says her friend.

"But all my *human feelings* got in the way," says the first girl.

"That happens," says her friend.

*

There's a voicemail on the house phone from That Home informing us there's been an incident with my father. My mother's still at botany class, so I call back. As it rings, I crouch down on the floor like I'm about to pee, some atavistic instinct that it's safer down there. By the time I get transferred to the nurse practitioner, I have my forehead bowed to the floor too. I rock back and forth on the balls of my feet and hum softly until she comes on the line.

She explains briskly that my father managed to squirrel an old credit card away and has ordered hundreds of dollars' worth of products from daytime infomercials to That Home.

"The packages have been arriving for the last few days," she says. "It's against policy for patients to receive mail that's commerce."

"You couldn't have mentioned in your voicemail," I say very quietly into the floor. "That the incident with my elderly, infirm father was one of *fucking commerce.*"

*

I drive over to That Home and find my father cowering alone in his room like a dog that's eaten the birthday cake.

"Hi, Pa," I say softly, kneeling beside his chair.

He's clutching the end of the curtain and rubbing the nubby corner back and forth with his thumb. Sunlight flocks through the window. I put my hand on his arm. He jerks it away.

"You're not in trouble, Pa," I say.

He fumbles to get a better handful of the curtain and tugs it slowly across his face.

★

The stuff he bought has been confiscated and held at the nurse's station. *Confiscated?* I want to yell. *He's a doctor! He went to Princeton!*

I borrow a pair of scissors and slice open packages in the lobby. There's a retractable cane, a hair crimper, two calligraphy sets, something called the "Fat Blasting Magnet," a purple neck pillow in the shape of a panda, and a scratch-proof saucepan.

"I'd advise you to return those," says the nurse.

I lug the boxes out to the car and sit in the front seat filling out return labels. There is, understandably, no box for neurodegenerative disease under "Reason for return," so I go with "Product did not meet customer's expectations."

I sit and watch the sky turn gray. A nurse in lavender scrubs steps out for a cigarette. A knot of pigeons corkscrews into the air. I grab the panda neck pillow and shove it under my arm.

"He's keeping this," I say as I march past the nurse's station.

★

Frank and I are working late, supposedly on the presentation for this real estate company.

"This is bad, but not as bad as my first copy job," Frank says. "It was for a Chinese restaurant. So many wok puns."

"Like 'wok 'n' roll'?" I laugh.

"All the obvious ones had already been taken," he says. "We were resorting to things like 'Chip off the old wok.' 'Laughing wok of the city' . . ."

"'Between a wok and a hard place.'"

"See, you're a natural," he says. "I wanted the tagline to be 'Don't be a woksucker,' but they didn't bite."

Frank lays his hand, palm up, on the desk. I think about kissing it. Just those two parts of us, my lips and his palm, are in communion. I sit on my hands, but my head keeps tugging forward like it's trying to bob for apples. It's listening to my mouth.

★

Levi calls to tell me he's working on a solo album about his breakup. It's called *Table for One . . . Not by the Window.*

★

I find this line of poetry by Sáenz and email it to my mother:
I want to dream a sky / Full of hummingbirds. I would like to die in such a storm.
She replies:
I think I'd rather die in my sleep like Auntie Louise.

★

"But are these concepts ownable?" asks the real estate client in pinstripes. "Are we using language and phraseology that's indigenously ours?"
"I'm going to have to stop you at indigenous," says Frank.
The meeting did not go well.

★

"You and I deserve a drink," says Frank as we leave the real estate client's bland midtown offices. "Or twelve."
We go to an Irish bar around the corner that smells of salted nuts and disappointment. I think Frank is worried about losing the client, which I assume is why he orders three whiskeys for every one of my wine spritzers. Soon he is looking at me as if trying to make me out through dark and murky water.
"All right, Mr. J. Daniels," I say. "Let's get you home."
I try to hail a cab for him on the street while he weaves around me in a looping half dance. He grabs a parking meter and leans his cheek against it forlornly, blinking at me through his glasses.
"I don't want to go home," he says.
My heart lunges. What can I say to this? *Why don't you come home with me to New Jersey, just try not to wake my mother?*

"Your wife will be worried about you," I say.

He sighs. "You're right," he says. "When you're right, you're right!" He twirls around the meter without taking his eyes off me. "You are such a nice person, Eleanor."

"You're a nice person too, Frank," I say over my shoulder as I flag down a free cab.

Frank shakes his head blearily.

"No, I'm not," he says. "I'm a bad man."

The cab pulls up, and I open the door for him.

"Bad, bad man," he repeats as he heaves his way into the back seat.

I lean down to speak to him before I close the door.

"You're not a bad man, Frank," I say. "You're just drunk."

"Same thing," he says, falling backward across the seats.

He is laughing as I close the door, but it doesn't sound like he thinks it's funny at all.

*

In the email inviting us all to the office holiday party, there is a warning that the company will not pay the bail of anyone arrested this year. I ask Myke if this is a joke.

"You didn't hear? Two years ago, an intern and an account exec got caught doing blow on the street. Frank had to bail them out. Legendary." Myke shakes his head in awe. "Absolutely legendary."

*

I spend approximately three and a half hours getting ready for the party, which is the longest I've ever prepared for anything in life, including my SATs. I have been soaked, scrubbed, rubbed, shaved, plucked, and slicked with lotion. My hair has been washed, blow-dried, re-curled, and doused in hair spray. I have applied every cream and powder I own to my face. I have spritzed perfume into the air and walked through its wet cloud.

*

I have also done something I never do, and that is buy clothes. I take a fresh pair of stockings out of their packaging and slide them on. They were insanely expensive, more expensive than one would imagine two tiny sheaths of nylon fabric could ever plausibly be, but the world of fashion is full of such oddities. I put them on with the utmost care, knowing that if I ladder them with one of my hobgoblin toenails, I will surely have to kill myself. I zip up into my new black dress and slip into a pair of patent high heels. I grab a birthday-cake flavored Lip Smacker I've had since high school and throw it in my purse, just in case.

Finally, I stand in front of the mirror, and I see . . . soft belly, coarse hair, thin lips, thick waist. I am a Jewish man in drag.

*

Okay, so I am not pretty. Some people have diabetes. Some people have six toes. Some people get caught in forest fires and suffer third-degree burns all over their body. Some people have headaches they ignore for months, then finally go to the doctor only to find out it's a brain tumor that kills them within weeks having never achieved their life's potential. I did not end up pretty. Big whoop.

*

I'd like to sneak out unnoticed, but my mother is in the living room, poured over one of her gardening books, waiting for me. She looks up with her glasses hooked on the end of her nose.

"Oh," she gasps. "You look beautiful."

I smooth the front of my dress.

"Not like a Jewish man in drag?"

"This nonsense you speak," tuts my mother. She gets up and gives me a kiss, squeezes my waist. "Go have fun. And remember to *suck in*."

*

I take the PATH train into the city. There are two college students sitting in front of me talking loudly about the club they're going to. Something about bottle service. The ends of their sentences all flip up, like whale tails, into questions.

Still, it must be nice to have the company. I'm carrying my mother's tiny satin evening bag, which could barely accommodate the Lip Smacker, let alone something to read. Sometimes it does not pay to make an effort, I'm learning.

★

The elevators doors open to reveal Jacky teetering on a stepladder, holding a disco ball above her head.

"Whoever that is, help me!" she yells over her shoulder.

"It's me, Jacks," I say, holding her steady as she pushes the pin into the spongy ceiling tile. She steps down and brushes glitter from her hands onto her red sweater dress. She is wearing a large pair of reindeer antlers.

"We had an extra, so I thought—" She scans me up and down, lets out a long whistle. "Wow. Look who decided to show up for the party."

★

Frank is talking to everyone but me. Somehow I get stuck in conversation with one of the suits from the real estate company. Clearly they're not planning on dropping us before they've enjoyed the open bar.

"Do you have any plans for the holidays?" I ask.

"I have to fly to fucking Ohio to see my ex-wife and our kids."

"Oh," I say. "Well, I've heard Ohio is—"

"I could have gone to Hawaii," he says. "But instead I'm going to nightmare."

"Uh-huh," I say, casting around for Jacky. "And will you be in nightmare long?"

"No," he says, grudgingly. "We have a schedule: milk, cookies, presents, fuck off."

I'm about to tell him I'd like to implement the last part of that schedule right now when I see Frank, like an archangel, descend upon us.

"Are you telling one of my writers to fuck off, sir?"

The client laughs uncomfortably and reaches for his drink. Frank makes an excuse for me and pivots us away. He puts an arm over my shoulder and leans his face next to mine. His breath smells of vodka and orange juice.

"Sorry about the other night," he says. "'Tis the season to embarrass yourself in front of your coworkers, apparently."

CLEOPATRA AND FRANKENSTEIN

"It was nothing," I say. "It was fine."

"Well, you're a champ," he says. "And thanks for handling that guy. He always looks like he just walked into a bad hotel room. Have you noticed that?"

I look at Frank. That was the thing about him. *He* noticed that. He noticed people. It was his gift. Or really, it was the gift he gave you. To be seen.

"What?" says Frank, looking at me.

"Nothing," I say. "You look nice."

"Look who's talking," he says.

★

"You having fun?" one intern wearing a Rudolph nose asks another.

"The only place I want to be at a party," the second intern says, "is under the coats asleep."

★

I am dancing slowly, arms outstretched, to Wham's "Last Christmas." This is my favorite song of all time. It is full of pathos and insight. Perhaps the real tragedy here is not that George Michael's heart was given away, but that this beautiful song is relegated to only one month of the year, when its message of unrequited love leading to a deepening resolve to choose more deserving partners is undeniably relevant year-round.

"You don't usually drink much, do you, hon?" is what Jacky says when I tell her this.

★

Myke and I are bouncing up and down, and I cannot stop laughing. His impression of an Irish jig is hilarious. We have both wrapped tinsel around our necks, and it is also hilarious, as well as hot and itchy. I feel a kindling warmth toward all mankind. There is no one I would not kiss on the mouth right now. Myke and I grab each other by the wrists and swing around in a tight, giddy loop. The room is an ecstatic cotton-candy machine swirl.

And then I see her. The pearl. Her hair is a golden curtain falling down her back. She is wearing what appears to be a silk jumpsuit and gold slippers. Beside her is an impossibly slim man wearing a mohair sweater and shiny vinyl pants. I drop Myke's hands and stop spinning. I look at her. All the light in the room reflects her. Myke looks at Frank, who is looking at me, who is looking at her. She is turning and saying something that makes her friend laugh.

Well, I think, this is a terrible blow to us all.

*

I am trying to make it to the bathroom when it happens: we are introduced.

"Hon, have you met Frank's wife, Cleo?" Jacky grabs my arm. I notice her antlers are askew, and a handful of hair has gotten caught in the top prongs. I fumble to unwind the tinsel from around my neck. "Lee's a godsend. Such a talent, *and* she's a woman."

"I can see that."

Cleo smiles at me. I try to take in her face. She is both prettier and less pretty than I expected. She is the palest shade of cream, with minty green eyes. Her eyebrows are invisibly blond above a narrow nose and elfin, pointed chin. Her lips are two thin streaks of pink. There is something barely there, washed out, about her, like a bright piece of fabric bleached by the sun.

"They're lucky to have you," she says.

The British accent—I'd forgotten. She is charm personified.

"Thank you," I say. "Goodbye!"

*

Could have gone better but definitely could have gone worse, is my honest appraisal of that meeting as I throw up in the bathroom stall.

*

I leave the bathroom to find that one of the junior graphic designers has wobbled onto a chair and is attempting to make a speech.

CLEOPATRA AND FRANKENSTEIN

"You guys are, like . . . you're like family to me," she manages to choke out before her face crumples into tears.

There is an uncomfortable moment while we all watch her being helped off the chair by her friend and ushered, still sniffling, away. Frank stands up and claps his hands.

"Okay thanks for that heart-warming message, Courtney," he says.

"Her name's Corey!" her friend yells over her shoulder as they shuffle out.

"Well, I agree with her," says Frank. "We *are* like a family." He looks around the room. People nod vaguely. "And I don't know about you." He raises his glass over his head. "But I need to drink heavily to be around my family. So mazel tov!"

Everyone is laughing. Everyone except Cleo.

★

"What's your New Year's resolution?" one intern asks the other.

"Get off my antidepressants for good," the second intern says. "I'm tired of feeling numb to life's joys. Yours?"

The first intern reaches down to pull up the hem of his pants.

"Fashion socks," he says.

★

I am standing by the snacks table downing water and Fig Newtons to sober up when Cleo approaches me. I look around. No Frank.

"I just love your hair," she says.

"Oh," I say, brushing crumbs off the front of my dress. "Thank you. Yours is nice too."

"Mine's all flat and blah," Cleo says. "Yours is much more exciting." I know this dance.

"No way," I say gamely. "I always wished I had straight hair growing up. Yours is exactly what I wanted."

"And I always wanted curls." Cleo laughs lightly. "If only we could swap."

"If only," I say.

We look at each other. Those two words, so full of longing, hang in the air between us.

"What's he like to work with?" she asks.

"Frank? He's very smart. And, um, funny. And just an all-around decent chap."

This last part I inexplicably say in a cockney accent. I wonder if I will ever be able to look myself in the eye again. Cleo smiles generously at me.

"I'm glad," she says. "That he's nice." She leans toward me conspiratorially and holds my gaze. I have the insane idea that she may be about to kiss me on the mouth when she says, "Lee, can I ask you something? It's a little delicate—"

Her friend in the fuzzy sweater interrupts us. "Cley, do you know if we're allowed to smoke in here?" He gives us a quick appraising glance. "Are you two about to make out or something?"

Cleo colors. She is so pale you can literally watch the blood rise to the surface of her skin.

"This is my friend Quentin," she says.

"*Best* friend," says Quentin.

I haven't heard anyone referred to as that since high school. That was it, I realized. Cleo, her life, her friends, were still that of a girl's. I looked older than her when I was eighteen. I probably *was* older than her when I was eighteen.

"You'll have to ask Frank if you can smoke," says Cleo.

As if conjured by his name, Frank appears with Anders in tow. I can't be sure, but I think I see a flicker of panic in his eyes.

"I see you're meeting Cleo's real husband," he says, patting Quentin on the back.

Quentin looks at Cleo with territorial pride.

"I'm Eleanor, by the way," I say.

"Frank, I'm smoking in here, okay?" says Quentin.

"Your name's Eleanor?" asks Cleo.

"You girls look great," says Anders. "Love the dresses."

"Cleo's is a jumpsuit," says Quentin.

"*You're* Eleanor?" Cleo says again.

"Love the jumpsuit then," says Anders.

"You can smoke out the window over there," says Frank.

Quentin rolls his eyes and removes the unlit cigarette from his mouth. "Coming, Cleo?" he asks, though it is more of a demand.

"One second," says Cleo, turning back to me.

"Do you . . . Did you think I was someone else?" I ask her.

"*Cleo*," whines Quentin.

"I said give me a second," says Cleo with the slightest edge in her voice.

She turns back to me. Watching Cleo compose her face is like watching a vase shatter backward. All the pieces suddenly zoom back together.

"I thought your name was Lee . . . I was confused."

"Cley, can you come help me bring out the Secret Santa gifts?" interjects Frank. His face is all twitchy and tense.

"Please excuse me," she says, following him away. She looks strangely dazed.

"Typical," spits Quentin and storms off to smoke out the open window alone.

And so I am left with Anders. He is looking at the Christmas tree, blinking one eye, then the other, in time to the flashing lights.

★

I take the elevator down to the lobby. A group of accounts people come in from smoking outside. I don't want them to see my face, so I bend over like I'm trying to lace my shoe. Their laughter bounces off the floors. I take out my phone. It only rings once.

"Ma," I say quietly.

"What's wrong?" she says.

"I have to tell you," I say.

"What is it?" she says. "Do you need me to come get you? I'm getting my keys."

I shake my head, even though she can't see me.

"He's married, Ma." I say. "He's married to someone else."

I put my hand over my mouth to quiet the little choking noises I'm making.

"Myke's married?"

"No, Frank's married." I laugh in spite of myself and rub snot on my sleeve. "Myke's an idiot."

There is silence on the other end. I hear her exhale.

"Oh, Ellie," she says. "I thought you were going to tell me something really terrible, like you were moving back to LA."

★

The next morning my mother makes me pancakes before work while I lay my head on my arms and moan. Outside, it is snowing. I try to inhale the flakes as I walk to the train. I need something pure inside me. Finally one lands on my tongue. Nothing.

★

"How's your day going?" Jacky asks me.

I lift my head up from my arms.

"It's no double dolphin kiss," I say.

Jacky roars with laughter.

"Nothing is, hon," she says.

★

It's the day before the office closes for two weeks. Frank and I are walking to lunch when an Orthodox Jew approaches us. He asks if we're Jewish. The wrong half, says Frank, but I tell him I am. He smiles and wishes me a happy Hanukkah.

The wrong half. I keep repeating the phrase in my mind as we walk. I want to tell Frank that there is no wrong half, no halves at all in fact, that if there were, we'd be busy halving ourselves again and again until we got to the little square of us that was good and then we would all be free to love and be loved.

"Let's go through the park," says Frank, nudging me in the direction of the gates.

I squint into the icy sunlight. The path sparkles with a thin layer of frost. Everything is hard and bright, like I'm looking out from inside a diamond.

"So, you're Jewish?" Frank says.

"You couldn't tell?" I say.

"My mother always wanted me to marry a Jewish girl," he says.

"I just realized that marriage is the definition of temp-to-perm," I say.

"What?" says Frank.

"Temporary to permanent," I say. "That's what I am."

"Oh, you're perm," says Frank. "You're about as perm as they come."

A breeze filled with light and ice circles us. A police officer sitting on a bench unwraps a silver Hershey's kiss. Children scream in ecstasy on a playground out of sight. We stop walking. Frank is looking at me. I am looking at Frank. This is a place of exquisite beauty and extreme danger.

CHAPTER NINE

January

S he's not happy," said Frank.

He was in his office overlooking Madison Square Park, which was covered in patches of dirty ice. The sky was a flat slate gray. It was the time of year when winter had ceased to be festive and become a test of endurance lasting until spring. There was maybe an hour of daylight left. Over the phone, he could hear the click of his mother's lighter, the first inhale.

"I don't understand this obsession with happiness," she said. "Happiness is like the Hollywood sign. It's big, it's unattainable, and even if you do make it up there, what's there to do but come back down?"

"Mother!" Frank said. "Please! I'm asking you for help."

"All right, all right. Tell me what's going on."

Frank misted the window with his breath and absently wrote his name in cursive.

"We're pitching for a new client," he said. "An energy drink called Kapow!"

"Asinine name," said his mother.

"You're telling me," said Frank. "The exclamation point is *part* of the name."

"I could hear that," she said. "Somehow I could hear that."

Frank laughed.

"Anyway, if we win it, I'm going to be traveling a lot more, even more than I am now. And, well, I'm worried about leaving her."

"What are the odds you'll get it?"

Frank smiled in spite of himself.

"We're the underdog, but we've got a shot. It's money, Mom. Like pay-the-rest-of-Zoe's-college-tuition-and-get-a-bigger-apartment kind of money."

"Good for you, Frankie." He heard her exhale smoke. "Go after what you want in life, no matter what anyone says."

"Mm," said Frank. "Like you did?"

Growing up, his mother was always on some ski trip or another. And, before she stopped drinking, at some bar or other. She didn't like the heat, so she packed him off to a Christian summer camp in Minnesota every year and spent August in Zermatt, Switzerland, where there was snow 365 days a year. She didn't like the other mothers, so she never went to his school plays or diving meets when she was home. *Just tell me about it afterward, Frankie. I'll enjoy it more hearing it from you.*

"I took care of myself," she said. "And I don't apologize for it."

"You sure don't," said Frank. He rubbed his name off the window with his sleeve.

"I know!" said his mother. "What about a pet? Remember how I got you Brigitte to keep you company? You loved her."

"Brigitte ran away," said Frank sulkily.

"Nonsense," said his mother. "Brigitte died of thyroid cancer. I just told you that so you wouldn't be upset. Do you still believe she sent you those postcards too?"

After Brigitte disappeared, he'd been inconsolable. His mother's cat, the arthritic Mooshi, who appeared to be prepared to outlive them all, had been no comfort. His mother herself had, of course, left for one of her trips soon after. A few days later, he'd found a postcard in the mail from Brigitte. She apologized for leaving and explained that she'd been invited to tour her off-Broadway show, a spin-off of *Cats* about her own life, around the world. A week later, there'd been a card from the Ritz Paris, then London, and later another from Zermatt, Switzerland.

"I'd forgotten," said Frank. "I loved those cards."

"Get her a cat," said his mother. "It will do you both good."

"She's allergic," he said.

"Then get her a hairless one. Get her a lizard! We all need something to look after."

"What about someone to look after us?"

"You're not children. You can look after yourselves."

"Yeah, but I was a child, Mom," said Frank. "I was one."

Frank hung up the phone a little while after and spun his chair round and round, watching the ceiling turn. Talking to his mother bewildered him. He wished he loved her a little more or hated her a little less, something to tip the scale. Instead, he lived in the fraught balance between the two, each increasing the intensity of the other: the more he longed for her, the more disappointed he felt by her; the more disappointed he felt, the more he longed. He tilted his head back, closed his eyes and exhaled a long *fuuuuuck*.

"That's pretty much what I want to do every time I talk to a client too," a voice behind him said.

Eleanor. Frank had once seen an image of a tsunami wave carrying hundreds of species of sea life within it, sharks and stingrays and schools of silver-backed fish, all lifted high in the wave's arc before crashing onto land. That was what it felt like whenever he was near Eleanor. They had never touched, never kissed, but his response to her was titanic. Everything in him rose to meet her.

"What about after talking to your mother?" he asked.

He opened his eyes and swiveled to face her.

"Ah." Eleanor nodded. "The original difficult client."

"Except she doesn't have any money."

"Come on." Eleanor grinned. "How bad could anyone who birthed you be?"

She was standing in his doorway. Her curly brown hair was piled messily on top of her head. She was the only woman he had ever seen who used a pen to hold up her hair not as an affectation, as Cleo some-times did with chopsticks or a long-stemmed feather, but out of absent-mindedness. Her face, which some would describe as plain, but which had never seemed so to him, with its pale skin and round cheeks, unruly eyebrows and restless, dark eyes, was on full display. When she smiled, her teeth were surprisingly small, tiny cream squares that revealed, momentarily, the child she had once been, roguish and precocious, still visible inside the face of the woman.

"What are your thoughts on hairless cats?" he asked.

"Demonic. I prefer tortoises."

"Live too long," said Frank. "I don't want a pet that will outlive me. It's for Cleo, by the way."

He watched for a change in her expression, but she was impenetrable, as per usual.

"A fish then?"

"*Too* mortal," said Frank. "We'll kill it in weeks."

"Have you vetoed dog already for being too provincial?"

"Not allowed in our building."

"I know! What about a sugar glider? My neighbors had one growing up. My brother and I loved it."

"How is Levi?" asked Frank.

"His girlfriend came back," said Eleanor. "So, happier."

"What happened to the Hell's Angel?"

"I don't think we want to know," said Eleanor. "Look up sugar gliders."

Frank turned to his computer and typed the words into his search engine. Images of a small rodentlike creature with huge dark eyes and a long tail populated the screen.

"It's crazy-looking," he said.

"Crazy beautiful," said Eleanor. "It's like a cross between a flying squirrel and chinchilla."

"You would think that was beautiful," he said.

"Look, they make great pets," said Eleanor. "I've gotta run. Think about it."

"Going on a date?" asked Frank before he could stop himself.

"No, I thought I'd spare myself that indignity tonight." She smiled sadly. "My dad isn't doing so well. He took a, um, turn, so I want to go see him before visiting hours end."

"Of course," said Frank. "I'm so sorry. If you need to take some time off to be with him, just let Jacky know. You can have as much as you need. Paid, of course."

This was not even remotely company policy for freelancers.

"Good luck with the pet," Eleanor said. "I'm sure Cleo will love whatever you get her."

After she left, Frank read about sugar gliders. Self-cleaning, affectionate, and inexpensive to feed, they did indeed appear to make excellent pets. He looked up to see if any were for sale nearby. The first link that came up was an ad on Craigslist. ~!~!~!~!**BABY SUGAR GLIDERS 4 SALE THEY R 2 CUTE 2 BELIEVE**~!~!~!~! Frank clicked on the link and read the brief description requesting interested buyers to call for more information. Frank got up and closed his office door, then dialed the number listed. The voice that answered was surprisingly sultry and kittenish.

"You want a sugar glider? Sure, I got gliders. I can do one for one seventy-five, two for three hundred, or three for four twenty-five. How many you need?"

"Um, just the one, I think," said Frank. "How many is normal?"

"You want to get it a friend?" she purred. "It's a good deal for two."

Frank looked at the wide-eyed creature on his screen and laughed.

"Okay, two it is," he said.

Frank took the subway to an address in the Bronx. It was early evening and the train was full of the usual commuter types with their headphones and paperbacks and air of mild hostility. He got off at 149th Street and walked the few blocks to the address he'd been given with his head lowered against the wind. The dark residential streets were close to empty. A car passed by blaring a reggaeton song that had been popular on the radio that summer; it felt as out of place on the barren street as a palm tree sprouting from one of the derelict front yards. He reached the house number he'd been given and looked at the unlit brownstone. Nobody appeared to be home. Frank blew into his hands and called the number from the website.

"Hey, I'm outside. You sure you gave me the right address?"

"You're late," the voice chided lightly. "My mom will be home soon." He saw the blinds of the bottom-floor window move. "I see you. Come to the door."

Jesus, thought Frank, walking heavily up the steps. How the hell did he end up buying a flying rodent from what now appeared to be an underage girl in the Bronx? What was so wrong with a fucking fish, anyway? He shook his head as he rang the bell. He was the only person he knew who could get himself into a situation like this. Except, perhaps, Eleanor. He smiled to himself at the thought of her. She, he was sure, was capable of anything.

The woman who opened the door was large, at least three times the width of Frank, and, if he had to estimate, in her late forties. She wore a lilac sweatshirt with a faded logo of Mickey Mouse on the front and a pair of thinned, bleach-stained leggings. Her skin was dark and smooth and poreless. Frank searched her face for signs that this was the voice. who had spoken to him on the phone. Her eyes were mahogany brown, lined by short, tightly curled lashes, and focused just past Frank with disconcerting intensity. Her full cheeks and heavy chin had a mournful quality, but her glossy lips were faintly upturned. There was not a straight line anywhere on her face or body.

"Are you Frank?"

There it was, that silky voice. Frank nodded, temporarily dumbfounded.

"Come in." She beckoned for him to pass her. "We gotta be quick. My mom finishes work soon, and she doesn't like it when I let people come to the house."

The smell of sawdust, damp, and an unnamable sour odor Frank instinctively knew to be human greeted him as he walked through the door. Piles of clothes littered the living area she led him to. A large plasma screen covered one of the walls.

"You don't have cats, right?" she asked.

Frank shook his head.

"Good, because cats kill the babies. I'll go get you one."

The woman disappeared up the unlit stairs. He looked around the room, which was illuminated by a single buzzing overhead light. Among the mounds of clothes were plastic shopping bags, all ostensibly filled with more clothes. Frank perched on the arm of the large sofa next to him, then stood up again. He rubbed his hands on his thighs. The woman returned with her hands cupped in front of her. He kept trying to decipher her age. She certainly couldn't have been younger than forty. Her thinning black hair was streaked with white. But she lived with her mother? The whole thing unnerved him.

"Okay, you ready?" she purred. "This one's a boy. I just woke him up. Let's hope he likes you."

She motioned for him to put out his hands and Frank did so. Very gently, she tipped the contents of hers into his. He felt the light, warm pressure of a living body and the tickle of fur against his skin. She pulled her hands away, and Frank saw for a moment a small gray creature crouched on his palm. Before Frank could look closer, it sprung into the air, pinged off the window blinds behind him, bounced off the sofa, and dove into a heap of clothes a few feet away.

"Oh no," she moaned softly. "He didn't like you. You wanna try another?"

"Jesus," said Frank. "You tell me."

He took a step toward the mound of shirts, which did not appear to be clean. This whole exercise was proving to be insane, as he should have known it would be. But he was committed now. He was going to get a sugar glider to like him.

"Should I . . . ," said Frank. "Try to retrieve him?"

"That's okay," she said lightly. "He'll come out when he's ready. I'll go get you another."

She disappeared back up the stairs, and Frank stared dubiously at the mound of clothes concealing the creature. It did not stir.

"You sure about that?" he mumbled to himself.

The woman returned, and Frank dutifully put out his hands.

"This one's a baby girl," she said. "I have a feeling you're better with girls."

A tumble of fur slipped from her hands to his, and there, sitting placidly in the center of his palm, was the baby girl sugar glider. She looked up at Frank. She was the palest gray, almost lilac, with a dark stripe down her forehead and back, reaching to the tip of her tail, which looked like it had been dipped in ink. Between her feet and hands was a fold of fur, ruffled like the underside of a mushroom. Her wings. Huge black eyes, wet, as if from crying. Petal-pink nose and pink-tipped fingers. Now she was lifting a hand to wrap it nimbly, monkey-like, around his thumb. She was soft as dandelion seeds.

"Oh," said Frank.

"You want her?"

"I want her."

"Yippee," said the woman and clapped her palms together. "Shall I go get another girl for you?"

"No, no," said Frank. "She's enough for me. Here—"

As tenderly as he could, he cupped the sugar glider against his chest with one hand and pulled his wallet out of his back pocket with the other. He could feel her heart pulsing softly beneath her fur against his fingers. He pulled out three $100 bills and handed them to the woman.

"You sure?" She looked down at the money. "But you're only taking one."

"Please," he said. "I insist. For having me in your home."

He accepted a shoebox with holes punched in the top to transport the creature home. It started to rain as he was walking back to the subway, so he hailed the first cab he saw and sat with the box held tightly on his lap the whole ride back downtown. The traffic lights smeared past the window in streaks of amber and green. Fat rain droplets glowed on the glass. Frank leaned forward in the steamy warmth of the back seat and found himself whispering quietly through the holes of the shoebox, little nonsenses and pleasantries that were foreign to his tongue. *Yes, that's right honey baby, sugar love, sweet thing, we're going home.*

Frank let himself into the dark apartment and found Cleo lying on the sofa under a pyramid of light from a lamp. She did not stir at the sound of the door. She had her back to him, curled into the sofa with a book in front of her face. She was wearing a baggy pair of jeans and a large cashmere sweater of his. The soles of her bare feet were brown with dirt. With the tips of his fingers, Frank touched the back of her head. Her golden hair was dulled by the winter, and knots were visible in the back.

"Cleo honey," he said. "I have something for you."

She twisted to face him. Her cheeks were flushed. A look of confusion and upset stained her face. He placed his hand on her neck, which was warm and damp, and pecked the side of her temple. He'd placed the box on the floor by the sofa, out of view.

"I was half asleep," she said. "Have you ever heard of Berthe Morisot?"

"I don't think so," said Frank. "But, honey, I want to show you something."

"Look at this," said Cleo.

She had a kind of feverish intensity about her. She propped herself up on her elbow and proffered the open pages of the book toward him. It was a painting of a woman sitting before a mirror. Her curved back was turned to the viewer, only her ear and a pale sliver of cheek exposed. The reflection of her face in the glass had deliberately been left blank, void of features or expression. Her hands were piling her dark hair on top of her head, as Eleanor's had been that day. The background was vivid blue, energetically painted, as if a breeze were moving through the room, stirring everything, the fabric that fell from her shoulders, the red flowers on the nightstand, into motion.

"Very good," said Frank. "Looks like Degas."

"No!" Cleo slapped the page in disgust. "Degas looks like *Morisot*. Degas, Manet, Renoir, Monet . . . They all admired her, copied her, but has anyone ever heard of her? No! Degas is a *hack* compared to her. I hate his insipid ballerinas. Look how full of life, of *agency*, her subjects are by contrast."

"Yes, yes, I see that," said Frank, looking vaguely at the painting, which really did look like a Degas to him.

"Degas can suck my dick," said Cleo fervently.

Frank laughed and took the book from her, setting it aside. He rested his hand on the curve of her waist.

"Did you paint today?" he asked.

She shot up to a seated position, sending his hand tumbling away.

"Why are you asking me that?" she said.

Frank was amused by Cleo in this mood, so impassioned and riled up, though he knew to be wary of it too. He preferred to see her like this, however, than in the dead-eyed despondency in which she'd recently been wallowing. She used to take such care with her appearance; he loved watching her get dressed each day for work. He'd supported her decision to quit doing the textile design, a job she'd sniffed at as beneath her fine art pedigree, to focus on painting. Now he suspected that was a mistake. It wasn't good for her, all this free time. He was happy to support her financially while she made art, but she'd been painting less and less. And this anger she had about women in the art world, women anywhere, really . . . Passion was one thing, but hysteria was another. It only seemed to be growing in her as her painting life dwindled.

"Look, I've got someone I want you to meet," he said. "She's been waiting very patiently, and—"

"Oh, Frank, you didn't bring someone home," groaned Cleo. "I'm not in the mood. Can we ever just spend time just us two?"

Frank picked up the box from the floor and held it in front of Cleo's furrowed face.

"Open it," he said.

Cleo widened her eyes. With the tips of her fingers, she lifted the lid. There, sitting in a little bed of sawdust, was the baby sugar glider. She looked up at Cleo with her big black eyes. Cleo shrieked. Frank felt his heart drop. She hated it.

"Oh Frank, you didn't!" The words came out all in a tumble. "You're crazy! You're nuts! What were you thinking? I love it! I love you. How could you—what are we going to do with it? We need food! What does it eat? I love it, really I do. It's beautiful but . . . What on earth is it?"

"It's a sugar glider," said Frank, grinning with relief. "It's kind of like a flying squirrel crossed with a chinchilla. Except small and cuter."

"It *flies*?" Cleo threw her head back in delight. "You're crazy, Frank. It's perfect. I love it."

"You've got to a pick a name for her," said Frank.

He couldn't stop smiling.

"It's a her?"

"Mm-hmm," he said. "A baby girl for my baby girl."

Cleo wrinkled her nose in distaste. She hated that kind of talk, he knew, which she deemed infantilizing. But sometimes he couldn't resist. Even in this disheveled state, there was something so disarmingly feminine about her, so undeniably *girlish*, it seemed crazy that he was never allowed to recognize it.

"Can I hold her?"

"Of course," said Frank. "She's yours."

Cleo scooped the sugar glider out of the box and cradled her to her chest.

"Hello, darling. What are we going to call you? What is your name, hmm?"

"What about naming her after that painter of yours?" asked Frank. "What was her name? Berthe?"

Cleo looked down at the creature in her arms, who was attempting to clamber up her sweater and into her hair. Aside from her tail, she was no larger than a packet of Sweet'n Low.

"I don't know," Cleo said. "It seems like an awfully serious name for such a crazy little thing."

"So . . . Not Berthe?" Frank was disappointed. He'd been pleased with himself for thinking of it.

"She can't have a human name," said Cleo. "She's too magic for a boring old human name."

"What do you want to do, then?" said Frank. "Give her a sign language name or something?"

"I love that!" said Cleo. "Do you know how to say anything in sign?"

"You're serious?" he said. "Well, I know this."

He made the movements with his hands.

"What does that mean?"

"'Oh Jesus, how I adore you.'"

Cleo rocked with laughter.

"Why on earth do you know how to say that?"

"Because my insane mother used to send me to a fundamentalist Christian camp every summer, where they taught us to sing the hymns in sign. That's the only part I can remember. Ironic for a half Jew, I know."

"All right," said Cleo. "Show me again."

Frank showed her how to spell out the words with his hands. They both looked down at the sugar glider.

"Oh Jesus How I Adore You," said Cleo. "Welcome to our little family."

That first night they went to the Petco, which inexplicably stayed open until midnight on weeknights. They left Oh Jesus How I Adore You in her shoebox with a single peanut, which they read she could eat one of a day as a special treat.

"Do you think she'll be okay without us?" asked Cleo as they walked to the store. She was already taking to her role as anxious mother.

"She'll be just fine." He put his arm around her shoulder. "We've got to get her some food and a nice big cage to live in."

Cleo nuzzled her face into his neck. Her nose was running from the cold. The rain had stopped, but an icy wind was barreling down the avenue, buffeting their coats and scarves about them. He'd forgotten his gloves. He put one hand in his pocket and reached the other farther around Cleo, pushing it between the buttons of her fur coat. It nestled against the warm wool of her sweater. She kissed the freezing tip of his ear lobe poking out from beneath his hat.

"I love you, Frankenstein," she murmured into his ear.

Inside the fluorescent-lit Petco the smell of cat litter and stale fish tanks encircled them. The place was almost completely empty, long vacant aisles stacked with neon chew toys and huge sacks of dry food. Frank loved it here; it was a welcome relief from ordinary life. They looked around and managed to root out one of the Petco staff somewhere near the birdcages.

"Excuse me, do you work here?" Frank asked.

"Work here? I'm the junior manager," said the Petco junior manager.

He had a long pallid face, made even longer by a waxed and pointed goatee.

"Great," said Frank. "Which of these, hypothetically, would you say is the best cage for a sugar glider?"

The junior manager inhaled so sharply, the tips of his nostrils blanched.

"I would say *none* of these are a good cage for a sugar glider," he said. "Because sugar gliders are illegal in all five boroughs of New York."

Cleo turned to Frank with a barely suppressed smile. "Well, isn't it lucky we don't have one then, darling?"

"Very lucky," said Frank. "We'd never do anything illegal."

"Never," said Cleo. "That's why we're speaking—"

"Purely hypothetically," said Frank.

"Hypothetically or not," sniffed the Petco junior manager, "it would be against my best interest to recommend anything to house, feed, or entertain a sugar glider to you or anyone else."

Cleo turned to Frank again.

"She needs to be entertained?" she said.

"I think you're highly entertaining," said Frank.

"I could do my Dolly Parton impression?"

"You do a great Dolly. And I'll juggle."

"I didn't know you could juggle."

"Only very round things."

"A man of many talents," said Cleo and kissed him.

The junior manager exhaled loudly.

"Entertainment as in *activities*," he said. "Sugar gliders are nocturnal and highly active, so it's imperative to provide them with hamster wheels, balls, or—"

"You got that?" said Frank.

Cleo nodded.

"Hamster wheel," she said.

The junior manager touched the tips of his fingers lightly to his lips. "I've said too much," he said.

"Oh, come on," said Frank. "Why the hell are they illegal?"

"Yeah, who are they hurting?" said Cleo.

"It's not a question of who they're hurting," said the junior manager.

They waited for him to continue but the man only gave them a mysterious and knowing look.

"What's it a question of, then?" asked Frank.

"Enlighten us," said Cleo.

"It's a question of breeding," said the junior manager. "While technically allowed in New York State, they're illegal in all five boroughs because of the proximity to eastern gray squirrels. Were a sugar glider to escape and breed with those squirrels, it would create a strain of flying squirrel that could prove, to say the least, unmanageable for city dwellers."

"Did you hear that, Cley?" said Frank

"Flying squirrels all over the city," nodded Cleo.

"It could cause an epidemic," said the junior manager seriously.

"Sounds—" said Frank.

"Wonderful," said Cleo breathlessly.

The junior manager's face fell.

"I'm going to have to ask you two to leave here," he said. "This is a place for law-abiding pet owners only."

"What about that cage?" said Frank, pointing to one past the manager's shoulder. "Looks pretty big."

"Did you hear me?" asked the junior manager.

"Sold!" said Cleo.

Frank pulled her after him toward the cages, both of them laughing like children. Cleo turned back to the Petco junior manager as she galloped along beside Frank.

"You've been such a dear," she called. "Terribly informative. We can't thank you enough."

Then she blew him a kiss with her pink-kid-gloved-clad hand and ran, hand in hand with Frank, down the aisle.

———

The next few days were ones of discovery. They found, for instance, that Oh Jesus How I Adore You loved apples, Gatorade, quinoa, and peach yogurt but no other kinds. They discovered why people generally did not give sign-language names that translated to six words or more to pets, and quickly began to refer to her as simply "Jesus." They learned that she woke up at around ten at night and stayed awake until ten in the morning, then slept for most of the day. Even with the cage in the living room, they could hear her through the walls trundling around in her wheel all night and occasionally emitting little bleating cries, which, they learned from researching on the internet, meant she wanted attention. They spent a lot of time researching her on the internet, reading aloud their favorite finds to each other.

"Listen to this," said Cleo. It was Friday night, and for the first time in a long time, they were spending it staying in together. "'While they bond to everyone in the family, each glider will almost always have a favorite person, usually the person who holds them the most, that will be their primary bond.'"

"Well, that's not fair," said Frank. "You're obviously going to be the favorite because you're home more."

"Tough luck." Cleo laughed. "Perks of being a stay-at-home mum."

"Hmmph."

"I read somewhere that she runs the equivalent of a marathon a night in her wheel."

"No wonder she needs to sleep all day."

"I think it's cruel to keep her trapped in her cage every night," said Cleo. "She should be free."

"But if we set her free, we'll lose her. The apartment's too big; she'll find a hole somewhere and escape."

"This woman on sugargliderlovers.com says she lets her gliders wander around her bedroom at night. You just have to keep the doors shut and proof the place the way you would for a baby."

"Cley, that's crazy." Frank poured himself another glass of wine. He went to refill Cleo's, but it was still full.

"Well, whosyoursugarmomma1956 doesn't seem to think it's so crazy."

"I'm going to ask you to think about what you just said," said Frank. "And then we'll talk about crazy."

But of course Cleo got her way. They moved the cage into the bedroom and left the door open at night. They researched how to sugar-glider-proof the room, which required blocking the electrical sockets, ensuring that the windows were tightly shut so she couldn't escape, and keeping the bathroom door closed with the toilet seat down so she wouldn't fall in and drown. Other than that, she was free to roam where she pleased. It was strange and exciting to hear her whirring around the bedroom while they lay in bed. It brought new life to their life. That first night, they lay awake listening to her.

"She's full of beans," said Cleo.

They were facing each other in the darkness, nose to nose.

"I gave her a nut late today, that might be why," he said.

"I gave her one, too! Frank, we've *got* to stop doing that, she's going to have a heart attack."

"But I love giving them to her. How else am I going to be her primary bond?"

"If we ever have a kid, she is going to be so spoiled," said Cleo.

"You . . . you want children?"

It seemed ridiculous that they had never spoken about it before. That was part of marrying in a hurry, he supposed. You had to do it before you knew enough not to.

"I think so," she said. "You don't?"

"No, I do," said Frank, surprising himself. It was amazing to him that they weren't speaking hypothetically, that this was how couples made decisions like this in real life. "I think you'd be a great mom."

"I've always been worried that I don't have that maternal gene. I don't think my mum had it, or she would never have, you know."

"You do," said Frank. "You definitely do. You're so nurturing. You look after everyone."

"You think?"

"Of course," he said. "You look after me." He reached for her hand tucked under her pillow.

"You'll be a wonderful father," said Cleo.

"How do you know?"

"You're kind," she said. "And playful. You'll definitely be a fun dad. And I see how you are with Zoe. You take care of people, too."

Frank squeezed her hand in the darkness. "I like how you see me."

Frank turned onto his back, and Cleo moved to put her head on his chest. He stroked the hair at her temples with one hand.

"I think I see you as you are," she said.

"I don't want to be anything like my dad," said Frank. "That's for sure. You know I went to Italy to find him once? In my twenties. Refused to see me. I found the restaurant he hung out at with his drinking buddies, went there one night, and told him who I was. Wouldn't acknowledge me. Pretended he didn't speak English. Asshole."

"Does your mum know about that?"

"No," said Frank. "I think it would hurt her too much."

Cleo rolled on top of him so they were face to face, her hands either side of his head. He could not make out her expression in the darkness.

"Frank?" she said.

"Yes?"

"I'm going to say something, and I want you to hear me."

"Okay."

"You are nothing like your father."

She rolled back off him, so they were side by side. Somewhere near them, Jesus leaped from one surface to another with a soft thud. Frank lay with his eyes open, trying to listen for her next move.

"Cley?" he said.

"Yeah?"

"What was your mom like? You never talk about her."

"She was a lot of different people," she said quietly.

Frank stayed silent. If Cleo was ready to talk, she would. He didn't want to push her.

"She made the best birthday cakes," she began. "I think it's because she was good at architectural models. Like one year, she made a cake in the shape of the Eiffel Tower with a little doll that looked like me at the top. We'd been to Paris for the Easter holidays and completely loved it, so the whole party was French-themed. It was me and twenty other eleven-year-olds all wearing berets and playing games like pin the mustache on the Frenchman. My mum even bought us fake cigarettes from a joke shop, which I think was pretty scandalous at the time."

"That's funny," said Frank. "What did she look like?"

"She had blond hair like me, but she was taller. She wore high heels every day and these tailored silk shirts. I used to go into her closet to rub them between my fingers, I just loved the way they felt."

"She sounds very glamorous," he said.

"She was," agreed Cleo. "But then she had to start taking this medication that made her gain a lot of weight and sleep all the time. She was very active, you know, so she hated that. I think that's why she stopped taking it eventually."

"When was that?"

"That was when she and my dad got divorced. I had to go stay with him and Miriam in Bristol because she needed to live in the hospital for a while. Then she got better, and I came home. When she was well, she could tell what kind of day you'd had just by the way you said hello. She'd want to know everything about what I was thinking, what I was reading in school. I'd sit on the kitchen counter and chat to her while she made dinner. But she'd have these bad periods where she'd stop sleeping or eating much. She'd get so focused on a project you could say her name ten times and she wouldn't hear you. I hated that. It was like you didn't exist. She'd talk to herself and laugh. She had a lot of random men over. I'd walk in on them in the bathroom sometimes. The first time she tried to kill herself was during one of those periods."

"I'm so sorry, Cley," he said. "Fuck."

"Then she got on a new medication," she said, the words pouring out fast now. "And she was normal again for a while. She went back to work, and I moved out to go to uni, and she started dating this guy seriously, someone actually nice for a change. He was another architect. Then something happened, I guess they broke up, and she went off her medication again. I didn't know that at the time, the doctors told me afterward. She died when I was in my final year. She had a little bit of money left, not much, and it all went to me. But I was depressed, like I told you, so that's when I came here to do my MFA. I started taking antidepressants and making more art and things got better. And then I met you, and that was the best thing really, the best thing that had happened in years."

Frank turned onto his side and wrapped his arms and legs around her. He held her as tight as he could without hurting her. He could hear the soft boom of her heartbeat beneath his ear.

"You're not going to be anything like your mom," he said.

Jesus leaped onto the bed near them and bounced off again, her tiny body barely leaving a dent in the covers.

"How do you know?" she said. Her voice in the dark was plaintive.

"Because you have me."

"But what about if something happens to you? Or you go away?"

"It won't. I won't."

"Promise?"

"I swear on Jesus."

———

He didn't deliberately avoid Eleanor at the office, but he was so busy working on the Kapow! pitch that their paths didn't cross much. Frank loved the brainstorming process, loved the feeling of ideas orbiting around him, and he felt confident in what his team had created. On the night before the pitch, Frank had managed to drink just enough to dull his nerves and knock himself out without, he hoped, impeding his performance the next day. He was just drifting into sleep when Jesus knocked over Cleo's book from the bedside table.

"Did you hear that?" said Cleo in the darkness.

"Mm," said Frank. "Sounds like she's having a grand old time."

"Will you hold me?"

"I'm too hot," said Frank. "My chest overheats. You hold me."

"Okay."

Cleo cradled herself around his back and tucked her nose into his hairline.

"My furnace," she said. "It's good to have you here."

"I live here," said Frank.

"You know what I mean," she said. "You're home more at the moment. It's nice."

He was almost asleep. He nodded with his eyes closed.

"Frank?" she murmured.

He stayed quiet. He really did need to sleep.

"Frank?" she said again, louder this time.

"Yuh-huh."

"I've been lonely."

He opened his eyes in the darkness. He could feel Cleo's breath on the back of his neck.

"You have?"

"Mm. And Audrey, Quentin, you know, they're no help. They're so . . ."

"Fucked up?"

Cleo let out a tearful laugh behind him. "Yes. But darling, I hate to break it to you, so are we."

"I'll try to be less fucked up." He yawned. "I promise."

"How?" she asked.

"You want specifics?"

"Not anything so specific . . . Except, maybe one thing."

He could feel her body stiffen into alertness behind him. Frank kept perfectly still and stared into the darkness ahead of him.

"Maybe, I don't know, maybe you could drink a little less."

"I could?"

"You don't think?"

"Is that what you think?"

"Well, I just thought that it seems to be getting worse . . . And if you could, I don't know, try to cut back a bit or try not to drink every night, it might, well, it might help."

Frank sat up in bed. "You thought the night before my big meeting was the right time to bring this up?"

"Oh," said Cleo. "Okay, I see your point. I just didn't think it had to be a big discussion or anything. I just thought—"

"I'm sorry, I must be confused," Frank interrupted. "Is there something I'm not providing for you?"

"What?"

Frank's voice, he realized with surprise, was slightly slurred. He slowed his voice to hide this, punctuating each word.

"*Is. There. Something. I'm. Not. Providing.*"

"Of course not," said Cleo very quietly. "You provide everything."

"What are you trying to say, then? Do I not pay our mortgage? Do I not go to work every day? Do I not work my ass off so you can basically do whatever the fuck you want with your life?"

"I'm not questioning how hard you work. I would never! I've just noticed—"

"What have you noticed, Cleo? Is it *you* who's paying for this apartment? With your . . . your paintings? You lived in a fucking dump when I first met you."

"Frank, stop!"

Cleo's voice was cracking. He knew he should stop, but he couldn't. There was a sick kind of pleasure in defending himself so ruthlessly.

"Don't you dare cry," he said. "You're not the one being attacked. I cannot believe you would sit here and criticize me after everything I've done for you."

"I'm not criticizing you," begged Cleo. "I just worry sometimes that you could—"

"I thought I married an artist, not some censorious housewife counting my drinks."

"I don't count your drinks—"

"What more can I do? Seriously, what more could I possibly do for you?" She tried to speak, but he barreled on. "No, tell me, Cleo, please tell me what it is I'm *not* providing for you. I work like a dog. I earn more money than all your little friends combined. I give you everything you ask for. I have never tried to control what you do. You paint, you don't paint, I support you anyway. And now you're going to accuse me of neglecting you, neglecting my duties."

"You're twisting my words! I . . . I never said that."

"You know what? It makes me sick, Cleo. It disgusts me that you could be so ungrateful."

"I'm sorry, I'm really sorry," she said. "I don't know what I was trying to say. Just pretend I didn't say anything."

"I thought you were an artist," he said again. "I never expected this petit bourgeois puritanism from you, Cleo. Anyone else, but not you. Honestly, it makes me sick. It makes me feel like I don't even know you."

"But you do know me," she sobbed. "You're the only one who *does* know me."

Frank was watching himself as if he was not himself. He felt gruesome and powerful at once. He had never been allowed to be angry growing up. He had never been allowed to feel anything. Now, the anger blanketed all other feelings. There was no shame, no remorse, no tenderness. He felt protected and untouchable. He felt drunk.

Cleo got up from the bed and shut herself in the bathroom. He looked at the yellow bar of light escaping from the doorframe. He heard her blow her nose and run the tap. He watched the shadow of her feet flit in the strip of light under the door. He heard her turn off the tap and open the cabinet. Let her cry, he thought. He had done nothing wrong. She still had not returned from the bathroom by the time he fell into fitful, dreamless sleep.

———

They won the Kapow! account. They pitched in the morning, and Frank got the call that very afternoon. The client said they just knew. Frank gathered the entire team together to announce the news, mandating that everyone leave work immediately to head to the bar down the block and celebrate. He was back in his office, trying to get Cleo on the phone to tell her, when Jacky led a crew past his door, singing "We Are the Champions."

"You coming, hon?" she yelled. "You're the man of the hour!"

"Cleo's not answering," he said. He grabbed his coat off the back of his chair. "I'm going to run home and see if she's there. Check on Jesus. I'll meet you there in an hour, less probably."

Jacky smiled at him. "Okay, family man," she said.

Frank let himself into the apartment and found Cleo on the living room floor with Audrey, crouched over pieces of cardboard with paintbrushes. She had Jesus on her shoulder, lightly tangled in her hair.

"Whats up, Frank," said Audrey. "Look what we're doing. We're protesting!"

"I tried to call you," said Frank to Cleo. "You didn't hear?"

"I left it in the other room," said Cleo without looking up. "Sorry."

"Jesus is up early," said Frank, bending down to kiss them both.

"She's still waking up," said Cleo, turning her face away. "She never usually sits still for this long."

Frank took the sugar glider in his hands. She was already a little bigger. He could see his reflection in her huge, dark eyes. He tickled her under the chin with the tips of his fingers. She closed her eyes in pleasure. He swore, sometimes it looked like she was smiling.

"You guys are so weird," said Audrey.

"Why?" said Cleo and Frank in unison.

"You have a pet rodent called Jesus," said Audrey. "That's the definition of weird."

"She's not a rodent," said Cleo hotly. "She's a marsupial."

"So?" said Audrey.

"Cley, can I talk to you quickly? In the other room?"

"Someone's in trouble," said Audrey in a singsong.

"I'm busy," said Cleo.

"Please," said Frank.

"We can talk here," said Cleo.

"Okay." Frank shot Audrey a sidelong glance. She was lying on her stomach with her chin propped in her palms, clearly prepared to be entertained. "Well, the first thing I want to say is that I'm sorry. I'm really sorry. And, um, about what you said last night? You're probably right and, well, I'll make some changes. I promise."

"Is that all?" said Cleo.

"No," said Frank. "The other thing I wanted to tell you is that we won it. I just found out."

"What?" Cleo brought her hands to her mouth. "But you only pitched this morning."

"I know, I know, it's crazy. They said they just knew."

"I can't believe it!" Cleo shot up from the floor to jump up and down. "I thought you heard they were leaning toward someone else?"

"Apparently not."

He tried to shrug nonchalantly, but he couldn't stop smiling.

"Can someone fill me in on what's happening?" said Audrey.

"He won a *huge* account," said Cleo. She turned back to Frank. "Gosh, I'm so proud of you. I can't believe it."

She threw her arms around him.

"We'll start shooting in South Africa next month," he said. "It's the middle of their summer. Eighty degrees and sunny, baby!"

Cleo let her arms drop.

"Wow, yeah, wonderful," she said, looking down.

He put his hands on her shoulders.

"What do you think, Cleopatra?" he said. "You want to come escape the cold with me?"

She lifted her eyes to his. "You want me to come?"

"Of course I do," he said.

"But you've never asked me to come on a shoot before."

"Well, you were doing the textile stuff before," said Frank. "And I didn't think you'd enjoy it. But you'll love South Africa. You can paint, get room service, hang out on the beach. It will be fantastic."

"Oh Frank!"

Cleo jumped on him and kissed his cheeks, his forehead, his mouth.

"So happy for you," drawled Audrey from the floor.

"The whole office is celebrating," said Frank. "I've got an open tab going. You girls want to come to the bar?"

"Fuck yeah," said Audrey.

"Well, actually . . ." Cleo glanced down at the cardboard they'd been painting on the floor. "We're meant to be going to this protest against art school tuition hikes. We made signs."

"But the bar," said Audrey.

"It's just, it's kind of important," said Cleo. "How is the next great generation of artists meant to grow if they can't afford to learn?"

"I was just going for the cute art school boys," said Audrey. "Let's go to the bar."

"Do you want me to?" said Cleo to Frank. "I can. I can protest another time."

"No, no, go to your thing," said Frank. "It'll be an early night for me anyway. I'll meet you back home and we'll have our own celebration."

"We will?" asked Cleo. "You won't want to stay out?"

"No way," said Frank.

Cleo looked down at the sign she'd been painting. It read "Make Art Not Debt!"

"Everything's changing," she said.

"Some change is a good thing, sweetheart," said Frank.

Cleo looked up at him and smiled.

Frank arrived at the bar, which was packed with people from his company. A balloon of pride inflated inside him. He had started the agency ten years ago out of a shithole office off the FDR. His first hire had been Anders, a former model who nobody took seriously as an art director. For the first year they'd only had one client, a men's silk suit manufacturer known as the suit of choice for the Italian mafia. He'd given himself a year-end bonus of one hundred bucks the first three years. And look at him now.

"Frank!" Jacky was waving him over. She was holding her phone in front of her. "I've got a reporter from *Admania* on the line. He wants a quote before they break the story tonight."

Jacky yelled for everyone to be quiet and signaled for the bartender to turn off the music. Frank held the cell in front of him. A crowd gathered around to listen. A tinny voice emanated from the phone.

"Hey Frank, congratulations on the win. Can I get a comment on the record about your recent success?"

"Sure," said Frank. "How did you know that's my favorite subject to talk about?"

"Just a hunch," said the reporter. "Now look, I'll be frank—"

"Aren't I already?" said Frank.

Everyone around him laughed.

"Very clever," said the reporter. "But seriously, you went up against some big dogs for this account, and well, I don't think anyone expected you to win it. We heard your pitch was spot-on. How does it feel for an agency of your size to officially be on the map as the one to watch?"

"Amazing," said Frank. "We can't wait to get our teeth into this brief. It's big, it's bold, it's brash, it's us. Look, we're not big dogs. We're wolves. And we're fucking feral."

Frank threw his head back and howled. A chorus of his staff joined in, and the air was momentarily filled with the sound of yelps and bays. Frank bared his teeth in a grin and motioned for them to quiet.

"That brings me to my next question," said the reporter. "You've made a name for yourself as the bad boy of advertising. Can we expect to see any more, shall we say, unruly stunts in this next chapter of your career?"

"No, no, those days are behind me," said Frank. He winked at Jacky.

"Any comment on the rumor that you're hoping to open a European office?"

"T'etait jolie comme enfant?" said Frank.

"I'm sorry?"

"That means 'Were you pretty as a child?' in French."

"So, I'll take that to mean Paris is on the horizon for you?"

"It means whatever you want it to mean," said Frank. "Now, why don't you come down here and get yourself a drink on me. Jacky, take this off me, please."

The reporter was still speaking as he handed the phone back to her. The music surged back on. He made his way to the rear of the room, accepting congratulations and handshakes from the throng around him. He was looking for Eleanor. He couldn't help it; he was always looking for Eleanor. He found her perched on a stool at the far corner of the bar, where the crowd was thinner and less raucous. He leaned on the wooden countertop next to her.

"Look who it is," she said. "The prodigal son."

"You're not wearing your glasses," he said.

"I got contacts," said Eleanor. "I was sick of seeing dead animals."

"What?" said Frank.

"Nothing," said Eleanor.

"Well," said Frank. "You look good."

"I think the real bar of adulthood is the willingness to touch your own eyeballs on a daily basis."

"That," said Frank. "And owning things like a wine aerator."

"You have a wine aerator?"

"I have *two*," said Frank. "We got given another one as a wedding present."

"Such maturity," said Eleanor.

She sipped her drink and smiled to herself in that funny, secret way she had. She always seemed to be keeping up an amusing dialogue with herself in her head, one that he was constantly hoping to become a part of.

"Anyway, as a man—," Frank said.

"Oh, you're a *man*?" She gasped. "I wish you'd told me earlier."

"Piss off," said Frank.

"A British man no less."

"That's Cleo's influence," said Frank. "Anyway, I was saying that yes, as a *man*, I always thought that contact lenses were kind of effeminate. I don't know why. But I keep losing my glasses at the moment, and if you're really near-sighted, like me, when you lose your glasses you also lose your source of finding them. Sight, that is . . . So, it's a conundrum."

What was he even talking about? He was blabbering. He had just wanted to talk to her.

"Truly," said Eleanor with her ironic half smile.

"What I mean is," he said, "it might be time for me to switch, too. Life is a constant renegotiation with one's own vanity, after all."

"Now that I agree with," said Eleanor.

"We agree on a lot," said Frank, realizing, as he said it, that it was true. "What are you drinking?"

"Soda with lime." She shook her glass. "Zesty."

"You're zesty."

Eleanor laughed and looked away. Frank cleared his throat.

"That sounds great," he said. "I'll have the same."

She raised an eyebrow as he ordered. "You're not drinking?"

The bartender shot soda from the tap and plonked the glass in front of him with a dehydrated-looking lime on the rim. Frank took a long, unsatisfying sip.

"Doing my bit to keep the bill low. This lot are going to bankrupt me." He nodded toward the crowd at the other end of the bar, where one of the account execs was already, inexplicably, shirtless with his tie secured around his head.

"Is that right?" said Eleanor.

"And." Frank gave her a sidelong glance. "I'm thinking of stopping."

"That's a lot of thinking," said Eleanor.

"You're telling me." He tapped his forehead. "Most dangerous neighborhood I know."

Eleanor laughed again. Her laugh was the sound of a slot-machine jackpot, a soda can cracking open, fairground music in the distance, a Corvette engine coming to life, a thousand hands applauding all at once. It was one of those truly beautiful sounds.

"You should try it," she said. "Do the things you've never done to get the thing you've never had. Or whatever."

"Whoa," said Frank. "Where'd you hear that? *Oprah?*"

"My mom has a magnet with it written on it."

"You should say you came up with it." Frank took another gulp of seltzer.

"But I didn't," said Eleanor. "So I wouldn't."

"You are so not cut out for advertising," said Frank. "It's a good thing, trust me."

Her hand was resting on the barstool between them, just beneath the view of anyone passing by. He patted it, then let his fingers linger on top of hers. The smooth planes of their palms rested one over the other like two tectonic plates shifting, finally, into position beneath the earth's surface. Eleanor looked at him with her funny, intent gaze. He felt it all the way through him.

"I cannot lie, Frank," she said quietly. "Even . . . even if I wanted to."

"I'm not asking you to," he said.

"Then what are you asking?"

If he could, he'd ask her if she remembered how the first time they met a current had passed from his hand to hers, an electric shock. It was a detail seemingly inconsequential, but which had come to signify everything to him. He would ask her if his emails were the highlight of her day, like hers were of his. He'd ask if her father was dying and if that was why she was always a little sad, even when she said she wasn't. He'd ask her what it was like to have a father. He'd ask her if she believed you could be in love with two people at once. If she knew what it felt like to love someone you shouldn't. If she knew what it felt like not to love yourself like you should.

"Nothing," said Frank. "Just, um, that you step up on the real estate account, since I'm going to be focusing my time on Kapow! now."

Crestfallen. That was the word for a face like hers. She pulled her hand out from under his.

"You got it, boss," she said. She swallowed the remainder of her drink, slammed the glass on the bar between them, and belched loudly. "Look at that, I'm done."

She shrugged on her homely puffer jacket and turned away. He watched her push through the crowd to the exit. Her curly hair was stuck in her hood. He watched her leave. The bartender came over to scoop up their empty glasses.

"You want another?" he asked.

"Sure," Frank said. Then, in spite of himself, in spite of everything, he added, "This time with vodka."

———

He must have left the bathroom door open when he got back. It was past midnight, and Cleo was already asleep. He'd stumbled home and taken a shower, trying to get the smell off him. He could hide it. If Cleo didn't smell it, he could hide it. He'd woken up a few hours later needing to pee. He was still in the shallow end of sleep, bleary from the hangover, when he'd glanced down to see the sugar glider bobbing in the toilet bowl beneath him. Her body was pitching in the stream of his piss. She was face down, unfurled in the shape of a star. She looked like a fallen star.

He'd flushed her down. What else could he do? He'd flushed her body away before Cleo could wake up and see what he'd done. She spiraled, resisted, and disappeared. Afterward, he'd vomited for the first time in years, that familiar bent-kneed position bringing him back to the summers of his youth. *Oh, Jesus.* He looked into the foul, frothing water beneath him. He flushed. It would not go down. He flushed again. It didn't work. The sullied water kept rising.

CHAPTER TEN

February

Anders was grudgingly attending the benefit auction at Cubed, a dumpling house turned independent gallery in Chinatown better known for its riotous after-hours parties than for any of the art it displayed. The space was packed with artist types, all dressed to express maximum individualism, yet all looking the same to Anders. You could recognize an art student anywhere in the world, he thought. The quest for individuality had resulted in the opposite: complete predictability. He peered over the bobbing crowd of beanies and bleached heads for someone he knew, spotted two women he'd slept with talking to one another by the far wall, and veered in the opposite direction toward the bar. New York, which had once fit him like a perfectly tailored suit, was feeling snugger every year.

On his way to the bar he bumped into Elijah, the creator of a cult-followed website that acidly reviewed the reviews of art shows, and whom Anders's magazine was currently courting as a staff writer. Elijah was busy looking unimpressed at a sculpture comprised of sex toys on a conveyor belt as Anders approached.

"Have you ever noticed how closely a butt plug resembles a Native American arrowhead?" he asked.

"Good to see you too," said Anders.

"I'm trying to find something to bid on," he said. "Though I appear to be the only one."

They made their way around the periphery of the gallery, Elijah declaring his opinions, mostly negative, in a loud falsetto. Anders absently scanned the photographs and paintings, keeping one eye out for the pair of women he'd spotted earlier. It never ended well for him when women united. If he was honest with himself, he was growing tired of the parade of beautiful creatures careening through his bedroom. Or rather, he was tired of himself. He had disappointed all of them. Not because he had broken any promises, but because he had refused to make any. He had offered them moments when they wanted months, years, marriages.

"You look lost in thought," said Elijah. "Considering making a bid?"

Anders looked around. Most of the work here was impenetrable to him. It all looked like it had been made by computers. He bee-lined toward an oil painting of a nude woman. This one, at least, wasn't bad. He liked that you could feel the painter's presence on the canvas, the brushstrokes equal parts expressive and restrained. He leaned in closer to read the artist's name. It was Cleo's.

"What do you think of this one?" Anders asked.

Elijah pushed his glasses up his nose and frowned.

"Timid," he declared. "Girlishly sentimental. I hate when you can look at a painting and just *know* it was done by a woman. Art should be unconstrained by the tropes of gender. Shame, really, because technically she's pretty good."

Shame for you maybe, thought Anders. You just talked your way out of a job.

"Well. Let's get a drink," he said.

"Oh, I don't drink alcohol." Elijah pressed his fingertips protectively to his chest. "I went to rehab for Adderall two years ago. Didn't you read the bio on my site?"

Anders smiled without opening his mouth.

"Sparkling water then," he said.

He spent the rest of the evening braced to run into Cleo. He scanned for her blond head among the crowd, felt the stomach twist of excitement when he thought he saw it, then the drop of disappointment when it was not her. After more plastic flutes of champagne than he could count, he bid on her painting. He offered twelve hundred, not much more than the last bidder, but enough to get the price up so she would sell at a respectable rate. He was surprised to receive an email the following day informing him that he'd won it. That afternoon at work, he got the call from her. Anders smiled at himself in the mirror above his desk as he pressed answer.

"Twelve thousand dollars," she said. "What on earth is twelve thousand dollars supposed to mean?"

Anders was sure his reflection had physically paled.

"Is this Cleo?" he stammered.

"Is this your way of apologizing for what you did?"

His brain whirred to digest this new information. Twelve hundred. Twelve thousand. The placement of a decimal. Eight, ten, twelve glasses of champagne . . .

"I'm glad you're sorry," she continued. "You should be. But it's been a year, and this—it's pretty extreme."

"How did . . . I thought the bidding was anonymous?"

"I couldn't believe it when they told me." Cleo laughed, ignoring him. "I even heard someone was contemplating outbidding you. Can you imagine? It's like 'The Emperor's New Clothes.' All you need is one person to believe, and it's true."

"Well, I certainly believe in you."

Anders was already recalibrating last night's events to suit this new narrative. Perhaps he *had* meant to bid such a large sum. It wasn't ideal, of course, but he could afford it, and it struck him now as charmingly spontaneous.

"Thank you, Anders. Really."

He heard her sigh with satisfaction down the phone.

"What are you going to do with the money?" asked Anders. "Buy yourself something pretty?"

"It was a benefit auction, Anders. *I* don't get the money. But it still looks good I sold for that much."

"Who gets it then?"

"I think it goes to the Avian Society of Central Park."

"What is that?"

"Bird conservationists."

"You're fucking kidding me. I gave twelve thousand dollars to a bunch of bird-watchers?"

"Apparently there are a couple of hawks that need protecting."

"Tell me you're joking."

"I never joke about money," said Cleo in a voice that neither confirmed nor denied whether this was true. "So, where are you going to put it?"

"Put what?"

"My painting, Anders."

"Oh. Isn't a wall the usual place?"

"Don't be clever. In your apartment?"

Anders hadn't thought about it. He'd never expected to end up actually owning the thing.

"Why don't you come over and see? You can help me pick a spot."

"We both know I've already seen your apartment."

This surprised him. Neither of them had ever openly acknowledged any detail of the night they'd spent together. It had happened shortly after she and Frank met, before any of them knew it would be serious. In fact, he realized, this was the first time they'd spoken without Frank present since.

"Never in daylight," he said.

"And whose fault is that?"

"No one's fault. Just a fact."

But it had been cold of him, he knew, sending her home in the middle of the night like that. It was guilt. Letting her sleep next to him, touching her in the sober light of morning, would have felt like a second betrayal of Frank.

"You humiliated me," she said quietly.

"Look," he said. "I crumbled my teeth over it, I did."

"What?"

"It's what we say in Denmark when we regret something we've said."

He could hear her smile in the silence. "How many teeth did you crumble?"

"All of them. Anyway, it's different now."

"What is?"

"My apartment. You should come see it."

"How?"

"It's got new . . . doorknobs."

Cleo laughed. It was as good as done.

It helped that Frank was gone for the next few weeks shooting a series of commercials in South Africa for a new energy drink that claimed to have hangover-curing properties. Millions of dollars of bullshit, he'd said, laughing, to Anders over beers before he left. Anders had been under the impression that Cleo was going with him, but clearly she'd stayed behind. He had never considered before what she did while Frank was on these trips. Paint, he presumed, though when he asked her about her work a few hours later, she waved the question off with a brusqueness verging on irritation.

Cleo was standing in his apartment, looking at the large white walls of his living room. Below them the evening traffic provided its usual complaint of car horns and sirens.

"How can you live with nothing on your walls?" Cleo asked.

Anders shrugged. He spent all day being ambushed by images at the magazine; it was a relief to come home to sparsity.

"Can I get you something?" he asked. "A drink, maybe, or . . ."

He strode toward her and picked her up. She wrapped her legs around his waist and let him snake his tongue inside her mouth. They toppled onto the sofa, but Cleo shook her head and pulled him down onto the floor. Of course. Last time they had been on the sofa. She was encased in layers. He pulled off a sweater, a turtleneck, a T-shirt, then unbuttoned her jeans to reveal a pair of tights beneath. He laughed as he tugged the stockings off her feet.

"You're like opening a Russian doll."

She offered him her slow, catlike smile.

"Worth the effort," she said.

She was spread naked on the carpet before him, her clothes scattered in a halo around her head. He ripped off his own shirt and pushed his trousers and underwear to his knees. He didn't even wait to kick them off before he spread her legs and was thrusting inside her, dipping hard and fast. He was in another world, no thoughts but the sensation of her wrapped tight around him. God, she felt good, even better than he remembered.

Cleo brought her hands to his chest and pushed him away. She stared up at him seriously.

"Anders," she said. "This isn't sex."

He looked down at her, panting.

"What do you mean?"

"I mean what you're doing—this jabbing thing—it's not sex. It's you masturbating with my body instead of your hand."

"I—uh. God, Cleo . . . Well, what would you like me to do?"

Cleo put her hands on his lower back and pulled him deeper inside her.

"Do you feel that?" she said. "That ridge at the top in the back? That's what you're trying to hit. Well, not hit, exactly, just stroke with the tip of . . . Yes, yes, like that, but *slower*. Roll up against it. Good . . . Good . . . Nice and slow. Mm-hmm, keep rolling and stroking, stroking and rolling. Yes, yes, that's it . . ."

He wasn't used to being told what to do. It irked him. He thought about pulling out, but it was Cleo, after all. The one he wanted most. The one he wanted to please most. She slid two long fingers into his mouth, swirling them around his tongue. They tasted ashy from her cigarettes, but he didn't care. Her eyes were looking up into his with that funny, furious intensity she had. They were an unusual dappled green, incredibly light. How had he never noticed before? She pulled her hand away and pushed it into the space between his stomach and hers. He could feel the curve of her knuckle moving against him as she touched herself. Her eyelids were fluttering open and closed like wings beating. She slipped her hand down to where he entered her, squeezing him between her fingers as he rolled in and out, in and out. He lasted another ten seconds, allowed himself a few quick pumps to finish off, then released inside her.

She laughed as he collapsed the weight of his body onto her with a groan.

"All right," she said, giving his back a pat. "We'll work on it."

He was getting too old to have sex on the floor like this. His lower back gave a twinge of complaint as he hauled himself off her and hastily tucked his shriveling penis back into his underwear. Cleo's pale body lay still on the rug next to him like a vase of lilies tipped over. She was staring up at the ceiling with a blank, inscrutable expression. What was she thinking? Did she regret it? She seemed suddenly to have receded from him. Her body was there, but he could feel her presence withdraw. It felt like stepping from the sunlight into shadows.

"Got a cigarette?" he asked, straining to sound casual.

She wordlessly rolled onto her stomach to reach for her bag and remove her pack, placing one in her mouth and lighting it with a grace born of practice. Exhaling, she passed it to him.

"You're not in South Africa," he said.

She shook her head.

"Did you have to work or something?"

Another head shake.

"Why then?"

She sat up and took the cigarette out of his mouth, bringing it back to her own. He could see a damp patch on the rug from where his semen had leaked out of her.

"You don't speak anymore?" he asked.

Cleo rested her light eyes on him. The softness he had witnessed in her just moments before was gone, replaced by a severity that unsettled him. Her voice, when she did speak, was low.

"What do you want me to say?"

"Why didn't you go to South Africa?"

She looked around for somewhere to ash the cigarette, then tapped the embers into her palm.

"Jesus. Here—"

He leaped up and grabbed a cup from the kitchen counter. That was the problem with Cleo, he thought, she never asked for help with anything. Kneeling back down in front of her, he took her hand in his and gently wiped the gray ash from her palm into the cup.

"I didn't want to go anymore," she said quietly.

"You two have a fight or something?"

Her pale shoulders were hunched close to her ears. "It doesn't matter."

"I'm sure it matters to Frank."

"Frank's a drunk," she said quietly.

Anders thought about this for a moment. Frank did drink a lot, he had to admit, though so did he. Of course, Anders being Scandinavian, it was just a cultural thing. And it wasn't like Frank was some homeless guy drinking himself to death under a bridge. If he was a drunk, he was a high-functioning one at least.

"Is that why you're here, then?" he said. "To get back at him for drinking?"

She shook her head again and looked down at her hand, which he was still holding in his.

"So what?" he asked. "You just wanted the company?"

She grabbed his fingers with surprising firmness.

"I wanted you," she said.

What astonished him most was how easy it was to be with her, how little guilt he felt. He had thought of her often since that drunken night they spent together, of course, but he had known to push any feelings toward her down to a deep, untouched part of himself. The day Frank told him they were getting married, he had felt a strange kind of betrayal—by Frank or Cleo, he couldn't tell—and had vowed to keep his distance from her. And he had managed for almost a year. Until now.

Every evening after work he raced home to see her, anxious to fold her back into his arms. They barely left his apartment. They ordered platters of sashimi and ate them with their fingers. They smoked weed out of an apple and had slow, trancelike sex. They watched movies, enfolded in each other. They ignored the snow softly falling through the window. They took baths. They drank tea. They squeezed each other's feet. They played each other music. They built a snowman on the balcony. They made soup from scratch. They snorted coke and stayed up talking until the morning chased them back to bed. They slept next to each other, sometimes fitfully, sometimes peacefully, every night for two weeks.

On the day Frank was to return, Anders woke with the light. Cleo was beside him, a bar of sunlight striping her face. Her expression, even in sleep, was worried. He pulled his arm out slowly from under her back and rolled out of bed. He thought about showering, but he wanted to smell Cleo on him all day. He dressed quickly in his usual dark jeans and turtleneck, then went to the kitchen. Tea and porridge, that was what Cleo liked in the mornings. Whistling between his teeth, he plugged in the kettle and pulled milk from the fridge. A plume of steam funneled into the room. He stirred the oats, added a swirl of granular brown sugar. Frank would be landing in a few hours.

The postcard Frank had sent him was propped on the kitchen counter. On the front was a picture of a man being mauled by a lion. The caption underneath it read "Send more tourists to South Africa!" Anders had received it with a jolt of fear—was Frank the lion?—when he remembered a long-standing joke between the two of them to each send the other the worst postcard they could find from every country they visited. On the back, scrawled in Frank's nearly illegible hand, were four words: "Thought of you, brother."

Anders checked his watch; he didn't have much time. Today was his day with Jonah, his ex-girlfriend Christine's son. Jonah wasn't biologically his child, but Anders had lived with him from the ages of four to ten and loved him in a fierce and uncomfortable way that he imagined was close to paternal. He looked forward to seeing him, though he didn't make time for it as often as he should. On this occasion, he was happy for the distraction. It would be good to take his mind off Frank's plane making its slow descent back into New York.

Cleo was spread like a star on the bed when he returned with breakfast. She'd thrown the covers from her, leaving her pale chest exposed. He liked her this way in the mornings, unadorned. Her silvery eyelashes gave her face an open, unguarded look. He sat down on the edge of the bed and very gently leaned over to kiss her nipple. She gave him one of her drowsy smiles, like a sunbeam struggling through an overcast sky.

"How did you sleep?" he asked.

"Pipes were clanging."

"It's an old building," he said. "I made breakfast."

Cleo sat up and gave him a serious look. "What do you think of Eleanor?"

"Who?"

"The copywriter at Frank's firm."

"She's nice, I guess? Why on earth would you ask?"

"I think Frank's in love with her."

Anders put the porridge and tea mug down on the bedside table with a plunk.

"Why are you bringing this up now?"

"You think he is too?"

"I think you're being ridiculous. Eleanor? She's . . . she's not Frank's type."

"I saw their emails."

"Just now?"

"No. A little while ago."

"So?"

"They send each other these jokes. Things they find funny."

"And?"

"It's the kind of thing people in love do."

"Or bored coworkers. You've never had an office job, Cleo. That kind of stuff is normal."

"It doesn't feel normal."

"Is that what all this was about then? You think Frank's having an affair, so you wanted to have one too?"

"I don't think they're having an affair exactly. I think he's . . . they feel for each other."

"You're crazy."

"*Don't* call me crazy."

Cleo sat up farther against the headboard and yanked the sheets around herself. Her face was pinched and white.

"Look—" He wrestled her hands away from where they were knotted at her chest and took them in his. "I know this is difficult, what with Frank coming back and us not knowing . . . Well, how to proceed. But we've had such a happy time together. Let's not fight now, please."

"I'm going to say something to him," she said.

He dropped her hands. "What do you mean?"

"I can't—" She stopped, trying to find the right words. "Something has to change."

Anders felt a pull in his stomach, as though a plug had just been yanked out.

"Cleo, please, whatever you do, do not say anything about us to him. Not yet. I need . . . I need more time."

"I won't bring you into it."

"Then what do you want to say?"

"I don't know! That I'm not happy. That I'm moving out. I have to do something. Can you just promise me one thing?"

She reached to pick up his hands from where they had fallen in his lap. Anders could feel himself physically inclining away from her as she grasped for him. He had to resist the impulse to leap up off the bed and out the fire escape.

"What?"

"Promise me you'll be there. You don't have to come out and tell everyone we're together. Just promise you'll be there for me."

"Look, I have to go," he said. "It's my day with Jonah, I told you. There's porridge for you there. Just please don't do anything rash, Cleo. Please."

He kissed her hastily on the cheek and pointed to the porridge, as if eating that would solve everything.

"Stay," she said, but he was already heading out the door.

He hailed a cab and headed west. He was running late. As they turned onto the West Side Highway, Anders relaxed his head against the back of the seat. Runners bundled against the cold jogged along the water, beyond which the unglamorous skyline of New Jersey stood. Eleanor was from New Jersey, he remembered Frank saying. Anders did not give much credence to Cleo's theory concerning their feelings for each other. Cleo was sensitive, imaginative, slightly paranoid; she read too much into everything. Frank would have told Anders if he had fallen in love with someone else. Anyway, what would possess him to pursue a woman like Eleanor when he had Cleo?

Anders's own feelings for Cleo were a riot of contradictions. His initial reaction to the prospect of her telling Frank about them had been terror, almost repulsion. Now, in the quiet of the taxi, the thought of Cleo being his all the time, out in the open, not just for a few stolen moments, kindled a warm blush of pleasure within him. But at what cost would that pleasure come? He'd known Frank for over two decades, Cleo only a year. But being with Cleo made him feel reckless, as though he could burn his life to the ground and rebuild it anew.

He arrived at Christine's and rang the buzzer for her apartment. He'd loved the place when he lived there, its curved walls and dusty skylights, but he'd been relieved to move back downtown when they split. He found the Upper West Side oppressive, with its unavoidable strollers and school talk. He'd always felt, perhaps delusionally, that he was too young to live there.

He stepped into the elevator and waited for it to be called up to her floor. Christine was an accountant for an architecture firm and made a good living without help from a partner, a fact she was extremely proud of. The doors opened to reveal her angular, familiar face. She pulled him in for a hug.

"Oh, Anders," she said, rubbing her face into his neck. "You haven't started smoking again."

"Only socially," he said.

"You smell like a teenager."

"You smell the same," he said.

He recognized the familiar scent, woody and a little spicy, of the cologne she used to steal from him.

"Jonah's in his room getting ready," she said. "Cities have been erected in less time."

He followed her to the kitchen.

"There's a chance I'll have to run a little early."

Frank would be landing now, he calculated. Then an hour, maybe two, to get through customs and back into the city. Would she say something the moment he walked through the door? He trusted that she would not betray him to Frank. But what would she say? Would she leave him? What if Frank suspected him anyway?

"That's fine," Christine said. "Have fun with Jonah, but not too much fun. He's on my shit list at the moment. Espresso?"

Anders nodded and checked his phone. Nothing from Cleo.

"What did he do?" he asked.

"He called me a bitch because I won't give him a credit card like all his other friends supposedly have. A credit card! He's *thirteen*, for God's sake. He should feel like a millionaire if he has fifty bucks."

She walked to the hallway and called Jonah's name. His name in her mouth was two long syllables, like an air raid siren.

"Woman, I'm coming!" he heard Jonah yell.

Christine rolled her eyes.

"Grows ten pubes and thinks he can call me 'woman,'" she said. "Sometimes I worry I raised a real brat."

"We raised," he said. "And all kids are brats at that age."

She smiled, then frowned. "I wasn't."

She turned toward the espresso machine and handed him the tiny, steaming cup.

"So, are you seeing anyone at the moment?" she asked. "Any more Russian supermodels?"

"Sasha was Ukrainian," he said. "And no."

"Well, well." Christine raised her eyebrows at him. "What have you been doing with all your spare time?"

Cleo, he thought.

"Working," he said.

Things had been going well at the magazine, despite his inattention. They were opening an LA office and, in fact, had asked him a few days prior to be head of the West Coast team. He hadn't mentioned it to anyone yet and now realized, with a surge of pleasure, that he could tell Christine.

"Actually," he said. "I've been offered editor in chief at the new LA office."

"Oh, Anders, how wonderful." She leaned over and kissed him on the cheek. "So, when will you be moving?"

"It's flattering, but I'm not going to take it," he said. "What with Jonah, you know, I should be here near him. And it's a lot farther for my parents if they ever want to come visit."

He had no intention of leaving New York. Not when his life had suddenly become so full of Cleo. Perhaps it would be better if Frank *did* know sooner rather than later. He would forgive him eventually. Especially if he was, as Cleo suspected and Anders couldn't quite believe, in love with Eleanor. Anders could be happy with Cleo. They could live together, get their own place. Uptown maybe, near the park. Jonah would like her, he was sure.

"Anders." Christine furrowed her brow at him. "Your parents have never once come to the States in all the years I've known you. And as for Jonah, you hardly see him every month as it is. He can go and see you out there. I'm sure he'd love that."

"I see him more than that, surely?" Anders ventured.

"Anyway, it's not Jonah you have to worry about. Frank's the one who really can't live without you." Christine took a sip of coffee and grimaced. "He's like the poster child for codependence."

"That's not true. And he's got Cleo now."

Just the sound of her name in his mouth gave him a feeling of warmth.

"I don't see those two lasting."

"You don't? Why's that?"

Because he had fucked her twice last night?

"Frank still acts like a child," Christine said. "And, from what I've heard, she virtually *is* a child."

"She's hardly—" He was mildly panicked by this description of her, not least considering that he was two years older than Frank.

"Ah!" Christine threw her hands in the air, looking past him. "And here is my child!"

"I'm not a child, Mom," Jonah growled.

Anders leaped up to hug Jonah, who submitted to, but did not reciprocate, his embrace. Jonah was in the awkward part of a growth spurt, his limbs somehow a little too long for his body. His shaggy brown hair partially covered the dusting of acne that was creeping from his cheeks to his temples. Despite all this, Anders thought, he looked pretty good. He was wearing a Chelsea jersey and a pair of slim selvedge jeans Anders would have worn himself.

"My god," Anders said. "You're almost as tall as me now."

"Yeah, maybe," said Jonah, staring at his sneakers. "But you're still mad tall."

"I thought we'd go to the Natural History Museum." Anders rested his hands lightly on Jonah's shoulders. "There's a butterfly exhibit."

The suggestion sounded deeply lame, even to him. Jonah gave him a look that could only be described as withering. When had he learned to look at someone like that?

"All right, fuck that." Anders grinned. "You want to go get steaks or something?"

"Language!" said Christine.

"Sure, whatever," said Jonah, shrugging on his parka.

The steakhouse they went to was dark and empty, unpenetrated by the sunshine or air of weekend merriment that permeated the streets outside. In keeping with the main item on the menu, the interior of the restaurant was blood red; carmine-drenched walls, congealments of dark maroon chairs, thick crimson napkins pleated on mahogany tables. It was like being inside an artery.

Anders ordered them porterhouse steaks with sides of baked potatoes and creamed spinach, plus a Peroni and a Coke. Real man's food, he observed dryly to himself, thinking of his weekly vegetarian brunches with Frank at Sant Ambroeus; their orders of organic eggs and many rounds of Bloody Marys to ameliorate the effects of the night before. He realized, with a start, that those brunches would be over for good.

"So, how's high school?" he asked.

"I'm young for my year," said Jonah, slurping his Coke in one gulp. "Everyone else is fourteen."

"But how is it?" said Anders. "Are you making friends?"

"It's all right," said Jonah. "What's it called when you have, like, letters standing for words?"

"Acronym," Anders said, relieved to have remembered.

"Yeah, that. You know what they say Dwight is an acronym for? Dumb White Idiots Getting High Together."

"And your mother's paying how much money to send you there?"

"A shit-ton." Jonah shrugged. "They've got a good soccer team."

Anders surreptitiously checked his phone. Nothing. He took a long pull of his beer in the silence that descended.

"So . . . high school is good," he attempted again. "Very different from middle school?"

"It's pretty druggy there," said Jonah, playing with his napkin. "A junior got caught doing coke in the library last week. You ever tried it?"

Tried it? He loved it. But he wasn't about to tell Jonah that. The memory of snorting powdery lines off Cleo's smooth breasts came to him like an electric jolt. He took another gulp of beer.

"No, buddy," he said. "That stuff rots your brains." Then, fearing that he was giving the kind of rote answer he would have ignored as a teenager himself, he added, "Stick with beer and weed. It's a safer bet."

"Good to know." Jonah smirked. "Hey, cool bracelet."

He reached across the table and touched Anders's wrist. It was the first time he had willingly made contact with him that day.

"You like it?" Anders said. "You can have it."

He unwound it and watched as Jonah haltingly wrapped it around his own slim wrist. It was made of blue maritime rope held by a silver fishing hook. Jonah looked at it, then back at Anders.

"Nah," he said. "It's mad gay."

Anders regarded the bracelet as Jonah removed it again. Eighty-five dollars at Barney's for something his father could have made from his tackle box. He slipped it into the pocket of his jeans.

"I can't believe you kids are still calling things gay," he said.

"It just means not dope, you know, lame. It's not about sexuality or anything."

"What do you know about sexuality?" exclaimed Anders. "You only have ten pubes!"

"Well," said Jonah, shooting up in his chair. "I already have a girlfriend. So fuck you."

Anders was thrilled to be given this confidence, however aggressively. Jonah had never talked to him about girls before.

"That's fantastic! Who is she?"

"She's only kinda my girlfriend, I don't know," said Jonah. He scrunched the napkin into his palm. "This girl Raquel."

"Raquel," repeated Anders. "Fantastic. What's she like?"

"She's in my grade," he said. "She's cool. She's not the hottest girl in the year, that's this girl Natalia, but she's like top four. And"—he smiled to himself at the memory—"she let me stick a finger in her."

"Whoa," said Anders, genuinely taken aback.

Jonah leaned back in his chair and picked up his steak knife, twirling the point against the tip of his finger. Likely the same finger, Anders observed, that had recently been inside a Dwight freshman named Raquel.

"I tried to get her to give me a BJ," Jonah said. "But she was all whiney about it, so I gave up."

This tone was entirely new to him. His Jonah was sensitive, kind. He'd cried at half the movies Anders had taken him to. Anders remembered something Cleo had told him about empathy, how it should be exercised like a muscle, particularly in boys, starting from a young age. She said it was the most important skill a person could have, the ability to feel as another feels.

"And, um, how do you think that made her feel?" he ventured.

"What do you mean?"

The waiter arrived to unload the porterhouses onto the table. Blood ran across the plates. Anders sliced open his baked potato and looked tentatively at Jonah through the cloud of escaping steam.

"When you, um, touched her," he said as the waiter retreated.

Jonah took a bite of his steak.

"Oh, I know how it made her feel," he said. "Wet!"

Anders's phone buzzed. He slid it from his pocket and felt everything inside him contract. Frank was calling him. She'd told him. He mumbled something to Jonah about a work call and stumbled from the table. He stepped out of the restaurant into sunlight, the phone still buzzing in his hand. It was an unusually warm day for February; even without his jacket, he was sweating. A group of girls walked past, singing along to a pop song playing tinnily from their phone. His thumb hovered over the answer button. He could not move. He willed his thumb to press down, but he was paralyzed. He stared at the name. Frank. Frank. Frank. Then the screen darkened. He'd missed it. The girls crossed the street, their music fading with them. He exhaled, patting his pocket for the cigarettes he already knew he'd left with Cleo. His phone vibrated again and declared a voicemail. He lifted it to his ear, his heart racing.

"My brother!" Frank's voice said. "I'm back. Best seafood I've ever had. Octopus legs as big as my arm. You would have loved it. Anyway, I'm about to get food with Cley. She wants to eat during the Arsenal game, of course. Come meet us! Or if you want a drink later . . ."

He heard a murmur in the background, a low female voice. Cleo.

"Anyway, call me back," Frank said. "I've missed your handsome Danish face."

Anders returned to the table. He felt relief and disappointment wash over him in waves, one sensation gaining force as the other retreated. She had not left him. She would not. He had been spared one sadness, only to be given another. He sat down, looked at his bloody steak without appetite, then stood back up.

"I'm just going to run to the restroom," he said in answer to Jonah's puzzled look. "Don't eat my steak while I'm gone." He attempted a smile.

He locked himself into a stall and unbuttoned his jeans, leaning one hand against the wall and positioning himself over the toilet bowl. He closed his eyes and saw Cleo. She was kneeling in front of him, naked, and smiling up at him. He rubbed his shaft and imagined reaching down to smooth the part of her golden hair. He stroked her breasts, pinched her nipples. Then he squeezed hard. He shoved his cock in her mouth, feeling her gag on it. He was gripping the back of her head, cramming himself deeper down her throat. Tears were sliding down her cheeks; he pulled out and slapped one side of her face, then the other. He was fucking her from behind now, hands spreading her cheeks apart. He was ramming into her puckered pink asshole. He was spanking her, spitting on her, pulling her long hair. He was flipping her over, yanking her legs apart. He was sinking back into her pussy now, smashing into her wet cunt. He was jamming his fingers down her tight red throat. He was pushing his thumbs into her eyes. Then he was punching her face, her beautiful, irreverent, heartbreaking face, pound pound pound, until his fist smashed through, into the hollow beneath like a china doll, and there was nothing but a black jagged hole where her mouth and nose had been. And then he was fucking the hole, fucking it, fucking it, fucking it, fucking the space where her face had been until, with one long ropy spurt, he fell into it and disappeared completely.

———

Somehow he made it through the remainder of lunch with only the slight mishap of distractedly agreeing to get Jonah a credit card. Christine would be irate, but he would deal with that later. They walked back from the restaurant up Columbus Avenue, stopping to wander around the flea market on Seventy-Seventh. Jonah was traipsing behind him on his phone, blind to the hodgepodge of junk on display. Anders felt the urge to throw his own phone in the trash. He drifted over to another table and leafed dispassionately through a stack of *i-D* magazines from the 1980s until, with a start, he found himself staring back.

The picture was in an alleyway in SoHo, black and white and deliberately grainy, so it appeared even older than it was. He had no memory of it being taken, but that was hardly surprising. He flipped back to the front cover: 1982. He'd been twenty years old. He was wearing an oversize pair of slacks and a suit jacket with no shirt, slouched against the brick wall, hands in pockets, in the timeless pose of youthful insouciance. He was impossibly slender; hollow cheekbones, hollow chest, pale hair flopped over one eye, the other staring straight into the camera, into him.

"Hey Jonah, come look at this!"

He held the magazine open so he could see.

"That you?"

"It appears so."

"There's a kid in the grade above me who's a model," said Jonah, slumping his shoulders. "Everyone likes him. Was it, like, fun?"

"Modeling? Sometimes. Mostly it was tedious."

And terrifying, which he'd never admitted to anyone. He rarely talked about those early years when he'd first moved to New York. How he'd been passed around by casting agents, managers, and stylists, all older than him, all clued into this world of suggestion and innuendo he could not decipher. There was one photoshoot where he'd been convinced to strip naked but for a smear of lipstick. He remembered keenly now the baffling humiliation of trying to appear unfazed in front of the photographer. He still didn't know what those pictures were for.

Jonah leaned to peer closer at the image in his hands.

"No, it's not you . . . Look, it says the model's name here. Jack."

"What?" Anders lifted the page closer to his face and scanned the text. Jonah was right. The model was credited under another name.

"Weird." Jonah shrugged. "Looks a lot like you."

Jonah wandered away toward another antique stall, leaving Anders staring at his nonself in embarrassment. On closer inspection, this model was thinner than he'd ever been, with a more symmetrical, American-looking face. Anders snapped the magazine shut and put it back on the pile. What was it his agent used to say? Everyone was replaceable.

"Hey Anders," Jonah called from a nearby stall. He was tossing a brown leather soccer ball from hand to hand. It was as old as Anders, the kind his father might have practiced with. "Want to kick this around? I have tryouts in a week."

A hundred bucks for a soccer ball ("It's hand-stitched," the vendor kept insisting), but it didn't matter. Jonah let Anders keep his arm around his shoulder for the length of two whole avenues as they walked to the park. He'd never been great at being an authority figure for Jonah, something Christine had often berated him for when they were together. But it was different for him. He'd known Jonah since he was four, two-thirds of his life but not his whole life. He wasn't guaranteed love.

They stood opposite each other on the Great Lawn, tapping the ball back and forth. Anders's mind settled in with the rhythm of the ball; his thoughts began to slow and order themselves. She wasn't going to leave Frank. She needed him too much. And even if she did, she and Anders couldn't be together. It was too messy, a relationship born of the destruction of a marriage and a friendship. And yet here he was convincing himself it was a good idea, like some romantic idiot. Enough.

"You've still got a pretty good leg for an old guy," called Jonah.

"Thanks," Anders called back. "But I'm not old."

"You're like fifty," Jonah said, moving closer.

"I'm forty-fucking-five," Anders said.

Jonah laughed. "Language!"

"Don't tell your mother."

"But you don't have kids," Jonah said suddenly.

"I have you."

"Yeah, I know, but real kids that live with you and shit."

"Language," Anders said, less convincingly.

"Look—" Jonah held the ball still with his foot. "I just think my mom worries about you. I heard her on the phone to Aunt Vicky, talking about you."

"Is Auntie Vicky the one with the kid in Model UN?"

"Ned? That kid's an ass."

"Total ass," said Anders and felt Jonah's smile warm him from the inside. "No one needs to worry about me. Now, show me your kick-ups."

Anders watched Jonah bounce the ball from his toe to his knee and back again. He counted along with him, *nine, ten, eleven, twelve* . . . He was forty-five. He didn't have real kids that lived with him and shit. He wasn't married, never had been. His longest relationship had been the six years with Christine. But he was still healthy, still had his looks. If he had a baby next year, he'd only be sixty-six when the kid was twenty. That wasn't so old. People ran marathons at sixty-six. He just needed to meet someone. Someone without all the baggage. Jonah lost control of the ball, and Anders ran to retrieve it.

"Hey Jonah," he said, tossing the ball back to him. "I'm thinking of moving to LA. How would you feel about that?"

"Like to the beach?"

"Maybe," he said. "Yes, actually. I could look around Venice Beach."

"Where the Z-Boys are from?" said Jonah.

"Exactly," said Anders. "And you would come visit, of course. We could go surfing. And I'll buy a car, a convertible, so we can drive out to the desert."

"Sweet," said Jonah. "Chelsea's playing at LA Galaxy soon."

"I'll get us tickets," said Anders and squeezed his shoulder. "You'd really be okay with that?"

Jonah looked at the ground and shrugged.

"I don't care."

He lunged for the ball and began bouncing it on his head. Anders intercepted it and called for him to go long. Jonah raced away across the lawn, the West Side silhouetted behind him. The sun was still setting early, but there was a good hour of light left. Anders took a few steps back, ran forward, and let the ball go. It was a perfect pass.

CHAPTER ELEVEN

Early March

F rank had left a note on the kitchen counter for Cleo to find, but it wasn't written by him. It was from their next-door neighbor. He was complaining about their "late-night soap opera histrionics," as he put it. The neighbor was a theater critic with impeccable hair, so he could say a thing like that. Cleo read the note once more, folded it neatly into a square, then set fire to it over the kitchen sink. It was noon.

Frank had left early that morning for a shoot that wouldn't wrap until long after sundown. She had not heard him leave; he had taken to sleeping on the sofa, ostensibly to avoid disturbing Cleo when he came home late, but mostly so he could return drunk with impunity. It went without saying that this arrangement meant they were no longer having sex. Cleo had spent the morning lying in bed, watching the sunlight creep accusatorily across the ceiling, until thirst drove her to the kitchen, where she'd found the note waiting. Frank had not messaged her or appended any note of his own to the neighbor's. He'd left it for her to discover alone.

She placed the matches back in the cutlery drawer. There were the hand-painted chopsticks she had made for him when they first met over a year ago. She was always making things back then, carrying them to Frank like a cat proudly dropping a sparrow at his feet. Not anymore.

The note was a new kind of humiliation. Someone had witnessed them. Worse, someone had confirmed what she already feared: they were not normal. It was not normal to fight like they did. Not normal for Frank to return drunk so many nights in a row. Not normal for her to react with such savagery when he did. In the past month, she had shattered a vase and an ashtray, she had hit his face and chest and arms, and last night she had hurled the blue orchid he'd bought her as a wedding present at him, snapping the stem in half.

"No one else is like this," she'd said the night before. They were sitting on the living room floor, the orchid's black soil scattered around them. "Are they?"

She looked at him.

"I don't know, Cley," he said.

"Well, what do you think?"

"I'm sure there are couples that are worse." He shrugged. "And better."

"You thought we would be better?"

He shrugged again. "I didn't expect it to be so hard."

"Being married?"

"Living together, everything. I didn't think you'd be so . . . so affected by me."

"What am I meant to be affected by, if not you?"

"I know, I know. It's just, I work hard. Life is hard. I don't want to come home and have . . . The fighting, you know. I don't like it. And you being upset with me all the time."

"But why is the onus on me not to be upset? Why can't you come home earlier? Or not spend every other night out? Why can't you . . . I don't know, be better?"

Frank cupped his forehead with his palms and looked down.

"What?" she asked. "Too many feelings for you, Frank?"

He looked up at her from between his hands.

"It's not fun, you know," he said quietly. "Always being wrong."

He'd stood up stiffly and left the room, and it was like all the light left with him, leaving Cleo in the shadowed world of her own thoughts once again.

———

Cleo turned the tap on and ran water over the ashes in the sink, scooping the black mess down the drain with her palm. A soap opera, the neighbor had called them, and it was true.

She knelt on the kitchen floor and punched herself once, twice, in the stomach. She fell forward onto her hands and knees, breathing heavily. She could feel her breasts and stomach pulling toward the floor. She balanced on one palm and punched her fist into her stomach again. It was pointless; gravity worked against her, softening the blow. She wanted the anger knocked out of her, to be left feeling quiet and still, but the punches had been too dull to dislodge it. It surged on.

She pulled herself up to standing and looked blankly around the kitchen. She and Frank had been given a block of chopping knives for their wedding, with beechwood handles. They never used them, of course, never cooked, never did anything remotely domestic. The whole apartment was full of practical objects turned purely decorative—an elaborate wine aerator, a miniature trampoline, expensive musical instruments neither of them could play. They owned a theremin, for goodness' sake. They couldn't even own a pet without . . . Cleo shook the thought away. It was too painful to remember.

Cleo pulled a knife from its wooden block. She stretched her arm stiff in front of her, resting the back of her hand on the kitchen countertop, and made a fist. The underside of her forearm was very pale, tawny skin gradually blanching to soft exposed white, like the belly of a dog. She needed to be shocked out of this feeling, control it so it would stop controlling her. She lifted the knife and did a couple of practice swipes. It made a satisfying swoosh through the air. She closed her eyes and inhaled. The trick was not to hesitate.

But she did. She opened her eyes. She put the knife down and walked back to the bedroom, to the unmade bed and its creased plane of sheets, and lay down. There was the ceiling again. The anger was ebbing away, but in its wake was a hollowness that could be filled by anything. She closed her eyes and waited. She imagined feathery slivers of ash falling from the ceiling. Silvery and soft, they depressed her body to the bed. Flakes caught on her eyelashes and gathered in the hollows between her arms and chest and legs. She was muffled under a mound of silver ash, it hushed all sound.

Only then, in the quietness beneath, did the new feeling arrive. It was shame. Shame that she had quit her job, shame that she did not paint, shame that she had married Frank, shame that he was in love with someone else, shame that she had run to Anders for comfort, shame that he had discarded her, shame that Frank drank like he did, shame that they let Jesus die, shame that Frank had let her tear apart the whole apartment looking for her before coming clean about what he'd done, shame that she'd covered for him and told everyone that Jesus had escaped, shame that it was her secret now too, shame that she was too afraid to leave him when she said she would, shame that her mother was dead and she could not ask her for advice, shame that her mother didn't want to be her mother enough to *not* be dead, just shame, shame, shame.

She wanted to pull apart the threads that held the last twelve months together, unpick the stitches like a dress being let out for someone new. She wanted to be the someone new. She lay there while sunlight filled and retreated from the apartment. Her phone rang once, then again. Cleo endured the sound for ten shrill rings, then pulled herself up from the ash heap and answered.

"*There* you are. Why do you pretend to be busy? I know you're not."

It was Quentin. He was going to pick up a vacuum he'd found on Craigslist and wanted her to come with him in case the seller tried to murder him.

"What makes you think they won't murder me too?" Cleo said. She was surprised by how natural and light her voice sounded. It frightened her how easy it was to fake her own happiness.

"Well, he won't be expecting you," said Quentin. "And it's much harder to murder two people at once."

The fact that Quentin was buying a vacuum secondhand was typical of his peculiar mixture of extravagance and frugality. He could happily drop thousands on a lambskin trench coat or Japanese anime figurine, but spending money on anything remotely useful, like cleaning supplies or cable, grieved him deeply. He was perhaps his pharmacy's most dedicated card member, collecting points with a fanatical enthusiasm. It was the side of Quentin she was oddly most fond of, however; the same side that meant he almost exclusively wore the socks given free on airplanes, the side that hand-drew a birthday card for her every year, that smoked cheap Polish cigarettes and ate cereal he bought in bulk off the internet. The other Quentin—scornful, rich, invulnerable—was harder to tolerate.

"This vacuum is really worth being raped and murdered for?" she said.

"Jesus, no one said anything about rape," said Quentin. "But it is a Dyson Ball Compact with *three* of the five original heads." Cleo was quiet, looking at her arm. Quentin exhaled down the phone. "That means yes."

Cleo let herself be cajoled into meeting him in an hour, felt the relief tinged with resentment that came with doing what other people wanted her to do. She stood in front of her wardrobe, frozen. Just the act of picking something to wear felt insurmountable. Very slowly, she slipped on a pair of jeans. Good, that was half the work done. She picked up one of Frank's cashmere sweaters and pulled it over her bare torso. It smelled of his cologne, tobacco leaf and spice, and another scent that was uniquely Frank. She tugged it off and put on one of her own sweaters instead. She looked at her shoes. It was bitterly cold outside, boots weather, but she was not sure she could remember how to tie her laces. She pulled on thick socks and cautiously slid her feet into a pair of slip-on sneakers. She was doing well.

Waiting for the elevator, she listened for the neighbor. Often, when walking past his door, Cleo could hear the opera music he liked to play seeping into the corridor. It was a beautiful, soaring sound. But today there was only silence.

When she met him outside his building, Quentin was wearing a midnight-blue silk pajama suit adorned with tiny gold arrows under a large fur coat with a pair of old running sneakers. Quentin had always had the dual ability to make expensive things look like they'd been plucked from dumpsters and inexpensive things look prohibitively expensive.

"Nice pajamas," said Cleo.

"It's my Jack Nicholson–goes-to-a-Lakers-game look," said Quentin pushing a pair of thick-framed gold glasses onto his nose. He eyed her approvingly. "You look thin."

Cleo had put on Frank's heavy camel topcoat and cinched it at the waist with one of her vintage belts. She did a little pirouette on the sidewalk in front of him.

"It's depression!"

Quentin shrugged. "Best diet I know."

Cleo found she was disappointed that he didn't bother to inquire further. They were walking toward the end of his block, where traffic was already building up on the avenue. The yellow light of headlamps splashed and pooled in slush puddles along the sidewalk. Quentin checked his phone.

"We're late."

"Want to run for this light?"

"Running is for children and thieves," said Quentin.

He was pulling off his gloves to light a cigarette when his eye caught something across the street. Cleo saw him inhale sharply. Quentin's face was preternaturally expressive; his emotions seemed to live just below the skin's surface, like fish that survive in the shallows. His eyebrows alone could register fear, hope, disappointment, relief, in the space of a breath.

"What?" asked Cleo.

"Nothing," said Quentin. "I thought it was Johnny for a second."

"Where?" Cleo scanned the other side of the street for Johnny's orange hair.

"Stop," he said. "It wasn't him."

They waited for the light in silence. It changed, and Quentin strode across ahead of her.

"How is Johnny?" she asked, catching up with him on the other side.

"How should I know?"

"I thought maybe you two still talked."

A crowd of schoolchildren ran past, trailing shrieks like colorful ribbons of sound behind them. Quentin pivoted to sidestep them, and Cleo saw him grimace just slightly as he turned away.

"Sorry," she said. "To bring it up."

Quentin faced her again and bared his teeth in a grin.

"That balding nobody?" He flicked his half-smoked cigarette into an ice-rimmed puddle scarred with light. "He's already forgotten. Actually, I'm kind of seeing someone."

Cleo raised her eyebrows in surprise.

"I didn't know you had a new boyfriend," she said.

"Alex is *not* my boyfriend," retorted Quentin.

"Oooh," teased Cleo. "It's Alex, is it?"

"I've told you his name before," said Quentin. "You just don't remember."

Cleo frowned. She was fairly sure he had not.

"Look," continued Quentin. "He's just this guy I . . . see sometimes. It's unpredictable. He's very dark and Russian."

"Delightful," said Cleo.

"I don't know if I'd call him that," said Quentin. "But he's definitely something."

Cleo gave Quentin a sidelong glance.

"But you're . . . good with the situation?" she asked. "He treats you well?"

"What do you care?" he snapped. "You stopped worrying about what I did the moment you married Frank. Don't act concerned now."

Quentin announced that they'd arrived with a finality that showed he would not listen to her response. The address the seller sent was in a prewar doorman building on a quiet street near Washington Square. A large Nordic landscape covered one of the lobby walls. Cleo usually found these paintings oppressive, with their dark mountains and shadowed pine forests, but this one had a beautiful gilded frame that reflected on the glossy lacquered floor in a pool of gold. Cleo imagined skating across it, as if across a dark, frozen lake. She thought of a song her mother used to play, a woman singing plaintively about wishing for a river to skate away on . . . How true that feeling was. Her mother had felt it; now she did too. That was the real inheritance from her mother, she thought, more defining than any facial feature or mannerism. They both wanted to disappear.

"I love going into strangers' homes," said Quentin as they padded down the thick-carpeted hallway. "It feels transgressive. Like, if we'd planned it better, we could rob him right now. I'm not saying we would. But we *could*."

The man that opened the door to them was red-haired with a broad, freckled face and eyes the color of sea glass under white-blond lashes. Redheads were, incidentally, Quentin's greatest weakness. This man's coloring reminded Cleo of Dutch Post-Impressionist paintings, all blues and rusts and creams.

"You're here to see a man about a vacuum," he said, crinkling his eyes in a smile. "Here you go." He lifted the unwieldy thing into the hallway in front of them. "As I said in the post, it's missing two of the nozzle things, but apart from that it's good as new."

Quentin made no motion to touch the vacuum or retrieve his wallet to pay. He was eyeing the man with a look Cleo had seen many times before. It was longing.

"So, um, if you have cash that's great," the man said, directing his attention to Cleo. "Check is good too, I guess. If anyone carries around a checkbook anymore."

"Do you mind if I try it?" said Quentin. He raised one eyebrow. "Check the . . . suction?"

"Oh, well, sure," the man said, stepping aside to let them pass.

The apartment was small and ordinary in every way, forgotten even as one stood inside it. The only point of interest was a framed poster of Mozart looking, as he always did to Cleo, highly lascivious. The red-haired man crouched down to plug the vacuum in behind a low bookshelf that lined the nearest wall. As he leaned forward, his checkered shirt pulled up to reveal a pale, freckled lower back. Milk sprinkled with cinnamon.

His wife was in the shower, he explained, dusting off his knees. It had taken them years to realize they didn't need two vacuums anymore. Hers was much smaller, a handheld, and she preferred it. He knew better than to argue with a woman about these sorts of things.

"Take it for a spin."

He passed the handle over to Quentin and pressed the power button. It roared to life, and Quentin began lackadaisically pushing it around the wooden floorboards. As if summoned by the noise, a woman appeared in the doorway of the bedroom, wearing a floral terry-cloth robe. She was visibly pregnant, full and curved as a shoreline. She took in the scene with a bemused smile.

"Sorry, babe," the red-haired man said. "They wanted a test drive."

"Do you mind if I try this on the carpet?" Quentin said.

Cleo shot him a warning look, which he ignored.

"Take it away," said the woman and smiled invitingly.

Quentin moved farther into the room to tackle the carpet under the coffee table, thrusting his hips in tandem. The three of them stood triangulated around him, watching the sight of silk-clad Quentin vacuuming the drab Turkish rug.

"It's good on carpet," the man said dubiously.

"I see that," said Quentin, and smiled as though they had just shared a secret joke. He pushed the off button with his toe, and the room was restored to quiet.

"Well, this all looks great," said Cleo, motioning to leave. "We should get going."

"No rush, *babe*," said Quentin.

"How long have you two been together?" asked the woman, looking from Quentin to Cleo perplexedly.

"We're not—," said Cleo.

"Two years," said Quentin. "Isn't that right, honey?"

The man raised his eyebrows in surprise. Quentin loved pretending he and Cleo were together. She always wondered if this was a way of fulfilling a secret fantasy for him, one in which he didn't have to lie to his family about who he was. Who could blame him? His family had taught him that the only way to be loved was to lie.

"Two and a half years," said Cleo.

"Oh, I remember the two-and-half-year phase," the woman said. "That was a long time ago for us old folks."

Cleo watched her share a look with her husband that contained unbounded pride, and something else too. Joy, she realized. They were in love. She was having his child. They lived in a one-bedroom in the West Village that no one had to lie to anyone to live in. Did Cleo want that? And if not now, ever? What had she done, marrying Frank? She should have married Quentin. She should have married no one. How did a person learn to live? Learn to be happy? She had surrounded herself with people who didn't know. This couple, with their his-and-hers vacuums, had figured it out.

"So where are you guys from?" the woman asked.

"England," said Cleo.

"I guessed," the woman smiled.

"Here," said Quentin curtly, turning from her toward the man. "Where are you from?"

"I'm from Philly." He looked to his wife. "But Anna's actually from here too."

"Yes, Anna by the way," said Anna. "And this is Paddy."

"I went to fat camp in Philly," said Quentin, ignoring her. "When I was eight. My parents sent me from Poland. It was right by the Hershey's chocolate factory. What a stupid place to put a fat camp. The air always smelled of chocolate or manure. Obviously only one of them was conducive to weight loss."

Quentin had directed this exclusively to Paddy with a fervent kind of intensity.

"You don't say," Paddy mustered.

"We went to that factory once—," Anna began.

"And then when I became a model in high school, I heard they put my picture up on the wall as 'thinspiration' or whatever for the kids. You know, to encourage them to eat healthy. But I'm like, *babes*, it's not that complicated. You just stop eating and start doing a bunch of blow."

Quentin laughed, and Cleo forced herself to join. She could see the couple nervously trying to digest this new information. Cleo was so tired of being the kind of person who made other people uncomfortable. She could see it when she was with Frank, strangers trying to work out their relationship to one another. Too young to be her father, too old to be her partner. And Quentin specialized in making people feel uncomfortable. She used to get a thrill from it—it felt like a repudiation of her stiff British upbringing—but now it only exhausted her.

Paddy moved to unplug the vacuum. "Well, we're about to have our dinner. So if everything with the Dyson looks good . . ."

"We eat so early now," Anna said apologetically and rubbed her protruding belly. "I can barely stay awake past nine."

"When are you due?" asked Cleo.

"You guys should go to the Duplex one night," said Quentin. "It's right around the corner from here. I sing there sometimes. If you can stay awake, I mean." Quentin looked meaningfully at Paddy.

"We should let you eat," said Cleo.

"Well, I hope you enjoy it," Paddy said, motioning toward the vacuum perched between them like a watchful animal.

"I always do," said Quentin with just the slightest wink.

———

"Why do you do that?" asked Cleo. They were back outside on the street corner, Cleo hopping from foot to foot to stay warm. An ambulance drove past, sirenless, illuminating their faces.

"Do what?"

Quentin lit a cigarette and handed the pack to her.

"Lie to strangers. About us."

"Why not?" shrugged Quentin. "It's not like we're ever going to see them again. Although I wouldn't mind seeing more of old Paddycakes." He wiggled his eyebrows over his glasses.

"I think he was aware," said Cleo.

"Good," said Quentin. "Always good to give a man options."

"And what about Alex?"

"What about him? He's not my boyfriend."

Cleo exhaled. Had Quentin always been this prickly and defensive? It felt impossible to talk to him—just when she needed to talk to someone most.

"Their life seemed so . . . simple," said Cleo.

"If you're using *simple* as a euphemism for *boring*, then yes, it was very simple," said Quentin, pulling out his phone. "There's a party with an open bar tonight, if we get there before ten."

"No, I meant it seemed nice," she said. "Happy."

"Oh god, Cleo, you're not going to let Frank knock you up, are you?"

"We'd have to be having sex for that happen." Cleo blushed. She hadn't told anyone that.

"Good," said Quentin without looking up from his phone. "You're not cut out for that." Quentin affected his elderly queen voice. "'We are not those kind of people, honey.'"

Cleo immediately regretted saying anything. Why should he care about her failing marriage anyway? Why should she expect anyone to care? Quentin tried to insist she come get a drink with him, but she pretended she was having dinner with Frank.

"Tell Frank about the party tonight," said Quentin as he crawled into the back seat of a cab with the vacuum. "You know *he* likes an open bar."

Cleo's smile collapsed as soon as the taxi pulled away. Her face was a white tent with the ropes coming loose, everything falling at once. The evening had brought a freezing wind and people were huddled together, hurrying into the warmth of restaurants and homes. She walked south toward her apartment, shivering. She was trying to think of a single person she admired who lived a happy life. Quentin was certainly no example. He wore himself like an elaborate, glittering costume full of pins.

It occurred to her that Anders seemed content, in his own selfish way. The thought was unbearable. She'd called him the day after Frank returned. No answer. It had taken weeks of silence for her to finally understand that she would not hear from him again. The phrase she kept thinking was that Anders had washed his hands of her. She was the smut, and he wanted to be clean. When Frank told her Anders had accepted a job in LA, she knew he had rinsed her off him for good. Frank had been looking to her for comfort, but she'd only stared at him mutely. On the night of Anders's going-away party, she'd feigned sickness and lay, unsleeping, in bed for the whole evening and night. Just his name sent a hot wave of humiliation through her. Of course she couldn't have been happy with Anders. She couldn't imagine herself being happy with anyone. Quentin was right. She was not those kind of people.

Cleo had reached the gardening store near her and Frank's apartment. She had always loved glimpsing the courtyard filled with palm trees as she walked past, an unlikely slice of the tropical between the blandly gray. Without thinking, she walked through the entrance. Plant life was all around her instantly. It was like being in a Henri Rousseau painting. Cleo closed her eyes. The air smelled green.

"Need help?"

A young man wearing overalls was looking at her.

"How did you know?" asked Cleo. She began to laugh. Why was she here? She was there to buy a new blue orchid, that must be it. She had broken the blue orchid. "Do you have orchids?"

"Most of them are in the hothouse. You want me to help you pick one out?"

Cleo shook her head and walked in the direction he pointed. The warmth of the hothouse enveloped her immediately. A sweet, pungent odor enfolded her. Cleo could feel the pores of her skin pop open like hundreds of curious eyes. Everything was so close, flooding back inside her. The orchids were arranged in rows; creamy white, hot fuchsia, buttery yellow, vulva pink . . . but no blue. There was only one indigo-blue orchid, and she had destroyed it.

She looked at the rows of pert little flower faces staring up at her. They were so fleshly, so human. Cleo stroked a crimson petal with the tip of her finger. She had expected it to feel supple, velvety, but it was waxen and stiff. So they were not faces at all, but cadavers. These flowers were all dead and pretending to be alive. They were rotting behind their waxen masks. The fragrance of flowers plugged her nostrils and filled her throat. She was choking on the sweet, putrid scent. She grasped for the door and escaped back into the cold evening.

Outside the glass structure, she gasped for air. She should have known on their wedding day when Frank bought her the blue orchid, dyed with poisonous ink, that he didn't understand her, never would. She needed to return to the earth, simple and unadorned. She had been living too long in Frank's false world. She thought she would find security there, but she had not. She entered the main store and bought a wheelbarrow and four large bags of soil, ignoring the quizzical look of the man in overalls. She understood what she needed to do now.

The wheelbarrow was a struggle, heavy and unwieldy, but she managed to maneuver it the two blocks home and into the building's elevator. She could hear the neighbor next door as she pushed it inside. Music and laughter, the clattering of plates and men's voices. She released the wheel-barrow in the center of the living room and smiled in relief. The humil-iation of the note that morning felt very far away.

First things first. She went to the record shelf and searched the sleeves until she found what she was looking for. She withdrew a stained copy of Puccini's *La Bohème* that had been her mother's. Cleo carried the record out of the apartment and gently propped it against the next-door neighbor's front door. All would be forgiven. He would not bother Frank.

Cleo came back inside and poured herself a glass of milk. She looked at her hand resting on the counter. There was her band of gold. She thought of the gold reflection on the marble floor of the lobby earlier that day. Slowly, she sank her finger into her mouth and withdrew it, pulling the ring loose with her teeth. She balanced it on her tongue, took a long draught of milk, and swallowed the ring in one smooth gulp.

She picked a knife from the block—the paring knife, curved like a smirk—and returned to the living room. The broken orchid still lay on the floor. She moved it aside and rolled up the rug, propping it against the wall. She tipped the bags out of the wheelbarrow and sliced open the first one. Dark earth poured out of the gash onto the floorboards at her feet. She placed the orchid on the pile and shook the remainder of the soil over it. When all the bags were emptied, the mound was the length of her and twice as wide. She patted down the earth with her palms. It was damp and rich, comfortingly familiar. One by one she removed her shoes, jeans, sweater, and underwear, folded them, and placed them in the wheelbarrow. She picked up the knife.

Cleo lay down on the earth and inhaled. How calm she felt. Frank would not be home for hours. She was alone, as she always had been. She pressed the blade to the tender skin inside her arm. The world, so close just moments ago, was falling away, a silken dress slipping off her shoulders. What she thought of was not Frank, Anders, Quentin, or any other selfish man she had selfishly loved. She did not think of her paint-ings, those canvases that used to breathe with life while she knelt over them in the night. She did not think of New York.

What she thought of was a summer evening fifteen years before. She was ten years old in her childhood home. A new bedroom was being built for her, designed by her mother. She was leading her by the hand to the top of the stairs, where a ladder had been left pointing to a skylight in the roof. The air was full of dust and light. Cleo was being hoisted upward with her mother's hands around her waist. Then her head and shoulders were free above the house, and it was all sky. *Look.* Her mother's voice below her. She saw a long exhale of indigo, impossibly large, incredibly blue. It was as though she had never seen the sky before. She felt her mother's arms around her. *Do you see?* A great expanse, unblemished by cloud. All blue, all beautiful. Her mother's arms around her waist. She saw. They had found it, the two of them, the escape hatch up and out, free and clear, launching them into the great, wide world.

CHAPTER TWELVE

Still March

On the day Frank called to tell him about Cleo, Santiago was declared Slimmer of the Week, a fact he was very proud of and would not be telling anyone. He had lost four pounds that week, fifteen in total. This was thanks to Begin Again, Slim Again, the weight loss program he'd been attending for over a month now. Every Saturday morning, he and ten or so other overeaters met next door to the Union Square Coffee Shop to talk about what they had or had not put inside their bodies that week.

The discussion was led by Dominique, a smiling Jamaican American who wore fuchsia lipstick and dresses made of swaths of bright, diaphanous fabrics. When she moved, her long braids swung across her back like ropes of twisted pastry. Santiago thought she was beautiful and would have liked to ask her out, but after being weighed in front of her, he'd lost his nerve. Dominique herself had lost over one hundred pounds thanks to the program and was a testament to the fact it was possible to not only shed weight but—hardest of all—*keep* it off. She was still not a small woman, but, as she told the group, she could reach down to tie her own shoelaces now, and that was priceless.

It had been a hard week for the group. One woman had been given a birthday cake at work she could not eat, another's daughter was complaining that she no longer had bagels in the house, one man had been on a date during which the only thing on the menu he could order was a large plate of broccoli, resulting in some untimely flatulence. Santiago had also been challenged. He was in the midst of opening his second restaurant, as well as a pop-up in LA, and between the menu tastings and photoshoots and outpouring of money—he had shakily written a deposit check for more than he'd earned in his entire twenties that week—it had been hard not to "self-soothe," as the group called it, with a binge. Sometimes Santiago envied recovering alcoholics and drug addicts; at least they could abstain altogether. Food addicts still had to eat.

But he had not binged, and now, in addition to the satisfaction of being able to buckle his belt on the tightest hole for the first time in years, he'd been rewarded with a yellow tote bag inscribed with the words "Slimmer of the Week!" in bubbly cursive. He was proudly carrying this prize down to the restaurant when Frank called.

It took Santiago several moments to understand what Frank was saying, in part because an ambulance siren was wailing in the background, but mostly because he kept using the word *accident* to describe what had happened to Cleo. *Cleo's had an accident.* Images of bike crashes, kitchen fires, and hit-and-runs flooded Santiago's mind, but eventually he pieced together that what had happened to Cleo was not an accident at all, but something achingly deliberate. Frank's voice caught as he went over the details.

"Thirty stitches," he was saying. "In her arm. Apparently, they have to hold patients in the psychiatric unit for at least seventy-two hours if they, um—" Here, Santiago could hear Frank struggling to find the right words. "Do what she did," he settled on.

"Ay, dios mío." Santiago shook his head softly. "I'm so sorry, man."

"But the paperwork took forever." Frank's voice hardened. "So they left her on a gurney in the emergency room hallway all night. The fucking hallway! She was pretty out of it on pain meds, but it was . . . Well, you can imagine the shit that goes down in an emergency room at night. It was rough, man. They finally transferred her up to psych yesterday."

"Is she okay there?"

"I just left," Frank continued. "And visiting hours don't open again until 2 p.m. But I have to go back to work. We have this huge client meeting I just can't miss. Basically, I was wondering if you could go sit with her at two? I'd ask one of her friends, but they're so—"

"Of course, brother," said Santiago. "I'll be there. Can I bring anything?"

"No, no. I dropped off her clothes this morning. Just bring yourself."

"And how are you doing with all this? Are you okay?"

Frank gave a dry, scraped laugh down the phone.

"To be honest, I could use a drink. But I'm fine, I'm fine. It's Cleo I'm worried about."

"Remember to take care of yourself too," said Santiago, repeating something Dominique had told him. "You owe yourself the same care you give to others."

"You won't tell anyone, will you?" said Frank suddenly. "About Cleo? It was a mistake, and I don't want anyone thinking . . . the wrong thing about her."

"I would never say anything that hurt you or Cleo."

"I know, man. Thank you. You're a good friend."

Santiago had unwittingly stopped walking; as he hung up, he suddenly became aware of the people streaming around him, nudging his girth with their elbows and bags. He was sick of taking up so much space. He stepped into the bike lane to avoid them and checked his phone again. It was midday, a couple of hours before visiting hours started. The thought of going to the restaurant to talk about barstool designs and table arrangements was incomprehensible. He would have liked to eat something, but he had already had his muesli breakfast and allotted morning snack that day, a single apple with a tablespoon of almond butter. Just across the street was the tantalizing orange and pink of a Dunkin' Donuts. He imagined biting into soft, warm dough, the powdered sugar coating his mouth, quieting his mind. He looked down at his yellow tote bag. He couldn't throw this week's progress away, not when Dominique had said she was proud of him.

If he couldn't eat, he could at least cook. He went home to make something for Cleo. He decided to prepare his favorite comfort food, arroz con leche, or Spanish rice pudding. It was what his grandmother made for him back in Lima when he'd had a hard day at school, "to sweeten your grief," she would say. He boiled the rice in milk and added a cinnamon stick, watching the thick, creamy mixture swirl against the wooden spoon. His grandmother told him that his ancestors in Babylon had made this same dish thousands of years ago, sweetening the mixture with honey and dates. Today, he would make it the way she had taught him, with vanilla and orange peel. He added the condensed milk and inhaled the cloud of sweet steam that enveloped him.

And there, in that fragrant fog, he thought of Lila, the woman who had once been his wife. Lila was from Bogotá, five feet to his six and a half. Lila spoke Spanish like she was cutting tall grass with her tongue. She could walk on her hands and cook a perfect chicken. She was always cold and never wrong. Lila won first runner-up in her local beauty pageant but had the most prized possession of all, an American passport, endowed by her half-American father. At fifteen, she was sent to high school in New York to learn to speak English like a white American and, upon graduating, dismayed her family by enrolling at Alvin Ailey to learn to dance like a Black American.

Santiago met Lila when he was still in culinary school, clearing tables at the diner on Fifty-Sixth Street. She would come in after class with the other dance students, all lithe as panthers in black leotards and sweats, all smoking cigarettes and drinking black coffee and talking reverently about people he'd never heard of. He'd catch the names as he cleared away plates of smeared ketchup and discarded burger buns, try to memorize them so he could look them up later. *Martha Graham. Merce Cunningham.*

He noticed Lila, of course. She demanded to be noticed. One evening, perhaps on a dare, perhaps because someone had simply suggested she couldn't, she jumped up from the table and did a series of backflips down the linoleum aisle while her friends whooped and hollered, her slim body arched like a tiny, turning rainbow.

She had noticed him too. Back then, he was lean and muscled from carrying heavy food deliveries, with a head of thick, curly hair women went wild for. It was she who first spoke to him in Spanish, under her breath, like she was sharing a secret with him, who invited him out with them one night to a club where the boys dressed as girls and everyone was high on E, who kissed him under the Brooklyn Bridge, who lay naked on his mattress and asked him to warm her up, who moved into his studio apartment above the laundromat and filled it with dry flowers and wet leotards.

It was Lila who married him so he could get his first legal job in a kitchen, who took him to dance performances that made him weep in the dark, who taught him that the body has its own kind of language that expresses what words cannot. And it was Lila who introduced him to heroin, who shot them both up for the first time with gear given to her by a choreographer who swore it was like being cradled by God. Santiago got sick that first time and didn't have the stomach to try it again. But Lila didn't get sick. She fell back into his lap, smiling, and said that she finally, at long last, felt warm.

Sometimes, when the restaurant was busy, whole weeks went by without him thinking about her at all. But ever since Frank and Cleo's wedding, she'd begun visiting him in his dreams again. Sometimes she was dancing, but mostly she was just there, watching him. Now he wondered if she'd come to warn him about Cleo. She was trying to tell him that Cleo was hurting herself like Lila had before her, for reasons he had failed to understand, in ways he had once again failed to stop.

With a start, Santiago realized that the rice pudding was beginning to stick to the bottom of the pan. He scooped the creamy mass into a glass bowl and sank two cinnamon sticks into its center. He bent over it, inhaling the familiar vanilla scent, then turned away. He would not ruin it by salting it with his tears.

———

Santiago took a cab to the NYU hospital on Thirty-First Street, the rice pudding balanced like a favorite child on his lap. He followed the signs past the lobby and the gift shop to the elevator, where the psychiatric ward was listed on the sixth floor. The doors opened onto a small waiting area with a row of seats on one wall and a stack of lockers on the other. Through the window of the locked steel door, he could see a long fluorescent-lit hallway lined with metal carts. He checked his watch—he was a few minutes early—and took a seat next to an older Jewish woman wearing a large purple coat. She nodded at the wall of lockers in front of them. The numbers appeared to have been assigned at random, with locker 1 located between 45 and 12.

"The crazy starts here," she said.

A loud buzzer from the steel doors announced the arrival of a nurse, who instructed the handful of visitors to place all their possessions inside the lockers. The ward, she said, did not allow any outside objects, including bags, cell phones, jackets, food, or drinks.

"I made this for one of the patients," said Santiago, holding his bowl in front of him with a hopeful smile.

"No outside food or drinks," repeated the nurse, turning away.

"But I—"

"Look, they're not going to let you take that in," said the purple-coated lady. "What if you hid a knife inside it?"

"A knife?" spluttered Santiago. "It's rice pudding!"

"Sure," said the lady and shoved her coat into the locker.

The ward was mostly full of sad-looking young women, NYU students, he assumed, shuffling around in cloth gowns and sweatpants with a mixture of bored and forlorn expressions. He passed what appeared to be a therapeutic art class, where the patients were gathered in a circle, painting sunsets.

Santiago found Cleo's room at the end of the hallway. When he came in, she was sitting on a low twin bed with her back against the wall, reading. She had on a silk kimono robe in a watercolor palette of peaches, lilacs, and creams. The long fabric of the sleeves folded around her like a nest.

Her eyes darted up at him in surprise. It was the first time he had seen her look anything other than beautiful. Her face was pallid, almost gray, with bruised violet circles around her eyes and yellow crust in their corners. The usual burnished gold of her hair was dull and bundled in a greasy topknot. Her dry lips were the same anemic color as her skin. Everything about her was muted, drained, except her eyes, which were even more pellucid than he remembered, a green so clear he found himself avoiding them.

"Mi amore," he said softly.

She dropped her book, pulling her kimono tighter around her.

"What are you doing here?" she asked. "Who told you I was in here?" Santiago began to feel panicked. He did not recognize this Cleo. And, worse, she did not seem to recognize him. She looked afraid of him. Her friend Santiago, who would do anything for her! He lowered his voice to a nonthreatening murmur.

"Frank told me," he said. "He didn't want you to be alone."

"Who else has he told?"

"Just me," he soothed. "Only me, and I will not tell another soul."

"You swear?"

"I swear on my grandmother's grave."

She seemed to calm at this. Her pale eyes flitted over him.

"You're so slim," she said.

He could not suppress his smile.

"I must look ghastly," she said, bringing a hand to her face.

"You could not. I brought you some arroz con leche, but—" He waved his empty hands up at the ceiling apologetically.

Cleo looked at him through half-closed eyelids like a cat.

"Greatest chef in the world," she said in a tone too accusatory to be entirely affectionate. "Isn't that what Frank always says?"

Santiago nodded.

"I'll make it for you again when you get out," he said.

Cleo was pulling her hair roughly out of the topknot. He realized, with a pang, that she was trying to make herself more presentable for him.

"So how are you?" she asked, straining to sound casual. "How's the new restaurant?"

"It's okay. I fly to LA tomorrow to do a—" He stopped himself. He didn't want to seem like he was bragging about his life while she lay here in a hospital. "It's all fine," he said. "How are you?"

Cleo raised an eyebrow. She didn't need to tell him what a stupid question that was. He pulled up a chair and sat opposite the bed, placing his hands on his knee, then clasping them in front of him. He felt too big for the chair, like an elephant perched on a toadstool.

"This place is actually, you know, pretty nice . . . ," he began.

The room was the size of a spacious studio apartment. It had a twin bed pushed against either wall and two bare writing desks with the kind of low, unobtrusive wooden chairs found in elementary schools. Through the window was a view of First Avenue to the Upper East Side and beyond it Harlem, where he had spent his first year in New York. Today, it felt no closer to him than Switzerland.

"It's the Carlyle of psych wards," said Cleo. "According to my roommate, anyway."

"Oh, you have a roommate. Where is she?"

"Getting a lobotomy."

Cleo's face cracked with grim mirth at Santiago's shocked expression.

"Art class," she said. "But she would know. She got taken to Bellevue last time. You know the people you see yelling on the subway and switch cars to avoid? It's pretty much just people like that there, apparently."

Santiago himself had visited Bellevue after Lila's first overdose and knew it was not the kind of place anyone wanted to return to. He could still remember the incessant shouting from the beds, like chained dogs barking, and the feral odor of human shit that hung in the air.

"You were smart to come here," he said.

"I didn't have a choice. The ambulance took us."

"Us?"

"Frank."

"He was with you?"

"He found me."

Cleo's face looked like a white napkin crumpled on the floor. He wanted to say something about how terrifying that must have been for Frank, but he stopped himself. He was saying all the wrong things, he knew.

"Do you know that I was married before too?" he said, trying a new tack. "It's how I remained here after school."

Cleo nodded. "To a dancer."

"Yes, Lila. You two would have liked each other, I think. She would be older than you now, almost forty, but you are similar, in your own ways."

He could not imagine Lila being middle-aged. She had been younger than Cleo was now when he knew her, with a rash, impractical nature ill-suited to anyone not very young.

"How were we similar?"

"She was an artist, like you. With a—I don't know how to say this well—an ego that is large but self-esteem that is small?"

Cleo let out a husky laugh. "Sounds about right."

"That is a dangerous thing. She was very eager to get into a dance company, very afraid she would not. Audition after audition . . . It hurt her."

"Did she ever make it?"

"It was competitive, but she would have."

"How do you know?"

"She danced like water."

Lila was gifted, nobody could deny that, but she was not disciplined. Between her talent, family money, and easy access to America, she never had to be. When the choreographer of a prestigious avant-garde company grabbed her crotch to better show her a lift, Lila did not think twice about throwing a water bottle at his head. It hurt her career, her unwillingness to capitulate to the men who groped and coaxed her in the name of correcting her. It was what made Santiago—so fearfully obsequious, so accepting of the white man's power to instruct—respect her more than anyone he had ever met. And yet, in the end, she had doubted herself.

"How long were you married?"

"Just a moment. We are still married"—he tapped his heart—"in here."

"But she died," said Cleo flatly.

"It was an accident," he said.

Accident, the same word Frank had used to describe what happened to Cleo. But with Lila it *had* been an accident. That first time they shot up was right before Christmas; he remembered using a string of tree lights to tourniquet their arms. By the end of summer she was dead. It was easy to overdose, everyone had said so. And Lila was so small, barely a hundred pounds with shoes on.

"Was it an accident?" he asked. "What you did? Frank said it was."

Cleo looked down at her arm. A gauze bandage the color of dry clay was discernible beneath her kimono sleeve.

"It's never an accident," she said quietly.

He felt a surprising surge of anger toward her, this young girl who was so wasteful of her own life. How dare she? She didn't know Lila. Lila had not wanted to die. She was more alive than anyone. And they were happy together, happy in their marriage. She just couldn't stop using. It was different.

"So you wanted to die?" he asked.

She looked at him with her severe green eyes. "I wanted things to change."

"But why?" Santiago's voice was almost a wail. "Frank loves you so much. We all do. Me, Quentin, Anders—"

"Anders!" Cleo spat the word. "He doesn't care about me. None of them do. They don't care about anyone—"

"That's not true!" interjected Santiago, but Cleo did not stop.

"They want me, they compete for me, but do they *care* about me? You think Anders ever even thinks of me after, after . . ."

She inhaled sharply and brought her hands to her throat as if to arrest the words at the source. She swallowed, and he watched her slim fingers slide over the skin of her neck with the effort of it. He waited for her to say more, but she appeared to be winning the battle to keep down whatever had wanted to come out.

"After what?" he asked.

She closed her eyes and knocked her head against the wall behind her. A single tear escaped from under one eyelid, made a dash down her chin, and disappeared into her lap.

"I'm sorry, Santiago. I think I need to rest. They give me these meds here . . . They make me so sleepy."

"Of course. Of course, you must take rest."

The anger had drained out of him just as swiftly as it arrived. He took the book from her lap, so she could turn herself around and lie down on the bed. She kept her eyes tightly shut as she curled sideways on the thin mattress. She seemed to recede inside the folds of her robe; he could no longer clearly see where her body ended and the bed began.

He sat watching her huddled form, his large hands clutching her book. It did not feel right to leave so soon, when Frank had asked him to stay with her. He opened his mouth, then shut it again.

"I could read to you?" he asked.

He decided to take her silence as assent.

"Please excuse my accent," he said, clearing his throat.

He was not familiar with the book, which was a collection of short stories with a sepia picture of an older woman standing in a field on the cover. She had a shock of white hair and a tough, good-humored look. The stories were very short, some only a page or two long, and it often seemed that nothing very much was happening in them, until something startling and irreconcilable did. In one, four young boys played between the train cars, annoying the other passengers, until one fell forward and was crushed beneath the wheels. In another, the narrator's friend called to tell her she was dying, to which the narrator replied, "We're all dying," but then the friend did indeed die, and she was very sad. In another, entitled simply "Wants," a woman ran into her ex-husband on the steps of the library. He accused her of not wanting anything, but she said she did have wants, which included being a different person, ending the war for her children, staying married to one person her whole life, and being able to bring back library books on time. Except the woman did not say this out loud, she said it only to herself and the reader, so no one would ever know but them.

From the bed, Cleo murmured something so softly he did not catch it. He leaned forward and put his ear close to her mouth. He could smell the sweet, yeasty scent of her breath.

"I want my mum," she said.

———

Santiago sat on the flight to Los Angeles, watching the meal cart trundle down the aisle as he took another dry bite of the cranberry quinoa salad he had prepared for the journey. Airline meals were definitely on the list of unapproved Slim Again, Begin Again foods. He had heard, but never been able to confirm, that each meal contained a full day's worth of calories in case passengers had to survive on them after a crash—which would explain why he found them so delicious. *In the event of an emergency, please refrain from gorging yourself on the creamed chicken and mushroom tortellini entrees.*

There were certain foods respected chefs like him just weren't supposed to like. This included in-flight meals, Mister Softee, string cheese, Flamin' Hot Cheetos, street cart hot dogs, microwave dinners, supermarket sushi, Twinkies, movie theater nachos, and all fast food chains (though an exception was made for In-N-Out). But Santiago loved these things. To him, they tasted like America.

Now, he was crossing the country to help set up a pop-up on the West Coast. The concept was to create some of the staple dishes from his new restaurant, but simplified, in reusable jars you could carry on the go. It was simple, sustainable food at a time when the trend in dining was to make everything as complicated as possible. Santiago thought it was light years ahead of what his competitors were doing and had agreed to have a special wooden capsule created at great expense, from which his team could sell the jars.

He had planned to stay at the Chateau Marmont, where the people-watching alone was worth the cost, but Anders insisted he stay at his place in Venice. He had submitted, though he knew it would be harder to stay on his meal plan around Anders, whose life, with its catered parties, six-course dinners, and never-ending supply of drugs, was hardly ascetic. Fair, lithe Anders always made him feel like the tubby brown friend—unassuming, unthreatening, unfuckable. Which, of course, just made him want to eat more.

And now he also had to keep the secret of what had happened to Cleo from him. He was still unsure if he should bring her up to Anders at all. Cleo had refused to say anything more about him at the hospital, and he had left the visitor's hours uncertain if he had just witnessed a confession or something else. But what? Had Anders done something to hurt Cleo or Frank? He decided to find out as much as he could from Anders without revealing what he knew. Which, he was realizing, was not very much at all.

When Santiago pulled up to the address that Anders had given him on Amoroso Place, his first thought was that Anders had managed to find a home in LA that looked exactly like him. The two-story house was mid-century Scandinavian in style, with a high, angular roof, blond wood panels, and glossy sliding glass doors. It was early evening, and the sky had turned a dusty lavender, against which the house glowed a warm, inviting gold. Or rather, it would have appeared inviting had Santiago not immediately felt two feet tall standing before it. He tried to smooth out the wrinkles in his linen shirt with the sweaty palms of his hands as he rang the doorbell.

There was the sound of a man's voice and the click of a dog's nails on wood, and then the door flung open to reveal a tanned, shirtless Anders and a scrambling golden retriever puppy.

"My brother," he yelled, yanking the barking creature away by its collar and pulling Santiago in for an embrace. "How was the flight?"

Santiago was sweating, and he worried Anders would be able to smell the sour odor drifting off his stale clothes. He took a step back and clapped his hands.

"All good, man, all good. And who's this?"

"My new friend!" grinned Anders. "This is Thor."

"Wow. You've only been here a month, and you already have a dog!"

"Six weeks. But, I don't know, I just wanted to settle down a bit."

"Well, California living suits you, man. This is quite a house."

Anders had managed to wrestle Thor into something like submission and was now kneeling beside him, ruffling his blond fur vigorously with both hands. Even his dog looked like him. It was ridiculous. Anders pushed a lock of his own pale hair from his forehead and grimaced with pretend humility.

"Eh, it's okay," he said. "Come on back to the deck. Me and the girls were just having some drinks."

Santiago followed him through a spacious open-plan living room decorated in shades of tasteful cream with palm-tree-green accents. A wide, modern staircase suggested an equally expansive upstairs. They passed through the glass doors to a back deck that functioned as a second living room, bordered by beds of heather and cacti. Long wooden couches covered in plush canvas cushions were positioned around a blazing fire pit. Lounging on these, drinking glinting glasses of wine, were about five women, all of whom appeared to be models.

"Girls," said Anders. "This is my friend Santiago. He's come all the way from New York to teach ignorant Los Angelenos about Peruvian food."

Santiago awkwardly shrugged off his leather duffel bag and lifted a hand in greeting. The models cooed a chorus of welcomes. The most striking of them came forward to embrace him. She moved with the hypnotic, liquid grace of a cobra. From her shoulders hung a sheer midnight-blue kaftan woven with stripes of glittering thread.

"So great to meet you," she murmured. "I'm Yaayaa. And"—she turned to Anders with a knowing smile—"it's just Angelenos, babe."

Anders grinned. "That's what I said."

He collapsed onto the couch and poured a glass of wine for Santiago, then another for himself. He was wearing a pair of loose linen pants with no shirt or shoes. The skin of his flat sun-browned stomach rippled into tight rolls as he leaned forward to give Santiago a glass.

"I'm not here to educate," said Santiago. "Only satiate."

"I love that!" cried one of the other women, whose pert, pointed face reminded him of a strawberry.

Yaayaa returned to curl onto a cushion next to Anders and look at him with a curious, level stare. Her nose was dusted with freckles that crept over her cheekbones to her charcoal-lined eyes. Santiago perched opposite them and sucked in his stomach. He wondered when he could make his escape and take a shower.

"So, you live in New York?" she asked.

"Yes, how is New York Shitty?" said Anders. "God, I'm glad to be out of that place."

Santiago bristled but kept his voice neutral. "Same old, same old, man."

"You should move out here," said Anders. "Everyone's doing it!"

"But I would miss my friends," said Santiago, treading lightly.

"It's not that far," said Anders.

"In fact," he continued, "I saw Cleo just yesterday."

He watched Anders's face in the firelight for a reaction, but he remained stonily impassive.

"Oh yeah?" he said. "How's she doing?"

"I think she's struggling."

"She's an artist. She's always struggling."

"Who's Cleo?" asked Yaayaa.

Anders opened his mouth to answer, but Santiago got there first. "His best friend's wife," he said.

Anders closed his mouth and gave him a tight-lipped smile. "I thought you were my best friend."

"We both are."

"How do you two know each other?" asked Yaayaa.

"We met a long time ago," said Santiago. "Probably before you were born."

"I'm older than you think," she said. "I just have good genes."

"We met back when I was modeling," said Anders. "His wife Lila and I were cast in a photoshoot together for *Paper* about the downtown dance scene."

"You were a dancer?" asked Yaayaa.

"She was. I was just there to look pretty."

Lila and Anders had become fast friends. They were both outgoing, reckless, fun-loving. Santiago had initially been threatened, but he soon began to enjoy having another straight man around to talk soccer with, a rarity in Lila's dance circles. The three of them frequented parties together during the ecstatic early period of the 1980s, when hip-hop, new wave, and dance music was colliding in clubs. In the dark years that followed, during which they navigated AIDs, the crack and heroin epidemic, and Lila's death, Santiago and Anders stayed friends. In fact, it was Santiago who convinced Frank, a regular at the restaurant he became a chef at, to give Anders a shot as an art director.

"I still have those pictures," said Santiago.

"Oh god, burn them." Anders laughed. "I can't believe how crap the style was back then. Those parachute pants." He hid his face in Yaayaa neck at the memory.

"I'm not going to burn a picture of Lila," Santiago said quietly.

Anders's face reemerged with a look of genuine contrition.

"Sorry, that was stupid of me. Anyway, Lila probably looks phenomenal. She always did."

Yaayaa, evidently bored by this turn of conversation, wriggled in her seat. "So . . . you're a chef?"

"Right now, he's *the* chef," said Anders. "Aren't you, big guy?"

"I have a small restaurant," he said.

"Ever do free catering for photoshoots?" she asked.

"No," he said.

Thor ran past them from inside the house and jumped onto Anders's lap in a blur of golden fur.

"Hey buddy," said Anders, beginning to play-fight. "You want some attention?"

"He probably needs another walk," said Yaayaa. "Have you taken him out tonight?"

"He's fine, aren't you, buddy boy?" Anders gently pushed the puppy off the sofa. "He can shit in the cactus if he needs to."

Yaayaa turned back to Santiago and looked at him again with her steady, serpentine gaze.

"And you are a model?" Santiago asked.

"Yeah. But I make clothes too."

"She's starting her own line of kaftans," said Anders.

She nodded. "And crochet bikinis."

"Right on," managed Santiago.

"That's why my girls are here. We're heading out to Joshua Tree tomorrow to take mushrooms and do a photoshoot. Anders is lending us his car."

One of the models looked up from her phone and emitted a lackluster whoop.

"This one's actually one of her designs," said Anders. "Go on babe, stand up. Show him."

Yaayaa rolled her eyes, but a moment later she was spinning before him, her arms outstretched so he could see the shimmering material and, beneath it, her. What must it be like to be so unselfconscious in one's body? His eyes traveled the long line of her tapered waist to the curve of her small breasts. The dark areolas of her nipples were just visible beneath the thin material. Anders was smiling like a pimp watching her. But in truth, Santiago was not attracted to her, nor to any of these women.

He thought of Dominique talking proudly about running her first 10K. Once, when she was bending forward, he had seen the pale stretch marks that streaked the surface of her ample breasts like fissures of lightning. Dominique's body had character and a story. It was substantial like her, generous like her. Seeing the beauty in her made him feel like someone could one day see the same in him. Anyone could see the beauty in Yaayaa.

"What do you think?" asked Anders.

"Que linda," he said softly.

"I wish I spoke Spanish," Yaayaa said.

"What about Danish?" said Anders.

A wrinkle of her freckled nose. "A little less useful."

"Did you grow up here?" Santiago asked.

"My parents are from Ghana, but I was born here. I lived in Paris for a while, then I came back here for college."

"What did you study?"

"Business at Stanford."

"I didn't know that," said Anders.

"You never asked," said Yaayaa.

"Well, we haven't known each other that long."

"Santiago's only just met me, and he asked."

Santiago's stomach rumbled, and he tried to cover the sound with a cough.

"Anyway," Yaayaa continued, "I dropped out after my sophomore year because Black models were finally starting to get some attention, and my career took off."

"I always worked with a ton of Black girls," said Anders. "And that was in the eighties."

"Babe, cover up," she said, patting his bare chest. "Your whiteness is blinding me."

Santiago snorted a laugh before he could stop himself. He'd never heard anyone talk to Anders like that. Anders narrowed his eyes at him across the fire pit.

"Sorry, I'm being a bad host," he said suddenly. "You want to go take a shower, man? I bet you stink."

The next two days were so busy, Santiago hardly saw Anders at all. Between setting up the pop-up and the endless meetings, meals, and phone calls with potential investors he was obligated to take (the "swine and dine," as his sous-chef called it), he simply had not had the time. He returned late each night to an empty house, Anders still out at whichever party or event he had chosen to attend that night, to find Thor at his post in front of the door, awaiting Anders's return with hopeful agitation.

Santiago would wearily unhook the leash from its peg and take the overexcited creature for a walk along the boardwalk, where Thor would delight in snuffling through piles of trash or sticking his nose into the lap of one of the many itinerants squatting along the beach. Thor relished in the pungent squalor of Venice, while Santiago felt more conflicted, both afraid of and concerned for the legions of homeless who populated the area. He was ashamed of how eagerly he wanted to turn away from them, to wipe the images of bare, cracked feet swarming with flies from his mind. He tugged Thor home to the comforting glow of Anders's house with a mixture of sadness and relief.

On his last day, he made sure to ask Anders if he wanted to spend the afternoon together. Anders surprised him by suggesting they grab juices, then drive up to Malibu with Thor to hike Sandstone Peak. Clearly, Santiago thought, it didn't take long for LA to change a person. But he was glad for the distraction of an activity, not only because it meant he would definitely reach his ten thousand steps that day.

He had given up on finding out anything from Anders about Cleo. Anders either knew nothing about what he had done to make Cleo so upset with him or he did not trust Santiago enough to share what had happened between them. Short of an out-and-out confrontation, which appalled Santiago's gentle nature, he must accept that he was simply not close to Anders anymore. They were growing in different directions. Santiago was looking for love, the kind Anders would not, he imagined, value or understand. At least he could enjoy a nice walk before heading home.

They left the car nearby and walked to where the trails began. It was midday on a weekday, and the carpark was empty save for a few other dusty vehicles. One of them had a novelty plate that read SPıRıTUALıST.

"We've got a couple of options here," said Anders. "There's short and steep or longer but easier."

"Short and steep," said Santiago. "I can handle it."

Anders slapped his back gamely. "That's my man."

They set off up the narrow path in single file, Thor bounding ahead. A stark blue sky stretched luxuriously above them, unscarred by clouds. They crossed a short wooden bridge, then began their ascent into the hills. Wild morning glory, honeysuckle, and spiky sagebrush draped over the banks surrounding them. Everywhere Santiago looked, the mottled green was punctuated by clusters of frothy white, sharp-cheddar-yellow, and magenta-pink wildflowers. The dusty path was smooth except for the occasional jutting rocks, one of which Santiago tripped over when trying to get a better look at an orange butterfly teasingly flitting just ahead.

"You doing okay back there?" Anders called behind him with evident amusement.

Santiago grunted in response. He did not want to give Anders the satisfaction of hearing that he was already short of breath. Losing that fifteen pounds had made him lighter on his feet than he had been in years, but he was still a heavy load to carry. Ahead of him, Anders leaped like a mountain goat from one rock to another on toned, agile legs.

They walked for almost an hour in silence through chaparral-covered hills and steep outcrops of rock. Finally, after a relentless uphill stretch that Santiago had to use all his willpower not to stop and lie down during, the path opened up with the suddenness of a curtain sweeping aside, and they were at the top. Layer after layer of sun-dappled hills sprawled beneath them, beyond which the curved shoreline gave way to a bright, flat blue sea. Anders sat down on a smooth patch of rock and wiped his face with his T-shirt. Santiago's own shirt was soaked through with sweat, and he took a bandana from his pocket to mop his forehead. Thor, whose endless reserves of energy had not been diminished by the climb, went bounding into a thicket of brush.

"You want some water, big guy? Looks like you need it." Anders proffered his algae bottle toward Santiago with a self-satisfied smile. Santiago took a large gulp and tossed it back to him.

"Hey, man?" he asked. "Could you do me a favor? Could you not call me big guy?"

Anders raised his palms in a gesture of surrender. "I didn't know it bothered you. Sure."

Santiago looked at the ground and kicked the dust with his sneaker heel. "It's no big deal."

"Are you okay? You've been, I don't know, distant since you got here."

Santiago was about to say something dismissive about being busy with the restaurant when he stopped himself. What was it Dominique had said? Nothing changes if nothing changes. He was tired of being the affable doormat. He looked up from his feet.

"What happened between you and Cleo?" he asked.

He caught the shock Anders's face momentarily registered before hardening into defensiveness.

"What makes you think anything happened between me and Cleo?"

"She's not doing so well, man."

Anders yanked a dry yellow hunk of brush and waved it dismissively in front of him. "Cleo's fine. She's got Frank. That's all she wants."

"No, man. She hurt herself real bad."

"What do you mean?"

Santiago made a cutting motion down his wrist. "It's serious, Anders."

"Are you fucking kidding me? Who told you she did that?"

"I went to visit her in the hospital."

"When?"

"Before I came here."

Anders leaped to his feet. He had turned a pale shade of maroon. He clutched his hair with both hands and cast around left and right, swinging his entire body, as if Cleo might suddenly appear before him. When he did speak, his voice was hoarse.

"Why didn't you *say* something? Or Frank? Why didn't he call me?"

"He asked me not to. I guess he didn't want . . . People knowing their business."

Santiago was gratified to see the sting of exclusion on Anders's face.

"I need to go see her," he said firmly.

He scrambled to grab his water bottle and leash. So it was true, Santiago realized. Anders and Cleo. The indignity of the situation hit him like a physical blow. He stood in front of Anders, blocking his way.

"How could you, man?" he said quietly. "Frank is like your brother."

"What flight are you taking? I'm coming back with you."

"Your *best friend*. What's wrong with you?"

"Look, you don't understand the situation . . . So, with all due respect, get the fuck out of my way." Anders sidestepped him and made to leave, then turned back. "Wait, where's Thor? Thor! Thor!"

He ran a few steps down the path, returned, then jumped into the thicket of brush and wildflowers, thrashing the greenery back with his arms as he yelled the dog's name. Santiago began to call for him too. The name sounded alien in his mouth, but he kept his voice clear and steady. Anders returned, looking sweaty and flustered.

"I can't see him," he said.

"Were you meant to let him off the leash?"

"I don't know. He's a fucking *dog*. They're meant to run around, aren't they?"

After fifteen more fruitless minutes of searching, they decided to retrace their steps in the hopes the puppy would find them on the way back. Anders set off down the path at a brisk clip.

"Keep up!" he yelled over his shoulder.

Huffing behind him, Santiago followed. It was easier downhill, and they made good headway on the narrow winding path. Every few feet Anders would yell Thor's name in a strained voice. Santiago tried his best to chime in, but he was concentrating on keeping his legs steady as he bounced down the steep slope. His thoughts rattled in his head with every step. Who did Anders think he was? How dare he say it was none of his business! Cleo and Frank were his cherished friends. He had prepared their wedding meal. He wasn't just some pudgy sidekick with no feelings, happy to play the part of the sympathetic listener without an opinion of his own. He was a part of this. He *mattered*.

"You're so selfish it's crazy, man!" he yelled at Anders's back.

"Fuck you!" Anders called over his shoulder.

Anders was beginning to put distance between them. Santiago took a deep breath and quickened his pace, leaping over a boulder with ease. He felt superhuman.

"You need to leave her alone! She's been through enough!"

"Don't tell me what to do!"

"You sound like a child!" he yelled.

"I need to do this!" Anders yelled back. "I need to see her!"

"It's not about what you need!"

Nimble Anders disappeared around a bend ahead of him. Santiago surged on; there was no way he was going to let him off the hook. He was flying, gathering more speed than he had in years, when he felt his ankle roll beneath him. A moment of giddy, weightless suspension, and then he was tumbling forward, arms outstretched, skidding down the path on his belly in a cloud of dirt. He could hear Anders's light footsteps recede as he became aware of the laughing chorus of cicadas surrounding him. He heaved himself onto his back and looked up at the bright stretch of sky above him. There was a dull pain in his right knee. Otherwise, he felt fine. He felt alive.

Santiago lay on his back, catching his breath. He placed a hand on his hammering heart and another on his belly, as he'd been taught to do in the yoga classes he'd recently started attending, and focused on slowing down his heart rate. He heard a thrashing near him and then, in a flurry of yelps and yaps, Thor was on him. He pushed his paws joyfully into Santiago's chest and stomach, licking his chin, nostrils, and even, most unfortunately, the inside of his mouth when Santiago opened it to protest. He sat up and gave Thor a couple of playful punches.

"Where have you been, hombre?"

Lying on the ground, where Thor had clearly discarded it in favor of the more entertaining plaything of a prostrate Santiago, he spotted the pulpy green form of a half-masticated lizard.

Santiago took his time burying the lizard under a pile of sage and brush, placing a single white flower on top of the small heap. Luckily, Thor was so intrigued by this behavior that he stayed close underfoot. Clouds were darkening the sky when he did make his way down, the puppy squirming in his arm. He reached the bottom of the trail to find Anders leaning against the car with his shoulders slumped, his entire body deflated. At the sound of their approach, he jerked his head up and met Santiago's gaze. Then he did something Santiago could have never expected. He burst into tears. The dog sprang out of his arms and raced over to Anders with a bark of delight. Anders dropped to his knees and buried his face in the golden fur.

———

Anders did not move to turn on the engine as they sat side by side in the dark car. Thor, finally tired out, was curled in the shape of a croissant on the back seat, snoring softly.

"I love her," Anders said quietly. "I know I shouldn't, but I do."

Santiago nodded slowly.

"Maybe you just think you love her because she's the one person you can't have?"

"Maybe. But it doesn't feel like that."

"Cleo's a special person," he agreed. "But she's not the woman for you."

"But what if she is?"

"She's not."

"How do you know?"

"Because if she was, she wouldn't be married to Frank."

"What should I do then? What would you do if you were me?"

"Let her go. She needs to heal. So does Frank. He can't take more pain right now. You know he was the one that found her?"

"Jesus. He did? Is he okay?"

"He won't be better if you come and declare love for his wife. Pretend it didn't happen. Let them both move on, whatever that means for them."

"I just want to talk to her."

"I know, man, I know. Talk to me."

Anders rubbed his eyes roughly with the back of his knuckle. "Do you think she really wanted to die?"

"She told me she wanted change."

Anders exhaled heavily. "What a way to go about it."

"She's young. Remember when we were twenty-five? The things we did? We were *loco*."

Anders traced the wheel with the flat of his hand. "I get wanting things to change. Why do you think I'm in this insane town?"

"I thought you loved LA!"

"I don't hate it. It's just . . . I've been asked if I need a shaman recommendation like three times since I moved here, man."

Santiago sighed. It was true. People in LA took spiritual smugness to a new level.

"What about Yaayaa?" he asked.

"Yaayaa?" Anders snorted. "She just wants me to put her kaftans in the magazine."

"I'm sure that's not—"

"You know all those models fuck each other, right?" he continued. "They don't really want a man around." He exhaled. "Unless they need to borrow a big car."

"Really?"

"Oh yeah."

Both men began to laugh. Anders turned in his seat so he was facing Santiago straight on.

"And what about you?" he asked. "What's going on? I thought you might hit me back there. Not just because of Cleo."

"I'm changing, man."

"I see that."

"All this time, you treat me like I'm just the—" It pained him to say the word aloud, but he must. "The *fat* friend. The sidekick. But I have feelings. I feel a lot."

"Nobody sees you like that, Santiago. Except, maybe, you."

"Don't tell me it's in my head. I know what you all think about me."

"That's what you've been saying to yourself all these years? Wake up, man! You're so successful. Everyone's raving about your restaurant. And you're charming, you're deep. Yaayaa wouldn't stop talking about how thoughtful you were. It pissed me off, honestly."

"Yeah, I'm the guy women like to *talk* to, but that's it. They don't see me as a lover."

"Well, do you ever ask anyone out?"

Santiago had to concede that he did not. He had been with women, but the last time he had been in love was with Lila. He was a young man then, sixty pounds lighter. Lighter in every way.

Anders searched his face with unusual tenderness. "You know I miss her too, right?"

Santiago nodded.

"In truth," Santiago said, "I am afraid."

"No shit. We're all afraid."

"You're not. You're the donjuán."

"Oh yeah, I'm doing great. Forty-five. Unmarried. In love with my best friend's wife. You didn't even want to stay with me."

"That's not true." Santiago shifted in his seat. He hated to lie.

"It's okay, I get it. The worst part is, Jonah won't come. I sent him a ticket and everything."

"Why not?"

"He's mad at me for leaving, I guess. I've been a shitty stepdad, or whatever I am to him. It's not like I had the best examples. You know my parents have never once visited me in America? Twenty-six years I've lived here."

Santiago's own parents had been out just last year. They had embarrassed him by eating at his restaurant every night, loudly declaring they were his parents to any nearby diners.

Anders tilted his head back against the headrest and looked at the roof. "No one loves me," he said. "Not really."

Santiago thought about how at Slim Again, Begin Again the group talked a lot about why people ate, the hunger that was beyond food. They ate because it reminded them of their parents feeding them and the times they were taken care of. They ate because their parents did not feed them, and it's how they learned to take care of themselves. They ate because they felt less alone when eating. Because they wanted to feel full, then wanted to feel nothing. Dominique said it was like that Bruce Springsteen song "Hungry Heart" from the 1980s. Everybody's got a hungry heart. The trick is to learn when you're eating to fill the heart instead of the stomach. Feeding the stomach, she said, is easy. That's just diet. It's learning how to feed the heart that's hard.

Santiago placed his large palm on Anders's shoulder. "I love you, man," he said. "I do."

Anders bent his head forward wordlessly. Then he patted Santiago's hand and put the keys in the car.

"You're just saying that so I drive you to the airport."

———

Before his flight Santiago did something he had not done in years; he went to the airport chapel. Most people did not know that many airports had churches. But Santiago had been raised a strict Catholic, and his grandmother always insisted that he stop inside and pray for safe delivery before taking off. He never did, though he would promise her dutifully, but he always scanned the terminal signs for the chapel icon and crossed himself just in case.

LAX's chapel was a long, unadorned room with two rows of wooden pews and a simple altar. The smell was what he noticed first. He could walk into any Catholic church blindfolded and know exactly where he was. From Lima to Los Angeles, they smelled the same. The lingering scent of incense and flowers, Murphy's oil soap, furniture polish, candle wax, the cheap newsprint of the missalettes, and something musty and indistinct that was simply time. The room was cool and dark, empty of people. A message board informed him that they performed Mass every evening, but he had just missed the last one. He didn't mind. He preferred to talk to God alone.

He squeezed into one of the pews and knelt. It had been a long time since he had been here. What should he say? Phrases from his childhood came to him, dusty and inchoate. Out of habit, he began reciting the Lord's prayer, but the real thoughts, his actual prayers, interrupted before he finished. He asked for his grandmother to rest in eternal peace. He asked for God to watch over his parents. He prayed that Cleo not be in pain. He prayed for her and Frank to be happy again. He asked for mercy for Anders. He prayed that Lila be allowed to dance, wherever she was. His grandmother had always told him not to pray for himself, but at the very end he did. He prayed for the courage to talk to Dominique. He asked for love to come to him again. Finally, he humbly asked God for the strength to bear his hungry heart, the heaviest weight of all to bear.

CHAPTER THIRTEEN

Late March

Upstate, what little snow was left had hardened to ice. Cleo had pretended to sleep for most of the train ride from the city, eventually slipping into a shallow, dreamless doze for the last few stops. Frank had alternated between anxiously staring out of the window, anxiously staring at his phone, and anxiously staring at Cleo. She had been released from hospital that morning.

They took a taxi from the train station, passing frosted white fields and quietly dilapidated houses in silence. One of the houses they passed was surrounded by a shoulder-height pronged metal fence. Hanging over the side was something brown and furry. As they came closer, it became clear that a deer had unsuccessfully attempted to jump over it, lacerating its stomach on one of the sharp spikes in the process. It was torn wide open down the middle, suspended in a drooping arc, its front legs hanging over one side and its hind legs trailing down the other.

"Was that what I think it was?" asked Frank, craning round to get another look as they rushed past.

"It was if you thought it was a dead deer," said the driver.

Cleo put a hand to her mouth.

"Is that normal?" asked Frank. "Is that a normal thing to happen? For a deer to commit suicide on your property?"

The driver chuckled. "I don't know if it's normal," he said. "But it happened."

It was late afternoon, and the sky had blanched to an anemic shade of gray by the time they arrived at Frank's cabin. The taxi pulled away, and the two of them looked at each other in uneasy silence. They were uncomfortable alone with each other, Frank thought as he turned to unlock the front door. Cleo's accident, the ensuing days apart, had dissolved whatever easy intimacy they had fostered over the past year.

He had visited her all seven days she was held under psychiatric observation, but they had done little more than exchange small talk about his work and the weather. He had imagined his visits would be punctuated by violent outbursts from the other patients or the chaotic ramblings of the palpably mad, but in fact the place was oppressively quiet. Most patients, it seemed, passed their days sleeping or staring into the air in front of them. Life seemed to stand still within the ward's walls. Frank hoped that now she was free, Cleo would open up a little. But it appeared she had nothing to say.

Inside, the house was dark and silent, with the thick, still quality air that develops when it has not been disturbed for many weeks. Cleo stood in the entranceway, shivering, and pulled her coat tighter around her.

"It's colder in here than out there," she said.

"The power's out," said Frank, toggling the light switch on and off. He walked into the kitchen and checked the taps. "The hot water works, at least. It must have just gone."

"Lucky us," said Cleo.

"We're in the country." Frank sighed. "It happens. It should come back on tomorrow."

Cleo thought that this suggested knowledge of country living was pretty rich, coming from a man who had just had paroxysms over the sight of a dead deer, but she decided against mentioning it.

"Do you have candles at least?" she asked.

"In the credenza. I'll make a fire."

Cleo looked at him over her shoulder and raised an eyebrow. "You know how?"

Frank shrugged off this slight. "If the cavemen managed it," he said. The cabin was not grand, just a living room, kitchen, and eating area with two sparse bedrooms upstairs. It was a summer house really, built for the warmer months, with a simple, unadorned interior designed to lead the eye outside, through the large windows, down the tree-studded hill in the back to the sparkling body of water that lay beyond. Frank had bought it over a decade ago mostly for this view of the lake, which was spectacular. Today, however, the water was covered in a layer of ice the flat, dirty gray of uncooked shrimp. It did not sparkle. Cleo returned with some tapered candles and a bag of tea lights. She looked around the room at the scuffed brown leather sofa, balding beanbag chair, and plain wooden coffee table.

"It's different than I remember," she said sadly.

Frank felt a mixture of defensiveness and deflation for this house, the first piece of property he'd ever owned.

"We'll make it cozy," he said.

They both fell silent, thinking of the last time they had come here, that happy sunlit weekend in May. It was as if they could dip their hands beneath the surface of the day and feel the current of that other life, only nine months earlier, running just beneath it. There was Cleo running naked through the living room, dripping lake water across the floor, and Frank laughing just behind her, trying to grab her slippery limbs. Here was the kitchen where they had eaten fresh fruit, cereal, or sandwiches for every meal because neither of them could cook. There was Frank dozing on the sofa, a book tented on his bare chest, and Cleo gently setting it aside to lay her head in its place. It was on the train home that he had asked her to marry him. She'd lifted her cheek from his shoulder in wonder. *How did you know that was what I wanted?* He'd laughed. *So that's a yes? Yes,* she'd said, *a thousand yeses, yes.* And it had felt like the beginning of everything.

Now, Frank stood with the fire starters in his hand, staring blankly at the empty blackened fireplace. He remembered vaguely being told how to do this, something about creating a base. Truthfully, he was lost. Cleo looked over at him and frowned.

"You have to check the damper," she said.

"The what?"

"Here, let me." She maneuvered him aside and dropped to her knees, poking her head up the chimney and reaching inside to adjust something. "If it's closed, the smoke all billows into the room. Should be good now."

Frank was struck, again, by the breadth of things he did not know she knew. She sat back on her heels and rolled balls of newspaper from the pile in the basket to stick into the grate, then stacked the kindling in a crisscross pattern on top.

"You're good at this," he said uneasily.

It was emasculating, just hovering there behind her. He picked up a large log from the basket and made to put it on top of the kindling, but she intercepted him and grabbed two others, arranging them in a tepee shape. In one deft movement, she lit several matches at once and placed them in the nest of newspaper balls.

"We had a working fireplace when I was growing up," she said, blowing on the flames that emerged. "My mum taught me."

This mention of her mother surprised Frank. He could not have known that, though Cleo had been assigned roommates at the hospital (a compulsive skin picker followed by a bipolar bulimic), her real living companion that week had been her mother. Her mother had sat with her during the long, leaden hours, waiting for the day's scant activities, either group therapy or art class, to start. Her mother had leaned against the sink as she scrubbed her teeth until her gums bled each night, an act of rebellion against the numbness taking over her body. Her mother had wedged herself between Cleo and Frank on each visit, leaving Cleo to peer round her to catch a glimpse of him. Worst of all, when Cleo looked in the mirror, it was her mother who now stared back. She was fighting to think of them both, her mother and herself, as something other than broken and suicidal. They were women, at least, who could make fires.

She kept blowing until the flames began to crackle, then wiped her hands on her jeans and looked up at him. Even in winter, her eyebrows were barely visible, almost white. She raised them now as if to say, *Don't look so surprised.* Her sternness was offset by a black stain of soot on the end of her nose. Frank thought she looked like some adorable chimney sweep. Very gently, he touched the tip of his finger to the smudge. Cleo recoiled as though he had held a lit match to her skin.

"You have some soot," he said, raising his palms in surrender.

Cleo scrubbed her nose roughly with the sleeve of her jacket.

"It looks cute," he said.

"It's terrible for your skin."

"Right." He turned away from her to conceal the hurt on his face. She would not even let him touch her. "Are you hungry?"

Frank had been to Dean & Deluca earlier that morning to get groceries before picking Cleo up at the hospital. Without either of them saying it, they both seemed to understand that it was too soon to return to their apartment together, to the place where he had found her, so Frank had suggested that they head directly to the train station and spend a few nights upstate. He wasn't sure what Cleo would feel like eating, so he had haphazardly grabbed a variety of foods not particularly suited to each other: sushi, crackers, pasta salad, curried chicken, salmon filets, a ball of buffalo mozzarella, fruit salad, a single lemon, and a large slice of buttercream cake. And of course he had stopped by the liquor store afterwards too.

"Still no." To appease him, Cleo attempted a smile. "But I'll let you know when I am."

"You have to eat."

"I'll eat when I'm hungry."

"You didn't have breakfast or lunch."

"The medications they gave me make me nauseous."

"It's still good to try."

"I'll try when I'm hungry."

"Okay."

They both turned to look at the fire again. Cleo raised her hands toward it and turned them front to back in an elegant twisting gesture. Her sleeve pulled down to reveal the top of her bandage. Frank looked at it and saw soil wet with blood. The skin of her arm sliced neatly open like a gutted fish. She caught his stare and dropped her hands.

"It's a little warmer at least," she said.

"Have you thought any more about what they said at the hospital?" Frank asked. "About seeing a therapist?"

"I only just got out," she said.

"It's just, the doctor said—"

"I don't want to talk about what the doctor said."

Frank exhaled. "I'm only trying to help."

"You're not."

"Okay," said Frank. "I'm sorry. You're too fragile to have this conversation right now."

Cleo turned on her heels and stood up. "I am *not* fragile."

"I didn't mean fragile." Frank waved his hand as if he could dispel the word like smoke between them. "Sensitive."

"I am not sensitive. *You're* sensitive."

"All right, whatever you say, Cleo." He turned away from her again. "I'm going to go chop some more wood."

Cleo restrained herself from saying anything derogatory about this display of manhood. After he left, she stood shivering in the living room. Soon she could hear the heavy, rhythmic sound of the ax. She lit a few more candles and stoked the fire with the poker, looking into the flames for a long moment. She had been so desperate to leave the hospital, but now she was out, she didn't know how to act. She knew Frank was trying to help, but it just made her feel like an invalid incapable of helping herself. She had spent so many years trying not to be defined by what her mother did, trying to be whole, trying to be happy and light. Now she had undone it all. She dropped the poker and turned to follow him outside. She was going to act normal. She was going to make nice.

Frank was at the back of the house, where a wooden porch and small garden overlooked the slope down to the lake. He looked up to see her standing by the rusty porch swing, lighting a cigarette. She tucked the pack back into her pocket as she watched him. Where had she squirreled those away? He certainly hadn't brought any for her. Cleo saw him notice this and smiled to herself. She had charmed one of the nurses into giving her his pack before leaving, which was why she was deigning to smoke

Camels instead of her usual Capris. She considered it the only real success from her time in hospital.

Frank, who had noticed this smile and assumed she was mocking him, decided to keep on chopping the wood as if she wasn't there. Of course, he missed the next swing, sending the ax skidding down the side of the chopping block to the ground. He couldn't do anything right. Swearing under his breath, he wrestled the blade out from where it was embedded in the earth. Cleo pinched the cigarette between her lips and clapped her hands, which were white from the cold.

"Give it another go," she called. "What do Americans say?" She affected a nasal accent. "*You got this.*"

He checked her face to see if she was making fun of him, but her eyes were shining faintly with good humor. He looked away, grinning to himself, then swung. He split the piece of wood in a perfect half. When he looked back at her, the eagerness was all over his face.

"Good job," she said, still in her twangy accent. "That was great."

"So you're American now?" he asked.

"Only when I'm being peppy," she said. "You know my favorite Americanism?"

"What?"

She lowered her voice to a gruff southern baritone. "Winners win and losers lose."

"Where'd you hear that?"

Cleo smiled.

"That American man from our honeymoon said it."

"He would," Frank scoffed.

He picked up the pieces of wood he had just chopped and cradled them in his arms. The thought of their honeymoon brought a terrible sadness. That was before he met Eleanor, before he bought Jesus, before anyone had irredeemably hurt anyone else. Back then, he did feel like a winner. He walked up to the porch and set the wood back down between them.

"I know you think I'm a loser," he said. "You wouldn't have done what you did otherwise."

Cleo looked up and exhaled smoke to the gray sky, shaking her head. "That's not why I did it. It was bigger than just you."

"Just me? I *found* you. I thought you were—"

"I didn't mean it like that," said Cleo. "I meant—"

Frank dropped to the porch swing and put his head in his hands. "I thought you were dead, Cleo."

She didn't know what it had been like for him while she was in there. First, the horror of finding her. His hands convulsing as he called the ambulance. Holding a towel to her wrist, feeling her blood throb through it. Still couldn't get the stains off the sleeve of his coat. The only thing that stopped his hands from shaking now was a drink. Then the days and nights without her, longing for her and hating her and worrying about her. The terrible, stultifying hospital visits where she barely seemed to recognize he was there. Lost, he felt as if he had lost her for good. Santiago, the only other person who knew, had left for LA. Eleanor had been avoiding him at the office since the Kapow! party. He had been desperate to confide in her, she who he trusted above all others, but he held himself back out of loyalty to Cleo. At least at the hospital, they knew. Outside, he had no one. Heading straight home after work, shedding his false smile along with his coat at the door. The relief of a drink. The relief of not having to pretend anymore. The relief of falling apart until the next morning, when he would pick up his bloodstained coat and worn-out smile and do it all over again.

Cleo shook her head with a pained expression on her face. "I wasn't trying to die," she said. "I was, it was . . . A moment of weakness."

Frank looked up at her from his hands.

"Eating an entire tub of Häagen-Dazs is a moment of weakness, Cleo. What you did was violence."

"Only toward myself. No one else."

"*Only?*" Frank spluttered. "You think what you did didn't affect anyone else? Didn't affect me?"

"No, I—" She paused to think. "I just don't want that one act to become the totality of who I am. It's no more definitive to me as a person than what you did to Jesus is to you."

Frank looked up at her in disbelief.

"That was an animal—not to mention an accident. This is *you*."

"She mattered just as much as me."

"Do you hear yourself? That's insane."

"Her life has just as much value as—"

"No. I'm sorry, it does not. Some lives are worth more than others. That's just a fact. Your life is worth a thousand sugar gliders' lives. Christ, it's worth a thousand *people's* lives to me. I know that's not ethical, but it's how I feel. It's how the human heart works. Your life is more precious than any other life to me. Even more—even more than my own."

"Is that meant to be romantic?"

"It's not meant to be anything. It's just true."

Cleo, who had felt nothing for seven days, felt an invigorating rush of anger pulse through her. She felt articulate and strong. It felt good. She paced up and down the porch, waving her cigarette.

"You have a funny way of showing that my life is so valuable to you when you make absolutely no concessions or changes to your behavior to account for or accommodate my happiness."

"Why are you talking like we're in a law court? Did the psychiatrist say this to you? Are you quoting him?"

Cleo stopped to stand directly in front of him. "I'm quoting me."

"You really think I made no changes to my life for you?"

"Can you name one?"

Frank opened his mouth, then shut it again. He stood up.

"Look, we're both tired. Let's just drop this."

"I'm not tired! I've done nothing but rest for a week!"

"Fine, *I'm* tired. Shall we make some food?"

"I told you I'm not hungry."

"Okay!" he yelled. He took a deep breath and tried to modulate his voice. "What would you like to do then? Read? Watch a movie?"

"I'm freezing. It's freezing here."

"Then let's go back inside."

"It's freezing in there too."

"I can run you a bath."

"I can't get my stitches wet."

"You can keep your arm outside the tub."

"But I don't *want* to. You're not listening to me."

"For Christ's sake, I'm trying here."

"And I'm not?"

"Just tell me what you want me to do, and I'll do it."

"I don't want to have to tell you!"

Cleo stalked back inside the house. Frank picked up the wood and followed her, wrestling to maneuver the screen door with his hands full. He dropped the logs by the fire and trailed her into the kitchen. He didn't want to fight with her, but he could not stop his feet from following her. They stood either side of the dining table, the bags of unpacked food between them.

"Look, I *get* it, Cleo," Frank said, rubbing bark residue off his hands. "I'm the asshole. I'm the corporate clown. I'm the bad guy who fucked up your life."

Cleo rolled her eyes at him.

"Don't do that. Don't victimize yourself under the guise of taking responsibility. That's not an apology, that's self-pity."

"It doesn't matter if I apologize or not! You don't *want* to forgive me. How many times can I say I'm sorry?"

"I don't need you to say it! I'm sick of your words! Words, words, words—" Cleo slapped the table in front of her for emphasis. "Words might be enough for Eleanor, but they're not enough for me."

Frank gave her a startled look.

"Eleanor?" he stammered. "What does Eleanor have to do with this?"

Cleo narrowed her eyes at him. "You know, Frank."

"I don't have any idea what you're talking about."

Cleo thought about pursuing this line of attack, then remembered Anders with a hot flush of shame and dropped it. Frank was racking his brains for how Cleo could have found anything out about Eleanor. He had never touched her, never told anyone about her, barely acknowledged his feelings for her to himself. They had not even spoken for the past month. So what could it be? Did Cleo know his heart that well?

"I can't believe anything that comes out of your mouth," she said, retreating to generalities.

"Fine, you don't trust what I say," said Frank. "But where are my feet? I'm still here, Cleo. At least give me some credit for that. *I'm here.*"

Cleo clutched her chest and gasped. "You want credit for not leaving me? Are you joking? Sorry, Frank, but you *married* me. For richer, for poorer, in sickness and in health. That was the deal. You said those vows. You made those promises. And now you want credit for, what, living by them?"

"We both know why we took those vows, Cleo. I was richer, you were poorer."

"Oh, fuck you. Don't give me that binary bullshit. And now what? I'm sickness, and you're health?"

Frank was about to say something, thought better of it, and retreated through the arched doorway to the living room. Cleo followed after him and pushed his shoulder to turn him back around to face her.

"What? What is it, Frank? Say it!"

"Don't push me, Cleo—"

"Say it!"

He exhaled slowly.

"I was going to say that *I* am not the one wearing a hospital bracelet." Cleo looked down at her wrist in surprise. She had been wearing the bracelet for so long she had forgotten it was there. How humiliating. She grabbed the plastic and began yanking at it.

"You're delusional," she spat.

The bracelet would not give. She clawed it into a tighter bind around her wrist. "Your sickness *became* my sickness," she said, still wringing the plastic band.

He grabbed her hands. "Look, stop. Just, just wait—"

He disappeared into the bathroom, then came back to grab a candle. "Too dark," he muttered.

Cleo glanced out the window. The sun had indeed begun to set, and the room was cast in a low gloom. Frank returned with a pair of nail scissors and beckoned for her to lift her wrist. Very gingerly, almost tenderly, he cut through the plastic. It felt like freeing the paw of some skittish wild

animal from a trap. Frank looked at her bare wrist. The bracelet fell to
the ground between them, spiraling like a slice of apple peel. He did not
want to let go of her.

Cleo could not bear the look on his face. She closed her eyes. When
he did speak, his voice was soft.

"Why did you do this to yourself?"

Cleo murmured something that was barely words.

"What?"

"You did this to me," she whispered.

He dropped her wrist and stepped back as if struck. He felt struck.
"You're just trying to hurt me."

She shook her head.

"No," she said. "I'm trying to survive you."

Frank took another step back.

"Survive me? What are you talking about? I supported you. I gave
you everything I had. *Survive* me? How could you say that?"

"Your drinking," said Cleo quietly. "I'm not talking about what you
did for me financially. I'm talking about your drinking."

Frank was shaking his head in disbelief as he listened to her. Yes, it
had gotten bad last week. Worse than before. But she couldn't know
that. He'd missed work for the first time ever, with a hangover. Started
drinking a little in the morning too, a new one for him. But who could
blame him when every time he closed his eyes, he saw Cleo bleeding
out on that wet black mound? Alcohol had soothed him, numbed him,
loved him, when no one else could. Without it, he would not have
survived last week. She had no idea what she was talking about.

"I always looked after you," is what he said.

"Not when you were drunk."

"I don't believe this." Frank spun away from her. "You want to
know what surviving an abusive alcoholic looks like? It's being raised
by my mother. She used to fall asleep with a lit cigarette in her
hand. She used to forget to pick me up from school—" He stopped
himself and took a deep breath. "You don't know what you're talking
about."

Cleo looked around the room in mock surprise. "Could it be? Are we back here again? At the Frank pity party?"

"You're hilarious," murmured Frank. "No really, that's hilarious."

"I *wish* I was joking," said Cleo. "How many times do I have to hear this? Poor little Frank wasn't raised right. Nobody loved you the way you needed. *Join the fucking club.* So your mother was an asshole. Big deal! My mother *killed* herself."

"I *wished* my mother would kill herself."

Cleo snorted with disgust.

"Do you hear yourself?" she said.

"Do you hear *yourself*? Are we seriously fighting about who had the worst childhood?"

"We're not fighting about it, because I know I did."

Frank threw his hands up. "Fine, you win. You're irrevocably damaged. Your life's been hell, and mine's been a cakewalk."

Cleo grabbed the hair either side of her temples.

"I can't talk to you! You're impossible. No one is saying your life has been easy, although let's be honest, it has. But at least you still have a mother."

"And you know who your father is! Mine never even acknowledged my existence!"

"Oh, and it's been such a blessing to have my father," said Cleo. "You met him, Frank. You know what it was like for me."

"And you know what it was like for *me.*"

They were at an impasse. Frank dropped himself to the sofa and stared up at the ceiling. "Do you have any idea how it's felt to be married to you?" he said quietly. "I could feel your disappointment in me from ten blocks away."

"No, you could feel *your* disappointment in you. Proximity to me just made you aware of it."

"See, you state that like it's a fact, like you have some higher knowledge of my psyche that I'm not privy to, but it's just your interpretation."

"It's the interpretation of someone not drunk half the time, Frank."

Frank shot up and stormed over to the fire to throw another log on it. Sparks flew back in his direction. He turned back toward her, his face flushed. She always managed to make him aware of how he was failing, how he came up short. It was demoralizing.

"I was never what you wanted," he said. "Right from the very start."

Cleo circled the coffee table so she could face him directly. She could see the machinations of his mind constructing this new narrative that he had been destined to fail. She was not going to let him let himself off the hook like that.

"Why would I have married you if that was true?" she asked.

"Because your visa—"

"Stop saying that! I could have married bloody Quentin for that. I *wanted* to be married to you. I wanted you to be enough. I wanted to be surprised by you every day." She began counting on her fingers for emphasis. "But I never knew when you were coming home. You're obsessed with your work and prioritize it over everything, over me. And you refuse to grow up and stop blaming your mother. Tell me, who would that be enough for? *Who?*"

Frank looked at her face, glowing amber in the firelight. Behind her, the sky through the window was deep blue-black. She seemed to delight in listing in his shortcomings. In that moment, he learned that he had the capacity to hate her.

"And you gave up on your dream when you met me," he said. "You were an artist. What are you now?"

"What are *you?*" spat Cleo.

"I am who I've always been. Sure, I work hard, that's how I made myself a success. And yes, sometimes I drink too much. But I never pretended to be anyone else. That's just who I am."

Cleo looked at him with pure contempt. "Those have to be the saddest words a person can utter."

"What?"

"'That's just who I am.'"

"Why?"

"Because it shows a total unwillingness to change. That is *not* just who you are, Frank. It's who you've become, who you choose to be. You just refuse to acknowledge the choice."

Frank threw his hands up in the air. "Fine! Who do you want me to be, Cleo? Tell me who you want me to be."

Cleo spun around and looked out the window. She could see tiny white stars beginning to appear, like salt spilled in the sky. In Manhattan, she forgot stars even existed. She wanted someone to tell *her* who to be. Frank was a forty-four-year-old man. Why was the onus on her to fix him? She turned to face him again and she felt emptied of all love for him.

"Do you know how easy it is to be you?" she said. "You live in the city you were born in. You're surrounded by people who love you. Even your mum, in her own flawed way."

"So are you!"

Cleo shook her head.

"I'm not from here," she said.

"But you chose here," he said. "It's your home."

"I have no family."

"That's not true."

"No," she said. "I have no one."

Her voice broke as she said the word, as she realized it was true. *No one.* She walked past him toward the fire so she would not have to look at him. Frank took a step toward her. He raised a hand to her shoulder, then let it fall. Cleo was watching the flames with such an intensity that her eyes started to burn. A film of tears blurred her vision.

"You have me," he said.

He let his hand cup her shoulder. She shrugged it off. Pity. She could hear it in his voice. Pity for her, the orphan suicide. She might be alone, but she still had her pride.

"I don't want you," she said.

She did not see Frank wince. When he did speak, his voice was hard.

"I'll get out of your life then," he said.

She didn't turn around.

"If I've been so bad for you," he said, "what are we still doing here?"

"Don't do that," said Cleo, and her voice was heavy with exhaustion.

He walked back into the kitchen and picked up the grocery bags, hefting them onto the floor for no apparent reason. He walked back into the living room.

"I'm going to call a taxi," he said. "This was a stupid idea. You obviously don't want to be anywhere near me."

"Fine," she said. "Do whatever you want."

He stalked back into the kitchen, pointing at her. "This is what *you* want."

He dialed the number, pacing back and forth to the fridge, then hung up and tried it again. He waited, then slammed the phone back on the table.

"Why did I never learn how to drive!" he shouted at the ceiling.

Cleo was slumped on the sofa when he came back in. Neither of them had taken off their coats yet.

"I'll try them again in a few minutes," said Frank. "You won't be stuck with me much longer."

"Shut up, Frank," said Cleo wearily. "Just shut up."

"I know you're struggling," he said. "But you're cruel."

Cleo slapped her hands down either side of her in exasperation. "Stop talking to me like I'm an invalid. I'm fine!"

He strode toward her and picked up her arm, the one she had hurt, holding it above her head like a boxer declared victorious.

"This is fine? You think this is fucking fine?"

Cleo ripped her arm away, cradling it toward her chest, and stood up. "Don't you dare touch me."

"Don't you dare tell me you're fine!" he cried. "We are not fine! This is not fine!"

"I know this isn't fucking fine!" Cleo shouted.

"Then tell me what to do to fix it. Just tell me what to do."

"Fix it?" Cleo looked at him with unadulterated rage. "You broke it!" she screamed. "You broke me!"

"You were already broken!" yelled Frank.

"Not like this," she screamed, windmilling her arm above her head. "You caused this pain!"

"And what about me?" Frank yelled back. "My pain?"

"I don't care!" she shrieked. "I don't care, I don't care, I don't care!"

Frank strode toward her and put his face close to hers. It was the culmination of every fight they had ever had, every cruel word they had ever spoken to one another. There was nothing left to protect.

"You are the worst thing that ever happened to me!" he roared.

Cleo shoved him away from her. He staggered backward over the beanbag and fell to the floor, smacking his head on one of the pieces of wood by the fire. He sat back up again, dazed, and brought a hand to the back of his skull.

"Oh god, I'm sorry." Cleo dropped to her knees as the rage drained from her face. "Are you hurt?"

"It's okay," said Frank, waving her off. "I'm fine." Then, catching himself, he added, "Well, as we've established, nothing's fine. But I'm not hurt."

"Let me see at least."

She scooted round so she could inspect him from behind, picking gently through his hair with her fingers. A memory of his mother inspecting his head for lice as a child rose to the surface of his mind. It was one of the very rare times that she'd willingly touched him, and afterward he had itched his head furiously whenever he was near her in the hope that she would do it again. *Get away from me, Frankie, you're like a dog with fleas.*

"Tough as a nut," said Cleo, knocking gently on his skull.

Frank crawled forward to collapse onto the beanbag and closed his eyes.

"I'm sorry," he said. "I can't fight anymore."

"You're sorry that you can't keep fighting, or for saying I'm the worst thing that ever happened to you?"

"Both," he mumbled without opening his eyes.

Cleo sat down on the floor and leaned on the beanbag next to him. They lay in silence, listening to the crackle and hiss of the fire as the room descended into a deeper darkness. One by one the tea lights burned down and snuffed themselves out, leaving only the pale-yellow glow of the tapered candles. Eventually, Cleo spoke.

"Do you remember when we were coming back from France, there was that couple in front of us at the airport?"

Frank opened one eye and peered at her. "From our honeymoon? Did we know them?"

"No. They were just this regular couple with two little kids, a baby and a toddler. They were going through security, trying to dismantle the pram and get their shoes off and remove the computer, all that shit, you know, and the baby was crying and the little girl was having a temper tantrum, screaming to be picked up."

Frank shook his head.

"I don't remember that."

"Well, in the middle of all that chaos, the wife looked at the husband, they caught each other's eyes over the heads of the bawling kids, and they started laughing."

"Why?" asked Frank.

"Because it was such a nightmare, you know? They had to laugh." Cleo thought about this for a moment. "Actually, that's the point. They *didn't* have to. My parents would have been screaming at each other."

"My dad wouldn't have been there to be screamed at."

Cleo nodded. "Exactly," she said. "But these two, they were in it together. They were laughing."

"And you remember that," said Frank.

"I do."

"Because you want that?"

"Because I realized that *that's* what life requires. When it gets messy and difficult and unglamorous. That kind of partnership."

"And we don't have that."

It could have been a question, but it was a statement.

"I don't think I can have that with anyone." She smiled ruefully to herself, remembering what Quentin had said to her the day she hurt herself. "I'm not 'those kind of people.'"

"Who told you that?"

CLEOPATRA AND FRANKENSTEIN

Cleo shook her head. "I thought we could be happy again," she said.
"I know."
"I thought we could forgive each other."
"I have nothing to forgive you for."
Cleo looked into her lap. "You don't know everything I've done."
Frank sat up to search her face. She turned it away from him, so it was
no longer illuminated by the fire.
"What have you done? You can tell me, Cleo."
"I'm so ashamed," she whispered.
"What is it?"
She bowed her head. She was thinking of Anders on top of her.
Anders's hands on her body, his cock in her mouth. How she'd begged
for him to stay as he rushed out the door. The days after Frank returned
from South Africa, sneaking calls to him that he never answered. The
humiliating realization that he never would.
"Sometimes the shame," she said. "I can't bear—" She clutched her
throat as if choking. "Have you ever felt like that?"
"I'm half Jewish and half Catholic, what do you think?"
Frank tried to smile at her, but he could see when she turned her face
back to him that she was tormented.
"But what could you have to be ashamed of?" he asked gently.
Cleo wanted to tell him about Anders. She wanted to reveal herself
exactly as she was, flawed as she was, and be forgiven. But the price of
that absolution would be more pain for Frank. Even if he could bear
it, she was not sure she could bear causing it.
In that moment, Frank felt intuitively that whatever Cleo couldn't
tell him was something he didn't want to hear. It had to be some humiliating infidelity, what else? Another blow to his manhood. And, in spite
of himself, he hoped she would spare him.
Very subtly, he shifted his body away from hers, turning back
toward the fire. Cleo looked at his glowing profile, and she knew he
did not want to know. She stayed silent, and they both sat in the
absence of her confession, each understanding the other, each
entirely alone in that understanding. Finally, he reached over and
took her hand.

"You're like ice," he said. "Let me run you a bath?"

Cleo consented with the slightest nod. He dropped her palm and picked up one of the tapered candles, retreating to the bathroom. She stayed seated as she listened to the gurgle of water filling the tub. Outside, the darkness was absolute.

CHAPTER FOURTEEN

April

F rank was sitting at a table by the window when Zoe arrived, sipping a Bloody Mary. She was relieved to see that he was already drinking, then immediately felt guilty for being relieved. It was she who had suggested they meet, though she had not mentioned her motivation. In truth, she was struggling. She'd lost her job at the boutique on Christopher Street earlier that month after the owner had run into her out one night wearing an expensive silk jumpsuit she'd borrowed from the store. But even before that regrettable encounter, Zoe had managed to rack up several thousand dollars' worth of credit card debt, which was becoming increasingly difficult to ignore.

Zoe hadn't exactly been scraping by on instant ramen and turnstile jumping, but she'd hardly considered her behavior dangerously indulgent—or, at least, not more so than anyone else's she knew. Her mistake had been forgetting that she was not like her other friends at Tisch. When they complained about being broke, they didn't mean it literally. When they went to postrehearsal drinks and dinner, split the cost of an eight ball, took a fleet of late-night taxis from one party to the next, or got a $12 green juice with hangover-curing properties before class, they did so with the knowledge that there was always some parent or trust waiting just out of sight to carry them back to the safe shores of solvency. Zoe, meanwhile, was adrift.

Her plan had been to ply Frank with drinks over dinner, then do her best puppy-dog plea for money, but he'd thrown her by suggesting break-fast at Santiago's new restaurant instead. Even as she'd agreed to the plan several days earlier, she knew she would be late. But really, what did he expect? It was before noon on a Saturday, after all.

She wove her way through the already full tables, looking around the restaurant appreciatively. The place was modern American with a tradi-tional Peruvian twist, and this meeting of old and new culinary styles was reflected by sleek stainless-steel furniture juxtaposed with colorful Andean textiles. Overall the space felt fresh, open, and relaxed—the exact opposite, incidentally, of how Zoe felt.

Frank had cut his hair since the last time she saw him, the cloud of dark curls usually surrounding his face sheared to only a few coils on top. It left his head looking strangely exposed, she thought, like a newborn. He stood up to give her a hug, then pulled away, clutching at his chest.

"What's wrong?" asked Zoe.

"Nothing." Frank waved her off. "A little burn."

"Heartburn? You're turning into Mom."

"Not heartburn. I . . . Well . . ." He paused, then exhaled loudly. "Fuck it. I was trying to dye some gray hairs there, but the stuff I bought was too strong, and it burned half my skin off."

In deference to Frank's embarrassment, Zoe swallowed the laughter that was rising in her throat.

"Let me see," she said, pulling the shirt aside to reveal what did appear to be an angry red burn covering his chest. "It's doesn't look too bad," she lied.

They sat down and eyed each other across the table in silence.

"So, you got a breakup haircut," said Zoe.

"That's not a thing," said Frank. "Men don't do that."

Zoe wanted to interject that men didn't usually dye their chest hair either, but she resisted.

"It was just getting too long," he said. "Anyway, what do you think?"

He took off his glasses and mussed the top. She thought he looked like a gay soccer player, but the sight of his pale scalp peeking from beneath the stubble, his naked squinting eyes, made her ache.

"It's cool," she said. "Makes you look younger."

She was happy to see him smile as she grabbed the cup of ice water from the table and pressed it to her forehead. Frank looked at her over his glasses and slid his Bloody Mary toward her.

"You're hungover."

"Only a little." She took a long sip.

"What did you do last night?"

Last night. She'd gone out with the aforementioned friends from Tisch, promising herself she wouldn't drink, but once she was there, it had seemed pointless not to have one glass of wine, and in fact if they split a bottle it worked out to only a little more, and then there was a movie producer she'd met once at an after-party who was offering to get her a drink, get everyone drinks, and it had seemed a good idea to have a bump in the bathroom, just one so she'd drink less, and then she'd heard there was a warehouse party in Brooklyn, and all right, she'd got in the cab, but just to see it, not to stay for long, and wow the drinks were so much cheaper than in Manhattan basically free did she have cash she got two got three and where were her friends they'd gone never mind there was the producer he was dancing and sweating and yelling something over the music she couldn't hear it sounded like I'MSOLONELYI'MSOLONELY and he wasn't bad looking really just a bit old and he was staying at a hotel and he had another gram back at the room he called them a car and black space she was yelling about diversity in Hollywood or something, she was angry and black space rolling on the bed laughing, saying don't get it in my hair black space naked on the bathroom floor trying to get clean something wet get up get a towel blackspaceblackspaceblackspaceblackspace.

"Drinks with friends," said Zoe, shaking her head to clear the thoughts. "Anyway, you're hungover too. I can tell."

"I've earned the right," said Frank.

"How convenient for you."

A blond server who didn't look much older than Zoe bounded over to their table, clutching his notepad. She gave him a little wink. To her satisfaction, he blushed to the tips of his ears.

"We'll have the *huevos*," said Frank, handing him the menus before he could open his mouth. "And another Bloody Mary. I'll have a beer on the side too."

"Me too," said Zoe.

"Um, which kind?" he asked, ferociously scribbling away.

"Corona," they said in unison.

He laughed. "You guys been dating a long time?"

"She's my sister," said Frank.

A profusion of embarrassed apologies followed while Zoe assured him that it happened all the time, which was true. No one would guess they were related by sight. Their mother might not have made her offspring in her image, but she had stamped them with her nature, a fact they both deeply resented. Quick to love, quick to anger, quick to self-destruct. The server brought their drinks and retreated, still bowing with contrition.

"How's the internship going?" asked Frank.

"Amazing. I'm working really hard."

Zoe was getting class credit interning at an experimental theater company in Dumbo. She was meant to be gaining hands-on experience in the Brooklyn fringe theater movement, but mostly she had been learning how to live on the minimum amount of sleep possible and still get to work and school on time. She took a gulp of Bloody Mary and chased it with the beer. She was trying to decide when to bring up her recent credit card bill when a current of nausea ran through her.

"That's the way to do it," said Frank. "You know when I started at Saatchi, I worked seventy hours a week. All the night cleaners knew my name."

"And you kept a spare suit in the broom closet," Zoe droned.

"All right, you're tired of hearing it," Frank said. "But I wasn't like you, all special and talented. I was hardworking, that's what I had." Zoe tried to contradict him, but he waved her off. "I'm happy for it now. Gave me the life I wanted. Helped me give you the life you want."

The life she wanted. Was Zoe living that? She was twenty years old, and the most she'd achieved was a callback for the role of Girl in Jacuzzi. She *did* think she was special, but she wouldn't have admitted it. She knew enough to know that there was nothing less special than thinking you were.

"Anyway," he said. "I'm proud of you, is what I'm trying to say."

Now was the time to bring up the money. He had served her the perfect opening. But when she tried to speak, the words would simply not come. Would he still be proud of her if he knew why she'd asked to meet? If he knew the trouble she was in? She took another gulp of her drink.

"Have you spoken to Cleo?" she asked instead.

Zoe had been sad to hear about Frank and Cleo splitting up, though, in her hidden heart, not totally surprised. She had often thought about what Cleo had said that summer night on the balcony. *Sometimes Frank is the hole.* Zoe didn't know much about relationships, but she knew that wasn't something someone happily in love said.

"We're giving each other space." He looked up at her hopefully. "Why? Have you?"

Zoe shrugged and tried not to look directly at Frank, whose face was aglow with anticipation. She regretted bringing it up.

"We text a little," she said. "Just about, you know, girl stuff."

"That's cool," said Frank, straining to sound casual. "That's great."

"You don't have to pretend to be happy about it," said Zoe. "I know it must be weird."

"I'm not pretending. I'm glad you two talk. You didn't always get on so well."

"That's because I was really immature last year," said Zoe magnanimously. "I really like her . . . But I can try not to if it makes you sad."

Frank shook his head. "She can still be your friend, even if she's not mine."

Zoe cocked her head. "But she was never your friend," she said. "Not really."

Frank looked down at his lap. "The thing is," he said, "she was my best friend."

Zoe stared at her brother and saw that he was suffering. She had not really stopped to think, with all her own problems, how Frank was feeling. She had assumed he was upset, of course, but now, looking into his creased, downturned face, she saw that he was really heartbroken. Zoe looked at him with concern and made a mental note to never, ever let herself be hurt like that. Frank downed the last of his drink and attempted a smile.

"Anyway," he asked. "Change of subject. How are your grades?"

She was saved from having to answer this by the appearance of Santiago, who emerged from the kitchen's swinging doors bearing their plates of eggs aloft like the scale of justice. He was slimmer than Zoe had ever seen him and looked several years younger.

"Look at this!" cried Frank. "It's the incredible shrinking man."

He slapped Santiago's still substantial girth appreciatively. Santiago bowed his head, glowing with barely concealed pride.

"I heard the most beautiful girl in New York was in my restaurant," he said, "and I had to come see for myself."

He slid the food onto the table and bent to kiss her.

"Frank's right," said Zoe. "You look great."

Santiago turned to Frank and put a large hand on his shoulder. "What about this guy! The hair is *muy guapo*."

"Uh-uh, don't change the subject," said Frank. "What's going on with you, man? You look good. You even *smell* good. What's new?"

"Nothing new! I've just been eating well, you know, taking my exercise, and . . ."

"You met someone, didn't you," said Zoe.

Santiago beamed. "I have a new friend, yes."

"You've been holding out on me!" cried Frank. "Who is she? When can I meet her?"

"Her name is Dominique," he said. "We have been on three dates."

"And?" asked Zoe.

"She is warm like the sun."

"Wow, man," said Frank. "Why didn't you tell me?"

"It is new," he said. "And with you and Cleo, I didn't want to . . ."

"Hey," said Frank. "Stop that. Just because we broke up, doesn't mean I can't be happy for my friend when he finds love."

Santiago pulled up a metal chair and straddled it. "I appreciate that, brother," he said. "Now Zoe, you tell me, has he cried to you yet? He needs to cry. When a marriage ends, a man should shed tears like heartbeats."

"I don't want to talk about it," said Frank.

"He doesn't want to talk about it," said Zoe.

"But you must talk about it," said Santiago. "It's the only way to heal."

Zoe had, in fact, never seen Frank cry. He often joked that their mother was so disgusted by tears, she had purged him of the habit by the tender age of five.

"Will you stay married?" asked Santiago. "For her visa?"

"If she wants to," said Frank. "Honestly, I don't know. Last I heard she was staying with Quentin. Who I'm sure is doing a good job of turning her against me."

"Last you *heard*?" exclaimed Santiago. "Why don't you call her, man? I remember the food I made for your wedding like it was yesterday. It *was* yesterday. She still loves you, I feel it. A girl like Cleo loves forever."

"I'm not sure that's true of anyone," said Frank.

"Pssh." Santiago made to cover Zoe's ears from this unromantic opinion. "I've been trying to call her," he continued. "The hospital would not let me give her my rice pudding. I wanted to make it for her again."

"Hospital?" asked Zoe.

Frank gave Santiago a furious look. Zoe noticed him immediately color.

"Not hospital!" he exclaimed. "Sorry, my English gets confused. I meant . . . hospitality team! My team would not let me give her my secret rice pudding recipe. They can be very strict."

"That's weird," said Zoe. "It's your recipe."

Zoe looked at Frank, who was shrinking in his chair, holding his chest again. She could feel in her gut that Santiago was lying. Her first instinct was to badger Frank relentlessly until he had no choice but to tell her—she was a theater kid, after all, and treated secrets as a vital source of sustenance—but she stopped herself. Suddenly she could see exactly what Frank had looked like as a child. That hopeful, fearful expression as he peered at the world from behind his glasses. She wanted to reach over the table and cup his skull in her hands. She wanted him to know that she would always choose him, always take his side, and that even if he never told her what happened to Cleo, she would understand. Because he was her brother and she was his sister. It was that simple and that complicated.

"Santiago, these eggs look amazing," she said instead.

She sensed that the greatest act of kindness she could do for Frank right now was to get Santiago off the subject of Cleo, and this would be most easily achieved by talking about food. She took another bite.

"Is that paprika?"

"You have to talk to her, man," said Santiago.

"Best eggs in the city," said Frank, forking what looked like half his plate into his mouth.

"I added a little *ají panca* too," Santiago said, relenting.

"I can tell," said Frank, choking into his napkin.

"Let's talk about Zoe then." Santiago turned and wrapped his arm around the back of her chair. "Tell me, how is it possible that a girl like you does not have a boyfriend? We need to find you a nice boy. Don't you know anyone, Frank?"

"As far as I'm concerned, Zoe's dying a virgin."

"Don't worry, *mi amor*." Santiago winked at her. "I'll find you a nice guy."

Zoe hated talk like this, in part because of a growing fear that she was not a nice girl. Nice girls blushed and got giggly when they drank, could order wine and leave a half-moon of liquid still in the glass. Nice girls went to spin class and had savings accounts. They did not have seizures. They did not have debt. They did not let old guys have sex with them in hotel rooms and leave before they woke up. They did not only see their brother because they needed money.

"I don't think I want a boyfriend," said Zoe.

"Good," said Frank. "Focus on your schoolwork."

"Of course, focus," said Santiago. "But youth and beauty are terrible things to waste."

Frank began to say something, thought better of it, and continued plowing through his eggs.

"Well, it's a beautiful day, and I'm happy to see you both." Santiago rested his hand on the table between them. "What is this beer you're drinking?" He shook his head and called to the server, who was anxiously wiping down the gleaming bar top. "A bottle of prosecco for my friends!" He turned and grinned at them. "What else are Saturdays for, eh?"

———

The day was already ending by the time Zoe opened the door to her apartment. Tali was out, and the place smelled like incense and cigarettes and trash. She needed to rest. If she went to sleep early, she could still have a whole day tomorrow, maybe check out a museum, then go to school on Monday refreshed for once. She lay down on her bed and listened to the Saturday crowd outside her window.

But her mind refused to settle. It kept reaching, instead, to fill the gaps from last night. She remembered opening a bottle from the minibar with her teeth, scattering M&Ms on the carpeted floor, being on her hands and knees . . . She kicked off her shoes with a violent shudder. She needed to think about something else. She opened her laptop, and the screen brightened onto her bank statement. She closed her eyes. She had not asked Frank for the money. She would not.

She was sinking into a fitful sleep when the sound of her phone chirping in her bag startled her awake. It was a message from her mother, asking how the internship was going. Mother messages were worse than no messages at all. She threw her phone back in her bag, then opened her desk drawer and inspected Portia's card. It was not the first time she'd considered using it since meeting her at the Climaxing to Consciousness group, but it was the first time she'd felt desperate enough to act on it. She plucked it out of its hiding place and carried it and her laptop to the kitchen. There was no wine or beer left, so she grabbed the half-empty

COCO MELLORS

bottle of spiced rum from above the fridge and sloshed some into her blue Tisch mug. Then she slid with her back against the cabinets to the floor and typed in the website address.

An image of an attractive couple in black-tie appeared on the screen beneath the words "Find a mutually beneficial relationship . . ." The website was simple and corporate, remarkably untitillating, until Zoe clicked on the Sugar Babies tab to reveal image after image of girls. Most were taken by the girls themselves, pouting faces staring up at a camera lens raised above their heads, but there were also girls at the beach, girls in cars, girls on the couch, girls on boats, girls in bed. At the top of the page it read: "Want to provide companionship in exchange for getting pampered like the princess you are? Sign up here and connect instantly!" Zoe drained her mug and clicked.

She filled out her details quickly and mechanically. Under religion she put "Marlon Brando." When it asked her to upload a photo, she scrolled through her pictures and chose a shot of herself in a black spaghetti-strap dress, taken after her opening night in *Antigone*. The sun had bronzed her skin and streaked her curls with gold; she looked honey-hued and wholesome. She pressed submit, and her profile populated onto the site. Hardly a rigorous screening process, she noted. She lay back on the cool tile floor. It had been almost too easy.

She was still lying there, balancing the empty bottle of rum on her forehead, when her laptop pinged with a message. Zoe was surprised to get one so soon. Did these men just sit around waiting for fresh girls to appear? She rolled up to face the screen, the bottle clattering behind her. It was from a man called Jiro Tanaka. She clicked on his profile before reading the message. He was Japanese, late thirties, with a wide tanned face that crinkled around the eyes. Under interests he had listed skiing, water sports, and Tina Turner. He was not what she'd expected. She had thought the men on the website would be gray and liver-spotted, like sex offenders in nicer suits. Zoe slid onto her belly and opened the message.

Hi Zoe!
What a beautiful name you have. And you are very cute! ☺

Will you be free for a drink tonight? I know an excellent sake bar
downtown I think you will enjoy.

Jiro.

She rubbed her eyes and read the message several times. Very slowly, using two fingers, she typed a response.

Hey Jiro,
You have a cool name too. I'm free to meet tonight.

She paused, replaced the periods with exclamation marks, and hit send. He responded almost instantly with the address and suggested they meet at 7:00 p.m. That gave Zoe just over an hour to get ready and walk there. It was all happening much faster than she expected. She pressed her cheek to the floor and moaned.

Zoe hurtled north on Bowery and looked for someone to bum a cigarette off. Three girls in jewel-tone coats skittered past, trailing perfume. The emerald girl on the end had a cigarette pinched between her lips. Zoe turned to approach them, but they spun away, laughing, refracting like light. Under her leopard coat she was wearing the same black dress she'd had on in the photo, and she wished she'd worn something else. She tried to reach into her bag for her lipstick, but she kept careening off-balance. Her fingertips touched the sidewalk. What difference could lipstick make anyway? She laughed. She was what she was!

The sake bar was tucked at the bottom of a slim building on a residential street. She stopped in a deli on the corner, to buy gum, she thought, but she left with a can of beer instead. She walked to the middle of the block and stood across the street from the bar in the shadows. She held her jacket closed with one hand and drank. Through the lit windows she could see a row of people sitting at the narrow gold counter. Only one man was alone, his hair a dark, shiny black. Clusters of pink cherry blossoms hung from the paper screen above his head like thoughts. What an adventure she was on. Just like a character in a film. It struck her that adult life was endlessly harsh and exciting, something to be overwhelmed by again and again, like a wave beating her down as she tried to stand.

———

Jiro in the flesh was, to her relief, not drastically dissimilar to his photograph. Same wide, bronze face and curious eyes. In fact, he looked slightly younger than he did in his picture. He had what Frank called the "money glow," a winter tan set off by an expensive-looking dress shirt, and the slight softness that comes from eating well and often. He was watching her approach along the narrow bar when his face momentarily twisted into an extravagant look of amazement; his eyebrows leaped an inch, his eyes bulged, his mouth flared open. Zoe blinked, and his features settled back into their previously serene gaze. It was the kind of face one might make at a child to amuse or frighten them, though it passed so quickly that she wondered if she'd been mistaken. Zoe paused an arm's length away from him.

"Wow, Zoe," said Jiro, hopping from his stool. "I'm so pleased you could join me."

His accent was clipped and American, but with a slight overemphasis on the vowels. He placed his fingertips on her shoulders and pressed his cheek to hers. Fearing she might smell of beer, she pulled away quickly. She wished she had bought gum at that deli. She had meant to enter the situation confident and charming, to relish this bit of playacting as a professional seductress, but she was so tired.

"Hi Jiro," she said softly.

"You are just as pretty as your picture," he said.

Zoe noted that he had not said *more* pretty and was immediately disappointed. "Just as pretty" was practically an insult.

"You too," she said. "Not pretty. I meant—I mean, thank you."

"It's okay if you think I'm pretty." Jiro's eyes crinkled with a smile as he climbed back onto his barstool. "Well, I hope you like sake."

"You need to give me five hundred dollars," said Zoe.

She had realized on the walk over that there had been no discussion of money. She'd decided on $500 because it seemed comfortably midrange, enough to prove she was no amateur, but not enough to spook him. She had not meant to blurt it out in that *exact* moment, but something was happening in her brain that made it harder to contain thoughts.

Jiro tilted his head to one side like a bird eyeing a scrap of food it is not sure it can carry, then reached down to grab his jacket from under the bar. Regret was everywhere, instantly. Five hundred was too much; she should have aimed lower. After all, a couple of hundred was better than nothing at all.

But Jiro did not put the topcoat on. Instead, he neatly laid it across his lap and removed an envelope from the inside pocket. He opened it, licked his thumb and index finger, and deftly separated a portion of the bills from the stack inside, then handed them to her. With a wrench that was quite physical, Zoe watched him slide the still-plump envelope back into his coat pocket. So she had asked for too little. Of course.

"And now that is dealt with," said Jiro. "You prefer hot or cold?"

One benefit of the fact Zoe had been drinking all night and day was that it had left her with a whining nausea that mandated she sip her sake, a drink she didn't particularly enjoy anyway, slowly with gulps of water in between. The coke comedown had left her feeling untalkative, so she was also able to do something she did not often do, which was listen to another person speak without focusing solely on what she was going to say next. Jiro had been telling her about his job in something called private equity while Zoe nodded vigorously along when he stopped himself short.

"Let's get some food too, shall we? I see you are not a big drinker. The bar food here is very good."

Zoe tried to assure him that she wasn't hungry, but he waved her objections away and ordered generously. He ushered one of the cloudy bowls of miso soup that quickly appeared toward her. To her surprise the earthy, sweet liquid slipped easily down her throat, fanning her appetite. A dish of pan-seared dumplings doused in scallion oil arrived, and Jiro watched with evident pleasure as Zoe plucked up one after the other, finishing all six, then dug into a bowl of rice. Next came plump white pork buns. Jiro split one open, freeing a tiny cloud of steam. Zoe bowed her face over the sweet escaping air and smiled.

He ordered more, and while she ate, he talked. What she heard from Jiro was this: the taste of loneliness is a glass of chardonnay and a turkey club sandwich at an airport bar. The shape of loneliness is his son's single bed, which he uses on the rare nights he's home, while his son sleeps in the master bedroom beside his wife. The beginning of loneliness was moving from Japan to Brussels when he was nine, then to Toronto at eleven, then on to Missouri, Paraguay, Switzerland . . . A new home every two years until he was seventeen. It was being given the nickname "Oh Wow" at one of the international schools he attended, an Americanism he'd picked up and used too often, until the other kids began to mimic him. It was returning to Japan for business school to find himself no longer Japanese enough. It was marrying a woman he barely knew before his father died so he could leave this world in peace. It was dutifully making love to his wife until he gave her a child, who in turn replaced him, which made him free and alone once more.

"Is that why you use Daddy Dearest?" asked Zoe. "Because you and your wife don't . . . anymore?"

Jiro shook his head with a look of distaste. "I will not do that with anyone but my wife. That would not be appropriate."

Zoe tried to hide the smile of relief that was floating to the surface of her face.

"So you just use it to . . . hang out?"

"I like to know what young people do in the cities I visit."

Zoe raised her eyebrows. "The young men too?"

"No." He smiled. "I am less interested in what they do."

Zoe had finished all the food Jiro ordered and now looked at the array of bowls and dishes in front of her with surprise. Jiro followed her gaze.

"Oh wow," said Jiro. "You did very well."

"Oh wow!" Zoe laughed.

"Yes." Jiro dabbed at a streak of soy sauce on the counter in front of her with his napkin. "It's an appropriate nickname for me. I am often amazed by things."

"That's a good thing," she said. "I am often underwhelmed by things."

"You're too young to be underwhelmed."

"Being underwhelmed is part of being young. My generation has higher expectations than yours."

Jiro looked at her. "You want to know what the key to a happy life is, Zoe?"

"There's just one?"

"Just one that matters," said Jiro. "No expectations. No preferences. If you prefer one outcome over another in life, you will likely be disappointed. I prefer nothing and am always surprised."

"So, you're saying that if you were given two options right now, one that I kiss you and the other that I punch you in the face, you'd have no preference?"

"I would try not to, no."

"But in your heart of hearts you'd prefer the kiss, surely?"

"Perhaps you kiss me and I get a cold sore. Perhaps you punch me and bring me a new perspective on pain. If I have no preference, the outcome shows me what is beneficial or harmful in my life. I don't impose that value."

"Are you Buddhist or something?"

"No. I'm just older than you. I've learned some things."

"How old are you?"

"Thirty-eight."

"Yes," said Zoe thoughtfully. "That is very old."

Jiro threw his head back in a laugh. His throat was the color of copper.

"You want to eat some ice cream with me?"

———

The ice cream parlor was quiet and warm, with light like butterscotch. Zoe and Jiro sat on high stools in the window, on display. She nudged the mass of ice cream in her Coke float with a straw and smiled. Something unexpected was happening; she was feeling better. Perhaps it was the knowledge of the five crisp $100 bills nestled in her coat pocket, or eating the first real meal she'd had in days, or maybe it was the palliative combination of sugar and caffeine she was currently consuming, but she felt her mind and body come together for the first time in what felt like a long while.

"See, I think it's cool you got green tea," said Zoe, poking her spoon into Jiro's cup and nudging herself against his shoulder. "Not afraid of adhering to stereotype, you know?"

"Because I'm Japanese?" Jiro laughed. "You know, green tea origi- nated in China. And please note I ordered chocolate too."

"*Everyone* orders chocolate."

"You ordered vanilla!"

"Yeah, but in a Coke float. That's old-school." Zoe licked the metal spoon and grinned. "I could say something inappropriate now, but I won't."

"About ice cream?"

"About you clearly liking chocolate." Zoe raised one eyebrow. "Because, you know, you're on a date with me."

"You think that is why I contacted you?"

"I think that's got to be part of it. I mean, dude, you listed Tina Turner in your interests."

"I like her music," Jiro said. He shifted on his chair so they were no longer touching.

"And her Blackness," said Zoe.

"Do you consider yourself Black, Zoe?"

"I don't *consider* myself Black. I am Black. It's a fact, not an opinion."

"But you are also white, no?"

"My mother's white. My father's Black. So yes, I'm white too. But that doesn't make me less Black."

"It seems to me that is exactly what it does."

"And what would you know about it?" Zoe could feel her face getting hot.

"My mother is half Korean," said Jiro. "So I understand a little. It was very difficult for her, growing up in Japan. I think she always felt, I'm not sure . . . less than."

"Well, *I* don't feel less than," said Zoe. Her voice was growing higher.

"Of course," said Jiro. He tried to put a hand on hers, but she flicked it away. "I hope you never do. I'm merely telling you my mother's experience."

"Well, I'm not your fucking mother."

"Please calm down," said Jiro. "I don't see things that way. Race is not important to me. I was simply—"

"Oh, come on." Zoe rolled her eyes. "That's like men who say 'I love women!' If they feel the need to say it, it's because they don't. Anyone who says they don't care about race obviously does. A lot."

"Do you know the joke about coffee and opinions?" asked Jiro. Zoe shook her head. "The difference between coffee and your opinion is that I asked for coffee."

"*Whatever*, dude." Zoe slammed her spoon down on the table. A couple with matching white-blonde hair looked over at them in alarm. "You come from one of the most racist countries in the world. You guys are all like skin-whitening creams and parasols and hating on the Chinese."

"Have you been to Japan?"

"No, but—"

"Then perhaps we should have this conversation when you have."

"Just because I haven't been there doesn't mean I don't know about it."

"Perhaps. But this does not seem to be the most productive conversation for us to have at this time. Especially since your judgments so far seem to be based on"— Zoe was pleased to see Jiro lose a little of his cool here—"on I don't know what! Cartoons, I think."

"Fine," she said. "We don't need to talk."

"If you prefer."

"Enjoy your ice cream and your latent racism," she said.

She immediately regretted it, regretted the whole turn of the conversation, but she was not about to apologize. Zoe glared at the contents of her glass and whipped her spoon until the ice cream dissolved into a frothy brown swirl. Across the street a group of kids around her age were walking toward a bar. One of the boys was carrying a girl on his back, and they were laughing. She had forgotten it was Saturday night.

Jiro reached across her to grab a straw. He removed the paper wrapper, scrunching it into a tight harpsichord, and placed the crinkled piece of paper in front of her. Then he put the end of the straw in his glass of water and carefully let a droplet fall on the paper. The folds opened, and it began to shimmy along the counter. It became a wriggling paper worm. Jiro let another droplet fall, and it grew again, twisting toward Zoe. She turned to look into his open, expectant face.

"Oh wow?" she said.

"Oh wow," he said.

"What do you say we blow this ice cream stand," she said. "I saw a place down the street we can get a drink."

———

Zoe woke up in another hotel room, this one a glass orb streaked with light. She patted down her body. Her jacket, dress, and tights were all still on. She was alone in the bed. She sat up and scanned the spacious suite. Factory windows overlooking the Hudson River, a sleek writing desk and bar, a coffee table adorned with flowers, and a stack of glossy magazines. Everything bright and airy and modern. Jiro was sitting some distance away on a plush gray coach, still in his suit, reading the newspaper. A blanket and pillow were neatly folded beside him. He looked up and smiled at her.

"Good morning, Zoe," he said.

"Hey," she croaked.

A glass bottle of water had been placed next to her on the nightstand. She cracked the cap and took a long gulp.

"You had a little too much to drink last night. I hope your head does not feel it too badly today."

Zoe ran her hands through her hair. A thicket of tangles.

"I still managed to beat you at pool," she said.

"That is shamefully true." Jiro laughed. "And you danced me—what is the saying?—*under the table* too."

Zoe let out a gurgle of laughter. "You had some moves. I saw you working that robot."

Jiro improvised a mini version of this dance move from the couch.

"You're just being kind," he said in a robot voice.

Zoe sat up in bed, still giggling. "Did you sleep on the couch?"

"It was quite comfortable," said Jiro. "I am used to small beds, as you know."

"Thanks," she said. "Really."

"I'm afraid I could not quite decipher your address."

"Seriously, you could have just put me in a cab." Zoe sighed. "I'm good at getting home alone."

Jiro frowned at her. "I would not allow that," he said. "And nor should you."

Zoe rolled her eyes and fell back against the pile of pillows behind her. "All right, Dad."

"I will give you my car account number, just in case," Jiro said. "You can use it to get home from now on."

Zoe blinked sleepily at Jiro. "All right, Daddy," she said more slowly.

Jiro laughed and looked away. "So, what is your schedule like today?"

She sat back up in bed. Her hair was standing on end around her sleep-creased face in a way she hoped looked tousled and beautiful and not simply electrified. She put her finger to her cheek, pretending to think, then smiled.

"Nada," she said.

"I have no appointments until the afternoon. Shall we take breakfast together?"

"You work on a Sunday?"

"I work every day."

"Is this the hotel you usually stay in?"

Jiro nodded.

"What do you think?"

"Very nice," said Zoe, clasping her hands behind her head. "But I always judge a hotel by its bathtub."

"Would you like to take a bath before going to breakfast?"

"We're in a *hotel*, Jiro," Zoe exclaimed, clambering out of bed. "We're ordering room service."

And so began what was for Zoe a perfect morning. She emptied a full bottle of bubble bath into the black marble tub and soaked herself until she heard the clatter of room service arrive. Jiro took a shower, and she was free to eat pancakes and bacon in bed with her fingers while watching reality TV. She drank a whole pot of coffee with two jugs of cream. When she complained about the state of her hair, Jiro called the front desk and asked them to procure a hairbrush for her, which was brought up with a flourish on a silver tray. Later, she and Jiro lay side by side on top of the bedspread, each bundled in a white terry-cloth robe, scrolling through the movies.

"Garbage, garbage, garbage," said Zoe. "Let's go to the classics."

"You are very sure of your opinions," said Jiro.

"I've seen *everything*," said Zoe. "You might know hedge funds, Jiro, but I know movies."

"I saw on your profile that Marlon Brando is your religion." Jiro shook his head and laughed. "What is it you like about him so much?"

"His mannerisms, his emotion, the way he *breathes*." Zoe kicked her legs in the air for emphasis. "I've had his poster above my bed since I was ten."

"And you have always wanted to be an actress?"

"Sure have, Jiro."

"Why?"

Zoe shrugged. "I just love it."

"But why?"

"I guess . . . well, when you're an actor you can kind of be both seen and not seen at the same time. You're speaking, but not your own words. You express feelings, but not your own feelings, or at least not usually. You can play a character without being judged by your own character. It's freeing, you know? Freedom from being yourself."

"You don't want to be yourself?"

Jiro looked at her, and suddenly his features contorted into the same exaggerated expression of surprise she'd seen when they first met. It was like watching a crack of lightning zigzag down the center of his face. Zoe looked down, playing with the cord of her robe.

"What is that face you make?" she asked.

He brought a hand lightly to his cheek.

"It has been happening for some years now," he said. "Since my father died. No one is quite sure why."

"Does it bother you?"

"Very much."

"I have something a bit like that," said Zoe. "Well, worse really. I get these kind of . . . seizure things sometimes."

Jiro turned his face toward her and widened his eyes. "You have epilepsy, Zoe?"

Zoe felt a lump form in her throat as she nodded. She so rarely said the word aloud.

"I'm sorry to hear that," said Jiro. "Does it scare you?"

She swallowed. It was an effort to get words out. "Very much," she managed.

Jiro nodded slowly. "You know, Aristotle believed seizures to be a sign of genius. He had them, and his teachers Plato and Socrates before him."

Zoe smiled ruefully. "But those are all dead white men."

Jiro laughed. "And Westerners! But we can still consider his point."

"I definitely don't think I'm a genius," said Zoe.

"Who knows what you will be? You are still becoming."

Zoe smoothed the robe over her lap and pointed her toes. "I guess that's true," she conceded.

"Is that why you went to the meditation group you were telling me about last night? Where you heard about Daddy Dearest? To help with the seizures?"

"Oh God! I told you about that?" Zoe buried her face in her hands. "I only went because my roommate dragged me. It's a long story."

"You seemed to be quite moved by it," said Jiro. "It sounded like a special experience."

Zoe shifted on the bed. She had no recollection of talking about that with Jiro. She closed her eyes. She wondered if it was the new seizure medication she was taking that caused these gaps in her mind when she drank, like a movie reel that suddenly runs out of film, sputtering into blackness. Or maybe it was just the way she drank. The same way that Frank drank. The same way that her mother apparently drank, when she drank.

"Do you believe in that stuff, then?" she asked. "Climaxing to Consciousness?"

"That, I had never heard of. But yes, I believe in the benefits of meditation. When I have the time, I practice zazen, which comes from Zen Buddhism."

"See," said Zoe, poking him in the shoulder. "I knew you were Buddhist."

Jiro laughed. "You would like me better if I was a Zen monk?"

"Monks don't get room service," said Zoe. "And I like you just fine as you are."

"I like you as you are too, Zoe," said Jiro.

They looked at each other and smiled.

"Okay," he said. "We watch your favorite Marlon Brando movie, and then I go to my meeting. Deal?"

Zoe twirled the cord of her robe happily.

"Deal."

———

When Zoe woke again, the room was bathed in shadows. The blinds had been drawn over the windows, but a faint square of light still glowed around their edges. So it was still daylight out. She rolled over and found her cheek crushed against a note on the pillow next to her.

I did not want to wake you (it is good for you to sleep I think). I will be back from my meeting at 6 and will bring food in case you are hungry. If you have to go before, please do not hesitate.
P.S. Marlon Brando is my religion now too ☺

The clock on the nightstand emitted its digital glow. It was already 5:30 p.m. She must have drifted off during the movie—but that never happened. Usually Zoe had to be drunk to fall asleep with a man. She sat up against the headboard and stretched her arms out in front of her, twirling her wrists. She felt a growl of hunger in her stomach and something else even lower, something new. She brought her hands under the covers to her groin. She could feel an ache of pleasure as she pressed down on it. That was the new sensation. Zoe had touched herself there before, but it had never felt like this. After a while, she had simply given up trying. She had always assumed that part of her body was broken, just like her epileptic brain. She had woken up, however, feeling different.

Zoe scooted back down in the large bed and opened her robe from below the waist. She hesitated, looking again at the clock. She would die if she was walked in on, but she estimated she had more than enough time before Jiro returned.

"Upper left quadrant," she said softly to herself.

She guided her fingers to the right spot and closed her eyes. Deep breath. Her fingers circled slowly. Nothing was happening. Then. Something was happening. Time passed, time began to disappear. It didn't feel like much . . . until it felt like everything. How to describe it, this burgeoning? An exquisite agony, every part of her tensed into unbearable stiffness, toes splayed rigid, a paralyzing concentration, the certainty that if she let up even a little, even this much, she could lose it, it could lose her . . . But no, she couldn't because it was here, she was right at the edge, suspended agonizingly above it, she was close, so close, and then, yes, it was now, it was here, she was falling, sinking, rushing into the red sweet center of it, like velvet, like velvet, one rolling wave after another, pure pleasure, there it was again, that immense intensity, that intense immensity, and again the velvet wave came, beyond words and better than any word, it had happened, she was there, there was here, and she was a real girl, a real girl, a real girl . . .

She opened her eyes and let her hand fall away. A new wetness coated her fingers. She felt empty and full at once. A delicious tenderness between her legs. So *that's* what all the fuss was about, she thought. And then she was laughing, pressing the side of her face into the hot pillow. A puddle of pleasure, that's what she was.

When she heard the door open a little while later, she was still melted on the bed. Jiro stood in the doorway, a takeout bag in each hand, smiling.

"I know you will say I'm a cliché," he said. "But I got sushi."

He paused, regarding her. She could feel that her cheeks were warm and pink, her eyes unusually bright. She tried to smile at him, but the laughter returned again, rising inside her like a crowd of colorful balloons. Jiro set down the bags and began to laugh too. Eventually, when they had both run out of breath, he sat on the edge of the bed and looked at her.

"Now," he said, wiping his eyes. "Why are we laughing?"

CHAPTER FIFTEEN

May

C leo had been staying at Audrey's for a week when she noticed the neighbor watching her through the window. She had just taken a shower and was standing naked in Audrey's bedroom, applying body lotion, when she looked up and saw him. She froze. To close the curtains would mean advancing toward him; to retreat would only offer him an alternate view of her behind. In a panic she dropped to the floor and crawled military-style back to the bathroom, leaving a glistening snail trail of moisturizer on the wooden floorboards behind her.

She pushed the door closed with her toe and sat curled on the tiled floor. It was not just that he had seen her naked. It was her scar. The thin purple trench running from her wrist to elbow, thirty stitches like tracks on a railroad. Why did she care if he saw it? He was nobody. But her scar felt more naked than naked, more secret than her sex. No one had seen it but Frank. And she had not seen Frank for two months.

When she opened the bathroom door again, the neighbor was gone. Cleo dressed quickly in vintage high-waisted jeans and one of the silk wrap jackets she'd painted earlier that year, splashing giant peacocks and shining black crows across the backs. She'd brought a few in her suitcase when she left Frank's; she'd packed anything with long sleeves. She checked the sleeves of the jacket now. They were slightly loose, sliding up and down her arm freely. She whipped it off and pulled on a mesh long-sleeved shirt underneath, then retied the jacket. She was grateful the spring had not yet turned warm.

Audrey was lounging on the sofa, with her new boyfriend Marshall rubbing her feet, when Cleo entered the living room. Marshall was tall and chestnut-haired, with a square, symmetrical face. He had what Cleo had once heard referred to as "understudy good looks," a generic handsomeness that lacked any discernible flaw or character.

"Wow, you look great," said Audrey.

"I think your neighbor was looking at me naked," Cleo said. She perched on the sofa arm to braid her hair.

"Pervert," said Audrey. "I caught him watching us having sex the other day."

"Babe, that's because you refused to close your curtains," Marshall said.

"Well, I prefer the way I look in natural light, my sweet."

"All I'm saying, *gorgeous*, is that it wasn't very private."

Cleo smiled inwardly at this exchange. The more petulant they grew with one another, the more saccharine their nicknames became. This, along with Marshall's gift for offering the most basic psychological insight possible into any situation ("Relationships are complicated," "People are full of surprises"), was a reliable source of amusement for her.

"That's the crazy thing about New York," said Audrey. "Not even your bedroom is private. All the world's a stage, I guess."

"And the men and women merely overcharged renters," said Cleo.

"New York is *so* overpriced," said Marshall.

Audrey stroked Marshall's cheek affectionately with her big toe. They'd met at Santiago's first restaurant, where she was still a hostess and Marshall had until recently been a server. Now Marshall made his living cheerfully harassing tourists into buying tickets to comedy clubs on MacDougal Street, where he also occasionally performed with his improv group. Cleo was spared having to attend these performances by Audrey, who didn't believe in theater where, as she put it, "no one has bothered to learn their lines." Marshall was Audrey's first boyfriend, the first man Cleo had ever known her to sleep with more than once, in fact.

"Anyway," said Audrey. "I should start getting ready too. You look so good, Cleo. I wanna wear something like that."

"Really?" said Cleo. "I have some more if you want to take a look in the pile by my suitcase."

Audrey sprung up and disappeared into the bedroom.

"Perks of having Cleo as a roommate!" she sang.

"Just houseguest!" called Cleo. "I promise I'll be off your sofa soon."

"Don't worry," Marshall said. "We love having you here."

Cleo raised one eyebrow. We? As far as she knew, Marshall lived in a loft in Red Hook with six other out-of-work actors. Audrey appeared from the bedroom wearing one of the jackets over a dress so short it ended up looking like a very tiny bathrobe.

"Ta-da!" Audrey pivoted on her pointed high heels. "What do you think? Good enough for the party of the year?"

They were going to the opening night for the artist Danny Life's new show, *Deathly Revelations*. Danny and Cleo had been in graduate school together back when he had adult braces and still went by Danny Rodriguez, which was how she'd managed to get them on the list for what was arguably the most hyped and exclusive party to come out of a circle of artists known for producing hyped and exclusive parties.

Located in an abandoned liquor warehouse on Randall's Island, the event was being sponsored by real estate developers hoping to drum up support for two luxury towers they planned to erect in the warehouse's place. It was the central thrust of an effort to rebrand the neighborhood as a viable home for creative urban professionals, most of whom had never heard of Randall's Island. But Cleo wasn't going for the hype, the guest list, or the pleasure of being able to tell those not invited she was there. Frank would be there. She was going to see Frank. She was going so Frank would see her.

Rightly guessing that an hour-long subway ride would deter the crowd they were hoping to court, the party organizers had arranged for a fleet of yellow school buses to shuttle the guests from Union Square to the warehouse. The buses were lined along Fifteenth Street next to a stand selling mango flowers on sticks, a kebab truck, and a woman offering palm readings. That was the thing about New York, Cleo thought as they walked toward the buses. It never knew what you wanted, so it offered you everything.

"You going to be okay if we run into Frank?" Audrey asked.

"It can be hard to see an ex," said Marshall.

"He's not my ex," Cleo said. "Yet."

After they'd returned from upstate, they'd agreed it would be a good idea to spend some time apart. Cleo had since gone back on her antidepressants and was finally beginning to feel like herself again. It would be good for Frank to see her at something social where she could appear carefree and normal, more like how he'd first met her, Cleo thought. And Frank was certain to be there. He'd bought one of Danny's early paintings and would never miss a party of this magnitude. Cleo undid her braid and began replaiting it. She hoped she looked pretty. She should have worn more makeup.

"Wow, it's so *suburban*," shrieked Audrey as they clambered onto the school bus.

Cleo scanned the seats. No Frank. He was probably on another bus. She followed Audrey and Marshall down the aisle, passing a man with a salmon-crested cockatoo perched on his shoulder. He was wearing a T-shirt with a picture of what appeared to be the same cockatoo printed on it.

"Cool shirt," said Audrey as they passed him.

He gave her a disapproving look and then turned, in unison with his cockatoo, to stare back out of the window.

Quentin was already seated in the back, looking twitchy and sneaking drags of a cigarette out the window. Next to him was Alex. Cleo had spent most of the past two months staying with Quentin until Alex, the Russian lover he had met through some shadowy means Cleo had known better than to interrogate, appeared. He claimed he was being evicted from his apartment near Brighton Beach, and Quentin had promptly invited him to stay, which Cleo took as her cue to move to Audrey's.

Alex was beautiful but ravaged, like opening a shiny mink fur coat to find a stained, moth-eaten lining within. He watched Quentin constantly with cautious, haunted eyes, accepting without thanks whatever drugs, drinks, or food Quentin offered to him.

"He's not a stray dog," Cleo had chided Quentin. "You shouldn't have to feed him to keep him around."

But that only prompted Quentin to nickname Alex *Pies*, the Polish for dog. Since Alex rarely spoke around her, Cleo never knew how he felt about his new name.

"Isn't this fun?" said Quentin when she reached him. "Like going on a school trip. Except with drugs."

Quentin was wearing a corset top under a leather jacket with slim black jeans and high-heeled motorcycle boots. His clavicle bones protruded sharply from above the top's plunging neckline, and his naturally high cheekbones had a hollow, gaunt quality. She couldn't believe he had shrunk so much in just a few weeks. Cleo had never seen him wear any of his women's clothing outside of his house and was careful not to let her face register too much surprise.

"You look wonderful," said Cleo. "Are you sure you're going to be able to walk?"

"I've been practicing," said Quentin and gave her a wink. His eyelids shimmered with black glitter.

Alex, Cleo noticed with some alarm, was dressed entirely in Quentin's old boy clothes. Cleo met his eye and realized that he had been watching her register his outfit with satisfaction.

"Woof," she said and took a seat by the window behind them.

The bus had created the ideal combination of childhood nostalgia and adult revelry; an atmosphere of almost frenzied excitement pervaded it as guests passed bottles up and down the aisles and unsuccessfully attempted group sing-alongs to 1990s hits. Cleo found herself, unfortunately, sitting next to Guy, a French makeup artist and old friend of Frank's who had gotten so drunk at their wedding dinner, he'd wandered into the building's trash room and vomited down the chute.

"Hi Guy," she said, unable to resist pronouncing his name the American way, which she knew to be a particular peeve of his.

"Come on, it's *Guy* as in gui-llo-tine," he said. "How long we know each other now?"

"Long enough to know better."

She smiled, pressing her cheek against his. She was careful to breathe through her mouth, since Guy smoked like a true Frenchman: constantly. But to her surprise she smelled only shampoo. She hoped he would not ask after Frank. It was not yet public knowledge that they were no longer living together. The best tactic, she knew, was to get him talking about himself.

"You look great," she said.

"I know," he said. "I am sober almost six month now."

"Seriously?" Audrey craned around in her seat to look at him. "I thought the French were supposed to be able to drink and smoke the rest of us under the table."

"I used to say the same," said Guy. "But then I went on tour."

As the bus turned onto the FDR Highway, he told them about the four months he'd spent doing makeup for a major rock band on a year-long reunion tour through the States and Europe. The endless cycle of free booze and drugs that surrounded him, the bar fight in Amsterdam where he lost half his earlobe, the prostitute in Brussels who robbed him at knife point, and finally the time he'd woken up completely naked in a hotel hallway, with no idea what time it was, what room he was staying in, or even if he was in the right hotel. He staggered down the endless corridor, lost, naked, and panicked. Ahead of him he saw a light shining from the half-open door of a broom closet. As if in a trance, he walked toward the light. He opened the door. Inside, he found a white fluffy robe on a hanger. Inside, he found God.

"So that was it?" Audrey asked. "You put on a dressing gown and stopped doing drugs?"

"No." Guy shrugged. "I flew to Mexico to take ayahuasca and trip for three days. Then I stopped doing drugs."

"What was that like?"

"First," Guy said, holding up a tobacco-stained finger, "you see the color orange. Then"—he mimed an explosion either side of his head with his hands—"you realize you've never really loved."

"Wow," said Marshall. "One moment can change your life forever."

Quentin turned to look at Cleo and rolled his eyes.

"Now, I am addicted only to meditating," said Guy.

"Meditation as medication," said Audrey, evidently pleased with herself.

"*Exactement.*" Guy nodded. "My goal is to one day own only a loin-cloth and a singing bowl."

"Don't forget a toothbrush," said Quentin.

Cleo was silent, staring out of the window at the dark East River rushing past, the lights of Long Island City beyond, the art-deco Pepsi-Cola sign in its dramatic ruby-red script. She was thinking of the day she got out of the hospital. Frank had undressed her in the dark bathroom upstate, slipping her shirt over her uplifted arms as though she were a little girl. She'd put her hands on his shoulders as he'd knelt to pull her jeans off over her ankles and feet. She could feel the air whispering around her stitches. He slid off her underwear. She stepped out of them gingerly. Her body felt drained of all sex. She was back to being a child. He rested his forehead on the slope beneath her belly button. She took his skull in her hands, his lovely curly hair sprouting between her fingers. Devotional. That was the word for two bodies like that. They should have been more devoted; she understood that now.

"Cleo?" It was Quentin looking at her. "You okay?"

"I'm fine," she said. "Carsick maybe."

"I'm just checking, you know," he said. "Being a good friend."

She wanted to tell him that a really good friend wouldn't feel the need to point out what a good friend he was being to her all the time, but she let it go. Quentin turned back to Alex, whose yellow eyes had stayed fixed on him. Without looking at him, Quentin pulled a plastic bag from his pocket and slid it into Alex's lap. Inside were what looked like shards of ice. She could see, in her sliver of view between their seats, just the corner of Alex's mouth twisting into a smile.

"Look, there's Zoe!" said Audrey.

They were overtaking one of the other school buses heading to the party. Through the window they could see Zoe's beautiful curled head resting on the shoulder of an older Asian man wearing a suit. Their bus sped up, and she disappeared behind them.

"That girl is an enigma," said Audrey, shaking her head.

Quentin threw his arms above his head and shook out his hands.

"Are we there yet?" he yelled.

Audrey laughed. "You can't seriously be bored already."

"You know me," said Quentin. "I'd rather be crying in a limo than laughing on a bus."

———

Thirty minutes later they arrived at the entrance gates of the warehouse and parked near a large courtyard. Across the dark river the spiky Manhattan skyline winked at them. The revelers piled out and were shepherded up a walkway lined with burning torches toward two statuesque women holding clipboards. Either side of them was a line of stone-faced security guards. Each of them gave their names to the tall girls in front, all except Alex, who stood there staring defiantly at them.

"He's not coming in," the girl with the clipboard said.

"This is Danny's ex-girlfriend," Quentin said, pushing Cleo toward her. "He's her guest."

This was an exaggeration, but Cleo had slept with Danny on and off for over a year until, in what turned out to be the savviest move of his career, he began dating the daughter of one of the largest contemporary art gallery owners in New York. She brought her father to his graduate thesis show, and two years later Danny was the most commercially successful young artist in the city, selling a painting for a quarter of a million dollars when he was only twenty-six years old. But recently Danny's career had taken a turn, and a series of strong-selling but critically panned shows had invited murmurs that he was becoming the latest example of how success too early can ruin the integrity of an artist's career.

After Cleo had proven with a series of hastily pulled-up text messages that Danny had personally invited her, the clipboard girl grudgingly allowed them all to enter. They passed through to a cobbled dockyard lined by two large outdoor bars, along with food trucks and a photo station. In the center was an ice sculpture of Danny holding a bottle from one of the party's liquor sponsors. The sculpture was comically petite, the size of a child, with only a few of his signature dreads sprouting from his head.

"They couldn't splurge for life-size?" said Quentin, pointing at the sculpture. "I mean, they have gelato."

As Cleo looked around, a liquid sensation of failure surged through her. What had she been doing these past years? She was already so far behind. Danny's technique had been less developed than hers in school, yet he'd already achieved all this. She had done nothing, made nothing of herself.

"You know what I love about art parties?" said Quentin. "You can look around and see at least three people wearing black turtlenecks at any given time."

"And at least one ridiculous hat," said Audrey, as a man in a fez walked past.

"All right, let's test this theory," said Marshall. He craned around the crowd and then began laughing. "Yup, I've got three turtlenecks."

Cleo looked around and counted one, two . . . And there, in the third, was Anders. She scanned the people either side of him. He was alone. No Frank. He looked, impossibly, younger than she'd ever seen him before, slim and tanned. Typical, Cleo thought. He was pushing through the crowd toward her. Then he was pulling her into him, wrapping his arms around her back and bumping his lips against the crown of her head. The smell of him. She couldn't bear it. She pulled away. His arms fell limply to either side as a look of pained embarrassment passed over his face.

"I'm happy to see you," he said, turning to her friends to greet them in his clipped Danish accent. "Hi, hi."

"We were just seeing how many people in black turtlenecks we could count in this place," said Quentin.

"Well," said Anders, looking down at his torso as if only just realizing what it was clothed in. "You got me! What does it mean?"

"That you're a cliché," shot Quentin. "Just kidding."

Cleo felt the familiar dual sensation of pride and humiliation; pride in Quentin's protectiveness of her, humiliation in the snide way he went about demonstrating it.

"Have you ever noticed," Anders said, turning to Cleo, "that whenever an American says 'Just kidding,' they are never really kidding?"

"Hello, I'm Polish," said Quentin.

Anders took Cleo's arm as he spoke to Quentin. "I am going to borrow your friend now."

He pulled Cleo with him to a quiet area by the torches. They stood facing each other, firelight licking their faces. Up close, Cleo saw that beneath his suntan Anders's face was not younger looking, in fact, but grooved by exhaustion. The light of the fire did not reach his eyes.

"How are you?" he asked. "You look good."

"You too," she said. "Very . . . Californian."

"Ah yes," he said, rubbing his cheek. "I live near the beach now. I even surf sometimes."

"Jonah must love that," she said.

"Actually, Jonah has not come out yet." He looked down at his feet.

"Oh, I thought he—"

"It's not a problem." Anders waved his hand in front of him. "You know teenagers." He slid his phone in and out of his pocket nervously. "But I love it out there. The fresh air . . . everything. And, you know, I met someone."

"I heard," said Cleo.

In fact, she had seen. She'd found out about his new girlfriend through some ill-advised googling. She was gorgeous, of course, a model. There were two photos of them together, both from the same event for his magazine in LA. The first was outside with their hands interlaced, heads cocked slightly toward each other. Then they were inside the party, holding flutes of champagne, both caught mid-laugh. Cleo had sat curled on Audrey's sofa, bathed in the blue halo of light from her computer screen, the sound of Audrey and Marshall's lovemaking permeating softly through the walls, and clicked back and forth between the images of them smiling and laughing, laughing and smiling . . .

"Is she here?" asked Cleo.

"No, sadly she travels a lot for work," he said. "She's in the Bahamas right now."

Cleo gave him a thin smile. "Nice life."

"I am only here for the weekend, in fact," said Anders. "I had hoped to take Jonah to the movies tonight, but he wanted to see his friends, of course." He avoided her eyes and looked over her head, registering the presence of someone else he knew in the crowd. He nodded at whoever it was and mouthed a hello.

"Where's Frank?" she asked.

"Frank?" Anders refocused his attention on her. "He didn't think it would be appropriate, since Danny was your schoolmate."

He ran his hands through his hair. It was lighter now, streaked almost white in places by the sun.

"I see," said Cleo. She focused on keeping her expression as neutral as possible. The disappointment, it was so physical, she was worried her face might actually drain of color. She felt desperate to go home, to be alone again, without all this pretense. But where? She was a long way from any home.

"He thought you'd be relieved," said Anders.

"And you?" she asked, raising her head to meet his eye. "You didn't think you should stay away too?"

"I wanted to see you. I wanted to make sure you were okay."

"*Now* you care if I'm okay?"

"Come on, Cleo." He pulled his phone from his pocket again, unable to hold her gaze. "We're still friends, surely? I wanted to give you space, you know, to work out how you felt."

"Space?" she hissed. "You call never speaking to me again *space*?"

She had often imagined what it would be like to see Anders again. In her fantasies she was like metal, shiny and cold and impenetrable. But all her feelings, her stupid hurt feelings, kept bubbling to the surface.

"What was I meant to do?" asked Anders, raising his hands as if to shield himself. "You said you would leave him. You didn't leave him. So I . . . I guess I tried to move on."

Cleo wanted to say that she could not leave Frank without the assurance that Anders would be there for her on the other side, an assurance he could not give her when she asked. She hated herself for asking for it. She had been too afraid. And she really had believed that she could love Anders, although now she saw that she had simply clung to him because she couldn't see another way out. She hated to think about it.

She was the one in her twenties, she wanted to remind him. He and Frank were in their forties. They had the careers. They had the money. They had the citizenship, the stability, the power. In comparison, she had nothing but herself.

"I called you," was what she did say.

"I made what I thought was the best decision," said Anders. "Please try to understand my side of things. I've known Frank for twenty years."

A chain of people making their way toward the bar broke between them, yelling excitedly over their shoulders to each other. Anders stepped away from her to let them pass.

"You didn't even say goodbye," she said.

"I'm sorry, Cleo. I don't know what to say. I did what I thought was right."

Anders looked at her, and his face was filled with pity. He must think she was pathetic. She wanted to reach up and pull his expression away like a sheet of drawing paper, crumple it between her hands. She crossed her arms and backed away from him. There was nothing more to say. He reached forward to lightly touch her elbow.

"Cleo," he said softly.

In his mouth her name sounded like something falling, two bounces down a flight of stairs. *Cle-o.*

"What?"

He began to say something, appeared to think better of it.

"Don't be a stranger?" he said instead.

"Some of my best friends are strangers," she said, and walked back into the crowd.

She fought her way through the people surging toward the bars and walked into the first room of the warehouse. A coffin riddled with bullet holes spun in a slow orbit from a thick metal chain suspended above a mound of broken mirrors. She looked down and saw hundreds of fragments of her face reflected back, a sliver of cheek, of throat, of eye. Who was she? An artist who didn't make art. A wife without a husband. A child with no mother.

"There you are!" Quentin grabbed her arm. His eyes were glossy black orbs. "Have you seen Alex?"

Cleo shook her head. Quentin's grip was tight enough to bruise. She put her hand over his and pried his fingers away. "Are you okay?"

"Marvelous!" Quentin said in a British accent and threw his head back in a dramatic openmouthed laugh. He snapped his head forward, his face suddenly severe. His eyes reflected no light. "Need to find Alex."

"What did you take?" Cleo asked, but Quentin was backing away from her into the crowd. She kept sight of the back of his head all the way into the warehouse's main room before she blinked, and he disappeared into the swarm of bodies.

She passed a hallway where guests were delightedly ripping up the floorboards like scabs from skin. The dance floor was already packed, the crowd moving to a song Cleo didn't know. She could feel the bass pulling at the hairs on her arms, vibrating against her skin. She saw Audrey and Marshall bouncing together by the wall.

"Over here!" called Audrey. She passed her a bottle of water. "Want some? We put a couple of hits in it."

Yes, she wanted some. She wanted something that would roll through her like a flood, wash away whole years of her life. Those final hopeful months believing her mother was getting better. Gone. The night she met Frank, his smile, his compliments, his hand snaking its way under her dress to find a nest between her legs. Gone. Those weeks with Anders. Gone. Every man, in fact, who had burrowed his way inside her, kissed her and fucked her, come in her, on her. She wanted them out. She wanted a river heavy with men's bodies sucked out of her. She wanted death by flood.

She took the bottle and chugged, dribbles of water escaping from either side of her mouth.

"Whoa, steady," Marshall yelled. "This stuff is strong."

"Good."

She tossed the bottle back to him and pushed past them into the mass of dancers. She was being elbowed and shoved on all sides. Everyone felt taller than her. A man with a skull tattoo covering his shaved head grabbed her waist and began dancing with her, grinding his hips against hers. She steadied herself against him for a moment as he pulled her in closer, pushing his damp face into her neck. She grabbed his arms, then dug her nails into him as hard as she could.

"What the fuck!" he yelped, thrusting her away from him. She could hear him yelling as she slipped back into the crowd. *Crazy bitch.*

She found her way to the edge and ducked into a side room filled with tall glass candles painted with images of the Virgin Mary. The whole room glowed yellow. And there, at the center of the light, was Danny Life. He was wearing all white, a tailored boiler suit and pristine leather work boots. With him was an art critic Cleo recognized. He was eagerly holding a recording device in front of Danny, though he appeared to be doing most of the talking.

"To what extent is your work autobiographical?" the critic asked.

"What do you mean, autobiographical?"

"You know," said the critic. "How have your own experiences with street violence informed your work? Do you—"

"Listen, man," Danny interrupted. "I grew up in Pound Ridge. My mother's an epidemiologist. Look it up if you don't know what that is."

"But the guns . . ."

Cleo stood behind him and mimed shooting herself in the head with her eyes crossed. Danny's handsome face cracked into a smile. His white teeth glowed.

"If you'll excuse me." He pushed past the critic and gave Cleo a hug. "Cleo the cat. I hoped I'd see you."

"Look at you." Cleo smiled. "The hottest thing in town."

"That's me." He laughed. "How are you?"

The critic gave Cleo a withering look and skulked away.

"Homeless." She shrugged. "Unemployed. Single. You?"

She could feel something inside her coming loose, like the first cracks in the walls before an earthquake.

"Shit, man. Doing better than you, that's for sure."

Cleo laughed. Danny wasn't prone to sympathy, something she'd always liked about him. *Fondness* was the best word she could think of to describe what they felt for each other. Fondness was warm but not tepid, the color of amber, more affectionate than friendship but less complicated than love. Back during their school days, they'd lie together twisted in his sheets, flicking ash from their joints into a Coke can by his bed, and chat comfortably about their work, the artists they were researching, the other people they were sleeping with.

"You seriously homeless?" asked Danny. "I just got asked to nominate someone for this residency in Rome. You want to do it?"

Cleo didn't know what she wanted. She was saved from answering by a girl wearing a leather bra and pants running toward Danny and jumping on his back.

"Love you, Danny," she screeched, kissing the side of his face.

"Love you too, babe," Danny said. "But I'm going to need you to get off me now."

The girl fell away from him, laughing, and went to join her friends taking pictures. Danny looked at Cleo and took her hand.

"You want to come with me? I need a break from these people. They gave me my own trailer. It's crazy."

The trailer was lined with thick carpet and contained a large velvet sofa and vanity table holding rows of liquor and champagne bottles. Overheard, a chandelier winked at her. She could feel its light like feathers on her skin. She felt as though her blood had been carbonated. Danny looked at her eyes and cracked up.

"You on something?" he asked.

Cleo nodded.

"You want a drink?"

Cleo nodded again. She could feel the glow from the chandelier warming her from the inside. She reached up and touched one of the crystal teardrops. A rainbow of light swung across her face.

"How do you feel?" he asked.

She closed her eyes.

"Groovy," she said. "We should use that word more. *Grooooovy.*"

"Here."

He walked over and unhooked a crystal from its strand on the chandelier. Very gently, he removed the stud from her right earlobe and pushed the crystal's wire through the hole. She could feel the sudden tug on her lobe as he pulled his hands away, the unfamiliar weight by her check.

"Now you look groovy too." He took a bottle of champagne and drank straight from the neck, then passed it to her. "You hungry?"

They sat on the sofa and Danny passed her the largest bag of potato chips she'd ever seen. He took a handful and crunched on them.

He shrugged. "Sponsors."

"This is bigger than your ice sculpture," Cleo said.

They began to laugh, and the laughter gained momentum until they couldn't stop, helpless tearful peals, pulling all breath from their bodies. Each time one looked at the other, it started up again. Cleo's stomach hurt from it. It had been so long since she'd laughed like that. Once the last spasms had subsided, Danny wiped his eyes and looked at her seriously.

"So," he said. "You think I sold out?"

Cleo touched the chandelier pendant hanging from her ear and regarded him. "I think you sold," she said.

"That's the same thing, according to them." He nodded his head to the trailer door, then let it fall back on the couch. "Everyone wants me to be the next fucking Basquiat. Basquiat surrounded himself with white people, then killed himself. God help me if I end up like Basquiat, man."

"I'd start by avoiding intravenous drugs," Cleo said. "And white people."

"Easier said than done," said Danny, nodding toward her.

"True," said Cleo.

She took another pull of champagne and passed the bottle back to him. He took a gulp and continued.

"Sometimes it's like they *want* you to be high all the time. My agent would shoot me up herself if she thought I'd sell better."

"At least you have all this," said Cleo. "Now you just have to decide what to do with it."

Danny nodded slowly and ate another handful of chips.

"And what about you?" he asked. "You showing anywhere? You know, you were one of the best in our program. All the teachers thought so. I remember your final show. It was . . . majestic, man." He took a swig. "Fucking majestic," he repeated and burped.

Cleo turned her body to face him. He had scattered chip crumbs all down his front. She reached over to brush them off. Danny opened his mouth to say something, then grabbed her wrist. She followed his gaze. It was her scar, protruding from her sleeve like an exclamation point. She saw his eyes widen to absorb its length. Cleo pulled her forearm gently away from his grasp. Danny looked at her, and his eyes were dark and liquid, incredibly tender.

"You want to talk about it?" he asked.

Cleo bowed her head. Very gently, he kissed her forehead. They stayed like that, his lips resting against the line of her hair, for what felt like a long time. He pulled away slowly.

"Come on," Danny said. "There's something I want us to do."

He took her hand and pulled her out of the trailer and back into the party. They fought their way through the main room and out into the hallway. Danny picked up a wooden plank from a pile the guests had torn up from the floor and motioned for her to do the same, then led her back out to the courtyard. He walked toward his ice sculpture and, in one swift movement, walloped its head from the body with the wooden plank. He turned to her and grinned.

"Your turn."

Cleo took the plank in both hands and thwacked it into the sculpture's torso. The reverberation of the impact shuddered up her arms. The top half of the body cracked off and skidded across the cobblestones. Shards of ice flew like sparks around her. Danny knocked the remaining legs and feet to the ground and continued to smash them into smaller pieces with his plank. People were gathering around to watch and take pictures.

"Is this part of the show?" she heard someone ask.

Danny pushed through the crowd, still clutching his plank overhead. He ran toward the warehouse and struck the first window he saw. Glass shattered around his feet and onto the people gathering behind him.

"Dancing fucking star!" he yelled.

The energy passed through the crowd like an electric current. Somebody climbed into the taco truck and began hurling food from the counter window. A burrito exploded against the warehouse wall with a splat. Bodies were colliding and ricocheting off each other, everyone jostling to be near Danny, the anarchic pied piper. A burning torch got pushed over as a throng of partygoers surged forward into the warehouse. Cleo turned in the opposite direction.

She saw him from behind. Tall Anders, handsome Anders, shiny Anders for whom life's difficulties slipped away like a silk dress sliding off a hanger. Someone was calling her name. She didn't care. He thought she was Cleo the china doll, Cleo who cracked and broke under the pressure, Cleo who was hollowed out. Not anymore. She dropped the plank and picked up a silver ice bucket someone had just plucked a bottle of vodka from. She hoisted the bucket onto her shoulder, felt its weight tilt backward for one teetering moment, then pushed all her force behind it to tip it over Anders's head. Icy water sloshed over his shoulders. The bucket landed perfectly over his head like a dunce cap. Ice cubes skidded across the floor around their feet. He scrambled to lift the bucket and turned to look at her, his hair dark and dripping, a look of profound shock on his blanched face. Someone grabbed her from behind.

"Jesus, Cleo." Zoe was grasping her shoulders, searching her face. "Have you gone nuts?"

Security swarmed around them. Anders had thrown the bucket to the side and was bending at the waist with his hands on his knees, trying to catch his breath. His eyes did not leave Cleo. He looked at her through a slash of hair. She could feel her hands being pulled behind her, her wrists pinched together. Then she was being lowered to the ground, her legs knocked out from beneath her.

"Let her go!" yelled Zoe.

Cleo's cheek was against the cold cobblestones. The dull pulse of a heavy bass traveled through the ground under her ear. She lay completely limp, drained of all fight. Her wrists were being zipped together with plastic cuffs. Her scar. She hoped they did not see her scar. Above her was shouting, the clanging of metal, footsteps rushing past. Electric riffs of guitar serrated the air. A crowd was chanting Danny's name. Somewhere a girl was screaming for Danny, out of time with the others, over and over in a long, pained wail.

Cleo closed her eyes. When she opened them again, Zoe's face was beside her own. She had scrambled onto the ground next to her, so they were at eye level. She put her hand against Cleo's cheek and made little hushing noises. Above them, a security guard was telling her to get up. His voice sounded like stainless steel.

"Just breathe, Cleo," Zoe said. "I won't leave you. I won't go anywhere. You're safe."

Cleo smiled into Zoe's gold-flecked eyes. Everything she had ever wanted to hear from a man was hers from the mouth of a girl. Zoe's eyes were the color of Lyle's Golden Syrup. Cleo had adored it as a child and poured it on everything. The logo was old-fashioned, even by English standards, an illustration of a dead lion surrounded by a swarm of bees. Underneath it were the words "Out of the strong came forth sweetness." That was what Zoe was like. A lion filled with bees.

"Beautiful strong Zoe," said Cleo.

Zoe's eyes creased into a smile.

"Beautiful strong Cleo," she said.

"What the fuck is happening here?"

Danny's white boots appeared in Cleo's eye line. Not one scuff. Zoe scrambled to her feet.

"Sir, this woman just assaulted a man." That hard male voice again. "We had to restrain her."

"Assaulted?" said Zoe. "She poured a bucket of ice on him. Big fucking deal."

"Who are you?" said Danny.

"Her sister-in-law. Who are *you*?"

"I'm Danny Fucking Life. Wait a minute, her sister-in-law's a *sister*? I thought she married some old white dude?"

"I did," said Cleo into the ground.

"Sir, we're going to have to ask you to step aside so we can detain this woman."

"Look, that's not happening. I hired you guys. You're not the police."

"She could have injured—"

"No, she could not have." Anders's voice sounded flinty and resigned. "Just let her go."

Cleo was lifted to her feet. She looked at Anders. Anders looked at her. She had cradled that face in her hands, kissed its eyelids, pressed its cheek to hers, circled the dark cave of its mouth with her tongue. She knew his face. He knew hers. There was no undoing that. Anders was opening his mouth to speak when the art critic from earlier ran toward them with a wild look in his eyes.

"The warehouse is burning!" he yelled. "The warehouse is on fire!"

Behind him the back end of the building was indeed funneling a black cloud of smoke into the air. Cleo saw a single orange flame lick the black sky.

"Oh shit," said Danny, and ran toward his life's work.

———

Twenty minutes later, the party guests were all gathered at the water's edge on a bank of rubble and rocks. The fire trucks' lights illuminated their faces in flashes of scarlet and blue. The fire had been quickly contained, but everyone had been evacuated nonetheless. Of course the drama of this would only make the party more legendary. Marshall went to search for Alex and Quentin in the crowd, leaving Cleo standing between Audrey and Zoe. They looked out across the inky East River to Manhattan. A gray blanket a fireman had inexplicably provided was slung over all three of their shoulders.

"Guess those paintings he made with gasoline aren't going to survive this," said Audrey, shivering in her tiny dress. "What do you think Danny's going to do?"

Zoe shrugged. "Call it performance art?"

Audrey laughed.

"Start again," said Cleo.

They watched smoke somersault across the water.

"So," said Zoe. She put her arm around Cleo under the blanket. "You and Anders?"

Cleo looked at her feet and nodded.

"Girl, I've been there," said Zoe.

"Me too," said Audrey. "That man has had a bucket of ice coming for a long time."

All three of them laughed. Cleo nodded at an Asian man in a business suit walking toward them with a hesitant expression.

"I think someone is looking for you," she said.

"Who is he?" asked Audrey.

"Just a new friend," said Zoe, laughing, and ran to meet him.

He whispered something in her ear, and she smiled.

"Enigma," said Audrey, shaking her head. "I should probably go find Marshall. You okay here?"

Cleo nodded and turned back to the water. The sirens flashed on, bathing the river in light. Red. Manhattan was stretched out before her like a handful of jewels. Blue. The city that never wanted you to leave. Red. So it offered you everything, anything. Blue. It was time to go.

CHAPTER SIXTEEN

August

Not so miraculously, I no longer have a job. I was not, however, "invited to leave," which is a step up from last time. In fact, I invited myself. Somehow, coming into the city every day to write about condo developments, body scrubs, and energy drinks no longer seems so important. My father is sick. Sicker than sick, he is dying. First he fractured his hip slipping on the linoleum floor of That Home. Then he got pneumonia. Parkinson's doesn't kill people, his doctors keep reminding us. Everything else does.

*

My favorite nurse at the hospital is Stacy from Trinidad. She wears colors like kiwi green and neon fuchsia and tells me all the best nurse jokes. *What did the nurse say when she found a rectal thermometer in her pocket? Some asshole has my pen!*

*

My mother is skimming through one of the magazines in the waiting room while my father does yet another round of tests.

"None of this makes sense to me," she says.

I assume she's talking about his illness, the precariousness of life, health and wealth and all its implications, but she points to a page of ads in the magazine.

"What are these even for?" she asks.

"Oh, that's easy," I say. "This one's for PMS. This one's for a fancy watch. And this one's for an old woman having a seizure."

"You have a gift," she says.

"Less than a year in advertising, baby."

*

Frank and I haven't spoken since I left the agency. It's been three months. I dream about him still, I'll admit. Last night, for instance, I dreamed he was brushing my hair. My head was resting in his lap, and I felt happy. Then I raised a hand to my scalp and felt only skin. I looked down at the floor, and my hair was scattered all around us like seaweed. When I sat up, Frank was gone. I was bald and alone. I'm no Carl Jung, but that feels inauspicious.

*

My father still has all his hair, at least. That is something I'm proud of. You'd be amazed how rare a full head of hair or set of teeth is around here. I hope his teeth are still intact, too. I guess if he ever smiles again, I'll know.

*

I'm in the living room when my mother calls something from the kitchen that I miss.

"What's that?" I yell from the sofa.

"What did you say?" she yells back.

"What!"

"What?"

"What!"

"What?"

"Never mind!"

*

I send the first two episodes of *Human Garbage* to my agent in LA. Amazingly, she never fired me, even after I called the showrunner of the clairvoyant cat show a cunt. She has, however, yet to respond. I guess a show about two parasites called Scrip and Scrap living on a garbage heap at the end of the world doesn't have the same commercial appeal as the show she wanted me to write for, which was about a hard-hitting yet sexually available lawyer having an affair with her drug dealer.

*

I step outside the hospital for some fresh air. All around me, old people tip forward in their wheelchairs and puff on their cigarettes with grim determination. If they want to convince teenagers not to smoke, they should really make them hang out here. Just try to still find smoking sexy after seeing a liver-spotted eighty-year-old shakily unhook the nasal tubes of his oxygen tank so he can light one up.

*

Stacy trundles by with a tray of catheters. Today she is wearing mango orange.

"How you doing, baby?"

"Oh, I'm fine," I say. "How's your son?"

"He has three girlfriends." She rolls her eyes. "Tell me, how did I give birth to my ex-husband?"

I laugh.

"Your father in surgery?" she asks.

I nod and feel my eyes prickle.

"You got to distract yourself," she says. "He don't want you sitting here worrying."

"I know," I say. "I will."

"Good girl."

She gives my shoulder a squeeze. "What do transplant nurses hate most?" she asks.

"What?"

"Rejection!"

*

I take Stacy advice and go down to the gift shop to find something to read. I flip open a fashion magazine. Right at the top of the masthead is the name of Frank's friend Anders. I think of his handsome face at the office holiday party, winking in time to the Christmas tree lights. It seems absurd to me now, standing in the harsh fluorescence of the hospital gift shop, that I ever knew such a person. I put the magazine back on the shelf.

*

My father wakes up from surgery. He is, we've been informed, in tremendous pain. I hover at his bedside, watching him, but he can't see me. He opens and closes his mouth in dumb protest. His eyes roll around the ceiling. His neck is sinuously thin, it cannot lift his head, but his mouth keeps working, reaching for words. He looks like the ancient tortoise my kindergarten class had as a pet; we used to hold a rose petal just out of reach of his mouth and watch as he grasped, mutely, determinedly, for it again and again.

My mother stands up and leans over his face, so he can see her. She strokes the creases between his eyebrows with her thumb and says "There, there." She kisses his temple. Tears are leaking out of his eyes into his huge soft ears. I leave the room.

*

"As long as there's chicken parmigiana in the freezer," a lady says into her phone as she walks past me, "everything will be okay."

*

My father is asleep. The night nurse wears a crucifix around her neck, crucifix studs in her ears, and a diamond ring in the shape of a crucifix.

318

"Do you think she's *crossing* the line?" I say to myself.

The pun machine marches on.

*

Our noisy dishwasher has finally kicked the bucket, so my mother and I are doing the dishes by hand. She washes, I dry.

"Why do you still look after him?" I ask. "You haven't been married for years."

My mother glances at me out of the corner of her eye and keeps scrubbing. I nudge her elbow. She puts the sponge down.

"When someone is sick like your father has been sick," she says, "it's a lot of responsibility. His family have never been much help, as you know, and I don't think it's fair for the burden to fall on you and Levi."

"Wait a minute," I say, casting around the room. "Has Levi been here this whole time? I must need a stronger pair of glasses."

"Fine, it's a lot for *you*."

"I appreciate that," I say. "But I'm fine, Ma, really."

"People who feel the need to say 'I'm fine' are never fine, sweetheart," she says.

*

My father can't talk, can't move, can't read or write, but he can hear. I have read him half of *Moby-Dick*, skipping some of the longer sections about whale anatomy because who has the time? In fact, we do. Time moves so slowly in this hospital, it is like we are given a bonus day with every day. There is a line in Shakespeare, I forget which play, where a character is described as having "a face as long as Sunday." That's what it's like here. Every day is Sunday.

*

Jacky comes to visit me. Since I live at the hospital now, there is nowhere to entertain her but the hallway by the vending machines. We sit on two plastic chairs and smile at one another. The machines emit a low hum beside us like they're meditating.

"Here you go, hon." She hands me a pita sandwich from my favorite falafel spot in the city. "Eat. So, how's your pops doing? How are *you* doing?"

"I'm fine. He's . . ." I shrug.

"Did you know my dad died when I was in college?"

"I didn't. I'm sorry."

I stare at the bag without opening it.

"Brain aneurysm. Just dropped dead one day. Only fifty years old, poor fucker."

"Do you miss him?"

Jacky shook her head and smiled. "He wasn't around enough to miss. That was what I found the hardest. I wasn't close to my dad, and then he died. End of story. At least while he was alive, there was this hope that one day that could change. And then that hope was gone, you know? That's what I grieved, I guess."

I nod. We listen to the low hum of the vending machines some more.

"My father left my mother for a lesbian," I say.

Jacky nods without judgment.

"Eat," she says.

I unwrap the silver foil and take a bite. It tastes like Frank. This was our favorite spot. Jacky regards me with her usual perspicacity.

"They split up, you know," she says. "She went to Italy on a painting fellowship."

I choke a little on my mouthful of falafel.

"Not that it's of any interest to you, right?"

I eat in silence until Jacky claps her hands in exasperation. "Just call him," she says. "Stop this pining, both of you."

"He's not pining for me."

"And how would you know?"

"It's too late for all that."

"Pssh. Nothing's too late when you're young."

"I'm thirty-seven. And a half."

"Hon, that's *young.*"

Inexplicably, my face becomes wet. Jacky pulls a tissue from her sleeve and hands it to me. She rubs my back and makes gentle *shhh*ing noises. I marvel, once again, at how prepared Jacky is for all situations, big and small.

*

Stacy and I are doing my father's circulation exercises, bending each of his legs at the knee, rolling his ankles, flexing his arms, circling his wrists. I perform each task with gentle gusto. The most dreaded word I've heard in here is *bedsores*.

"Have you seen a lot of people die?" I ask.

"Mm–hm," she says.

"And does it make you sad?"

"Mm–hm."

"What do you do not to feel sad?" I ask.

"I let myself feel sad."

*

What do you give to a man who has everything?

Antibiotics.

*

Another dinner for two, another night of washing dishes.

"How come you never remarried?" I ask my mother.

"You know, there's a study that says widowed women are the happiest demographic."

"You're not widowed. Yet."

"I wanted to try something new."

"Being a divorcée?"

"I think I'd call it being my own person."

"Okay. So is the study right? Did you get to be happy?"

"Well, I got to be the talk of the synagogue for a good few years until the rabbi's son came out of the closet. That was something."

"Fuck those people," I say.

"Watch it," says my mother. "Those are your people."

"*You're* my people."

She squeezes my hand.

"Hang the dish towels out to dry, or they'll smell," she says.

*

I switch to reading my father poetry. I read from the books I found on his old bookshelf—Rudyard Kipling, W. H. Auden, Wallace Stevens. And, because those are all dead white men, I slip him some from my bookshelf—Anne Sexton, Terrance Hayes, Tracy K. Smith. It's never too late to expand your horizons, I figure.

*

My father is being washed, so I take a break from reading to sit in the hallway. A white-haired woman shuffles past me, trundling her IV along beside her. She looks me up and down.

"I'm trying to pass gas," she says. "Do you mind?"

*

Nobody's in the hospital rec room, so I grab the remote from behind the TV and flick through channels. There's a lot of life still happening out there, I see. A twenty-one-year-old got a million-dollar book advance and spent the money without writing the book. Health insurance rates have reached an all-time high. *People*'s Most Beautiful Person of the Year is a dog. A Hollywood couple's divorce has turned ugly. There's a new reason not to eat cheese.

*

I need to make money. I need to write today. I need to clean the bathroom. I need to eat something. I need to quit sugar. I need to cut my hair. I need to call Verizon. I need to savor the moment. I need to find the library card. I need to learn to meditate. I need to try harder. I need to get that stain out. I need to find better health insurance. I need to discover my signature scent. I need to strengthen and tone. I need to be present in the moment. I need to learn French. I need to be easier on myself. I need to buy organizational storage units. I need to call back. I need to develop a relationship with a God of my understanding.

I need to buy eye cream. I need to live up to my potential. I need to lie back down.

*

"Right," says my mother. "You're going out."

I'm dozing on one of the hospital hallway chairs, a pack of Fritos open on my chest. She gives my legs an indelicate kick.

"It's not good for you, moping around in here all day and night," she says.

"Ma, I'm not *moping*," I say. "My father's dying."

"Yes, and he'll still be dying tomorrow. Here—" She crunches a wad of cash into my palm. "Go into the city. Meet a friend. See a Broadway show. Just be anywhere but here, please."

"But Ma—"

"Good night and good luck!"

My mother turns on her heel and walks away.

"I don't even like Broadway shows!" I yell after her.

"Good! Night! And! Good! Luck!" she shouts over her shoulder.

*

I take the PATH train into the city. Somebody has thrown up at the far end of the carriage. Vomit on the train is an event usually confined to major holidays like Saint Patrick's Day, or at least a long weekend. I already miss the clinical asepsis of the hospital, where all rebellions of the body are accounted for and hidden.

*

I get off the train at Sixth Avenue and stand on the corner. In the past year, the bookstore has closed down and the burger joint's been turned into a juice bar. There's a strung-out couple with a pit bull begging for change outside the health food store, but even they felt the need to specify that they're vegan on their cardboard sign. I don't mind. I have no nostalgia for old New York, with its hookers, heroin addicts, and constant threat of robbery or rape. I'm happy to sacrifice fast food and hardcover books for general personal safety, which I guess makes me about as uncool as they come.

*

I wander south toward the basketball courts near West Fourth. I have, I realize, nowhere to go and no one to see. I pass the underground karaoke bar on Cornelia I went to with a gang from the office a few months back. Myke revealed himself to have a beautiful baritone and performed a rendition of Tom Jones's "It's Not Unusual" that made Jacky and I just kill ourselves laughing. I half expect to find them there when I step inside, but the bar is quiet. What the hell, I think, and book myself a private room.

*

Drinking a margarita out of what looks like a fishbowl and singing three Stevie Nicks songs in a row. Just try to tell me I don't know how to have a good time.

*

Back outside, a woman bums a light off a man and looks him up and down.
"Your shirt is telling me you live in Brooklyn," she says.

*

I'm trying to decide if it's late enough to satisfy my mother or if I should kill another hour getting a foot massage at one of the places on Eighth Street. I enjoy any form of massage that doesn't require nudity.

I'm looking up to check what street I'm on when a taxi passes. Inside it is Frank. He's in profile, leaning forward to say something to the driver. It is just a flash. The taxi slides past the green light, and he is gone. It takes everything in me not to drop to all fours and chase the cab across town like a dog let loose.

*

I sit on the PATH train and try not to think about Frank. This is impossible. I try to focus, instead, on listing all the different types of cheese I know off the top of my head. Camembert. Gouda. Swiss. Cheddar. Manchego . . . Could he really be pining for me? But if he was, why wouldn't he tell me that Cleo had moved? Maybe he thinks I don't care?

How could he think I don't care? Provolone. Feta. Stilton. Mozzarella . . . I didn't even say goodbye to him the day I left the agency. But he knew how to contact me . . . Brie. Pecorino. Ricotta. American. He doesn't think of me, or he would have reached out. This whole thing is in my head. Pepper jack.

★

Not satisfied with my romp into the city, my mother insists I accompany her to her bonsai class. The teacher is dressed like an ancient boy scout, with his socks pulled tight over his knees and shorts cinched at his belly button. His only teaching aid is a piece of paper covered in sketches of variously shaped bonsai held shakily in front of him. He has the tendency to say "This is what we call . . ." about the most obvious things—*This is what we call a leaf*—but terms like *ramifications* and *apical bud*, apparently, need no additional explanation.

★

"So what did you think?" asks my mother on the drive home. "Bet you'll never look at a bonsai tree the same way again, eh?"

"This is what we call a waste of my time," I say, gesturing to the car, this conversation, the state of New Jersey, the entire world.

"And this," says my mother, gesturing to me, "is what we call an asshole."

★

My brother Levi comes down from upstate.

"Man, I hate hospitals," he says, scuffing his heels against the linoleum floors.

"This one's not so bad," I say. "The nurses are nice, and they have a TV room."

"Ellie," he says, "it's a dump. Dad deserves better than this."

I have the urge to punch him swiftly in the neck, but I restrain myself. It was typical Levi, artfully sidestepping any responsibility, then showing up last-minute to offer a thoughtful critique.

"That's great feedback, Levi," I say. "You want us to write a Yelp review or something?"

Levi gives me an outraged look.

"Did Mom tell you I got banned from Yelp?" he says. "I *specifically* told her not to."

*

I'm reading to my father from one of his dog-eared volumes of collected poems when I stop at a page faintly marked with pencil. He has under-lined two stanzas of a Derek Walcott poem very finely, almost tentatively, as though trying not to muss up the page.

Days I have held,
days I have lost,
days that outgrow, like daughters,
my harboring arms.

Next to them is a faded check mark. A restrained little check. My heart.

*

I can't sleep, so I'm up late watching a documentary about Middle Americans and their battle with crippling methamphetamine addictions. The man currently being interviewed has dry red sores all over his face that he picks at absently, almost tenderly, as he speaks.

"I never had a real birthday," he says. "No presents or nothing. My parents didn't care. But on meth I can have a birthday whenever I want. I can have my birthday seven days a week."

*

Levi is playing his new solo album *Table for One, Not by the Window* loudly over the speakers in the living room.

"Turn that racket off!" yells my mother.

He turns the volume dial down, not all the way, but enough that the house is no longer vibrating.

"My eardrums, good grief," says my mother, collapsing onto the eating couch.

"It's not racket," says Levi.

"It is the definition of racket," says my mother.

"Listen," says Levi. "When the first radio programs came to India during British rule, people would gather from all over and sit together and listen to English radio shows. It was the first time a lot of them had heard Western music, basically ever. After the programs were over, there would be long periods of white noise, just static. And the Indians would all stay and listen to that as well."

"Your point?" asks my mother.

"They'd never heard it before, so to them that was music too."

"So?" says my mother.

"So, don't you see that it's all just *perspective*, Ma? Our white noise was their music. Your racket is my masterpiece."

"That's a cool fact, Levi," I say diplomatically. "About the Indians."

"You're going to have to travel a lot farther than India to find someone who thinks that's a masterpiece," says my mother.

*

He died.

*

Outside the hospital I wait for my mother and Levi to arrive. Next to me, an elderly woman wrapped in a pink blanket despite the heat sucks on her cigarette between great hacking coughs.

"Can I bum one of those?" I ask.

"Trade you for a dollar," she says.

"I don't have a dollar," I say. "My father just died."

She looks at me from under her wiry eyebrows.

"In that case," she says, "no."

*

My mother has driven over to speak to my father's brother. Levi is upstairs on the phone with his girlfriend. I sit in the garden and watch the birds dart around the feeder. Today is almost done. The sky is apricot with golden clouds. A chorus of grasshoppers surrounds me. The earth is alive. I am alive. I wait to feel whatever I'm meant to feel, but nothing comes.

*

I practice ways of telling people the news. He is no longer with us. He has departed. He's six feet under. He's deceased. He passed away. He croaked. He rests in peace. He is no longer of this world. He went to meet his maker. He bought the farm. He's with the big guy in the sky. He's pushing up daisies. He expired. He's dead as a doornail. He kicked the bucket. He's no more. He's been reincarnated, we don't know as what, but we're hoping anything but a Jets fan.

*

"The rabbi called," Levi says. "He wants to know why we're not sitting a week of shiva."

"What business is it of his?" I say.

"I'll deal with it," says my mother.

"What are you going to say?" asks Levi.

"I'm going to say, 'Who has the energy for all that sitting?'" she says.

"What if he disagrees?" I ask.

My mother shrugs. "So what?"

"That's it?" says Levi. "Ten years of Hebrew school, and it comes to that? So what?"

"Let me tell you something," says my mother. "Those are two of the most powerful words in the English language. Right between them is a free and happy life."

*

My father has been buried. I'm in the garage looking for birdseed for my mother. I clamber over piles of life's detritus. Boxes of school yearbooks. A rusty stationary bike. A vase Levi made in middle school. Finally I see a bag of birdseed on the top shelf.

I'm just reaching up for it when I trip over some electrical cord and skid my knees against the cement floor. I'm on all fours. Pain shoots through me. I grab the baseball bat and use it to prop myself back up. Then I start hitting. I pummel a cardboard box filled with holiday decorations. I thwack the stationary bike. I hit a deflated soccer ball like

a piñata. I hit the metal door of the garage until it dents. It sends rever-
berations through the walls that are so strong, Levi's vase wobbles and
falls off the shelf. It shatters on the floor just as Levi appears in the
doorway. He looks at the vase, then at the bat, then at me.

"Birdseed," I say.

*

I find Levi crouched on the basement floor, gluing his vase back together.

"God, Levi," I say. "I'm sorry. I didn't realize you cared about this."

He looks up at me, a shard of vase in his hand. "I don't." He shrugs.
"I'm doing kintsugi."

"What?"

"Kintsugi," he says. "It's the Japanese art of mending broken pottery."

"Again, what?"

"They use a special gold lacquer, so the mended pot becomes more
beautiful than before it was broken."

"But you're just using superglue," I say.

"Yeah," says Levi. "But the principle still stands."

I sit down on the floor across from him. "How do you know all this
stuff?"

"What stuff?"

"About India and Japan and everything. You've never left America."

"I've been to Canada."

"Okay."

Levi looks up at me from the piece he's gluing distractedly. "All day
I sit behind the hot food counter," he says. "And I read."

I nod. "You really think the vase will be more beautiful now?"

"Oh yeah," he says. "More character."

"Good," I say.

Levi continues gluing with quiet concentration. His large, knobby
hands are just like my father's.

"People are like this too, you know," he says eventually. "We break.
We put ourselves back together. The cracks are the best part. You don't
have to hide them."

"You really believe that?" I say.

"Mm-hm," he says, without looking up. "Believe it. See it in you."

"This is very after-school special of you, Levi," I say.

"What can I say," he says. "I'm a sentimental motherfucker."

⋆

I'm trying to write another episode of *Human Garbage* when an email pops up on my screen. I almost fall off my seat. Just seeing his name feels like I've been punched in the vagina.

Dear E,

Jacky told me your father passed away. Please know how sorry I was to hear it. I remember you talking about him and he sounded like a good man. I know you will miss him. I wish I could be there to comfort you because . . . Well, Jesus, Eleanor, I miss you.

Please let me see you again.

F.

⋆

It's the day of the shiva and half the synagogue is coming over. My mother and I wake up early to finish setting out the bagels, gefilte fish, cream cheese, and an array of other beige foods.

"They're not going to think it's weird we're holding it here?" I ask. "At his ex-wife's house?"

"What did I tell you about what other people think?" asks my mother.

"'So what?'" I say.

"Exactly."

⋆

Levi's girlfriend has come down for the day. It seems there are a couple of things Levi neglected to tell us about her. First, that she is a very small Korean woman, which I guess isn't something that necessarily needs to be mentioned. Second, that she is pregnant, which I feel is probably higher on the list.

"Ma, Eleanor," says Levi. "This is Min."

CLEOPATRA AND FRANKENSTEIN

Gobsmacked. That is the only word I can think of to describe my mother's face.

"It's such a pleasure to meet you," says Min. "Do you have a place I can plug in my curling iron?"

*

That guy I went on a date with, my mother's friend's broker's son, is here in my home, along with my mother's friend and the broker. None of this is good news.

"Mayhismemorybeablessingareyoustillsingle," says my mother's friend, just like that, without even a breath, then smears her lipstick on my cheek.

*

The broker's son comes and finds me later, looking as smug as ever.

"Sorry about your dad," he says.

"Thanks," I say.

"He was pretty old, right?" he says.

"Not really," I say. "Late sixties."

"That's old by some standards," he says.

"Right," I say.

"So," he says. "You still wishing you could cut off men's penises?"

"Not all men," I say. "Just the rapists."

"My mistake," he says. "That's much more reasonable."

"You should really learn to listen," I say.

"And you should probably learn to filter," he says.

"Okay," I say. "Good night."

It is not yet noon.

*

My father's younger brother, Bernie, stumbles over. Every family has a drunk. Bernie is ours. As a child, I was charmed by him. He smelled of peach schnapps and pulled quarters from behind my ears. Now I feel less generously inclined.

"Elly Belly, how are you?" he slurs.

"Half orphaned," I say. "But holding up. How are you?"

"Psssh," he says. "Orphaned? My parents survived the camps. *They* knew a thing or two about orphans."

My mother rushes past, holding a tray of baked kosher salami, and gives me a knowing look. "Just keep offering him seltzer," she mutters.

"There she goes," says Bernie, waving a hand loosely in her direction. "Busy, busy, bzzz bzzz." He leans conspiratorially toward me. I can smell the warm, yeasty scent of beer on his breath.

"Can I tell you something?" he says. "A secret."

"Must you?" I ask.

"I'm weird." He shrugs. "You've probably noticed I'm a little weird."

I give a vague sort of head nod.

"Well, *I* always knew I was weird," he says. "And now I know why. The doctors told me."

"They did, did they?" I look around the room to see if I can drag my mother back, but she has disappeared into the kitchen. Bernie pulls me in closer.

"I have an extra female chromosome," he says. "Just found out. Me! Six four! Strong as an ox. But it explains a lot, it does."

"Right," I say. "Wow."

"Mmm," he says. "Freaky, eh?"

I manage a nod.

"I have an appointment on the tenth to find out more," he says.

"So, tomorrow."

"On the tenth."

"Yes, the tenth is tomorrow."

"Tomorrow, you say? Then I'll know more very soon indeed," he says with satisfaction.

"Well, good luck with the doctor." I am trying to drift away.

"It explains a lot," he says again. "To be sure."

With a swift, snakelike motion, he thrusts his head toward mine and pushes his hot mouth against my ear. "I have a small set of breasts," he whispers.

"Seltzer?" I ask. "You want a seltzer?"

"No, no need," he says, patting my shoulder. "But you're a good girl. You understand it all. Good girl."

*

The broker's son is holding court in the living room with a couple of old guys from the synagogue.

"Stoop to conquer," he's saying. "That's what we're doing with the Randall's Island waterfront. Buying at a loss to eventually make a threefold profit. It's true of property and"—he gives me an indiscreet look—"women. Sometimes you've got to go down to come out on top."

"And yet," I say as I pass, "you don't look like you've ever gone down on a woman in your life."

*

The rabbi is coming toward me with his benign smile and huge ears and polite, deferential air. I'd like to drop to all fours and crawl under the paper tablecloth.

"May God comfort you among the other mourners of Zion and Jerusalem," he says.

"Thank you, Rabbi," I say.

He takes my hand in his. His papery soft skin reminds me of the pinches of dried food flakes I used to feed to our goldfish. "We miss you at the synagogue."

"I know, I'm sorry," I say. "It's just . . . I'm not really a believer."

"What don't you believe in?" he asks.

"You know," I say, avoiding his eyes. "God. Prayer. That kind of stuff."

"You don't pray?" the rabbi asks mildly.

"Um, no," I say.

"That's a shame," he says. "It can be such a comfort."

"I don't have anything to pray to."

"You don't have to pray to God," he says. "Sometimes it helps just to talk to the air in the room."

★

Mimi, one of my mother's friends from bridge, comes over and gives me a powdery kiss on the cheek. She smells of Chanel No. 5 and Werther's Originals and rubbing alcohol.

"Sorry about your pop-pop," she says. "You taking care of yourself?"

"I am," I say.

"Mm." She inspects my face. "Look at those dark circles. Are you sleeping?"

"Enough," I say.

"Are you masturbating?"

"What?"

"Masturbating," she says again. "It's the best sedative, you know. If you're not sleeping, you need to masturbate more."

"Please stop saying masturbate," I say.

"Movie, melatonin, and masturbation," she says, tapping out the words on my hand with her finger. "Best night's sleep you'll ever have."

★

I catch Levi hiding in the kitchen with a plate of potato salad.

"Ma's friend Mimi just instructed me to masturbate more," I say.

"Dad's cousin Ezra told me he got chlamydia twice last year," Levi says. "He's eighty-two."

"You win," I say.

"Apparently it's all over the assisted living facilities. Frisky widows and widowers, you know. He kept asking me if I was using protection."

"Well, clearly not," I say.

"Sorry, I was going to tell you about Min and the baby," he says. "But then Dad died."

"That's right," I say, slapping my forehead. "Dead dad! I forgot!"

Levi gives me a tired eye roll. "Mom gave me an earful about it too. Then she cried and tried to give me money."

"Did I say congratulations and all that crap yet?"

"Nope."

I pull Levi in for a hug. "Congratulations," I say. "And all that crap."

*

The rabbi is leaving when I tap his elbow gently.

"What would I say?" I ask. "If I wanted to, you know, pray?"

Two of my mother's synagogue friends eye me jealously from across the room. I would die if anyone overheard this conversation.

"Well, there are books. But you can also just say what's in your heart. Say what feels right to you."

"But . . . where would I even start?"

"Oh, you can start very simple," he says. "Two of my favorite prayers are 'Help me' and 'Thank you.'"

"Those are prayers?"

"Those are excellent prayers."

He smiles and begins to retreat, then turns back to me one more time. "You want to know one of my personal favorite prayers?"

"What?"

"Wow," he says.

*

My mother and I are on the patio, taking in the last warm hour of the day, when Levi comes out.

"Where's Min?" I ask.

"Napping," he says. "I think she was overwhelmed by all the Holocaust talk. She's retreating into sleep."

"Smart woman," says my mother.

Levi pulls up a chair next to us and removes a joint from behind his ear. He lights it, takes a long drag, and proffers it toward us.

"Levi Jeremiah Rosenthal," says my mother. "What on earth do you think you're doing?"

"Ma," he says as he exhales the smoke. "Come on. Dad's dead. I'm having a baby. Take a fucking hit."

"It's never too late for a first time," I say and take the joint.

My mother shakes her head and emits what can only be described as a cackle. "First time! Who do you think you're kidding? When your father and I were in high school we used to smoke pot and make out to Bob Marley records. And it didn't end there! When I was doing my teacher training and he was on residency, we loved to smoke a little grass in the evenings. How do you think you two were conceived?"

"Gross!" I yell.

"Ma!" says Levi.

My mother takes the joint from me, inhales deeply, and blows a perfect smoke ring. I catch Levi's eye and raise my eyebrows. We pass it around one more time and watch the sun dip behind the next-door neighbor's hedges.

"Wow, my baby's having a baby," says my mother quietly.

"My mom used to *be* a baby," Levi says.

None of us know why we're laughing.

*

That night I go to my computer and open my email. If Levi can have a kid and Bernie can have an extra chromosome and Mimi can masturbate herself into unconsciousness, I should be able to do this. I ask for help from the air in the room, then open Frank's email and type one word.

Come.

*

Levi and Min are heading back upstate. The hot food counter, apparently, waits for no man. My mother insists on strapping a pillow around Min's stomach for the car ride, as though that could protect the baby from all that life will throw at it. We stand in the driveway with our arms around each other as they drive away. I guess that's what life should feel like; setting off on a long car ride with all your worries and hopes strapped around you, the people who love you most frantically waving you off as you go.

*

I'm looking up how to make a grilled cheese, wondering what the hell I've been so busy doing all my life that I never learned this, when the doorbell rings. Frank is standing in the doorway. Ah, here is the man I love, I think. The thought comes so swiftly, so unapologetically, I almost say it aloud. Instead, I say, with an insane level of cheer, "New Jersey welcomes you!"

*

Frank and I pull up two chairs and sit looking out over the garden. The patio furniture is old and partially covered in bird shit. I consider being embarrassed by this, then decide it's not worth the effort.

"You grew up here?" Frank asks.

I nod.

"You're lucky," he says.

An emerald flash darts toward the bird feeder in front of us.

"Did you know hummingbird nectar is just sugar boiled in water?" I say.

Frank starts to laugh.

"What?" I ask.

"Why do we make life so fucking complicated?" he says.

*

We've been in the garden for about an hour, chatting in a general, nonrevealing way about what's been happening at the office, then lapsing into meaningful silences filled with shy smiles, when my mother comes home. We both leap up like we're teenagers who have been caught fellating each other and turn toward the screen doors.

"Sweetheart, can you help me with this!" she yells.

"Ma, I have a visitor!" I yell back.

"A what?" she yells.

"A visitor!" I yell.

I open the doors and lead Frank back inside.

"This is Frank," I say.

My mother turns from the wooden crib she's lugging across our living room floor.

"Frank who?" she says.

"Frank from work," I say.

"Oh!"

She flicks her eyes up and down him so quickly it would be imperceptible to anyone but me.

"So great to meet you," says Frank. "Can I help you with—"

"No!" My mother raises her palm. "You're our guest. I'll get tea."

This is not a good sign. The more solicitous my mother is to a person, the less she likes them. Get in her good graces, and you'll be cleaning the gutter. Fall out of them, and she'll insist on making you herbal tea. It's a counterintuitive but undeniable fact. We follow her into the kitchen as she puts the kettle on.

"That's a beautiful crib," says Frank.

"For my new grandchild," says my mother. "So he or she will have somewhere to sleep here once they're born."

Frank glances at my stomach with alarm.

"My brother," I say.

"Phew," says Frank. "I mean, congratulations."

"Do you have children?" asks my mother.

"Not that I know of," says Frank.

My mother sniffs and pulls the blackbird mug off the shelf. She only gives the blackbird to people she doesn't like.

"Frank has to go now," I say. "It's late."

"I do?" says Frank.

"Uh-huh," I say, ushering him out the kitchen and toward the front door as he calls a goodbye to my mother.

"Can I come see you again?" he says. "Tomorrow?"

"Tomorrow."

I go back into the kitchen and take the blackbird mug and throw it in the trash.

"What on earth—," says my mother.

"We need to talk," I say.

★

I take the eating couch. She takes the visitor's one.

"Is he still married?"

"No. Well, technically, yes. I think. She moved to Italy."

"And so now he wants to be with you?"

"I think so."

"And you want to be with him?"

"I think so."

"And you're in love?"

"Ma, we've never even kissed."

"And that has anything to do with it?"

"Okay, fine. Yes, I think so. But don't tell anyone. Don't even repeat it to yourself."

"Why?"

"Because it's humiliating."

"Sweetheart, love *is* humiliating. Hasn't anyone ever told you that?"

"Who would have told me that?"

"Do you know the word *humiliate* comes from the Latin root *humus*, which means 'earth'? *That's* how love is supposed to feel."

"Like hummus?"

"Like earth. It grounds you. All this nonsense about love being a drug, making you feel high, that's not real. It should hold you like the earth."

"Wow, Ma."

"What? I have a heart, don't I?"

"You also have a blackbird mug."

*

The next day I do something I almost never do, and that is get a haircut. Honestly, a root canal would be preferable. At least there are no mirrors at the dentist. I endure an hour and a half of lathering, combing, snipping, and small talk, all while avoiding eye contact with either the hair stylist or myself.

"So," says the stylist. "What do we think of bangs?"

"I don't know," I say. "What do we think?"

"You've got a great face for bangs," he says.

"Sure," I say. "Let's go crazy."

*

Crazy, that's what I am. Crazy. No one looks good with bangs. Bangs are just a beard on your forehead, a hair hat that you can never take off.

As soon as I get into the car, I check the rearview mirror to see if it's as bad as I thought. Even in that little sliver of reflection, the results are clear: I am a boiled egg in a wig.

*

Frank comes over that night promptly after work.

"Why are you wearing a baseball cap?" he asks when I answer the door.

*

Luckily, I have less time to worry about what Frank is thinking of my hair because I am now worrying about the fact that my mother has insisted on making us dinner. The dinner is stir-fry in a wok, which is the only thing my mother can make except meatloaf.

"Looks great," says Frank when he sees what's happening in the kitchen. "Wok 'n' roll."

"You *are* an advertiser," my mother says, then tells him to find the cutlery and set the table.

*

"You look pretty tonight," says Frank as we're clearing the plates away. "Did you change your hair?"

"I look like a boiled egg in a wig," I say.

"Hey," he says, grabbing my shoulders. "I want us to try something."

We are looking directly at each other, his hands tight on me. This is the longest we have ever touched each other. My heart is a jackhammer.

"Okay," I say.

"I'm going to say 'You look pretty,'" he says. "And then you're going to say 'Thank you.'"

"But—" I say.

"No boiled egg jokes," he says. "No jokes of any kind. Just 'Thank you.' Can you try that for me?"

I nod mutely.

"Eleanor," he says. "You look very pretty with your hair like that."

I want to slither down the sinkhole, turn on the garbage disposal, and grind myself into nonexistence.

"Thank you," I choke.

He laughs.

"You're welcome," he says. "We'll try again tomorrow."

★

I forgot to tell Frank what the rabbi said about "Thank you" being a prayer. A prayer can be a hope, a request for help, and an act of faith. When I say it to Frank, "Thank you" definitely feels like a prayer.

★

A few days later, we're back in the garden. The hose is sprawled between us, lazily watering my mother's rhododendron bush. The bees weave happily from flower to flower. It is the last week of summer.

"It's been different without you," Frank says. "At the office, I mean. No one to give me shit about my bad puns. My confidence is skyrocketing."

"Soz about that," I say.

"What's that?"

"Soz." I shrug. "It's how British teenagers say sorry."

"How sorry can you be if you can't even spring for the second syllable?"

"Since when was word length correlative to sincerity? 'I hate that' sounds a lot sincerer to me than, say, 'I anathematize that.'"

Frank laughs. "Like 'There's truth in that' versus 'There's verisimilitude'?"

"Exactly. Or 'I love you' versus . . ."

I stop. So I said it. Accidentally and to illustrate a linguistic point, sure, but I said it.

". . . I can't think of a longer way to say that," I say.

"Adore," says Frank softly. "Cherish."

"Love is better," I say.

"It is," he says. "And I do too. Love you, that is."

*

I am in his arms.

"Soz about how I acted after we got the Kapow! account. I was an idiot. And scared."

"Soz I disappeared on you. Soz I didn't say goodbye."

"Soz I let you go. I should have handled it differently."

"Soz I didn't give you the chance."

"Soz I waited the whole summer to tell you Cleo left."

"Soz Cleo left."

"Soz your father died."

"Soz you never met him."

"Soz I made such a mess of it all."

"But not for this? You're not soz for right now, are you?"

"No. Right now I have never been less soz for anything in my life."

And then he kissed me.

*

Frank tells me about how his mother used to pick him up from school drunk. He tells me how Cleo's mother died. He tells me about finding her bleeding out on their living room floor. He tells me what happened to their sugar glider. It's not pretty. He tells me that a couple of weeks ago, he stopped drinking and started going to meetings. He tells me he always thought he would hate AA because of his mom, but actually he feels like he's beginning to understand himself for the first time, maybe in his whole life.

"Could you ever . . . ," he says. "Could you ever be with a man who did all that?"

I put my hand on his.

"Have you ever heard of something called kintsugi?"

*

Amazingly, my agent emails me back about my animated TV show *Human Garbage*.

You're a weird one, cookie. But get me three more episodes and I think I can sell it.

★

Today, I will write.
"We'll see about that," I say, and go to run a bath.
"Better believe it," I say, and turn on the shower.
"Never going to happen," I say, and saunter back to the bed.
"Just try me," I say, and march myself to the desk.

★

Frank and I go to the movies together and make out for two hours straight. We visit the galleries in Chelsea. We go bowling in Brooklyn. We eat egg and cheese on a roll in Washington Square Park. We swap books. We go back to sending each other funny emails. We go to a jazz club, then realize neither of us likes jazz and leave to get ice cream. We take walks. We eat pizza slices.

Even though it's getting cold, we take the ferry to Rockaway to watch the sunset. From that distance, the whole city is one big reflection of the sky. Pink skyscrapers like temples of Himalayan salt. It looks like a mythical city for the gods, which in some ways it is.

"The ferry is really just the public bus with a better view," I say.

"That's what I love about you," says Frank. "Cynical even in front of sunsets."

★

I go to the Rose Reading Room in the New York Public Library to work. Aside from the squeaky chairs, it is writer's heaven. In fact, the heavens are quite literally painted on the ceiling above. Powdery blue skies and soapy clouds. I sit at one of the long mahogany tables dotted with emerald reading lamps and smile at my fellow workers. Who knows how many hit shows and best-selling novels have been written within these book-lined walls? I'm just getting into my flow when a man sits down across from me, opens an encyclopedia on his lap, and begins furiously masturbating beneath it.

*

Frank lets me use a spare conference room at the agency to write. At least this way, he says, the only person I have to worry about masturbating in front of me is him.

*

The best part of this new arrangement is that Jacky and I can go to lunch again.

"So, you're banging the boss," she says as we sit down at the diner. "*Dish.*"

"We're not banging," I say. "We're dating."

"How high school of you," she says. "Let's be bad and share some fries."

I take a deep breath. "Actually, in high school I dated a forty-year-old man," I say. "He used to make me do things like wash his laundry and swallow his cum." I exhale. "It was not great."

Jacky leans toward me over our huge sticky diner menus. "Oh hon," she says. "One spring break in high school I got drunk, and a group of seniors locked me and another boy in a hotel closet and told me they'd give me a hundred bucks if they could watch me give him a blowjob."

"That's awful," I say. "Did you do it?"

She shrugs sadly. "I liked one of the boys who was outside the door, and I thought . . . I don't know what I thought. I was sixteen and a hundred and ten pounds and had just discovered the Long Island iced tea."

She takes my hand across the table and squeezes.

"I'm really sorry that happened to you, Jacky," I say.

"I'm sorry about you too." She shakes her head. "Fuck that old man."

"Well, he died in a lawn mower accident," I say. "So there's a happy ending at least."

"God is not always just," she says. "But he does have a sense of humor."

Our server comes, and we order our salads and fries.

"And a chocolate shake for dipping." Jacky winks at me. "I think we need it."

We both lean back in our booth chairs and look at each other, smiling.

"Did you get the hundred bucks at least?" I ask.

"Oh yes, hon." She laughs. "I took my girlfriends to Benihana for dinner. Those shrimp volcanos were worth it!"

*

The leaves have turned, I'm wearing a jacket, pumpkin spice is everywhere, and someone actually invited me to go apple picking. It is definitely, officially fall.

*

I'm waiting in line for coffee by Cooper Square and listening to the art school students in front of me talk.

"What happened with that guy, the Icelandic performance artist?" the first friend asks.

"We broke up."

"How come?"

"He slept in a Victorian nightgown, had a baby called Jean-Pepe with his lesbian neighbors, and yelled 'Look me in the eye!' every time he came."

"So . . . How come?" asks the first friend.

*

Frank has been sober ninety days. We still haven't slept together. He wants to wait, and I don't mind. I figure I've waited long enough for him. What's a few more months? We celebrate the best way I know how with someone both celibate and abstinent. Illegal fireworks.

*

I can't believe it, but my agent liked the new episodes. She's pitching them to an animation studio in Japan. *Japan!*

*

Turns out, my father has left me some money. It's not much, but it's enough for me to move out of New Jersey and get a place of my own in the city. Now all I have to do is find an apartment and a way to tell my mother I'm moving out. I wonder if I could get breaking the news to her included in the broker's fee?

*

Frank and I spend a Sunday looking around open houses downtown.

"These all look like apartments people have been murdered in," he whispers to me.

"I think the 'natural death' apartments are out of my price range," I say.

"A few months in one of these dumps, and you won't have to worry about that," he says. "Because you'll have hung yourself from the ceiling."

"Don't be ridiculous," I say. "None of these places have high enough ceilings for that."

"I think I could find us a place with higher ceilings than this," he says.

"Us?" I say.

"You and me," he says. "A fresh start somewhere new. Think about it."

*

I do think about it. I think about it for a week straight. I find my mother in the garden potting her fall perennials. She looks up at me and rubs soil on her forehead with the back of her gardening glove.

"Do you know how Nietzsche defined a joke?" she says. "As an epigram on the death of a feeling."

"Ma," I say. "I want to talk to you about something."

"Isn't that brilliant? Nietzsche rocks my world."

"It's about my living situation."

"I gave you *Thus Spoke Zarathustra* when you were fifteen and having your first existential crisis," she says. "Do you still have it?"

"Frank asked me something the other day."

"Nietzsche had a poet's soul," she says. "Like you."

I grab a trowel and start digging. I am never leaving.

*

A group of owls is called a parliament. A group of emus is called a mob. A group of larks is called an exaltation. A group of doves is call a piteousness. A group of ravens is called an unkindness. A group of flamingos is called a flamboyance. A group of peafowl is called an ostentation. A group of parrots is called a pandemonium. A group of starlings is called a descent. A group of turtledoves is called a pitying. A group of finches is called a charm. All of these words can also describe a group of Jewish women.

*

I go pick Frank up from his evening AA meeting on Perry Street. Outside, people are smoking and laughing. They look pretty normal to me. A couple of suits, a couple of older Village artist types. One person appears to be in surgical scrubs.

We go to the Italian restaurant on Tenth Street where the terrible service is inversely commensurate to the excellent food. Frank tucks his napkin into his shirt before the meal begins, as is his way, and pulls off a hunk of bread from the plate that is plonked in front of us.

"Best bread in the city," he says, swirling it in olive oil.

"How was the meeting?" I ask.

"Incredible. So moving. The speaker had twenty-five years and was so spiritually fit. And *grateful*, you know? His prayer and meditation practice was off the hook."

I raise an eyebrow. Frank rubs his forehead and laughs. "I sound insane," he says.

"You sound happy," I say.

"I am," he says. "Still feels weird even saying it."

"Well, get used to it, baby," I say. "You are not, thank the heavens, going to be your family's Uncle Bernie."

"My family's who?"

"My Uncle Bernie has a drinking problem," I say. "And, apparently, an extra female chromosome."

"Right," says Frank. "You want to share a starter?"

"The tomato salad looks good," I say.

"How about the asparagus?"

"You need to go see Cleo," I say.

Frank swallows the mouthful of bread in his mouth with difficulty. "I need to what?"

"You need to go see Cleo," I say again. "Your wife."

"I know who she is."

"First of all. You're still married, which makes what we're doing right now technically an extramarital affair."

"I had no idea you were so puritanical."

"And second of all. You need to make sure she's being taken care of over there."

"Cleo can take care of herself," he says.

"If she could do that," I say quietly, "what happened would not have happened."

He looks at me, and I see how that experience has brought a sadness to his eyes that was never there before. "Go on."

"She's still very young, and she doesn't have much family, which means you and I are her family. We have a responsibility to make sure she's set up."

"You mean financially? I can send her money."

"Some things take a little more than money."

"I never knew you were so concerned with her well-being. Is this some *First Wives Club* stuff?"

I try not to look at him like he's the stupidest man on the planet.

"No, Frank," I say very slowly. "It's sisterhood."

Frank takes my hand gently in his across the table.

"Eleanor," he says. "You are a good woman."

"We're getting the tomato salad," I say.

★

My mother and I spend an evening watching an old season of *Sing Your Heart Out*. We have become, I think, perhaps overly invested in the success of young Harold, who put his singing aspirations on hold to look after his ailing, diabetic mother. Every time he performs, they replay the same footage of the two of them together in their small, shambolic home in New Orleans.

"He is my only pride," the mother says in her big floral dress. "My heart beats for him."

My mother turns to me and puts her hand on mine.

"Frank called me," she says. "Go."

★

Frank has come over to help my mother prepare a farewell meal. Incredibly, it does not seem to involve a wok. I've spent the whole day packing and need some air, so I throw on a coat and head out into the garden. It is very quiet, dark and still. My breath makes little gray clouds in front of me. Above my head, the stars are just barely visible. I can smell the earth. I can hear Frank and my mother laughing in the kitchen. Somewhere, a dog barks. I can feel the night pressing against my skin. It is cold, but I am warm. My breath meets the air.

★

Wow.

CHAPTER SEVENTEEN

January

Rome was in the middle of its mildest winter in fifty years when Frank arrived. A breeze with a tropical lilt licked at him through the taxi window as he headed toward the Fine Art Institute, where Cleo lived. The building he found was painted a faded fuchsia, with tall palm trees planted around its gates. A pink palace. It felt ancient and muted, precious and slightly forgotten. He couldn't imagine a better place for her to be.

From out of sight behind the window sash, Cleo watched him wind his way up the stone pathway to the entrance with his familiar bouncing gait. She had been standing there waiting for him to arrive for some time, her heart beating like a trapped bird inside her chest. She watched from above as Frank reached the door and searched the list of names, ringing the button next to hers. He stepped back to look up at the empty window from which she had just ran.

Footsteps, the sound of fingers scrabbling on wood, whispered swearing, a lock scraping back, and there was Cleo. His heart swelled like a wave returning to her shore.

She had cut her long hair into a bob, a golden hood framing her face. Her beautiful heart-shaped face, he wanted to take it in his hands and hold it up to the light like a snow globe. She was wearing sun-faded jeans and a nubby butterscotch cardigan he recognized. Her slim ankles peeked out above canvas shoes splattered with paint. What a lovely girl she was. Like a white butterfly in a bar of sunshine.

"Your hair," he said.

"Short," she said and ran her fingers through it.

"Good." He nodded.

"Not too short?" she asked.

"It's beautiful," he said. "Like a nun's wimple."

"You mean veil. The wimple's what they wear around their necks."

"See! This is why I need you in my life. Who knows how long I've been making that mistake. What if I had been talking to an *actual* nun?"

Cleo stepped out of the doorway and held his shoulders to take him in. Something about his face was different. His eyes looked clearer; she could see now that they were not brown, as she had always thought, but a golden hazel. It was as though the lights had come on inside him. She wrapped her arms around his neck and pulled him toward her until they were cheek to cheek. He felt like a great tent collapsing around the central pole of her body.

"Come inside," she said into his ear.

Frank followed her into the dark, cool entrance hall. She led him up the stairs to a sunlit landing, pointing out the kitchen and laundry with the shy pride of a student on Parents' Day. Scattered on the kitchen table were several empty wine bottles left standing from the night before, deep crimson rings marking the wood's surface. Frank stared at them with a mixture of relief and longing. He would never again sit after dinner like that, talk passionately about absolutely nothing like that, refilling glass after glass while evening unspooled into night. Cleo followed his gaze. Frank had told her he'd stopped drinking when he called from New York to suggest visiting. Six months, he'd said, but she'd had trouble believing it. Now, she could see that he was different sober, softer. Whatever defense alcohol had given him was gone.

"Do you want water?" she asked. "Or tea? Milk? Tea *with* milk?"

"I'm okay," he said. "It's just my first time traveling like this, you know. I feel a bit . . ."

"Tender?"

Frank smiled. "Yes," he said. "That's exactly the word for it." They looked at each other, and a frisson of warmth passed between them. "Why don't you show me your room?" he asked.

Her bedroom looked like a mixture between a hospital room and a dormitory, with speckled linoleum floors and a single bed covered with a pink comforter. Postcards of paintings by Lee Krasner and Jay DeFeo covered the wall above her small desk. The Fine Art Institute seemed to Frank like a boarding school for adults, a space both personal and impersonal, reflecting a group of inhabitants who would necessarily leave. Cleo loved it for this very reason; it was a place dedicated to creating.

Frank perched on the bed and felt something hard beneath him. He reached under the blanket and pulled out a smooth oblong stone. It was a pale opalescent pink veined with white, about the length of his hand, cool to the touch and heavy to hold. He looked at Cleo, who laughed. "Whoops, I didn't realize that was still in there."

She lifted it from his palm and slid it into a cluttered desk drawer. Inside were leaves of thick inkblot paper streaked with watercolors, a tapered white feather, a pen with a plastic sunflower on the end.

"What is it?" Frank asked.

"It's a crystal." Cleo leaned against the desk to face him. A thin strip of belly between her T-shirt and jeans appeared, like the sun peeking between clouds. "To put inside you. Actually, Zoe told me about it. You can use it to open your chakras, heal trauma, that kind of stuff . . . You're rolling your eyes."

"I am not!"

"You're rolling them on the *inside*. I can tell."

"You cannot."

But she could. Cleo's ability to see into Frank had always irked and thrilled him. He had never felt seen, really seen, until he met her.

"Put it inside you how?" he asked.

"Well, I don't swallow it."

"It's a sex thing?"

"It's a healing thing."

"You need that?"

Cleo smiled. "I need everything."

"That's the gift of being twenty-six," said Frank. "You can try anything and appear hopeful. At forty-five you're merely ridiculous, even to yourself."

Cleo snorted. "What nonsense! Look at you and your meetings. You're a whole new person!"

"Do you really think so?"

"You're lighter. It's a good thing."

"What about you!" exclaimed Frank. "You chopped off all your hair."

Cleo shook out her tulip-shaped bob. "I guess I'm lighter, too," she said.

Frank nodded, smiling. "Did Zoe tell you about that sex-positive feminist group thing she started with the kids from Gallatin?"

Cleo eyes shone with amusement. "She sure did."

"If she extols the power of the female orgasm to me one more time . . ."

Cleo threw her head back in a laugh. Zoe had indeed regaled her with stories about this the last time they spoke. She did behave as if she was the first woman to discover the clitoris, but her youthful enthusiasm was also charming.

"It's good for her," Cleo said. "She's exploring, you know. And—" She looked at him shyly, proudly. "I have a therapist now too."

"You do?"

"She's a Buddhist lesbian from Ireland, but she's lived in Italy for years."

"I couldn't imagine a better description of a therapist for you."

"I trust her," she said. "She's the first person I've trusted in a long time."

"I get it," said Frank. "That's how I feel about my sponsor."

"Wow, Frank," said Cleo. "Look at us forming healthy relationships."

They regarded each other in silence for a moment, both so familiar and unfamiliar to one another at the same time.

"I'm happy to see you," he said eventually.

Actually, he felt a swirling mix of elation and terror and relief upon seeing her, as did Cleo seeing him, but neither felt ready to get into that yet.

"Me too," she said. "I didn't think we would until next year."

"Why's that?"

"Santiago and Dominique's wedding."

"Oh yeah, of course! Can you believe that's happening?"

"I can. He's written me two letters so far, and they've both been odes to his love for Dominique, plus a pasta recipe."

Frank laughed. "He's the last living romantic. Remember the speech he made at our wedding?"

"I do. He said we were both made of gold or something."

"I don't know about me, but you certainly are."

Cleo smiled. She really did look golden to him.

"Want to see my studio?" she asked. "It's in the other building."

Frank followed her out of the room and down the hall. He watched her liquid, soft-footed walk.

"Has anyone else been here to visit you? Quentin?"

"We don't speak anymore," said Cleo quietly.

Frank waited for her to elaborate. She stopped walking and turned to face him.

"Meth," she said. "I guess Alex got him onto it. He's not doing well."

The last time Cleo saw Quentin, she explained, he had invited her to a cheap hotel in midtown. When she arrived, there were three other hollow-eyed men pacing the room with him. Quentin was half naked and manic, his thin, pale body jolting as if with electricity. He needed money, he'd said. He'd run out of the substantial monthly allowance his grandmother provided, and there was still a week left in the month. When she tried to get him to leave, he had attacked her. *Don't you dare judge me, you fucking cunt.* Cleo fled the room and called Johnny, but he was no help, and she didn't have the number of any member of Quentin's family. There was nothing to do but leave him there. Frank shook his head as she recounted this.

"I had no idea."

"He gave us cocaine as a wedding present. You didn't think he might have a teeny-tiny drug problem?"

"He's a character?" offered Frank. "I just didn't think it would get that bad for him. I mean, if doing a bit of blow and drinking too much makes you an addict, then everyone we know—" Frank stopped and pinched his brow. "Jesus, Cley. Everyone we know in New York is an addict, aren't they?"

Cleo nodded grimly. "Looking like it."

"You haven't tried to reach him again?"

She gave him a pained look.

"I did, of course I did. Countless times. I called rehabs and found free beds, but he refused to go. Then his number got disconnected. At this point, I'm not sure who I'd even be getting in touch with."

"You mean someone else got the number?"

"I mean, I don't know who he *is* anymore."

"Are you okay?"

She looked up at him with her exhausted smile. "One of us has to be."

"You're lucky you got out of New York when you did."

"By the skin of my teeth," she said.

She guided him to her studio, which was cluttered and small, not exactly the light-filled factory space he'd been imagining. Low wooden ceiling beams, the chemical smell of paint thinner in the air, a dusty concrete floor streaked with dark red. Frank's heart jerked. Was it blood? No. It was paint, of course. He spotted the same rust color on the canvases lining the wall.

Frank remembered Cleo's work as florid and fleshly, the colors of a bruise in the ugly part of healing, sour yellows and dark violets and crimson-tinted creams. These canvases were much simpler, clean red lines on white or gray backgrounds. He looked more carefully and saw that the lines were abstracted parts of women's bodies, twin spread buttocks, a roll of stomach, the heavy curve of a breast.

He had never really known if she was any good as an artist. She had certainly been unhappy enough to be good. But what did that mean? Talented people were often unhappy, but unhappy people were not often talented. Frank always thought that Cleo's main gift was her way of being. She was uniquely attractive, not just in her looks but in her essence. She had a way of bringing the light into a room with her, like a window being flung open.

Cleo watched Frank as he knelt to examine a small square canvas and the subject, which before had been the curve of a bent knee brimming with human movement, became just a line. They were bodies presented as absence; as you drew closer, they retreated. She was proud of these paintings, which were less obviously figurative than her previous work, lending her the freedom and anonymity of abstraction. She watched his face, trying to decipher his thoughts.

Frank looked up and saw Cleo was watching him with that curious intensity of hers. She was expecting something from him, he knew, some response he didn't know how to give. What he understood was language. Branding. What a dirty word that had become, but there was a straightforwardness to it verging on the sublime for him. All interactions were, at heart, transactional; at least advertising didn't pretend. This subtle world of shade and lines Cleo occupied, ostensibly so full of meaning, potentially so meaningless . . . Frank felt like he was trying to open a package with the instructions written on the inside.

"It's really smart, Cleo," he said. "So . . . artistic."

Cleo laughed. She could see he was mystified, but she was surprised to learn she cared less about his reaction than she'd expected. Regardless of what he thought, she was satisfied with the work.

"I'm having a show next month," she said, unable to conceal the pride in her voice. "In a little gallery in Monti."

"Do you have a title?"

"*Life Lines*," she said.

"Appropriate."

"How so?"

"Just appropriate," he said again vaguely. "For you."

"There's an installation piece too," she said. "I think it's the best part. If you want to see it?"

She was so earnest, so hopeful. Frank felt for her. There was no guarantee she would succeed at this; in fact, most likely she would not. He remembered the first time he met her, walking along the streets of New York declaring she was an artist with a proud little flick of her head. He saw the same confidence in Zoe's fight to become an actor, trading on her youth and beauty, wearing them away without return. They did not yet know what he did. That you could be gifted, hardworking, tenacious, even touched by a little bit of luck, and *still* not succeed, or if you did, not have it last. That never to experience achievements commensurate to your talent, never to receive adequate payment for your efforts, was a terrible, demoralizing thing.

Frank followed Cleo out to the courtyard that separated the buildings. The unseasonably warm Mediterranean breeze circled around them like a cat rubbing against their ankles.

"The installation's in the shed," said Cleo. "I just wanted to smoke a cigarette first."

She rolled a cigarette and passed it to him, then made another for herself.

"I don't smoke," he said, putting it between his lips.

She smiled. "Everyone who quits drinking starts smoking, just a little."

It was quiet except for the tinny sound of a radio from an open window above them. Cleo tucked the tobacco pouch into her back pocket and crossed her arms. It was time they talked about what he had come here to talk about.

"So," she said. "Tell me about Eleanor. Not your mother."

Frank coughed up the smoke he'd just inhaled. He'd assumed he would be the one to bring Eleanor up. He did not know that Cleo had heard about the relationship from Zoe weeks earlier. For Cleo, hearing that Frank was in love with someone else was like being stung by a jellyfish; after the first surprising pain had worn off, there was only a dull ache. It would never hurt as much again. And Cleo was determined to be happy for him—but first, they had to talk about it.

"I read your emails last year." She shrugged, a movement equal parts contrition and dismissal. "It's funny because I was so upset, but I was laughing too. I like her." Cleo forced a grin. "Maybe even more than I like you."

"I do too," he managed. "Certainly more than I like me."

What could he say about Eleanor? She was handsome, not beautiful, and didn't attract the attention Cleo did merely by walking into a room. But she was made of deeper, sturdier stuff. The best sense of humor he'd ever found in a woman, in anyone really, except maybe his mother. But she was kinder than his mother, tenderer too, with a writer's true capacity for empathy.

COCO MELLORS

"We're . . . very fond of each other," he said.

"I gathered that. You've been together a little while now, no?"

Cleo was trying to keep her voice casual, but it had taken on the flinty edge of interrogation.

"We just got a place in Brooklyn," he said. "I was going to tell you."

"Brooklyn!" Cleo's voice jumped an octave. "Wow, things must be serious."

Frank scrubbed the back of his neck with his hand. "Not far into Brooklyn," he said. "Just across the bridge."

"Brooklyn," Cleo repeated to herself incredulously. "That's very grown-up. Well, I guess you *are* both grown-ups. How old is she?" Somehow she had been flustered out of all her intended graciousness.

"Thirtysomething," Frank said, equally rattled. "Does it really matter?"

"I was just wondering," said Cleo. "She seems mature, is all. More mature than me."

This could have been a dig, but her voice was matter-of-fact.

"She turns thirty-eight next week," said Frank uneasily.

Cleo took a deep inhale on her cigarette. The embers tumbled down the leg of her jeans.

"That's great," she said, ferociously batting the ash off her knee. "Tell her happy birthday from me. *Buon compleanno*, Eleanor!"

She had been straining for cheerful, but she had overshot and ended up in the territory of manic. Frank gave her a long look, then dropped his cigarette and stepped toward her. He clasped her narrow shoulders in his hands.

"I'm sorry I didn't tell you before I came."

Cleo looked at her feet. "You don't owe me anything."

He shook his head. "I owe you everything," he said. "And I'm sorry."

Cleo raised her eyes to his, and her expression softened.

"I left the country, remember?" she said. "You're allowed to leave Manhattan."

Frank exhaled. Now was the time to bring up the divorce. It couldn't be a more natural time. After all, Cleo had landed herself in hospital trying to end their marriage; a divorce was a remarkably gentle approach by contrast. But something stopped him.

"It was actually Eleanor who suggested I come here," he said instead. "To make sure you were okay."

Cleo's fair eyebrows creased into a frown. "She did? You didn't want to come yourself?"

"Of course I did," he said quickly. "I just meant— There's no animosity on her part, is what I mean. She cares about you. I think she admires you." He was talking too much, but he couldn't stop. "She'd like to get to know you if, um, circumstances should ever allow."

Cleo's brow furrowed further. So Frank had come because of Eleanor. Of course it had not been for her. And there it was, the feeling she had been trying to deny, the dark, oily jealousy rising in her that Frank would do for Eleanor what he would never do for her. Eleanor got *this* version of Frank, the sober, thoughtful man who took her suggestions, while Cleo had endured the drunken predecessor like a fool.

The urge to puncture the smooth surface of his new love shot through her. It would not have been hard; she had met Eleanor, after all, and knew she was hardly the kind of glittering person Frank liked to see himself reflected in. Just one remark, and she could pierce his happiness like a poison-tipped needle.

But she stopped herself. She would only regret it. And in her heart, she knew Eleanor was good for him. She had not been lying when she said she liked her. Cleo and Frank could not make each other happy, no matter how hard they'd tried. Better to let him go, better to send him off with her love at his back like the warm Roman breeze, even if it carried him toward someone else.

"I'd like to get to know her too," she said. "She seems . . . sensational."

Frank smiled with relief. "She'll be pleased to hear that," he said. "And she is. You both are."

"You two . . . you *are* happy?" Cleo searched his face with her usual concentration.

Frank thought about how to answer honestly without hurting her. The first time he and Eleanor had slept together, he'd thought he might die of happiness. He had never waited to have sex with anyone before, certainly never fallen in love with them beforehand. He'd been incredibly nervous, as had she. Everything went wrong; he couldn't unhook her bra, she'd elbowed him in the stomach, half winding him, and then when he finally did enter her, he'd lasted about thirty seconds before exploding. They had both laughed until tears came. She'd collapsed onto his chest, his arms tight around her back, and fallen asleep right there, right at the center of him, her heart beating against his, and he'd slept too, pinned under her, happy, yes, happy at last.

"We're trying to be," he said eventually. "And you? Are you happy here?"

Cleo cast her eyes around the courtyard. It struck her that somehow, miraculously, she was. In the seven months since she came to Rome, she had made art every day, rediscovering the pleasures of both solitude and community. She ate breakfast in the kitchen with the other artists on residency and reconvened with them every evening to discuss the day's work over wine and pasta. She had seen the single bed where Keats took his final breath and walked with her face upturned through the Sistine Chapel, devouring the medley of gold and flesh and sky.

She loved New York, but it was not her city, she knew that now. It suited her to be part of this intricate network of European capitals, each only a few hours away from the others, each containing its Caravaggios and Sorollas and Soutines. She had even started talking to her father more, now they were only an hour time difference apart.

And she was discovering that the slower pace of Rome soothed her. She was industrious, but never exhausted. She slept deeply and alone. She had not yet taken a lover, though one of the other artists, a shy Swiss designer her age, had confessed his feelings for her late one night in the studio. She needed more time, she'd told him gently. In the afternoons she drank espresso standing at the bar and watched the Italians flit busily around each other like butterflies. She had finally learned to be by herself in public without thinking about what others were thinking of her. It was a relief to live from the inside out at long last.

"Trying too," she said.

Frank nodded, satisfied. "You want to show me the installation piece?"

She led him to a small shed behind the studio building. Cleo opened the door to reveal a square white room with a projector set up in the center facing the ceiling. Dark soil covered the floor. The smell of it hit him in a nauseating wave, earthy, rich, and sweet.

"Cley . . ." He hovered in the doorway.

"I know," she said. "Please. Just lie down."

He lay down on the earth, still sick with the smell of it. Cleo turned the projector on, and the room turned red. She lay down next to him. Crimson light wavered across the ceiling like the wrinkles on a poppy petal. The smell of soil was everywhere, tugging him back to that moment . . .

What surprised him was the rush of anger he felt returning to it. *He* had been the one to find her and call the ambulance, kneeling in the soil all blackened with her blood, and now here was Cleo, making it into art. Sticking a crystal up herself and calling it healing. The room had turned a blood-drenched carmine. Well, good for her. He was glad to be rid of her. He had used that violence too, to propel himself out of their marriage into a relationship with a sane woman. Thank god. He wanted to sit up and tell her about the divorce papers. He wanted a drink. He wanted a thousand drinks. He wanted to take fistfuls of earth and grind them into his eyes and scream like a baby. He wanted his mother, not his actual mother, that self-involved drunk, but his real mother, still unfound, the woman who could truly take care of him. He wanted Eleanor.

"Cleo," he sat up. "I can't, I can't."

Cleo put her hand on his arm, but he pushed it away. "It's too *much*, Cley." He shocked himself by bursting into tears. "Too much."

He bowed his head in his hands and sobbed. He could not remember the last time he'd cried. It was an exorcism of tears. Cleo pulled him forward and cradled his head in her lap. She had not wanted to hurt him, but she needed him to see this. Their whole marriage, she had submitted to other people's versions of her, retreating into the shape of their desires. She thought of Frank's vow on their wedding day. *When the darkest part of you meets the darkest part of me, it creates light.* Now she had completed that process on her own. She had met the darkest part of herself and created this.

Around them, the room changed color to a deep amber. Music began to play. It was an undulating juggernaut of keening guitars and synthesizers, a deep, swelling, expansive sound. Then the shed turned a brilliant blue. They were in a box of sky, streaked with the white vapors of clouds. *Life Lines.* Here were hers. She had found a way to choose her life. So must he.

"Divorce," he said into her lap.

"I know," she said, stroking his hair. "I knew."

———

They sat outside a café near Piazza di Spagna as rosy light bathed the streets. The workday was done, and the languor of evening hung heavy in the air like pollen. After the intensity of Cleo's art installation, it was a relief to be out in the gentle hum of public life. An ease had returned between the two of them.

"It's lovely here," said Frank. "I didn't always have the best associations with Italy because of my father. But now that you live here, I'll think of it differently."

Cleo bit into one of the salty circles of salami that had been set before them without ceremony upon seating. Her face was glowing in the peach evening light.

"I'm glad," she said. "He shouldn't get to take Italy from you."

A teenage waiter came to offer them an aperitif, clearly delighted to have the opportunity to practice his English. Frank gave Cleo a panicked look, but she ordered them two sparkling lemonades in Italian with impressive smoothness.

"I never thought I'd be able to visit Rome and not drink," he said, as the beaded glasses were placed before them.

"Wine is the least interesting part of Rome," Cleo said. "And of you."

Frank gave her a defenseless smile. "Thanks, Cleopatra."

"You're welcome, Frankenstein."

And there, suddenly, it was, the memory of their first Halloween together elbowing to the front of Cleo's mind. They'd dressed up as their nicknames, Cleopatra and Frankenstein's monster. Cleo had spent the whole afternoon getting ready, painting a golden headpiece and pinning a dress out of loose linen. She'd worn a long black wig with thick coats of coal eyeliner, transforming into her own dark twin.

"Do you remember Halloween?" she asked suddenly.

They had gone with friends to a party at Anders's, everyone crammed into a cab, fighting over which radio station to play, the first baggie being passed around the back seat like a lover's note.

"Of course," said Frank. "What made you think of that?"

Cleo shrugged. Her mind still had a habit of tossing up painful memories, a reminder, she supposed, to keep moving forward. Unlike Frank, she was not prone to nostalgia.

"When I think about drinking, I have a habit of remembering the best part of every night," said Frank, as if reading her mind. "My sponsor says this thing to me, 'Play the tape forward.' I have to keep remembering until I reach the point where it stopped being fun."

"Okay," said Cleo. "So, play it forward. You know how that night ended."

Frank fast-forwarded to being at the Halloween party, where he had been uncomfortable in his costume, which consisted of a monster mask that smelled like chlorine. Anders was dressed, to devastating effect, as some kind of sexy murderer. Fast-forward to feeling ugly and forgotten, like an actual monster, to drinking too much, to fighting with Cleo on the way home, to the sound of her crying into the pillow as he lay beside her, watching the ceiling turn. Yes, there were the pillowcases in the morning, all tarred with black makeup that wouldn't wash out; he'd stuffed them into the bottom of the trash, just as he used to as a child with his piss-soaked sheets, so his mother wouldn't find them. That was why he hated to remember. Fast-forward and he always got to the dark current running beneath each seemingly happy night, to the secret sadness at the heart of Cleo that he couldn't heal, to the black scars on the white sheets he couldn't get out.

"I'm ashamed to remember it," he said. "How I hurt you."

Cleo nodded. "You did," she said. "But there was one upside to that night." She gave him one of her mysterious, knowing looks. "You were so hungover the next day, I finally won Pinch Punch."

Frank began to laugh. Cleo had once mentioned offhandedly that it was a tradition in England on the first day of the month to say "Pinch, punch, first of the month!" As long as the victor declared

"And no returns!" afterward, they were free to enact these pinches and punches without retaliation. The loser then had to wait a whole month before having the chance to say it first again. Frank, who had a taste for the nonsensical, had sprung upon this game with a fanatical competitiveness, waking up early on the first of every month and hovering over Cleo's sleeping figure until, at the slightest sign of awakening, he would launch his attack, screaming the singsong rhyme with the kind of zeal that, Cleo was sure, caused middle-aged men to have heart attacks.

"I forgot about that." He chuckled. "You sucked at Pinch Punch."

"Because I didn't want to set my alarm for the crack of dawn on the first of every month like a maniac!"

Frank looked at her seriously. "That's what it takes to be a Pinch Punch champion, Cleo."

He tried to maintain a straight face, but they were both quickly reduced to laughter.

"Well, now you can play with Eleanor," said Cleo, as their amusement subsided.

Frank shook his head, serious again. "I wouldn't do that. It's our game. Anyway, she's not British."

Cleo looked at him tenderly. "Okay," she said. "It stays ours."

"Is it weird for you?" he asked. "That I'm with someone else? You can be honest."

"It is a little," she said slowly. "But in some strange way, you and Eleanor give me hope. It makes me feel like I can find what you have one day too."

"That won't be a problem for you. You'll have men lining up."

Frank finished his lemonade with a satisfied slurp.

"I'd like to be married again," she said. "For a little longer next time."

"You will. Just don't pick someone like me."

Cleo raised an eyebrow. "You mean an active alcoholic almost twenty years my senior?"

"Pah!" Frank fell back against his chair as if shot. "But yes, that's exactly what I mean," he said, coming back to life.

"You didn't pick someone like me."

"No. Eleanor's not like either of us."

"How is she different?"

"You really don't mind talking about her?"

"I'm curious."

"Okay, well, Eleanor has this mother. She intimidated me at first actually because she just—she's *fierce*. Fiercely loving. And Eleanor grew up in a house in the suburbs with a garden and something called a visitor's couch and, you know, three different types of bird feeder."

Cleo nodded. "The height of domesticity."

"Exactly. And it wasn't perfect—her parents divorced when she was young, and she had this weird relationship as a teenager with an older guy—but I could tell she felt safe in that house. She grew up feeling safe and fiercely loved."

When he looked up, he was surprised to see that Cleo's eyes had glazed with a thin film of tears. "That sounds nice," she said quietly.

"And you and I didn't get that, not because we didn't deserve it, we just got dealt something else. But the people who did get that love, they grew up to be different from us. More secure. Maybe they're not as shiny or successful as you and I feel we have to be. But it's not because they're not interesting. They just don't feel they have to do the tap dance, you know? They don't have to *prove* themselves all the time to be loved. Because they always were."

Cleo smiled sadly. "But how do you stop tap dancing if you're like us?"

"I just got too tired, Cley," he said. "The shoes didn't fit anymore. And when I stood still, Eleanor was there standing with me. And I think you deserve to be with someone like that, who can provide that safety and that stillness for you in a way I never could. Even though God knows I wanted to, Cleo. I really wanted it."

Cleo took his hand across the table. Frank's freckled hands. She remembered them always in motion, flitting across surfaces, adjusting his glasses, accentuating words in the air with an emphatic, flared-palm gesture that was, just, *him*. She squeezed his fingers between hers.

"I know you did," she said. "I wanted to do that for you too."

The young waiter brought the check to sign, and as Frank often did when feeling a little low, he attempted to lift his spirits with a burst of unnecessary generosity by tucking a fifty-euro tip inside the bill.

As the boy took it away, a minor commotion began to take place on the square. A young couple was running with loose-limbed abandon across the large flat stones and laughing loudly, shouting to each other for no reason, it seemed, than the joy of being youthful and beautiful somewhere ancient and beautiful. They're not much younger than Cleo, Frank thought. They're so much younger than me, Cleo thought. An old bearded man they passed was laughing too and waving his cane, calling after them in Italian. Cleo and Frank watched the couple's faces, flushed and free, as they raced past.

"Do you understand what the man was saying?" Frank asked.

Cleo shook her head as the waiter appeared beside her.

"Signor, this is not right!" The bill was open between his hands like a prayer book. "It's too much!"

"No, no, it's all right," said Frank. "It's for you. Did you hear what that man was saying? To the kids running?"

"Yes, I think so," said the boy. "But this—"

"Can you translate it?"

"But this tip," said the boy. "It is . . . too American."

Cleo laughed when she saw the bill. "I'm glad not all of you has changed," she said.

"Can you tell me what he said?" Frank asked again.

"How strange you are," said the boy looking from one to the other. "It's an Italian saying. It is something like, 'Wherever you are going, it is waiting for you.'"

"Wherever you're going is waiting for you?" repeated Frank.

The boy turned to Cleo apologetically.

"It doesn't sound so good when he say it," he said.

———

Cleo and Frank left the café and walked arm in arm down the Spanish Steps toward his hotel, where the divorce papers were waiting. Outside the restaurants, clusters of people sat enjoying the clement weather, their glasses of wine glinting in the light. Above them a black flock of starlings filled the sky. People turned their faces upward to watch. The birds swirled and pulsed, contracting to a dense black swarm, then twisting wildly into a dipping, fluxing swirl, a loose constellation of Vs. Frank stood mesmerized as they transformed from a dancing cloud to a pulsing wave to a lung breathing in and out.

"It's called a murmuration," said Cleo, surprising him, again, with the breadth of things he did not know she knew. "It's warmer here in the city, so they return every evening from the surrounding areas."

"It's beautiful," he said.

"And destructive. They cover everything in shit. You can see people all over the city in the morning washing it off their cars and mopeds."

"But how do they do that? All move together?"

Cleo had read about this when she first moved here, and she was happy to know the answer. "Each starling is only ever aware of five other birds," she said. "One above, one below, one in front and one either side, like a star. They move with those five, and that's how they stay in formation."

"But who's the leader? Who decides which way they go?"

"There isn't one." Cleo smiled. "That's the mystery."

They walked through a piazza where tourists idled around a marble fountain. A warm breeze lifted the hair from the back of their necks. The air smelled of petrol and olives. They passed a cobbled alley mottled with shadow where a pair of teenagers kissed against a moped. At the other end, a gypsy woman hiked up her skirt and urinated into a puddle. They walked on.

"Who are your five, then?" asked Cleo. "The ones you watch?"

"My five people?" Frank thought for a moment. "Well, Zoe's one, of course. Santiago, too." He looked at the ground, which indeed was scarred with bird shit. "And Anders."

"I'm glad," said Cleo, meaning it.

"And now Eleanor." Frank glanced at her from the corner of his eye. She was nodding slowly.

"And you. That's five."

"Me?"

"You," said Frank. "Always you."

They looked at each other. Cleo's face was serene as a cathedral. All around them the city was settling into evening. A child cried for its mother. A bottle popped open. A motorbike roared. The starlings flew on.

ACKNOWLEDGMENTS

This novel took over seven years to complete, during which it was nurtured and improved by many, many people. I am grateful to the following:

My agent Millie Hoskins, who understood the heart of this story and championed it from the start. My wish for all writers starting out is that they are lucky enough to find a Millie.

My editors Grace Mcnamee and Helen Garnons-Williams, who made editing this often unwieldy story a true collaboration and a joy. It is so much better for having had both your brilliant minds on it (it even has a plot now!). Also Jordan Mulligan and Sade Omeje, who came on board with such enthusiasm to see it through to publication.

The NYU MFA program, in particular my teachers Amy Hempel, Nathan Englander, Darin Strauss and Rick Moody. Those two years changed my life irrevocably for the better.

My writing cohort Isabella Hammad, Steve Potter, Liz Wood, and Allison Bulger for your insights and edits after the MFA.

My wonderful friends Adam Eli, Olivia Orley, Zoe Potkin, Sophia Gibber, Sean Frank, Dayna Evans, Corey Militzok, Margot Bowman, Max Weinman, Maya Popa, and many others. Thank you for encouraging me to keep going, and for everything else.

The sober community of downtown New York, who really did love me until I could love myself. I am here because you carried me.

Emily Havens, for all the phone calls, and for always reminding me that there is a plan in place infinitely better than mine.

Karen Nelson, for providing a safe place to go deeper and get honest. I am a better person, and writer, for knowing you.

My mother, my first reader, who taught me to throw my heart forward and run to meet it. This book is for you.

ACKNOWLEDGMENTS

My father and the love of language you instilled in me. Thank you for knowing I was a writer before I did.

My funny, beautiful, clever, audacious big sister Daisy Bell. I will always be your kitten.

My beloved biggest siblings Holly and George, and my cousin Lucie, for showing me the way.

My grandmother Judy, from whom I inherited a love of both sugar and mischief.

My grandmother Edie, whom I never met, but whose dream of becoming a writer lives on in me.

And finally, my Henry. Thank you for loving me, for marrying me, and for creating a life with me far too honeyed and harmonious to ever make for interesting fiction. I'm yours.